AF422748

RICK PARTLOW

www.aethonbooks.com

EXILE

©2017-2020 RICK PARTLOW

This book is protected under the copyright laws of the United States of America. No part of this publication may be reproduced, stored in a retrieval system, or transmitted, in any form or by any means, without the prior permission in writing of the publisher, nor be otherwise circulated in any form of binding or cover other than that in which it is published and without a similar condition including this condition being imposed on the subsequent purchaser. Any reproduction or unauthorized use of the material or artwork contained herein is prohibited without the express written permission of the authors.

Aethon Books supports the right to free expression and the value of copyright. The purpose of copyright is to encourage writers and artists to produce the creative works that enrich our culture.

The scanning, uploading, and distribution of this book without permission is a theft of the author's intellectual property. If you would like to use material from the book (other than for review purposes), please contact editor@aethonbooks.com. Thank you for your support of the author's rights.

Aethon Books
www.aethonbooks.com

Print and eBook formatting, and cover design by Steve Beaulieu. Artwork provided by Tom Edwards Design.

Published by Aethon Books LLC.

Aethon Books is not responsible for websites (or their content) that are not owned by the publisher.

This book is a work of fiction. Names, characters, places, and incidents are the product of the author's imagination or are used fictitiously. Any resemblance to actual events, locales, or persons, living or dead is coincidental.

All rights reserved.

ALSO IN THE SERIES

THE ACHERON
THE PRODIGAL
HYBRID
EXILE

PROLOGUE

Han-Kan-Ten-L'ral hadn't felt the air on his face in days. The skin-tight control suit was plastered to him with sweat and the oils produced by his body, and the itching threatened to drive him insane at times, but what really ate at his psyche was the claustrophobic confines of his battlesuit's helmet. He'd never thought of it as tight or restrictive previously, but that was before he'd come to the world that the humans called Andalusia. Spending ten of the local days stuck inside his armor, on the move constantly, sleeping on his feet for an hour or two when they happened to stop, had made him hate the helmet.

He hated this place, too, this valley. It might have been beautiful once, with the rolling, green hills climbing out of it up to the white-capped mountains...and it might be beautiful again, someday. It was a wasteland now, burned and scraped flat by high explosives and energy weapons and kinetic-kill projectiles, and wiped clean of anything worth fighting for. The smoke and haze mixed with the morning fog and the low clouds and hung like a shroud over them, blotting out the sky and giving everything a look of devastated sameness.

The humans had chased them here, out of their base near

the city and into this valley of death, chased them with their orbital strikes and assault shuttles and their Marines and their Emperor-cursed commandos, clad in shadows and killing swiftly and horribly. The humans had carved at them and hammered at them and ground them down until all that was left was the pitiful force arrayed into the defensive perimeter around the edges of the clearing. There was no natural cover here, but they'd dug fighting positions as best they could.

"We are all going to die here."

The words slipped out, and he checked quickly to see if his transceiver was active. It was, but he was still on a private channel to the one male among them who he trusted with the truth.

"Indeed we are, my brother," Shin-Tan-Vala-Kel responded with no fear in his voice. "It is the Emperor's will, it seems."

Kan-Ten looked at the face of Vala-Kel, visible despite the opaque faceplates of their exoskeletal armor thanks to the computer projection on his Heads-Up Display. His oldest and closest friend was the very image of a Tahni warrior, as if the God-Emperor had molded him that way, his features sharp and jagged like the mountains west of the sea back home. He refocused his eyes and suddenly he could see the exterior of Vala-Kel's battlesuit, and the perfection vanished. The suit was battered and scored, caked with mud and dirt and carbon, its armored chest-plate splintered and cracked in places where enemy shots had nearly penetrated. Their unit crest was obliterated, seared away by the war, along with their reasons for being here.

"I fear we may have sinned too greatly," Kan-Ten admitted. His breath felt labored, as if his battlesuit's servomotors had frozen and he had to support the massive weight of the thing himself. "His favor has abandoned us."

"Commander!" The voice was strident, edged with panic.

Kan-Ten turned ponderously, the circular footpads of his battle-suit scraping grass away from the moist, brown soil.

He didn't remember the male's name; he was just one of a hundred lightly-armored ground troops who'd fled the city with them. He didn't even have the same communications net as the battlesuit troopers, and was yelling to be heard. It was unnecessary; Kan-Ten's helmet had exterior pickups that amplified and clarified.

"It's the humans, sir," the soldier said breathlessly, his face flush with exertion from the run back from the outposts. He was an older male, put out to pasture on this conquered world to guard the human slaves, and long past his prime years as a warrior. His armor was faded and dented and poorly-maintained, and his weapon was held with an awkward discomfort that probably reflected a lack of familiarity with it.

"They're coming?" Kan-Ten frowned; he should have received warnings from the drones they'd left along the way. "Armor? Assault shuttles?" He looked upward automatically but his suit's sensors showed nothing.

"No, Commander." The older male tossed his head, his ill-fitting helmet flopping around loosely. "It is one human. I don't know how he got so close without triggering the sensors, but he speaks our language...he says he wants to talk to you, that he guarantees you won't be harmed."

"One man?" Vala-Kel demanded with the typical disdain of a combat trooper for a rear-echelon soldier. "Why didn't you kill him?"

"We can't see him, Vice Commander." The male made a gesture of helplessness. "We hear his voice somewhere in the surrounding trees, but he is invisible on thermal or infrared..."

"If he's there," Kan-Ten interrupted, "then they know where we are and it is pointless to fire blindly into the trees. I will go."

Kan-Ten left the old soldier and his friend's objections behind with long, swift strides powered by servomotors and an isotope reactor buried deep in his armor's backpack. The other battlesuit troopers were scattered at key positions around the perimeter, but there were far too few of them left, and it hurt him to number them. Each was a treasured comrade, more of a brother than the blood he'd left behind on Tahn-Skyyiah so many years ago, and he'd seen so many of them fall in those years.

And for what? he wondered. *The Imperium is dead, though it still walks. No one will admit it even to themselves, yet we all know. The humans will win this war in months, and this time they won't leave us to threaten them again. They'll occupy our worlds and grind us under their boots.*

The southern edge of the perimeter looked out across a hundred meters of open plain to the towering trees that the humans called a "pine," something they'd imported from their world to this colony over a century ago. Kan-Ten found them oddly dark and menacing, far too tall and slender compared to the flora of his own homeworld, which made them well suited to conceal the dark, shadowy figure threatening them. There were no battlesuits at this section of the line, else they would have radioed him about the situation instead of sending a runner. The rear-guard troops were huddled fearfully in their fighting positions, eyes rarely topping the edges of the hastily-dug holes.

Kan-Ten walked through them without hesitation, past them a good twenty meters before standing defiantly in the open, holding the massive arms of his battlesuit casually at his sides. He keyed his external address system and set it for maximum volume.

"You wished to speak to me," he challenged, hearing his own, amplified voice echoing back at him. "Show yourself. You have my word that we won't fire on you unless you fire first."

He blinked. It was as if the figure had appeared out of the air at the edge of the trees, clad in gray shadows. His armor, if armor it indeed was, for it looked skin-tight, seemed to shift with the patterns of the background, and it showed on thermal imaging not at all. The human's face was covered with a hood, but as he approached he pulled it off, revealing a close-cut matt of light brown hair and a face that was probably natural for one of them, but seemed far too thin and skeletal for the aesthetic of a Tahni. He had a sidearm holstered at his waist, but carried no other visible weapons.

"Are you the commander of the ground forces?" A human's voice box was poorly suited for the Tahni language, but the man's words were understandable for all that.

"What's left of them," Kan-Ten replied, unable to keep the bitterness he felt out of his tone, though he didn't know if a human would be able to pick it up.

"I'm Captain Savage of Commonwealth Fleet Intelligence." The word "Captain" probably didn't mean quite the same thing in their tongue as it did in Tahni, but Kan-Ten got the idea that the human was a middle-grade officer of some sort. "I've come to offer you a chance to surrender."

Kan-Ten *knew* that this word had a different meaning. In Tahni, the term referred to the formal ending of an internal dispute for the throne, when one side would acknowledge the superiority of the other's claim to be a more suitable physical host for the Spirit Emperor and pledge itself to restoring harmony and unity. The Tahni didn't have the human concept of giving up and throwing themselves at the mercy of a conqueror...because the Tahni had never before been conquered.

Yet he had heard the term. There had been a communique from the garrison priests warning that anyone who attempted to surrender to the humans would be executed.

"What will happen to my warriors if I agree to this?"

He spoke the words, yet doubted his own mind as he did. It seemed to him as if someone spoke through him, an ancestor's spirit perhaps.

"They'll be housed, and fed, and treated well," Captain Savage assured him. "They'll be taken to camps for Tahni prisoners for the time being, but we hope that when this war is finally over, they'll be allowed to return home."

"You are that sure that you will beat us." He wasn't arguing the point. He was fairly certain of it himself, yet the casual confidence the human's words implied was staggering.

"If I wasn't sure," the human responded, "I wouldn't bother talking to you." He motioned up with an expansive gesture. "You don't think we have orbital assets that could kill every last one of you without risking a single one of our soldiers? Your picket ships are gone, and we control the laser defenses. This world is ours again."

"Then why *do* you let us live?" Kan-Ten was genuinely curious. He knew that he would not have offered the same courtesy if the situation had been reversed.

"Because when this war is over, we're going to make sure we never have to fight you and your kind again. We could do this by wiping you from existence, but most of us don't believe that to be ethical or moral. So, we need individuals we can study, to figure out how to make a new government for you after all this is over and you go back home again."

Kan-Ten made a gesture of assent, though the human couldn't see it and might not have recognized it in any case. The man was brutally honest, not inclined to couch his words in any conciliatory tone.

"What would you have me do?" Again, that sensation of someone else speaking through him. Was he actually saying this? Was he actually considering it?

"Order your troops to disarm. Those in battlesuits," he motioned to Kan-Ten's powered armor, "will need to crack them open and climb out. Then you'll leave the weapons in the clearing and march everyone up to the edge of the trees and wait for our vehicles. If anyone refuses, I'm going to run," he motioned behind him, "*that* way as fast as I can, and the guys upstairs are going to start dropping big, heavy rocks on top of you all."

"I will give the order. I do not know if everyone will follow it."

The human slipped his face hood back on and disappeared into the shadowed wood so quickly that Kan-Ten could almost believe he was a death spirit, sent by the Emperor to punish them. He shook the thought off and turned back to his own lines. Vala-Kel was waiting for him there, silent and motionless, a scarred and weathered statue, a monument to this war and their own foolishness.

"What have you done, brother?" The tone was not accusatory, not angry, not even sad. Instead, there was a sense of exhaustion in his old friend's words, of the acceptance of a fate he was too tired to fight. Kan-Ten knew the feeling well.

"Our war is over," he said. "Our lives need not be."

He touched a control inside his glove, inputting the correct sequence and then confirming it when the suit's systems asked if he was really sure that was what he wanted to do. The front plastron of his suit swung ponderously open with a hiss of escaping air, and with its support removed, Kan-Ten nearly collapsed. His muscles were cramped and weak and he felt the sudden pain of aches and bruises and abrasions hidden from him by the suit's medical systems over the last few days. He grabbed at a support handle affixed to the interior of the chest-plate and pulled his lower body out of the battlesuit, finding purchase for his feet on the steps of the open plastron.

When he lowered himself down out of the suit's helmet, the chill morning air slapped him in the face, as if he'd stepped out of one reality and into another. He staggered when his feet touched the ground, feeling the cold leeching up through the thin boots he'd worn inside the battlesuit. Kan-Ten sucked in a deep breath of air, savoring it despite the touch of frost that made his chest hurt.

"If you do this, brother," Vala-Kel told him, his voice sounding odd and mechanical through the exterior speakers of his suit, "there will be no going home for you. You'll have no family, no place in the worship feasts, no prayers from our ancestors. You'll be an exile."

"Let the sin be on my head," Kan-Ten whispered, the steam of his breath taking the words away as if to the very ears of the spirits, "and not on these." He stared upward into the faceless helm that hid his friend. "Live, brother. Live, and I shall bear this burden."

Kan-Ten turned and found the closest of the rear-guard soldiers, still cowering in his hole, his mouth agape.

"Tell the others," he instructed the male. "Lay down your weapons and gather beyond the lines. We are surrendering."

CHAPTER ONE

"Get ready," Ashton Carpenter warned. "We're on the ground in five."

Sandrine Hollande felt the acceleration pushing her back into the liquid cushion of the copilot's seat, somehow more real and urgent than when she was sitting in the left-hand chair and plugged into the ship's neural interface. The armor she wore felt bulky and unnatural, and her palms were sweating inside her tactical gloves where they held tightly to the receiver of her pulse carbine. She was a pilot, not a gunfighter; but in their business, she had to be both. And it was her turn.

"Wish you were in this chair?" Ash asked her, eyes focusing for just a moment as his concentration shifted from the interface to her, a crooked grin on his open, square-jawed face. He still kept his hair cut regulation-short even though he'd left the military over two years ago now, and he still looked like he'd stepped right out of a recruiting ad for Space Fleet. His appearance certainly didn't give any clue that he'd fought his way out of one of the roughest slums in Trans-Angeles, or that he was wanted by the military for desertion and by the Patrol Service for murder.

At least the murder charge is false.

"Keep your eyes on the road," she shot back, nodding towards the main view screens.

They were nearly a kilometer above the surface of Grand Terre and fifty kilometers out from the planet's only real city and everything was roiling, burning chaos. Lasers turned swathes of superheated atmosphere into plasma as they speared upward from the city, and proton cannons answered them like scintillating lightning bolts out of the dark, low-hanging thunderheads. And all around their ship, the exhaust flares of rocket engines and fusion-powered turbojets lit up the night like a swarm of malevolent fireflies, their course jerky and erratic as a dozen assault shuttles, landers and converted military cutters like their own tried to avoid the lasers and missiles from the ground defenses.

"I still don't know how the hell the Sung Brothers cobbled together this bunch." The voice was scratchy and hoarse and immediately identifiable, but she turned her head toward it instinctively anyway.

Strapped into the Navigator's station between and just behind her and Ash, Korri Fontenot was wearing the same sort of matte-grey body armor as Sandi, but on her it looked natural, comfortable, as if she'd been born to it. *Born a long, long time ago to it*, Sandi amended silently. Fontenot's hair was silver and cut nearly as short as Ash's, and half her face was lined and weathered from a century spent out in the wilds of the Periphery and the Pirate Worlds. The other half seemed unnaturally smooth, with a sort of blocky, unbalanced look to it that came from concealing the metal cybernetics that had replaced half her skull under a layer of synthskin. That concealment was a concession to their status as wanted criminals, an effort to be less conspicuous, but Sandi liked to think it was also Fontenot's attempt to try to be more human.

"They smell blood," Sandi answered her question. "They know the *La Sombra* cartel is losing their grip on the outposts and they're pouncing on them like a pack of wolves."

"Still must have cost them a fortune to hire out this many mercs," Fontenot scowled with a frugality learned from decades on her own, living hand to mouth. "Can't be worth it just to get control of the markets on a shithole like this."

"Two minutes," Ash interrupted.

Fontenot sighed and slipped on a battle helmet, sealing it to the collar of her chest armor, and Sandi did the same. The Heads-Up Display flickered to life in front of her eyes, a rush of information streaming up the corner of her vision, telling her what her current elevation, speed and geographic position was. When she focused on the tiny map in the right-hand corner of the display, it expanded to show her the city only twenty kilometers ahead, squatting in a river valley on the planet's only continent, more a large island on a large world of mostly water.

It wasn't what she would have called a city when she'd lived on Earth, wasn't even the size of a housing district in one of the megalopolises like Trans-Angeles or Capital City. Life in the colonies was harder and rougher, and usually shorter, and the populations were still small. Even the oldest Core colonies like Hermes or Eden barely boasted a half a billion people, compared to the nearly thirty billion jammed into the megacities of Earth. Out here in the Pirate Worlds, the illegal squatter colonies controlled by the cartels, populations were in the tens or hundreds of thousands, crammed into the tiny habitable zones of planets not well suited to human life.

And yet people were going to die fighting over this little collection of wood and stone buildings barely ten kilometers on a side, die for status and control.

At least they're a good distraction.

"Hold on," Ash mumbled, barely audible over the roar of the jets. "We're going in."

Her stomach seemed to drop away, a feeling she'd grown used to over so many years as a pilot, and the privateer *Acheron* plunged into a steep dive, cutting below the trajectory of the Sung Brothers attack force and heading straight into the city of Barataria Bay. The crenelated wall that surrounded the city rushed by underneath them, and then the belly jets were screaming in desperation and something was trying to drive her bodily through her chair and through the hull and into the pavement. The landing gear impacted and her safety harness bit into her shoulders even through the armor as the tread assemblies sank into their housings and recoiled slowly with a hiss of hydraulics. There was a roaring in her ears, and lights flashing in her eyes, and a haze of confusion over her thoughts from the brutal deceleration and for just a moment, she couldn't move.

"I took out the guard shack with the Gatling." Ash's voice reached through the haze and pulled her back to the moment. "Street's clear for now."

Sandi yanked the quick-release on her restraints and pushed up out of the acceleration couch, but Fontenot was already moving ahead of her, through the narrow passage that led back from the cockpit to the utility bay. The belly ramp was rumbling open, and standing beside the control was a figure nearly two meters tall, armored but lacking a helmet, since nothing made for a human would fit him.

He was a Tahni: humanoid, close enough that he could pass for a tall man on a dark night, but in the glare of the work-lights in the utility bay, the differences were obvious. The bend of the knees and elbows and wrists was just slightly off, the fingers longer than a human's and boasting an extra joint, and then there was the face. The ears were plastered to the side of his head, the nose nearly flat and the nostrils elongated, the mouth a thin line over jaws like a steam-shovel. The eyes were the most obvious, though: small and dark and beady and sheltered under bony ridges that ran across the forehead. He had hair, coarser and thicker than a human's but still hair, shaved except for a strip down the center of his head that ran into a tightly-braided ponytail wrapped around his thick neck like a scarf.

Sandi had known him for two years now and was still no closer to being able to read his expressions or his body language, but she thought he considered her a friend. If anyone had told her back during the war that she'd someday trust a Tahni with her life...

"Kan-Ten," she told the alien, "secure the landing zone. Korri," she turned to Fontenot, "you have the map, find us a route to the compound. I'll be right there."

The Tahni moved down the ramp without a word, shouldering a heavy Gauss rifle, while Fontenot paused to retrieve an obsolete drum-fed assault gun from an equipment locker before she followed him. Sandi was alone in the bay with the other woman. She was strapped into one of the spare acceleration couches that folded down from the utility bay's rear bulkhead, and Sandi was pleased to see that she'd followed instructions and *stayed* strapped in.

Unadorned brown hair hung limply to her shoulders, matted with sweat from the strain of the g-forces they'd all undergone on the descent, and skin that was normally deeply tanned had gone pale, but the expression on that attractive, oval face was full of determination. If you'd dressed her in armor instead of civilian clothes and put a weapon in her hand, Sandi could have imagined her roaming out into the perils of the night to find her child on her own, rather than leaving the job to the professionals.

"Ash'll stay at this landing site as long as it's safe," Sandi told her. "If he has to take off, we can signal him when to swing back around and pick us up, once we find your daughter." She hesitated, unwilling to say the next words but knowing they were necessary. "If we find her."

"You will find her, Ms. Hollande," Stephania Willow said, her voice strong and calm, her gaze steady. "I have no doubt."

The words could have been a statement of hope, but the look in those dark eyes wasn't one of hope, and Sandi felt a slight chill as she realized it had more the sound of a threat.

"I want you to remember, Ms. Hollande," she went on, voice turning colder, "that I wasn't just Eduardo Santonio's wife, I was his business partner until I decided it would be better if my daughter had a chance at a more stable life. When I took Adriana to the Periphery, Eduardo did not have the power to stop me, and when he came to steal her back, he made no move against me because he knew what a grave mistake it would be. So, do not be misled by the fact that I am staying here on your ship while you go retrieve my little girl; I am not staying here because I fear what my husband or his goons would do to me, I am staying because this is your job and you've proven competent at it."

There was just the slightest quiver of her lip, the first sign she'd allowed that she was, besides being a badass former cartel enforcer, also a mother.

"Don't let me down."

Sandi had the feeling that this woman wouldn't care for empty promises, so she left her in the hold with the words unspoken.

Her boots thumped with hollow, rhythmic impacts on the belly ramp of the ship and the lights of the utility bay followed her, a golden halo in the drifting smoke and steam still rising from the scorch marks the landing jets had left on the pavement. Even with the enhanced optics in her helmet, it was difficult to make anything out through the billowing clouds roiled by the idling turbines, their shrill whine a constant background noise that her brain barely acknowledged. Above it, she could make out the roar of engines in the night sky, the distant thunder-cracks of beam weapons stabbing into targets on the ground, but nothing close and no warnings from Fontenot or Kan-Ten. She paused and hit the control to raise the ramp.

"We're out," she radioed to Ash.

"I'll stick here as long as I can," he replied.

The hum of servos off to her left drew her eye and she saw the *Acheron's* Gatling turret extending out from the portside wing, scanning back and forth for threats. There was still a faint glow on its cooling vanes from the burst that had taken out the guard shack on the wall. She couldn't see the wall from the ship, even though it was only fifty meters away, not with the thick haze, but her helmet's thermal filters showed her the hotspot where the shack had been, still burning. The *Acheron* rested in an empty lot at an intersection in Barataria Bay's industrial district, and around the massive, silvery delta of the cutter, she could just make out the looming sheet-metal walls of ware-houses and fabrication centers.

Glowing blue haloes in her HUD led her to Fontenot and Kan-Ten where they'd taken up watch positions on either side of the intersection, down on a knee, weapons trained outward. Sandi came up behind Fontenot and put a hand on her shoulder.

"You got a direction for me?" she asked, kneeling down beside the cyborg.

Fontenot gestured to their left.

"Two kilometers, more or less," she said.

"You're point, Korri. Kan-Ten, you watch our backs."

"I dislike walking backwards," the Tahni admitted, rising with a strange, inhuman motion that seemed more like he was unfolding. "My joints are not built for it."

Sandi snorted, patting him on the arm as she passed by.

"Then buy a helmet that fits you," she suggested, "or let us have one made for you. Otherwise, you don't have a map overlay and you can't walk point."

"I dislike helmets as well."

Sandi followed Fontenot from ten meters back, hoping the cyborg could make out more of their surroundings than she could. Explosions and gunfire echoed through the night from the other side of the city, the population centers, but all she could see here were the flares of street lights, shining like their own, discreet stars in the haze and fog but adding nothing to the visibility. A drizzle of dirty rain distorted the view out of her faceplate and she began ignoring the visible light display and concentrating on the infrared and thermal filters. Through their cybernetic eyes, everything around them was an indistinct blob, but she could tell they were alone on the streets.

Everyone with two brain cells to rub together is in a shelter, or heading for one, she reflected. *Guess that doesn't say anything flattering about us.*

"How sure are we about this intell?" Fontenot wondered. "Sure, this is where the dragon lady *says* Eduardo would send their kid, but she's been gone, what? A year now?"

"It's what we've got." Sandi fought back a sigh; they'd had this argument on the trip from Sylvanus, and she was already tired of it. "And it's more than we usually get, especially thanks to Captain Fox."

The Intelligence officer had clued them in to the Sung Brothers' pending attack on Barataria Bay, accelerating the timeline for extracting the little girl. They'd done some good work for him over the last two years, so it wasn't *exactly* suspicious; but dealing with spooks always made her nervous, and in her experience, they never gave away anything free.

She wiped a gloved hand over her faceplate to clear it of

excess water and realized that the fog had thinned; she could see the fine details of the buildings on either side of the street, see the cheap sheet metal of the industrial district giving way to storefronts of local wood and stone, their windows and doors covered by metal security shutters. Probably to keep out offworlders, she reasoned, since the locals wouldn't put up with anyone inclined to steal or vandalize.

She thought about the families who owned and ran the stores and wondered if the Sung Brothers' troops would allow them to keep the businesses, or kick them out and put their own people in place. It was always the innocents who suffered, always the children who paid the price for the greed and lust for power of people like Jordi Abdullah and the Sung Brothers. There'd been a family on Asiento, another of the smaller *La Sombra* outposts, who had given her shelter when she'd been caught in the middle of a fight between Jordi's people and the Rif cartel. They'd lost a son to the violence and were so desperately afraid they'd lose their young daughter to it as well...

"This way," Fontenot gestured down an alley to their right, holding the theoretically crew-served assault gun easily in the crook of one bionic arm.

They cut across two more parallel streets full of businesses until the dark, shuttered workplaces gave way to the bright lights of the city's one hotel and a handful of small bars and clubs. This place had a small landing field outside the city, but the traffic was mostly *La Sombra* flight crews taking out cargoes of illegal weapons from the caches stored in the warehouses here, far from the probing eyes and sensors of the Patrol, and outlaw spacers didn't have the sort of money to throw around that Corporate Council freighter crews might. Still, the hotel and the bars hadn't had enough warning to close up and shutter the doors, and now they were paying the price.

Sandi knew that the main body of the Sung Brothers ground

force would be hitting the *La Sombra* compound about a kilometer west, toward the landing field---she could see the smoke billowing upward into the clouds, see the flames rising already, and could still hear gunfire echoing through the streets from that direction. At first, she thought the hotel and the clubs had escaped notice, but then Fontenot threw up a hand and Sandi and Kan-Ten halted and went down to a knee just short of the exit of the alleyway, the Tahni turning back to cover their rear approach.

"There's a squad of them coming up the street," Fontenot said, her voice as calm and steady as if she were ordering dinner, a stark contrast to the twisting in Sandi's stomach and the drumbeat of her heart trying to pry its way out of her chest.

Sandi fought to control her breathing, trying to follow Fontenot's gesture with her eyes and the muzzle of her pulse carbine. She could see them now, ten of them, moving slowly and cautiously up the road from the direction of the landing field and the *La Sombra* compound. Their armor was mismatched, their weapons the mini-rocket-firing carbines so ubiquitous out in the Pirate Worlds, easily fabricated. They weren't the Sung Brothers' best troops; she figured them for hired guns, not even professional mercenaries. They'd seen the lights, she guessed, and been sent to investigate.

Unfortunately, they were heading the same place that she was, and she couldn't let them reach it first.

"Korri, take them out, if you can," she ordered, the words seeming to pry their way out of her mouth. She was sentencing them to death. Maybe they deserved it, but who was she to say? "If you can't, keep their attention. Kan-Ten, come with me."

She used the butt-stock of her carbine to lever herself to her feet and ran. She didn't have to check the transponder display to see that Kan-Ten was following; she knew he would. The Tahni wasn't human, but he was as dependable as the motions of the planets. Fontenot's assault gun thudded with a report she could feel in her chest, lessening as she drew away from the cyborg's position. She didn't look at the Sung Brothers troops, either, counting on her friend to keep them busy; her focus was the largest of the bars, the one just behind the hotel, the one festooned with the flashing holographic image of a wolf howling at the moon just above the stone archway that overhung its front entrance.

None of these sorry fuckers have ever seen a wolf, she thought irrelevantly. *Except in a video.*

There were people here; people too stupid to be off the streets, probably not locals. They were running, too, running from the report of the assault gun, from the return fire of the rocket carbines. They were dressed like spacers and they were running for the hotel where they likely had rooms, as if it offered some sort of supernatural shelter against the death and violence outside. She remembered that night on Asiento and felt a sudden pang of guilt for looking down on them, but there was no time for that.

The front door to the Howling Wolf was newly closed, likely locked, but it was local wood and the latch would be of local metal, nothing exotic enough to resist a tungsten slug travelling at 2,500 meters per second.

"Open it," she told Kan-Ten, her voice breathless from the sprint across the seventy meters to the bar entrance. She tried to stay in shape, but when you spent most of your time in a starship, long-distance running wasn't on the regular workout list.

The Tahni barely slowed down, just levelled the Gauss rifle and fired half a dozen rounds. The armor-piercing slugs punched through each corner of the door and the latch mechanism, and Kan-Ten followed them with his shoulder, slamming his full hundred and twenty kilograms into it. The massive, wooden door toppled inward and Kan-Ten pitched forward with it, not resisting the motion but following it, letting it take him to the floor and out of the line of fire.

Inside the door, arrayed in the entranceway, were two men and a woman, all rough-looking, and all armed with compact carbines. Sandi recognized them from Stephania's very complete files; they were Eduardo Santonio's hired guns, his most trusted, and the ones he would have sent to take his child to safety when he'd detected the incoming Sung Brothers' ships. Which meant Sandi was in the right place.

She spared just the space of half a second making sure the child wasn't in the room with them, that the area behind them was clear of targets, before she touched the trigger pad of the laser carbine. It was almost too long; they were good and they'd opened fire on her immediately. But they were also distracted by Kan-Ten's explosion through the door, and the spin-stabilized mini-rockets from their carbines went wide, detonating against the rear wall in a spray of plaster dust. Sandi's carbine was linked to the targeting system in her helmet's HUD, and she didn't miss.

Laser pulses shed white flashes of ionized air like optical afterimages visible long after the actual burst of coherent light had passed. Brilliant ropes of actinic lightning connected Sandi's weapon to center-mass on the closest of the three, a tall woman with purple hair shaped into a starburst around her head in a style that had been out of fashion on Earth or the Core colonies for decades. The big woman wore an armored vest under her rain jacket, but it wasn't enough to stop the laser from point-blank range; there was a flare of fire as cloth vaporized and metal sublimated and the cartel enforcer jerked backwards, her weapon slipping from nerveless hands.

Sandi shifted to the next of the three, her motions economical and smooth after much practice with Fontenot, who'd been shooting at people who were shooting at her for longer than the other three of them had been alive, combined. She ignored the mini-rockets flashing by to her right, coming closer as the man turned, and kept her finger mashed down on the trigger. She hadn't let her eyes focus on the man before now, but as her shots tore through his throat and upper chest, she noticed that he was strikingly handsome, his features even and sharp enough to have been professionally restructed, or maybe he'd just hit the genetic lottery. That handsome face twisted with pain, and terror, and then forlorn resignation, as his life sprayed across the hardwood floor in gouts of red.

As fast as Sandi had become, as much as she'd trained, the third shooter would still have killed her; he had a clear shot and the time to aim. But Kan-Ten had rolled over onto his side, against the right-hand wall, and opened fire with his Gauss rifle. The slugs punched upward through the last man's chin. She never got the chance to see what he looked like, if he was handsome or ugly, angry or desperate or despairing, because his head disappeared in a volcanic explosion of brain and fluid and skull fragments, and what was left of him lurched forward, hitting the floor with a sickening, wet thump.

Sandi rushed past the bodies, pausing to kick the guns away from their hands and trying not to focus on the tacky, sticky sensation as the soles of her boots made tread-marks in the swiftly-spreading pools of crimson. Again, guilt tried to well up inside her; these people had been assigned to protect a child, and she'd killed them for it. Kan-Ten was up and following her through the entrance hall and into the main dining room; it was deserted, chairs kicked over and food still on the tables...and a man's body, sprawled on the floor between the dining area and the bar, a handgun near his outstretched fingers. Eduardo's people had kicked everyone out when they'd brought his daughter here, and someone hadn't wanted to leave. Suddenly, she didn't feel as guilty anymore.

Sandi kept her carbine trained on the bar and the doors set in the wall behind it, careful of anyone hiding there, ready to ambush them. Steam drifted off the cooling vanes of her carbine, the shimmering waves of heat carrying away the beads of water that had accumulated in the light rain outside. She came around the edge of the bar and ducked under the gate, ready to hose down anyone she found there, but there was nothing. She held the gate up for Kan-Ten and they both picked their way through pressurized kegs of beer and crates of locally-bottled liquor to a rubberized matt on the floor near the center of the bar. Sandi kicked it aside, revealing a metal trapdoor with a hinged handle at the front edge.

She pulled her carbine into her shoulder and crouched above the trapdoor, then signaled to Kan-Ten. The Tahni reached down and yanked the handle upward, revealing a wooden stepladder descending into an unlit basement. Sandi hesitated for just a moment, afraid there might be another guard stationed in the cellar, but no gunshots were forthcoming.

"Adriana," she called. She realized that her helmet's external speakers made her sound distant and mechanical; with a muttered curse, she jerked at the quick-release and twisted the helmet off. The air inside this place was warm and dry, and the space behind the bar smelled of stale beer, and breathing it made everything feel so uncomfortably real.

"Adriana!" she repeated. "Your mother sent us to bring you back to her!"

Another long pause, and for a moment, she thought the girl wasn't down there, that they'd found a different hiding place for her.

"Who are you?" The voice was a little girl's, halting and tremulous and scared.

"My name is Sandi. Your mom, Stephania Willow, sent me. She was worried about you and wants me and my friends to take you home." She made a face, realizing she sounded awkward. *Probably comes from having a fucking admiral for a mom.* "Your mom is with us, back on our ship, just a few minutes from here."

She thought she'd reached the girl, but then there was another stretch of silence. She checked the time on her wrist display and cursed.

"Why didn't Mom come herself and get me?" Adriana demanded, a bit of petulance sneaking into her voice.

"Because it's dangerous outside." Sandi forced calm into her tone, trying not to sound impatient. "There are bad men coming to try to hurt everyone here and your dad is fighting them. That's why your mom wants you to come home. That's why she sent us."

Sandi shot Kan-Ten a look of exasperation, mouthing "Jesus Christ," and knowing both were probably wasted on him.

"All right, I'm coming."

Sandi hissed out a sigh and shifted the muzzle of her carbine upward, relaxing her crouch into more of a squat. She could see movement in the darkness below them, and then a mop of dirty blond hair ascending the ladder. Adriana's face was cherubic, but then most well-fed eight-year-old girls seemed fairly cherubic until you got to know them. Her clothes were expensive, and tailored, and fit in poorly in a place like Barataria Bay, but perfectly with her mother's tastes. Adriana paused at the top of the ladder and looked Sandi up and down appraisingly.

"You're too pretty to be a soldier," she declared, her green eyes narrowing.

Sandi laughed; she couldn't help it.

"That's because I'm really a pilot," she admitted. "I'm only a soldier when I have to be."

"I want to be a pilot!" Adriana announced, smiling as if they weren't on a world settled by gunrunners and in the middle of an invasion. "Mom says I can learn how to fly when I get older!" The little girl glanced over at Kan-Ten and gasped. "Are you a Tahni?" she asked, pushing herself up out of the trapdoor to stand next to him. "I've never met a Tahni before!"

"I am Kan-Ten," the alien told her with what would have sounded like earnest sincerity in a human. "We must leave this place now. You need to stay close to Sandi."

Sandi pulled her helmet back on, pushing shut the seals, then touched the control to transmit over her 'link.

"Korri," she called. "We've got the girl and we're heading out. Are you okay?"

She could see the older woman's transponder on her HUD, and it showed her about fifty meters from the bar and moving in an arc back toward it.

"Roger that." Still that relaxed voice, like this was nothing to her. "I got what was left of the squad running in circles, chasing where they think I am. I'll meet you at the entrance in one minute."

"I'm going to have to carry you for now, Adriana," Sandi told her, slinging her carbine and picking the girl up, then pulling her sidearm.

"I can walk," the girl protested, though she didn't struggle.

"I know you can, but we're going to have to move fast, and I'm wearing enough armor to protect the both of us."

Kan-Ten led them out the front door, and she tried to shield the girl's eyes from the dead bodies in the entrance hall; she wasn't sure how successful she'd been, but the child didn't react either way. Outside, Kan-Ten turned to the right, looking for Fontenot, and Sandi stepped off to the left, near the corner of the bar...and stopped short. She was staring into the yawning muzzle of a rocket revolver, a massive, obsolete weapon held in an equally massive hand.

The face behind the hand was good-looking in a rough and

rugged way, tanned and lined, strands of grey streaking his close-cropped beard, and his eyes were the same shade of green as his daughter's.

"Dad!" Adriana blurted, like he'd caught her snacking between meals.

"Put her down," Eduardo Santonio ordered tightly, his words a barely-controlled hiss.

Sandi sensed more than saw Kan-Ten turning, bringing up his rifle.

"Hold your fire," she said quickly. "Fontenot, if you can hear me, do not fire."

"Are you sure you know what you're doing, girl?" Fontenot sounded dubious, but Sandi ignored the question.

Sandi slowly and carefully holstered her pistol, then reached up and pulled off her helmet, looking the cartel enforcer in the eye.

"Mr. Santonio," she said, trying to keep the intense fear out of her voice despite looking straight into the explosive warhead of a mini-rocket, "I work for your wife. She sent us to take Adriana home. She knew this attack was coming." She waved a hand back toward the landing field and the *La Sombra* compound, and the gunfire still clearly audible and getting closer. "She knew Adriana wouldn't be safe here. You have to know it, too."

The look on the man's face changed from barely-chained fury to a halting confusion and hesitation, and the barrel of the revolver wavered. He knew she was telling the truth. Then his expression hardened again and the weapon straightened.

"She's my daughter," he insisted, "and she's staying with me. Put her the fuck down now before I blow your head off."

Sandi felt her mouth set in a grim line and she turned her body, angling the little girl away from him.

"No," she said. "Not here. If you want to keep your

daughter safe, if you want to be with her, you'll come with us, get her safe on our starship and fly out of here." She nodded toward Kan-Ten, then out to where Fontenot was approaching, assault gun levelled at the man. "You can shoot me, and maybe hit your daughter, and then she can watch them kill you. Or you can be her father and protect her."

Santonio's lip quivered somewhere between frustration and desperation and he slowly lowered the gun.

"All right," he sighed. "Goddamnit, you're exactly the kind of person Stephania would hire. Let's go."

Sandi nodded, then put her helmet back in place and sealed it.

"Korri, lead off. Kan-Ten, watch my back." She paused and made sure her exterior speakers were turned off before she continued. "And if this asshole looks at me sideways, shoot him."

Something exploded less than a hundred meters away in a globe of white fire, and the ground shook hard enough that it nearly threw Sandi off her feet. Fontenot didn't need any more encouragement; she loped off back the way they'd come, and Sandi surged into a sprint to keep up with her.

"We're heading back, Ash. You still good?"

"So far, but I don't know how much longer we've got," he answered her. "The fighting's getting closer."

"You don't have to tell me. Hang tight."

Then she was breathing too hard to speak. For a little girl, Adriana was damned heavy, and the only reason she didn't have Kan-Ten or Fontenot carry her was because they were both better gunfighters than her. She *could* have let Santonio carry his daughter, but she was afraid he'd seize the opportunity to take off and leave them there. She *thought* she'd gotten through to him, but she wasn't willing to bet Adriana's life on it.

The walls of the alleyways seemed closer together somehow than they had on the way in, as if the echoes of the gunfire chattering from a couple streets over was physically constricting her, closing around her and Adriana. She gritted her teeth and tried to keep her finger away from her sidearm's trigger pad as she ran, despite the instinct to clench her fist. They were one street away from the *Acheron* when Fontenot skidded to a halt just at the alley entrance and opened fire to her right, scuttling backwards to cover.

Return fire pounded into the left-hand wall of the alley, a block-and-mortar fabricator and small equipment repair shop, the warheads of the mini-rockets flashing with flares of vaporized metal that ate pockmarks out of the corner of the building. Sandi put her shoulder against the right-hand wall, shielding Adriana with her body, while Santonio and Kan-Ten swept past her to take up positions next to Fontenot. The cartel enforcer moved with a careful recklessness, like he knew the knife edge of the situation intimately and came just as close as he could to it. He went to the center of the alleyway, edging around Fontenot, out just far enough that he could see the shooters. The heavy revolver was an extension of his arm, pointed as naturally as Sandi might point her finger in a casual gesture.

Flame erupted from the barrel as rockets the size of a man's little finger launched one on the heels of another, just enough gap to make sure the exhaust of the first didn't alter the course of the next. He emptied the cylinder in one, long burst before taking a single, casual step backwards just ahead of a dozen rounds of incoming fire. They couldn't have missed him by more than centimeters, Sandi judged. The man had balls, but that was no surprise; Jordi Abdullah didn't hire cowards to run his businesses.

"We got two squads out there," Fontenot informed them, "less two or three individuals now. They've learned their lesson and are behind available cover. Can we bring the ship in for fire support?"

"The angle's wrong," Sandi estimated reluctantly. Calling in air support was always her first instinct. "He couldn't bring the *Acheron* in low enough to target them, and the streets are narrow enough that a straight-down shot wouldn't reach them."

She paused, grunting with effort as she shifted Adriana's weight. The little girl was pale, eyes wide, arms clinging around her neck tightly, as if everything was finally getting to her, just now sinking in. *Poor kid.*

"I'll circle around," Santonio declared, sliding a fresh load of ammunition into the cylinder of his weapon. "Keep them looking this way."

"I will accompany you," Kan-Ten said.

The cartel enforcer sized the Tahni warrior up and nodded curtly.

"Take care of my daughter," he warned Sandi. "Or I'll kill you."

Then they were both gone, down the other end of the alley, and Fontenot was leaning out and firing again. Everything felt distant inside the helmet, as if it was happening to someone else, and perhaps the distance let her keep her cool, because everything inside her was screaming with a desire to panic and run. She set Adriana down but kept one of her small hands clasped in her own left glove, held onto it like a talisman and kept her secure against the wall while she leaned out over where Fontenot crouched down.

Down the street, the Sung Brothers' mercenaries were less than fifty meters away, darting from cover to cover, from alleyway to sheltered doorway to the lee of an ancient cargo truck, on fire now with its thin metal engine cover shredded and splintered. The incoming fire was sporadic, unorganized, but daunting for all that due to their sheer numbers and Sandi jerked back as a burst of mini-rockets impacted the wall just around the corner from their position, throwing up a cloud of fiery fragments of rock and plaster.

Sandi leaned out again, quickly like a snake striking, and fired off most of a magazine from her pulse pistol. The weapon was high-signature, the passage of the laser pulses clearly marked by flashes of superheated air, and its impacts were equally as dramatic. Stone and brick and plaster and buildfoam and metal vaporized or sublimated in showers of angry red sparks, and a man dressed in black armor with impractically stylish red decoration fell backwards clutching the stump where his right hand had been a moment earlier.

Then Sandi was huddled around the corner with Adriana, crouching protectively over the girl to guard her from the burning fragments coming off the opposite wall as mini-rockets tore at it in raging futility. Fontenot braved the hail of fire with resolute calm, the report of her assault gun just as slow and steady, like a drum beating somewhere in the distance. The consequences of her shots were somewhat more drastic than Sandi's; the rocket-assisted rounds were like giant versions of the incoming fire, with warheads that sprayed targeted spears of plasma in four directions.

Sandi risked another look and saw another of the enemy down, probably dead, being dragged behind cover by his fellows, while the rest of them were staying further back than before. It still wouldn't be enough to get them across that street, though---it was fifteen meters of open space with no cover, and she had to carry the girl. It would be at least two to three seconds, and she and Adriana would both be good and dead before they'd hit the halfway point.

Then she heard the shouts. Two, maybe three voices yelling a warning, and someone screaming in pain. The reports of the weapons changed in pitch as the impacts on the wall lessened and then ceased; the shots were being aimed the opposite direction, toward where Santonio and Kan-Ten were attacking from the rear.

"Go!" she yelled at Fontenot, scooping up Adriana and breaking into a run without hesitation.

Two and a half, maybe three seconds, yet it stretched on forever, and Sandi was sure *someone* was going to look back, start shooting and she and the child would both die bleeding on the cracked pavement. They didn't; the next alley over swallowed them up and Fontenot behind them, and they were across.

"Go, Kan-Ten!" Sandi tried to shout it, but it came out as a dry rasp. "We'll cover you from this side."

"Get the child to the ship," the Tahni replied. The 'link pickup cleaned up his words in software before transmitting them, so she could understand what he was saying, but she could still hear in the background the sound of weapons discharging and rounds impacting all around him. "We will meet you there."

She wanted to argue with him; it felt right to say no, to insist on covering the two of them. But the girl was the mission, and more than that, she was their responsibility. She made a motion at Fontenot to move out and the older woman didn't argue.

The Sung Brothers troops hadn't made it as far as the interior wall of the city, and the *Acheron* was exactly where they'd left it. She looked, Sandi thought, incredibly beautiful and otherworldly sitting there in her silvery, streamlined glory among so much squalor and destruction. The fog had cleared, and she realized that the system's primary had risen somewhere behind the jealous grey of the clouds, giving just the slightest glint to the cutter's reflective finish...and making her feel suddenly very exposed.

"Open the ramp," she called to Ash when they turned onto

the last street, past the warehouses, nothing between them and the wall but the ship.

An expanding pie-slice of welcoming light flooded out to greet them as the ramp lowered, and stretched out in backlit shadow at the top of it was Stephania Willow. She stood like an ancient stone sentinel, waiting and watching; but when she saw her daughter she flew down the ramp with her feet barely touching its metal surface.

Sandi didn't remember handing the girl over, but suddenly Adriana was out of her grasp and in her mother's arms and she didn't know how she'd ever considered the woman cold and unfeeling.

"What are you crying about, Mommy?" The words were muffled, spoken against Stephania's shoulder as it shook with sobs. "I'm okay, I promise."

"I'm going back for Kan-Ten," Fontenot said, shifting her assault gun to her left hip as she pulled a spare drum for it from a pouch slung over her shoulder.

"There is no need." The Tahni's voice was in her headphones, not her external audio pickups, and his transponder signal showed him coming in from the next street over from the one they'd traversed.

Sandi turned and saw him running in that curious, shuffling gait that no human could have quite duplicated; it looked awkward as hell, but he covered ground as fast as any unaugmented human she'd ever seen. The armored pauldron over his left shoulder was charred and cracked, and she saw blood running down his left arm beneath it, though it didn't seem to slow his pace.

He was alone. There was no sign of the enemy or of Eduardo Santonio. She felt a hiss of breath go out of her. Whatever else the man might have been, whatever sins he might have committed, he was a father to his daughter. Fontenot scanned the approaches, covering the Tahni as he stomped up the ramp, then hitting the control to close it.

"Get us out of here, Ash," Sandi said, then began pulling off her helmet and walking towards the cockpit.

"Where's my Dad?" Adriana asked plaintively.

Sandi paused and looked behind her, saw the little girl standing in front of Kan-Ten, hands bunched defiantly into fists. The alien looked down at her, at her liquid green eyes, and then up to her mother, who wore a pleading expression that she wasn't sure the Tahni recognized.

"Your father remained to protect you," he answered, after a moment's pause. To her, his face looked expressionless, though she knew by now that there were cues to it that she couldn't reliably pick up. "He wished to make sure that the ship could get you to safety."

"Come on, darling," Stephania said, tugging at the little girl's shoulder as the whine of the turbines spinning up grew louder. "We need to get strapped in."

"Daddy didn't want to come with us?" Sandi clenched a fist and fought back an old, old pain deep in her chest at Adriana's words.

"He has work to do," the girl's mother explained softly, securing the straps of one of the fold-down acceleration couches. "But he loves you very much, and I know he's going to miss you."

"He told me," Kan-Ten spoke again, surprising Sandi and, from the look on her face, Stephania as well. "Your father told me before I left him," the Tahni expounded, "to tell you that he loved you, and that he was sorry."

"I'll stay back here with them," Fontenot volunteered, working on getting the mother strapped into a seat.

Sandi headed for the cockpit and Kan-Ten followed. She

wasn't sure, but she thought he wanted to be away from the girl and her mother.

"Thank you," Sandi said quietly as they walked. "There are some things kids shouldn't have to hear."

"None of us may go home again,' Kan-Ten said, not looking at her, or at anything on the ship around them. "She'll learn that lesson soon enough."

CHAPTER TWO

Kan-Ten didn't care for Sylvanus. He knew the others did, that they appreciated the mild weather here, and the comparative sophistication of the capital city, Dolabella, and that it was the most civilized place they could go even out on the Periphery without being arrested. He had to admit that the architecture was pleasant and the dry, temperate climate was a relief from the bitter cold on many of the Pirate World colonies, but he could never be comfortable here.

He sat on a chair not designed for his body, at a street café that served nothing he could stomach, under street lights that were the wrong frequency for his eyes, in a city almost devoid of any of his people, and he felt an almost constant subsurface tension. Nothing was right here, nothing was familiar and there was nowhere he could fit.

I should be used to that, he thought. *It has been my life for years now.*

He sipped water out of a glass not designed for his mouth and tried not to spill it, and listened to his companions engage in the human custom of "small talk" as they sipped their noxious "coffee" and waited for the other human, the one none of them could stand. That, at least, he had in common with his friends: he, too, did not trust Captain Richard Fox.

When they saw the man walking their way up the busy street, the conversation died and four sets of eyes turned toward him. He was an average-looking human, not especially tall or particularly short, though all of them seemed short to Kan-Ten. Fox had a certain roundness to his face that still didn't imply softness, and a quality to his dark eyes that the humans told him looked cruel. He was not in uniform; he never was when he met with them. Instead, he wore a multicolored shirt with patterns that seemed to match the plants he'd seen on some of the human colonies. Fontenot had told him it was a "Hawaiian shirt," whatever that meant. He assumed Hawaiian was one or another of the human worlds.

"Good evening, ladies and gentlemen," Fox said in his typical, casual manner, pulling out a chair with a scraping of metal on stone, and sitting down opposite them at their outdoor table. "I trust things went well at Barataria Bay."

"As if you don't already know," Sandi scoffed. "Hell, you probably knew before we did."

Fox chuckled softly, then waved for one of the café's human waiters, ordering his own caffeine-laden drink from the young man and waiting until he was gone before continuing.

"We should get down to business. Things are not going well for your old friend Jordi Abdullah," he confided, the corner of his mouth turning up.

Humans, Kan-Ten thought not for the first time, made an inordinate number of expressions with their mouths. It was unsettling; mouths were useful for eating and speaking, while meaning was rightly transmitted with hands and stance and the set of one's shoulders.

"Grand Terre isn't that big of a loss for him or *La Sombra*," Fontenot said. She tore a section off of the muffin she'd ordered and put it in her mouth with what seemed like amazing delicacy for hands that could rip apart metal. "It's a setback, but I've seen him come back from worse."

"This time is different. The other cartels are joining forces against him. The Sung Brothers have recruited what's left of the *Novya Moscva Bratva* and the Rif, and they're working and planning in concert. He can't beat them all, not with his power base in the Pirate Worlds shrinking."

"Good riddance," Ash Carpenter muttered, hiding his expression behind a coffee mug. Kan-Ten had the sense that the former Fleet pilot still resented the things he'd been forced to do when he'd been trying to help get Sandi out of debt with Jordi Abdullah and his cartel. The young man was still an idealist, and Kan-Ten had no idea how he managed that.

"He won't go quiet into that good night," Sandi warned, putting a hand on Ash's arm. "If Captain Fox is telling us this, I'd bet it's because Jordi's about to try something drastic."

"Perceptive as always, Ms. Hollande," Fox told her. The waiter returned with his order and Kan-Ten hissed impatiently as they had to wait for him to leave once again. "Jordi is running low on ships, on troops, and on money. So, what I've heard is, instead of spreading all the resources he still has out on three or four fronts fighting to keep his hold in the Pirate Worlds, he's going to put it all together to seize a new foothold somewhere the other cartels can't touch him."

"Don't tell me." Fontenot's eyes---the biological one and the cybernetic one both, the latter's motions slaved to the former---went wide. "That crazy fuck's going to try to take over a Periphery colony, isn't he?"

"What?" Ash blurted, nearly spilling his drink. "That's fucking impossible!"

He realized how loud he was being and paused, glancing around self-consciously before continuing at a lower volume.

"He'd have the Patrol all over him in days, if not the Fleet! He can't believe he can get away with that!"

"Normally, no," Fox admitted. Then he frowned, a more serious and troubled expression than Kan-Ten remembered seeing on his bland face in the two years they'd known him...and been in his employ. "But things are in a flux right now. I'm not at liberty to go into details, but there's, well...a sort of political power struggle going on right now between the military and parts of the civilian government."

"Shit," Sandi breathed the word and the hand that had rested lightly on Ash's arm clamped down with a sudden alarm. "Are we talking a military coup?"

"Not as such," Fox dithered. "It's complicated, and it has to do with things that don't matter much to people out here in the Periphery, much less the Pirate Worlds, things like the influence of the Corporate Council on the DSI and the Patrol."

Kan-Ten didn't know what the Corporate Council was, but he had heard of the DSI: they were the civilian intelligence agency that was somehow the rival to the military intelligence service Captain Fox worked for. That sort of dynamic made no sense to Kan-Ten, but then he found that humans frequently made no sense.

"The long and short of it is," Fox went on, "everyone's distracted. There are things going on you may never even hear of out here, but it's a great time to act if you want to pull some shit off and have it be a *fait accompli* by the time anyone in the Commonwealth federal government notices it." He spread his hands. "And Brigantia is the perfect place to do it."

"Brigantia," Ash tasted the word, eyes narrowing in thought. "I've heard the name, but I can't remember any details."

"It's one of the smallest Periphery colonies, down an orphan Transition Line with no other connections, and no wormhole jumpgate." Fox had shifted to a tone that Fontenot had told him was something like a human teacher speaking to children; it was one of the reasons the cyborg couldn't stand talking to him. "It was settled the very first year the Transition Drive was invented, but it doesn't have much to offer except a habitable ecosphere. During the war, the Tahni," Fox glanced directly at Kan-Ten, "conquered it almost as an afterthought, mostly because it was so lightly defended."

"There is a Tahni community there," Kan-Ten said, recalling the name now himself, from reports he'd read. "A large one."

"There is. And from what we've been able to piece together, they aren't happy. There have been acts of violence recently, by humans and Tahni, after years of both sides leaving each other alone." He paused significantly. "Almost as if someone was stirring things up."

"Jordi Abdullah is trying to turn the Tahni and the humans against each other," Kan-Ten presumed, feeling an odd tingling in his neck, a premonition that something bad was about to get much worse.

"Let's just say there have been a lot of new faces in the last couple months. And some of them have been Tahni immigrants. There's been one Tahni male in particular who's been connected to a separatist faction that's been instigating for independence from the human colonial government. He's former Imperial military and he's already been kicked off the Tahni homeworld by the provisional government; been kicking around Tahni settlements ever since, getting himself into trouble."

Fox's eyes had never left him the whole time he'd been speaking, as if the human knew something that he didn't, as if he was waiting for a reaction.

"The male," Kan-Ten asked slowly. "What is his name?"

Fox nodded, as if he'd been waiting for the question.

"Vala-Kel."

———

The transport driver was a gaunt, skeletal old man with skin the texture of cured leather, and he gave Kan-Ten a long, suspicious look as the Tahni climbed out of the passenger compartment ahead of Fontenot.

"You got a problem?" Korri Fontenot demanded, never one to shrink from a confrontation. Her glare was challenging and her broad shoulders would seem imposing even to someone who didn't know they were mostly metal.

"You keep strange company," the man muttered in a sour voice that made her think he might have caused trouble about it if he'd been younger or her smaller...or if she hadn't been very openly carrying a rather large handgun at her hip.

"That's my business," she snapped, tossing a twenty-dollar Tradenote at the man then slamming the door behind her.

The old truck creaked and shuddered as it rolled away from them, its electric motors humming softly in comparison to the plaintive groans of the worn-out shocks and suspension. Fontenot squinted at the glare of the system's primary star, Belenus, reflecting off the angry red sandstone that stretched from the spaceport to the edge of Gennich, Brigantia's largest city. It wasn't nearly as big or as modern as even Dolabella or other Periphery world capitals, much closer to a Pirate World town in size and scope.

The planetary Constabulary loomed over everything else on this end of town, an edifice of stone and steel meant to act as a shelter from exterior threats, though it hadn't done much to deter the Tahni when they'd invaded early in the war. It was undeniably impressive though, a fortress three stories tall and two hundred meters on a side, with walls ten centimeters thick, and from their mission brief, she knew it was also the center of the planetary government, such as it was.

This place had been bustling and growing, not that long ago. There were four or five half-constructed buildings visible just from this end of town, dinosaur skeletons only half-assembled in this outdoor museum to life a hundred and fifty years ago in the Core worlds. No workers congregated at them, no machines poured buildfoam or locally-made cement, no trucks hauled materials from the spaceport.

Because there are *no materials*, she thought with a sense of disgust at the waste.

"That's the other half of Jordi's plan," Fox had explained to them nearly a week ago on Sylvanus. "Since the system has no wormhole jumpgate, Brigantia gets one hundred percent of its mineral resources from asteroid mining in the outer system. The returns aren't large enough for the Corporate Council to get involved, but there's an independent mining consortium that works in conjunction with an import group in Gennich. It's an efficient, inexpensive system: reusable barges with primitive, cheap fusion pulse drives take loads of nickel-iron to planetary orbit, where it can be brought down by heavy-lift cargo shuttles or used for orbital construction."

The Fleet Intelligence officer had paused, cocking an eyebrow. "Well, it *used* to be cheap and efficient, until the attacks started."

"Shit," Sandi had muttered, as if she'd seen it coming.

"They thought it was pirates at first, but they didn't steal anything." Fox had shrugged. "Not that there'd be any money in stealing processed nickel-iron. Then they thought it was blackmail; they thought at some point, there would be demands for money to stop the attacks. But that hasn't happened either."

"I don't get it," Ash had interrupted, his face twisted into a confused frown. "If it *is* Jordi behind the attacks on shipping, what is he hoping to accomplish? Can't they just get minerals from surface mines?"

"There *are* no surface mines. They were never built because asteroid mining was cheaper and it was a good setup for everyone involved. And they certainly can't start any now without either equipment or the raw materials to fabricate it." Fox had leaned back in his chair, steaming mug held in both of his hands. "As for what he wants to accomplish, that's easy. He wants to destabilize the planetary government, and denying them key resources is a good start. The system has no armed spaceships other than a couple shuttles out in the belt with jury-rigged mining lasers." He had nodded towards Ash and Sandi. "That's where you two come in. The mining consortium has put out a call for armed ships to guard the cargo runs, and particularly Transition Drive ships. You're going to answer that ad, and while you're out there, you're going to end that threat."

"All by ourselves?" Sandi had asked, a skeptical tilt to her eyebrow.

"There can't be that many of the pirates; Jordi doesn't have enough money to have hired more than a handful. Use those tactical minds that served you both so well in the war."

"And what about us?" Fontenot had wondered. "We're going to solve the whole Tahni-human kerfuffle, just the two of us?"

"There *isn't* anyone else. There's no backup, no cavalry to call in if things go wrong. But I think one of you," Fox had said, looking at Kan-Ten, "may be uniquely suited to handle this situation."

And that had been that. There'd been no further explanation coming from either Fox or Kan-Ten, despite several attempts to press her friend for details on the flight out. He'd simply said it was a private matter and he'd tell her more if it proved necessary.

The streets didn't seem crowded for mid-day in the late summer. It was a bit on the hot side, but dry for all that, and she'd have expected to see more workers and children and just citizens out on the streets getting a quick lunch. But the only people out were in vehicles, or just in front of businesses, half-heartedly unloading cargo from ancient trucks. No Tahni on this side of town, either.

"Maybe," she said to Kan-Ten, "we should have had that guy drive us right to the Tahni neighborhood."

"I do not believe he would have been willing," Kan-Ten pointed out, with what she had to admit was admirable insight into human nature, for an alien.

She found herself glancing over at her old friend every few seconds, still taken with his clothes. In all the time she'd known him, he'd worn combat fatigues as if he'd lacked anything else. Now, he was dressed in what she knew was traditional garb for a Tahni male: a complex garment somewhat analogous to a tunic and slacks, but composed of multicolored strips of cloth connected together with what looked like spit and good wishes. It was fascinating to watch; it seemed as if it would fall apart at any moment, yet it never did.

He wasn't visibly armed; he'd thought it wouldn't be a good idea since they'd be dealing with a human population already keyed up about the Tahni, and she had to admit that, too, was admirable insight. Seeing the stares and dirty looks he was getting from humans in storefronts or vehicles as they passed by, though, she wondered if it had been a sound tactical decision.

"Maybe we should rethink our plan," she said quietly, walking beside Kan-Ten. "I don't know if you're going to be welcome in human businesses here."

"The mission remains the same," the Tahni reminded her, eyes fixed straight ahead. "This only works if word spreads that I'm here."

Fontenot shrugged and scanned their surroundings. The Constabulary was out of sight and the neighborhood was changing. The mostly-shuttered industrial businesses gave way gradually to the hospitality district, which seemed nearly as hard-hit by the downturn in imports. The largest hotel was boarded up, its holographic projectors stripped off, replaced by a "for lease" sign, its size as small and pitiful as its prospects of finding a buyer. A few small restaurants were still open, though, most with connected bars, and their destination was one of the smallest.

It was little more than a hole in the wall, sandwiched between a closed-down pleasure doll rental shop and a custom bakery.

The sex doll place is closed, but the fucking bakery is still open? Fontenot thought, chuckling softly in disbelief. *These people must really like their cakes.*

The sign above the door wasn't holographic, or even electronic; it was shaped from what looked like tarnished brass and mounted with old-fashioned bolts on a frame attached to the stucco front. "CAP ROCK GRILL." The words were twenty centimeters tall and tarnished green with neglect that matched with the cracks in the facing and the scratched, clouded transplas of the windows. Fontenot paused on the step up to the front door, about to ask Kan-Ten one more time if he was sure, but he pushed past her and opened the door with a shoulder against its faded brown paint.

A blast of cool air hit Fontenot as she stepped inside behind him, and she felt sweat she hadn't realized was there drying abruptly, sending a chill down the natural part of her neck. The grill wasn't terribly crowded for what was, ostensibly, lunchtime, but everyone inside was human and all of them turned to look at Kan-Ten as he and Fontenot moved to the counter.

"So much for this place being a mixed establishment," she muttered half to herself. Their reports had listed the Cap Rock as a business that catered to both humans and Tahni, but times, she noted, had changed.

She sidled up next to Kan-Ten at the lunch counter, pulling out a stool and more leaning into it than sitting down. There was one woman working behind the counter, haggard and drawn, with the hope drained from her pale, blue eyes. She wiped greasy hands on a greasy apron and regarded Fontenot with an expression too apathetic to be a scowl.

"You know," she said with a voice like feet shuffling on the pavement, "we don't serve any of that Tahni food here anymore." She rubbed at her face with her forearm, scratching at an itch she didn't want to stain. "You should probably take your friend somewhere else."

"Well, damn," Fontenot replied, sniffing a disappointed sigh. "We'd heard good things about this place."

"There are restaurants for his kind out in the District." The waitress shook her head, and Fontenot thought she saw a bit of sadness in the woman's eyes, the first sign of life the walking corpse had shown. "Things haven't been that good here lately, especially between us and the Tahni. You should go."

"You are hungry, my friend," Kan-Ten said to her. "If you wish to eat, I would be happy to wait and drink water." She wasn't sure if he was feigning concern, because she honestly didn't know what a concerned Tahni sounded like.

"You heard Tammy," a deep, booming male voice came from the kitchen of the grill. "You and that damned freak get the hell out of here."

The man was tall and skinny, with a stringy brown beard; he was as ragged and greasy as "Tammy," but not quite as apathetic. There was a fire behind his eyes, the rage of having been wronged, and the satisfaction of finding a target to take it out on. There was what looked like a short-barreled shotgun cradled in his hands, the muzzle pointed low, towards

Fontenot's gut. Her hand went automatically toward her holstered Gauss pistol.

"That gun doesn't scare me," he told her, taking a step forward. "You'll be puking blood before you get the chance to use it."

"All right," she said coolly, backing toward the door. That civvie popgun didn't scare her either, but some things were better left unsaid. "We're leaving."

The air seemed heavier when they exited the diner, as if a front was moving in and the storm was about to hit. The sky had clouded over and on the street...she saw the shift in the patterns, the people circling where there had been none before. Some were watching, eyeing the two of them as they walked out of the hotels and restaurants and into close-packed apartments and rowhouses. The minutes dragged with their steps, and as she and Kan-Ten moved deeper into the residential district, the buildings seemed to crumble and degrade with each block; she could see them watching in doorways and open windows and front porches, children and younger teenagers and older people, grandparents, perhaps great-grandparents.

Others were moving, circling, trailing them like a wolfpack tracking prey, looking for weaknesses. The walls seemed too close now, the street too narrow, although it hadn't shrunk a centimeter. They weren't locals; she could tell that by the way they carried themselves. They might have lived in this city, but they weren't from this neighborhood. They were too well-fed, dressed too nicely, far too confident. They stayed thirty or forty meters back, just keeping the two of them in sight but not close enough to give her an excuse to draw her gun, not even close enough that she could have a clear idea of their numbers.

"They are driving us," Kan-Ten said. She couldn't see his eyes moving under the ridged brows, but she knew him well enough to know they were scanning from side to side, the same as hers, taking everything in.

"Tell me something I don't know."

"You have been alive a long time, my friend. I am not sure there's anything you don't know."

Fontenot buried the laugh in a snort, trying to keep the smile off her face. It would give the wrong impression at the moment. Then they rounded a corner and even the hint of a smile faded. An old cargo truck was parked sideways, blocking the road, the canvas cover hanging across the metal frame over its cargo bed flapping in the warm wind funneled between the rowhouses. Seven men were arrayed across the breadth of the road in front of the truck, a few with lengths of metal pipe held in rough hands, one with a handgun, and another carrying a short-barreled shotgun.

She slowed her pace, the soles of her combat boots dragging across the pavement, and she drew the Gauss pistol from its holster, holding it at her side. The ones behind them were closing in now, at least ten of them, cutting off their retreat. None of those had guns, but she saw a few knives and clubs.

All of them were men, she noted with amusement, not one over thirty by her best estimate. Were they just hardcore frontier types, she wondered, who thought "womenfolk" were too soft for this sort of dirty-work, or was it just that young men were the only ones stupid enough to get talked into it?

The eternal mysteries of life.

"You can't get us all with that one handgun," one of them said from behind her.

She turned and regarded him, keeping her gun at her side. He was tall, fairly good-looking she thought, though too young for her tastes. He was well-built, with biceps and shoulders that strained against the new-looking work shirt he was wearing, and a mop of brown hair that threatened to fall into his eyes. He had a black-bladed dagger grasped in his left hand, held in a knife-fighter's grip like he'd used it before.

"No," she agreed, raising the Gauss pistol one handed and lining its muzzle up with his head. "But I can make sure I get you first."

"So what?" the younger man scoffed, with depressingly convincing bravado. "You think there's so fucking much to live for here that we care about dying anymore?"

"I think we're about to find out," Fontenot muttered, mostly to herself. Then, aside to Kan-Ten: "I'm going to kill the two with guns. Get ready to make a break for it."

Everything seemed to happen at once. Someone off to the side, maybe one of the crowd encircling them, maybe one of the spectators, threw a rock, a piece of pavement, something---there was less than a second between the time she saw it and the moment it hit, and it connected in just the wrong place. Fontenot felt a spear of pain in her right temple and polychromatic flashes danced across her vision as she staggered backwards, sensing more than hearing the warning from Kan-Ten that the crowd was attacking.

She still had the pistol in her hand, but everything seemed to be floating behind a veil of fog; she could see and hear, but the sights and sounds were disconnected from reality, and her response to them seemed to come minutes after the stimulus. She lashed out with her fists, slowly and clumsily, but there was enough power behind those fists to make even clumsy blows devastating. One hand missed entirely, but the other connected with a meaty shoulder and she heard the crack of bones breaking and the high-pitched scream of pain, felt whoever she'd struck flying away from her.

Then there were more of them, three, four, half a dozen, clenching at her, trying to pull the gun out of her hand, trying to take her down. Fists struck at her, most bouncing ineffectually off synthskin-covered metal but one connecting with the human side of her jaw and causing another explosion of light in her vision, another jolt of numbing pain. She thrashed wildly, freed from her normal restraint by an incipient concussion that dulled her thoughts.

Bones broke and men fell and the only reason she hadn't shot anyone was that there were three of them holding desperately onto her right arm, weighing it down, keeping the barrel pointed downward. She pulled the trigger anyway, the tungsten slug discharging into the pavement and sending fragments exploding upward, and someone howled in pain as they were struck in the face by the bits of concrete.

There was the crack of a pistol discharging; it was, she realized dimly, a long-obsolete projectile weapon, not even rocket-assisted or guided, just a propellant and a slug, and the round bounced off the body of the cargo truck with a petulant whine. She snarled at the three men holding her left arm and grabbed one by the ribs through his flesh, feeling the bone crack beneath unyielding metal fingers, then throwing him into another man.

Shouts and screams and pain and blood and she had a dim, distant sense that Kan-Ten was fighting too, and not doing nearly as well. She thought she saw him go down under three of the men, heard a shout of triumph from one of them and she knew she was going to have to start killing people...

Something hit her hard in the right hip, sending her tumbling out of control over the pavement, scattering her attackers with the dull thump of metal on flesh; and, as she hit the street on a metal shoulder, she could see the front end of the cargo truck spinning inward, the left side crumpled from the devastating impact of the transport van that had run into it at top speed. The truck skidded to a stop, bouncing rhythmically on its suspension before settling forlornly into a cockeyed rest, leaning into the ruin where its left wheel had been bent inward.

The van should have been in just as bad of a shape, Fontenot thought, but then she saw the bulldozer blade welded to the front of it like a snowplow, saw the edge of it dig into the street as it jerked violently to a stop. Tall, powerful figures in multi-colored strips of cloth jumped from doors on both sides of the transport, tumbling out recklessly, hands filled with clubs of wood or metal, a couple of them holding oddly-shaped blades. They swarmed over the humans who'd piled on top of Kan-Ten, clubs swinging up and down like the keys of a piano, the notes muffled thumps and cries of pain.

When was the last time I saw a piano? Fontenot wondered irrelevantly, still in a haze. *Was it on Earth, two hundred years ago?*

They were Tahni, she realized abruptly, some rational part of her brain struggling to seize control once again. The people in the van, the ones attacking their human assailants, they were all Tahni males. They looked like shards cut from the same stone, all of them adults of an age that they could have served in the war, their cues grown long and wrapped around their necks in the style of Tahni warriors.

The shotgun roared; she'd nearly forgotten about it, but the man holding it blasted a round toward the Tahni, ignoring the danger to the men they were fighting, and Fontenot saw a splash of blood from the flechettes striking one of the males in the leg. She rolled over on her side, bringing up the Gauss pistol and aiming carefully, her finger just touching the trigger pad. The electromagnetic slug-shooter bucked and the tungsten projectile smashed into the receiver of the shotgun, slicing through two of the fingers of the man's right hand and then through his right bicep as well before it died in the rear wheel well of the battered cargo truck.

He was a long-limbed, rangy young man with jet-black hair braided down his back, and those braids thrashed as he screamed and flopped to the ground, clutching at his ruined hand and broken arm, blood seeping through his fingers. The one who'd had the handgun turned towards her, raising it, and she came up to one knee, shooting him through the right ankle to make sure the round dug into the street afterwards instead of heading off into the apartments. The Gauss pistol's discharge was a hum-snap-crack, its impact a flat, echoing slap interrupted by his cry of pain. He went to the ground and she rose, putting another round into the fallen pistol and watching the cheap, pot metal fly apart.

Behind her, the engine of the van roared with a snarl of alcohol-burning power and it backed down the street, tires screeching. The Tahni had piled into it in the seconds she was turned the other direction, taking with them their wounded man, and Kan-Ten, and leaving scattered, battered humans...and her.

"Goddamnit," she muttered.

She clambered back to her feet and began to run.

CHAPTER THREE

Images swam across Kan-Ten's vision, distorted and dreamlike, towering over him like the spires of the Imperial Center, back on a home he'd never see again. He rubbed at his eyes to clear them and the swirling, chaotic shapes turned into faces, Tahni faces, warrior faces, regarding him with what might have been concern or just interest. He felt cold metal against the back of his head, felt the vibrations and occasional bumps of tires on a roadway; he was in a vehicle, though he didn't remember boarding one. He slowly rolled onto his side and pushed himself up to a seated position, cataloging the aches and pains his body registered as he moved.

"Are you injured, brother?" one of the males standing over him wondered. He held on to a plastic handle affixed to the bare, metal wall of the van and swayed slightly with the bumps in the road. "I am Rhin-Jan," he added, as custom demanded.

"Not badly." Unless there was a bleed in his brain from one of the blows he'd taken, but lacking an auto-doc or a fully-equipped medical lab, there was no way to know that. "I thank you for coming to my aid. I am Kan-Ten."

"Oh, I know of you, brother."

Kan-Ten thought the remark curious, but the male did not elaborate. He looked around him, trying to get a sense of his surroundings now that his head was clearer. The van's cargo compartment was large, but it was packed with at least ten Tahni males, crammed in shoulder to shoulder except for one sitting with a leg stretched out across the floor, wrapped in a blood-soaked bandage.

"Will he be all right?" Kan-Ten wondered, gesturing towards the wounded male.

"The bleeding is controlled." Rhin-Jan made a sign of equivocation. "The Emperor knows the Emperor's Will."

Kan-Ten very carefully did *not* react to that, much as the sentiment angered him. The Emperor's Will had done, as Fontenot might have put it, fuck-all to save them from human Marines invading their homeworld and destroying their temples.

"We are nearly there," the male went on. "We have trained medics at our base."

"Our base," he'd said, a peculiar choice of words. As if this were a military operation and all of them still warriors. His eyes went to the metal and wood cudgels, some stained with blood, and decided maybe that was the case.

The van's brakes squealed and the pavement grumbled beneath it, and those standing were jerked against their handholds as the vehicle came to a stop. One of the males pushed open the side doors, and hands from outside lifted the wounded man out, supporting him. Kan-Ten pulled himself to his feet, intending to exit behind them, but the rear doors were thrown open from without, and a tall, strong-faced male leaned in, the very image of a Tahni warrior.

"My brother," Vala-Kel said, holding out a hand. "It is so good to see you once again."

. . .

The building had once been a metal-working shop, deep inside the Tahni district, kilometers outside the main part of the city of Gennich. Like all Tahni workshops, it had apartments above and below it, but the shop itself had been cleared out, its machinery moved elsewhere, leaving only a fine dusting of metal shavings to prove it had ever been there. Vala-Kel had led him inside, through the old shop, and he'd noted the small collection of weapons there: guns, not clubs, though few of them. They'd stepped through lines of pallets, simple matts on the floor where males could sleep, and into a small back room that had been turned into an office of sorts.

Offices are such a human thing, he thought silently as Vala-Kel closed the door behind them and secured it. *A place where work is done alone, apart from others, as if work is such a dirty thing that no one should see it, or such a private thing that no one should share it.*

This one almost seemed a room for humans, with chairs and a table such as they used, and data terminals connected to the planetary nets through antennae he'd seen on the roof. The only Tahni thing in here was an imperial crest engraved into a stone column set upon that table, in the center. He hadn't seen one since he'd left Tahn-Skyyiah, so many years ago, and certainly never thought to again.

"I am surprised, Vala-Kel," Kan-Ten said as his old friend turned back from the door.

"Surprised to find me here?" the male finished for him, reaching out a hand to touch the crest. "Surprised that I am not home, under the thumb of our conquerors?"

The male had not changed a bit since the war, not one strand of grey in his hair, not one additional crease or line in that patrician face, not a quaver in that orator's voice. He could have led an army, if things had gone differently.

"Surprised that you do not still despise me as a blasphemer,"

Kan-Ten elaborated softly. "As a heretic, for surrendering to our enemies. For not believing in the Will of the Emperor."

"Of course not." His tone was dismissive, as if it were a trivial thing. Kan-Ten might have thought the male was toying with him, but his face was sincere, even enraged perhaps. "You were right, my brother. The mortal being we called an Emperor was nothing but a fraud, a false god. He led us to destruction and disgrace, and here we are wallowing in it, trying to live beside those who despise us."

"And yet you still believe." Kan-Ten gestured toward the crest. "You still hold to the old faith. How, without the Emperor?"

"The True Emperor is still out there." Vala-Kel paced around the table, hands across his chest in a restless pose. There was a manic nature to his expression, something fervent and fundamental. "He waits for us. Our sin as a people is in not searching for him, seeking to find the proper physical vessel for the Spirit Emperor. We have given up on our faith when we should have merely given up on the individual."

"And the others here believe so?" He stepped over to the crest himself, seeing the way the dim lights of the office played shadows from its deep engravings. It was hypnotic, in a way. "They, too, seek the new Emperor? For what purpose? Do you believe this new physical vessel can reclaim our heritage?"

"If he cannot," Vala-Kel countered, "then he is not the true Emperor. When we find him, we will know it."

"I do not understand," Kan-Ten admitted sadly, turning away from the crest and back to the male. "I do not understand how you can still hold true to the faith after all that has happened to our people."

"Faith is nothing if it is never tested, brother."

There was no arguing with the spirit behind those words, so Kan-Ten didn't try. He was constructing his next question carefully when a kick came at the base of the door. He still found that vaguely scandalous; back on Tahn-Skyyiah, only outer doors to homes were kept shut, and only on them would visitors be required to announce themselves. The door opened and the one who'd introduced himself earlier as Rhin-Jan stepped through.

"We have an intruder," he said, though his demeanor was not that of fear or alarm, but merely curiosity. "It is the human who was with your old comrade."

"You travel with one of them, Kan-Ten?" Vala-Kel wondered, eyes fixed on his. "When last we parted ways, you seemed determined to never live under the rule of the humans."

"And I never will," Kan-Ten assured him. "She is not my ruler, she is my friend, and has fought beside me more times than a mortal may remember, including just now when the other humans would have killed me."

"Is this so, Rhin-Jan?" Vala-Kel asked of the male who had been there for the battle.

"It is." Rhin-Jan made a gesture of assent. "The human even shot two of her own kind to protect our people from their guns."

"Then I would meet this rare human." He motioned to Kan-Ten and followed him out of the office and into the main room that had once been a shop floor.

Nearly two dozen males were gathered there, surrounding Korri Fontenot, tensed and waiting for a signal to attack. The woman didn't seem intimidated by them, despite the fact that she'd turned over her handgun; Kan-Ten saw one of the males examining it carefully and he hoped the warrior wouldn't accidentally shoot himself. Fontenot had a pressure cut over her right eyebrow that was still oozing blood, and an incipient bruise along her jawline on that side, but she was steady on her feet and she'd quite obviously run all the way here to make it this quickly. He wasn't certain how far they'd come, but if the maps of the city he'd studied during their flight were accurate, it had to have been at least four or five kilometers.

"Are you all right?" she asked when she saw him approaching behind the crowd.

From the look on her face, he assumed that his appearance was as battered as hers, and he certainly remembered being punched and kicked more than once while on the bottom of a pile of humans.

"I shall endeavor to continue my existence," he told her, and he saw her lip quirk. He had insisted many times that he didn't understand the human concept of humor, but he wasn't quite being truthful; he simply thought it would be funnier to them if they didn't think he was doing it on purpose. "This is my old companion from my service in the Tahni High Guard," he went on, gesturing in a human way toward the other male. "His name is Vala-Kel."

"I'm Korri Fontenot," the woman introduced herself, doing a good job of pretending the name didn't mean anything to her. "Thank you for saving my friend from those assholes."

He saw a look of momentary confusion on Vala-Kel's face and translated the human insult into the Tahni language for him. The warrior showed a vague amusement and replied to Fontenot in halting English.

"I am no lover of humans, female. But you have been a friend of my friend, so no harm will come to you from us." He looked between her and Kan-Ten. "But though you be welcome here for as long as you like, my brother, the human cannot stay. It would make too many of us uncomfortable."

"I will escort you back to the hotel," Kan-Ten told Fontenot in English, then switched back to his native language to address Vala-Kel. "After that, I would most appreciate if I could return here in the morning, so that you might tell how you wound up on this world."

"That is a story that will take some time, my brother." Vala-Kel's face and stance were of satisfaction, as if things had progressed just as he anticipated.

"As the humans say," Kan-Ten made a gesture of leave-taking as someone handed Fontenot back her weapon, "I have nothing better to do."

———

"This place is a dump," Sandi murmured in Ash's ear.

He grunted agreement but didn't look up from his feet. Walking in magnetic boots in microgravity was a pain in the ass at the best of times, but here on Brea it was a nightmare. The tunnels carved through the guts of the nickel-iron asteroid were narrow and claustrophobic, and the strip of metal lining the "floor" was barely a meter across; every few steps they were forced to slide to the side, their toes barely hanging onto the lining, to let someone else pass.

Chemical strip-lighting ran along the ceiling, cheap and easy to install but illuminating poorly and casting swathes of eerie shadows in their wake. The walls were damp, dripping with condensation and slimy to the touch, and the temperature in the corridors, away from the main ventilation fans, was kept at just above freezing. "The Belenus Independent Mining Cooperative" was a fancy name, but the whole thing seemed to be run on a shoestring.

"Next left," Sandi said, nudging him. He looked up and saw the light glaring from the open doorway a few meters down the corridor.

It's a fucking tunnel, not a corridor, he corrected himself. *I've seen better engineering in the Pirate Worlds.*

The light and heat swallowed them like a blanket as they stepped into the conference room. It wasn't much as these sorts of things went, no big holographic projection tanks, no virtual reality headsets, just a ring of two-dimensional flat-panel displays surrounded by concentric rings of metal strips for attendees to anchor themselves. The room was already packed, at least thirty people crammed into a chamber only ten meters in diameter, and Ash was suddenly wishing for the wide-open spaces of the *Acheron's* cockpit.

The crowd inside the conference room was a motley bunch of ne'er-do-wells, closer to what he'd seen at gang summits in Trans-Angeles than a military pre-mission briefing. Vat-grown spacers' leathers were mixed with remnants of old military and Corporate Council uniforms and flight suits, cheaply-fabricated bright-colored flash, and, in one case, a bright yellow fedora. Beards, long hair, braids and tattoos were the norm rather than the exception, and the only ones who looked at all conventional were a pair of young men in blue utility fatigues with some sort of unit patch that Ash didn't recognize.

Everyone was armed, which was also unlike any other asteroid station he'd ever been on, and he and Sandi had buckled on gunbelts as well when they found out they could. Because, well, why *wouldn't* you, when everyone else was?

The woman at the center of the circle of display screens had the typical, string-bean body of someone born in lower gravity and the slump-shouldered, bleary-eyed look of the chronically overworked. She wore utility trousers and magnetic boots and a stained and faded t-shirt under a heavy, armored jacket, and her dark, curly hair was tied into a pragmatic bun. She speared Sandi and Ash with a glare as they found a spot on the metallic strip and Ash suddenly realized they must be the last ones to arrive.

"Sorry," he mumbled, stepping into place beside one of the uniformed men. "Our ship just docked."

"You're from the *Acheron?*" the tired-looking woman asked,

her expression suddenly turning from disapproval to laser-focused interest.

"Yeah," Sandi told her. "Hollande and Carpenter."

"Welcome, I'm Trisha Nassir, Chief of Operations for the Belenus Mining Cooperative." The woman nodded to them. "Sorry to put you on the spot, but the *Acheron* is going to be the star of the show for us."

"We are?" Ash blurted, eyes going wide as he looked over the rest of the pilots and crews in the room and saw them staring at him.

"Let me get to the briefing," Nassir touched a control on her 'link and the displays switched from an image of the Co-op logo to one of a huge, ungainly mineral barge.

"Ugly motherfucker, isn't she?" Nassir asked, but Ash could hear a fondness in her voice that belied her words. "She's a big-ass fusion pulse drive at one end and a big-ass maneuvering thruster package at the other and nothing but magnetic clamps between them. But she can haul up to a hundred standardized shipping cylinders at a time, and each of those can hold 400,000 metric tons of iron ore powder suitable for use in industrial fabricators. She and the others like her are the lifeline of the Brigantia colony and the space station, and the contracts with them are the only thing keeping us in business at the moment, since the work on the moon base has stalled."

A deep scowl passed over her face, and Ash had the sense she'd been scowling a lot lately. "Unfortunately, this is what's happened to the last half a dozen barges we sent insystem."

Another touch on her 'link and the image became a video stream, and fusion fire bloomed from the drive of the ship, propelling it through the black, drowning out the starfields around it. It had, Ash thought, a certain grace to it in motion that it lacked at rest, the difference between a blue whale stranded on a beach and one breaching majestically from the Pacific waves.

"This is from a drone camera kept out at the edge of the belt," she added. "We didn't receive the transmission until hours after."

There were twin bursts of light, miniature novae that were unmistakable to a pilot: two ships Transitioning in, cutters much like the *Acheron* in origin, though less refined. The *Acheron* had seen the benefits of Jordi Abdullah's munificence as well as Captain Fox's government funding, where these ships were pirates working for hire. Their fusion drives ignited as they matched velocities with the barge, pulling even with its bow and then using their maneuvering thrusters to angle their noses toward the cargo hauler.

There was only one reason for them to assume that attitude, and the long, fat cylinder that ran the length of the spine of each of the ships warned him what they were going to do before it happened. Both ships ignited their fusion drives for just a heartbeat, the thrust meant to counteract the recoil from the railguns. Ash winced as the electromagnetic weapons opened fire, pumping meter-long metal projectiles out at 20,000 meters per second.

Railguns and Gauss cannons were proscribed weapons for use in any shipping lanes; the projectiles just kept going long after they missed their target, permanent hazards for any vessel in that orbit. The military hadn't even used them in the war for anything but planetary bombardment. The pirates didn't have those sorts of reservations, nor were they concerned with Patrol inspections or Spaceflight Safety Board fines. The huge, tungsten slugs sliced through the barge's maneuvering thruster assembly, their impact almost anticlimactic. There were no explosions, no light shows, no shower of sparks or clouds of burning gas, but the barge was doomed, for all that.

The two raider ships, their work done, disappeared with twin warp coronas, passing back into Transition Space as if they'd never been. The barge continued on, its computer systems still shepherding it insystem, oblivious to the attack.

"For those of you who rode here on the short bus," Nassir explained, "the pirates just took out the barge's maneuvering unit. It can't make a deceleration flip, can't even maneuver enough to use the gravity well of the star or any of the planets for a slingshot back to its destination. It's a fucking dart now, heading straight for the star Belenus." Her voice was bitter and ragged. "We've tried everything we could by remote commands, but the best we can do just using the main drive is to send it into interstellar space rather than crashing it into the star. Either way, no mineral shipment, no payment, no barge."

"There's no way to use Transition drive ships to take a new maneuvering unit?" someone asked---Ash couldn't see who'd said it.

"Do you have any idea how *big* that maneuvering unit is?" Nassir demanded, sounding almost outraged at the question. "It would take a ship the size of a Fleet cruiser to haul something like that through T-space, and I don't have a fucking Fleet cruiser on standby!" She raised a hand to forestall the next question, patience abandoning her demeanor. "And before you tactical geniuses ask, no, we can't afford to equip the barges with deflector shields or defense lasers or magic fucking beans!"

She stalked back and forth, hands on her hips, the effect spoiled somewhat by the jerky motions of walking in microgravity with magnetic boots.

"This is a shoestring operation, ladies and gentlemen! We are living hand-to-mouth! We use fusion pulse drive barges because they're stone cheap, but even then, there's only so many of them we can afford to build in any period! All this," she waved at them expansively, "all of you, this is a short-term desperation play. You are our last hope, our Hail-Mary, and if you don't come through, we're all going to be looking for jobs sweeping floors on Brigantia by this time next month!" Her dark gaze swept over each of them and Ash felt like shrinking back from its ferocity. "Do you all track what I'm saying? Any more stupid questions? Good."

Nassir manipulated her 'link and the image went back to the pirate cutters, zooming in on them.

"As you can see, these are your standard converted military surplus missile cutters." She shrugged. "They might have been stolen, they might have been pieced together from parts, might have been bought on the black market, who knows? But someone slapped a railgun on each of them and hired them out to whoever's trying to run us out of business, and they're a huge pain in the ass. And yes, we *have* tried arming the barges, but the best we could do was some industrial mining lasers, and these cutters can just jump out and jump back in before we can get a lock on them."

She clasped her hands behind her back, thoughts gathering behind her eyes. "All of you came here in Transition drive ships, of course: small freighters, transports, even one lighter."

She was looking at the two uniformed mercenaries with that one, Ash noted. He was impressed. If their company could afford to send a lighter out here, they must have some serious juice. "Lighter" was a generic term for any medium-size Transition drive freighter that had been converted to a paramilitary vessel by adding armor and weapons, but it was still expensive enough that most guns-for-hire couldn't slap one together.

"Your ships and your help will be important to the mission, but you all face one problem; freighters and even the Savage/Slaughter lighter don't have the multiple jump capacitors that a missile cutter does. You go after them, they jump a few light seconds away, then jump back somewhere out of your weapons' range and by the time you build up the charge for another Transition, they'll have fired on the barge and gone their merry way."

She pointed a long, delicate finger at Ash and Sandi.

"That's where you two come in. The *Acheron* is our only cutter, and from the specs you sent in, it's got enough firepower to take on the pirates. So, while everyone else will be cruising in formation around a single barge, you two will be our reaction force. We want you doing multiple minimum-duration Transitions to stay within commo range from the barges, and if there's an attack on any barge, you're the ones we call."

Ash groaned inwardly as he thought of the reactor fuel that would burn, and the miserable experience of navigating dozens of micro-jumps.

"We'll have reactor fuel available for you on one of the freighters," Nassir said as if she'd read his mind. "And yes, it's going to be a stone bitch. But we're up against it here. Can we count on you?"

Ash looked at Sandi and she rolled her eyes impatiently at the dramatic tone.

"Well, yeah," she snapped. "What the hell else are we gonna' say? We took the job, and when we take a job, we complete it."

"We'll do the best we can," Ash added, trying not to sound as strident as Sandi.

"That's all we can ask," Nassir said. "Everyone, your watch assignments will be sent to your 'links. Report to your ships at 0200 local time…that's three hours, so if you have anything you need to do here first, do it quick."

People began filing out of the conference room and Ash held back with Sandi, letting the others go first to avoid the crush at the bottleneck into the corridor.

"You're *the* Ashton Carpenter and Sandrine Hollande, aren't you?"

Ash winced when he heard the words; it wasn't the first time, and it usually ended badly. He turned, his magnetic soles scraping against the metal floor plates with a sound that set his teeth on edge. The voice had been a clear alto, a bit high for the face that had produced it. It was one of the mercs in uniform, a straight-backed, earnest-faced man about his age, with skin the color of well-aged teak and hair cropped so close to his scalp that it was barely a shadow. The one with him was shorter and stockier and much paler, with the look of a man who didn't want to be here and didn't care if you knew it.

"Depends," Sandi equivocated, cocking a skeptical eyebrow at the man. "Do we owe you money?"

"You two were awarded the Medal of Valor for the Battle for Mars," the mercenary said, and Ash could almost see the capital letters coming out of his mouth, wreathed in awe. Then his face twisted in confusion. "What the hell are you doing here?"

"As it turns out," Sandi said with a dry grin, "you can't actually eat glory. I know, it was a shock to me, too." She squinted at him. "Who are you again?"

"Lt. Benítez," the dark-complexioned man introduced himself. "This," he waved at the pale, stocky fellow behind him, who didn't seem interested in the conversation, "is Lt. Jacobson. We're with Savage/Slaughter...contractors," he added, a bit defensively.

"What the hell is 'Savage/Slaughter' anyway?" Ash wondered, gesturing at the unit patch on the arm of the man's fatigues. It sounded like some sort of sick joke.

"Captain Keller Savage of Fleet Intelligence," Benitez told him, sighing as if this was a question he'd been asked too many times, "and Captain Vontez Slaughter of Fleet Marine Force

Recon. They formed the company after the war, and yes," he admitted, hands held up, "it sounds incredibly lame, but how do you tell your bosses not to name the company after themselves?"

"You guys are pretty big now?" Sandi asked him, arms crossed as she regarded the two of them with a professional curiosity.

"We got a whole fuckin' planet to ourselves," Jacobson put in, his tone a bit surly. "I don't know why the hell we're working for this two-bit mining co-op. They *can't* be paying our usual fee."

"As long as we're getting paid," Benitez pointed out to his fellow contractor, "what do we care? Just do your job."

"Oh yeah," Jacobson scoffed. "I'm the fuckin' ground assault team leader...what the hell am I gonna' be doing on this op? At least you're a shuttle pilot...you might get to take a shot at something. I'll just be stuck running ViR simulations with my platoon on the lighter."

"Either of you ever wonder," Ash asked them, "who's pulling the strings behind this? I mean, someone is obviously bankrolling the raiders; otherwise, they'd be demanding protection payments. And these people," he jerked a head towards where Nassir had walked off, "would probably rather pay them than us."

"What the hell does it matter?" Jacobson wanted to know. "We have to fight them either way."

"Know your enemy and know yourself," Sandi quoted at him and Ash felt the corner of his mouth quirk, "and you need not fear the results of a hundred battles."

"Sun Tzu." Benitez grinned in appreciation. "The whole art of war consists of guessing at what is on the other side of the hill."

"Wellington," Sandi shot back, her own lip curling.

"War is mainly a catalog of blunders," Ash put in.

"Churchill," Benitez said with a laugh. "My favorite."

"Jesus Christ," Jacobson blurted, shaking his head and shuffling towards the door, "it's like the fucking military history class in the Academy with you jokers. I'm going to go get a drink while I have the chance."

Benitez looked after the man, sighing heavily.

"God deliver me from my friends," he murmured. "I'll take care of my enemies myself."

"The Iron Duke," Ash added. "Nice meeting you, Lieutenant." He stuck out a hand and the man shook it.

"And you, Commander," Benitez returned. "Commander Hollande." He nodded to Sandi, and then turned and was gone, and the two of them were alone in the conference room.

"I'm worried about Korri and Kan-Ten," Ash admitted to her. "There's just the two of them down there, and we have no idea what they're walking into."

"Let's concentrate on our part of this," Sandi urged him, tugging at his arm and leading him towards the corridor. "Come on, let's go make sure the ship is ready for a fight. We aren't going to win this by throwing quotes at them."

CHAPTER FOUR

Stepping through the street-level doors of the Brigantian Planetary Constabulary in Gennich was rather like crossing the siege lines into some medieval castle, Fontenot thought. A line of solid metal bollards were set in the concrete ten meters from the entrance to prevent vehicle attacks, and the doors themselves were small and narrow and easily blocked by steel shutters that could roll out of the massive concrete block overhang of the face of the building.

The rising sun disappeared beneath the oppression of that block of reinforced concrete, and she was inside, passing through narrow lanes into security scanners under the watchful eyes of deputies dressed in dark blue armored vests, rocket carbines slung across their chests.

They should be wearing helmets, she thought, looking them over with a critical eye. Instead, each of them wore a blue billed cap and goggles probably linked to the sights of their weapons. *Maybe they can't afford good helmets,* she allowed with a mental shrug.

The man in front of her, a short, dumpy sort with the look of a shopkeeper, passed through the scanners unhindered, barely paying attention to the deputies as the indicator lights turned green and he stepped forward. When she took a long step into the scanning bay, the lights began to flash red and she saw eyes widen behind those tactical goggles, carbine muzzles beginning to swing around.

"Easy," the woman monitoring the scan results cautioned from behind the bank of displays at her raised dais. "She's carrying prosthetics, but I don't see any weapons."

The three men and a woman arrayed around the scanner banks seemed to relax, their weapons going back to rest against their slings. Their fingers still seemed a bit closer to the triggers than before, though.

"You don't look like a Skinganger," the highest-ranking of the deputies opined, eyes going up and down her in a professional assessment. He was a big man, most of it muscle but some of it a bit of comfortable spread that, together with the weathered look of his face told her he was probably coming up on the century mark, which she estimated put him about sixty years up on the other deputies.

"That's because I'm not," she agreed. "I got the prosthetics in an accident when I was younger...I've lived my whole life way out in the Periphery, never had the money or the access to Core World medical tech to get it replaced with cloned tissue."

That wasn't entirely honest, but it was close enough. They also didn't need to know how overpowered her bionics were, and wouldn't, unless one of them was an engineer.

"What's your business here?" the big man wanted to know.

"I'd like to speak to the Constable, if he has a moment. It's about a shooting I witnessed in your residential district yesterday afternoon."

The deputies glanced at each other significantly, a cloud going over the face of the older one. He shifted his weight and his carbine came down a few centimeters across his chest and she could see a name tape affixed to his armored vest. It read "D. Blackard." She wondered if there was another Blackard some-where on the force that made him have to put the "D" there to differentiate them.

"What was your part in all that, ma'am?" Blackard asked her.

"I'd rather discuss that with the Constable," she said coolly. "If he's not too busy."

"Just a minute." The older deputy stepped away, and she could hear him speaking softly over his 'link. He listened for a moment, nodded out of habit even though whoever he was talking to couldn't have seen him. Then he turned back to her and the three deputies around her. "Let her through. I'll escort her up."

"Up" was stairs rather than an elevator, narrow stairs that wound up like switchbacks and she heard the subtle, winded sigh from Blackard as they topped the last landing and headed back to an office suite. The climb hadn't bothered her bionics a bit, but she imagined it got a bit tiresome for someone his age.

The Constable's door was unlabeled, just simple, unadorned grey metal, more like a military base than a police station. Blackard murmured something into his 'link and the lock released with an audible click; he had to yank hard on the handle and the door opened with a reluctant, weighty squeal.

The office was Spartan, telling a tale of a man who liked to keep his life and his work separate. No family videos or stills, no awards, no mementos, just a framed, physical certificate of the Constabulary's charter from the planetary governor on the wall. The desk was large and metallic and massive enough to use as cover in a gunfight, and the man behind it seemed nearly as massive. He was, she thought, older than Blackard even, maybe as old as her. He'd kept himself well, and enjoyed the best modern medicine had to offer out here in the Periphery, but you could tell by the lines in his craggy, weathered face and the set of his eyes and his mouth. Things like that couldn't be disguised by the nanite injections that kept the rest of your body young, couldn't be changed by anything but restruct surgery, and he didn't seem the type to go in for that.

His hair was long and streaked with grey, tied into a pony tail that hung down to the center of his back when he stood from his chair to meet her. He was tall, just a few centimeters short of two meters, and she thought he weighed in at over a hundred kilograms, easy, maybe a hundred and twenty, most of it in his shoulders and chest. After seeing the deputies downstairs, she would have expected him to be dressed in the same, uniform blue; instead, he wore something more akin to what she would have imagined a frontier marshal would have worn in the Old West on Earth. His jacket was leather---real leather, if she was any judge, from an animal and not grown in a cloning vat---and the civilian work shirt under it was as plain and unassuming as his office. His jeans were faded and worn, with a knife clipped into the corner of his left hip pocket.

He looked her over for just a moment, then stuck out a meaty hand.

"I'm Chief Constable Abel Freeman," he told her. Her hand, as big as it was, was swallowed up in his grip, but his handshake was surprisingly gentle. "What can I do for you, Ms...?"

"Fontenot," she supplied. "Korri Fontenot."

"Have a seat, Ms. Fontenot," he invited.

She pulled one of the cushioned office chairs up from the opposite wall and sat across the desk from him, noticing Blackard exiting and closing the door behind them. Freeman waited until she'd sat before lowering his bulk into his own seat, a well-constructed and well-padded office chair that squeaked softly beneath him.

"So, David tells me you were there for the dust-up in the Canyon?" he asked, tone casually conversational.

"'Fraid you have me at a disadvantage," Fontenot replied, hands folded in her lap. "David?" She shook her head. "The Canyon?"

"Sorry." He grinned self-deprecatingly. "David is Deputy Constable Blackard, the fella' that walked you in here. And 'the Canyon' is what we call that area of town where we had third-hand reports of a shooting."

"Third-hand?" She cocked an eyebrow. "Don't you have surveillance drones or at least security cameras?"

"You'd think," he agreed, spreading his hands over the surface of the desk like he was fighting an impulse to make fists with them. "But every security camera we put in the Canyon or the Tahni districts seems to get vandalized before the day's out, and every time we put drones up, they just stop reporting for some reason. So, you can understand how interested I am in hearing what you have to say about this little skirmish." He smiled thinly. "I don't suppose your 'link might have recorded the incident?"

She raised her palms apologetically.

"I'm afraid it was inside a pocket, so there's no video, and the audio would mostly be worthless."

"Of course." The expression on his face made it obvious how much he believed that. "Anyway, go on."

She gave the man a highly-edited version of the story, leaving out the part where she'd shot two people and allowing him to think that it had merely been the Tahni fighting the humans. By the end, he was nodding with what seemed to her like a depressed acceptance of a familiar story.

"Your Tahni friend is lucky he didn't wind up dead," Freeman commented. "Why didn't he come in with you?"

"Well, Constable, after what happened," she pointed out,

"he wasn't sure what sort of reception he'd get here, and honestly. neither was I. There's an awful lot of anti-Tahni sentiment in this city. Did the war hit you guys harder here than I'd heard?" She waved around them at the Constabulary building. "I mean, this place has got to be post-war and it looks like it was built to hold off another invasion." She snorted. "Unless you just wanted to make it such a pain in the ass to get to see you that no one would ever bother to come report a crime."

Freeman chuckled with appreciation.

"Well, there was a bit of paranoia after the military took the place back from the Tahni," he admitted. "But in the last couple years, things had been going pretty well. I don't think you were ever gonna' see humans and Tahni mixing it up at the Friday-night socials, but they ran businesses together, and things were pretty peaceful."

"So, what happened?" she prompted.

"Damned if I can tell you the why," he admitted, "but the what is easy enough. A few months ago, there was a series of attacks on the Tahni districts. Firebombs mostly, which was pretty damned effective since they build out of local wood a lot. Every time, before the attack, the security cameras on that street would get sabotaged, so I couldn't prove anything; but I heard rumors that it was off-worlders, men and women who came in at the port and left right after, which didn't make a damn bit of sense." The Constable shook his head. "The kicker, the thing that really tipped the situation over the edge, was when they attacked the female compound."

He pushed up from his seat and paced over to the framed certificate, looking at it as if it held the answers. "You know much about the Tahni, Ms. Fontenot?"

"A little," she allowed. "What I've learned from my friend."

"You know their males live separately from the females and pre-adolescent children?"

"I'd heard that," she said. "But I've never been around the females."

"From what I've heard, the males get out of control when they're around females of breeding age; like being in heat except times a hundred. They only get together for prearranged mating, to produce children, and the rest of the time the males live in neighborhoods, running their shops and doing their jobs, while the females share a compound outside the town and raise the children. The males pay for part of their keep, and the females make their own crafts and sell them."

He put his hands on his hips. "Well, one night a couple months ago, someone set off an improvised car bomb just outside the walls of the compound and killed eight of the women, and a couple children, too. That about drove the males bugnuts, as you can imagine, and they began to strike back. Like most people in pain, Tahni or human, they struck back at those closest and least deserving first, and burned out the human-owned businesses in their neighborhood."

He sniffed. "We were damned lucky they didn't kill anyone. And it's only gotten worse since then. The men and women who owned the shops have gathered paid thugs to go after any Tahni they catch alone, and the Tahni..." He tossed a hand in frustration. "They've brought their own people in from off-planet as well, and one of them is organizing their own little hit squads. It's a fucking nightmare. You can see it if you walk these streets; everyone is either angry or frightened."

Fontenot frowned, eyes narrowing.

"Why are you telling me all this?" she asked. "In my experience, cops aren't generally this forthcoming."

"You're a concerned citizen like I'm a fucking school teacher," Freeman said drily, eyeing her sidelong. "I know a hired gun when I see one, Ms. Fontenot. I just want to know which side hired you."

Fontenot smiled. The Constable wasn't some dumb, back-country hick, after all. She could appreciate that.

I'll be straight with him, she decided.

"I can't divulge that information. But I *can* tell you this: you're right about the source of this being external." She leaned back in the chair, hands propped under her chin. "Have you ever heard of *La Sombra?*"

———

Kan-Ten chewed the sour-sweet root automatically, hands and head going through motions he'd learned as a child, the smoke of the incense fire filling his nostrils. He tried to remember the last time he'd partaken of the sacrament, the last time he'd shared the Life Root with his brothers, and found he couldn't. It must have been on Andalusia, sometime before the humans had launched their bid to retake the colony, but he couldn't picture the ceremony, couldn't remember the day.

The shadowy innards of the old shop floor seemed a strange place for it, its flat drabness a far cry from the recesses and raised platforms of the worship chambers of home. And yet, perhaps it was appropriate, clinging to the edges of a human world, clinging to life as a people, clinging to a dying faith, that the chamber should be so rough and shapeless.

I should be thinking of the Emperor, he mused. *I should be deep in reverent contemplation of his perfection, in gratitude for the gifts of life and the food that provides it.*

Instead, all he could think of was that he'd grown to prefer the way the *Acheron's* food processors prepared the root to the traditional Tahni dishes, and how much he missed salt. Salt was an incredible seasoning and he was shocked it hadn't spread to the homeworld. Maybe, he thought, there was a future in becoming a salt merchant to Tahn-Skyyiah...

"You seem deep in contemplation," Vala-Kel said, and he suddenly realized that his old friend was standing beside him and that the worship fire in the center of the chamber had been extinguished. "Surely there is much to consider, after all this time."

Kan-Ten dropped what was left of the Root of Life back into the hollow of the carved stone tray, then bent to lift the thing over to where other males were stacking theirs in a corner. The uneaten food would be collected by the adolescent males and taken to the compound of the females, as per tradition.

"I would like to hear," he said when he turned back to Vala-Kel, "the tale of how you came to be here."

"Are you certain? It is a long and sad story, and not one to brighten your mood." At Kan-Ten's insistent look, the other male assented with a set of his shoulders. "Then let us walk."

Belenus was hanging midway down the western sky, and it cast a forest of shadows in the streets of the Tahni neighborhood, a curious image that made Kan-Ten feel as if the place was more illusion than reality. At least out here, in their own neighborhood, he saw male Tahni outside their houses and shops, running errands and pushing hand-carts loaded down with their wares through the street to other shops and houses for trade, rather than huddling inside, terrified to step into the light.

"When we parted at the repatriation center," Vala-Kel began once they were safely away from the house, "you were determined to get as far away from our home and the war and the human government as you could. How did that work for you? How did you live?"

"I lived by the gun, as that was the only trade for which I was trained." Kan-Ten felt no guilt at the declaration; it wasn't as if he'd been killing his own people. "I moved from one place to another out in what the humans call the Pirate Worlds. That was where I met my human friend. We came here on the word that there might be work for our sort here, that there was violence to be done." He paused, motioning to his friend. "And now you know how I came to be on this world. I await your own account."

They walked together in silence for a moment, the only sound the scrape of their sandals on the crumbling pavement.

"I went home, as I said I would," Vala-Kel finally spoke. He kept his eyes straight ahead down the street, his stance stiff and unbending. "I imagined that I would continue the fight against the humans, that I would lead our people in throwing off their rule. But our people were weary of fighting, and their spirit had fled along with their faith. The Emperor was dead, killed by a human Marine, some nameless leader of a squad, and our society died with him."

He paused again before he went on, as if the next part was almost too painful to remember. "You know my father held a high position in the civil government of the capital city. He was recruited by the humans to be one of the leaders of their puppet government, and he arranged for me to work for him. At first, I agreed, hoping to somehow use my position to sabotage the efforts of the humans to rule us. But we had already turned into a planet of informers, each male ready to betray the next in order to keep what power he had. I made the mistake of trusting the wrong 'friend,' and I was given the choice of being sent to an 'education center,' for further 'assimilation' or going off-world to a planet with a Tahni population. I chose the latter and wound up on the world the humans call Anansi."

"I have heard of it," Kan-Ten acknowledged. "There is a large Tahni presence on that colony."

"And they get along very well with the human population." There was bitterness in his voice. "Very well...and to that end, they are prepared to turn in anyone who causes trouble. I fled that world just ahead of the human police, working my way on a private freighter to Jahn-Skyyiah, hoping that there, on a Tahni colony, I would find a warmer reception."

"And did you?"

"At first." The words were grudging, as if he didn't want to admit it but was forced by innate honesty. "The Commonwealth military ruled that world with a clenched fist, and there was much discontent. It was a fertile field to sow revolution, and I had many allies. And I had a son."

"What?" Kan-Ten couldn't keep the disbelief from the set of his shoulders. "Your pardon, brother, but you were a refugee, with no prospects other than fighting a desperate war against our conquerors. What female would make a contract under those circumstances?"

"Surra-Kei was a believer." A posture of grief came over his friend's stance and Kan-Ten knew that this was the story Vala-Kel had not wished to share. "She thought me an instrument of the spirit-Emperor, and she didn't wish my bloodline to die with me. When the humans finally came to arrest me, I was with my son in the visitation center outside the commune of the females. Surra-Kei was coming back to claim him." A long pause, as if the words required a solid push to bring them to the surface.

"There was a battle and I was wounded and taken prisoner. They were both killed."

"I grieve with you, my brother," Kan-Ten said, and meant it. Nothing was more devastating to a warrior than the death of a son before he had the chance to prove his own worth in battle.

"I was languishing there in a cell," Vala-Kel went on, not acknowledging Kan-Ten's words, "my spirit broken, when a brother named Taarak-Sul told me of an opportunity, a way to take the battle to the humans and carve out a place for Tahni on a world where we still had a chance. He told me of a human named Jordi Abdullah, and how he could make this possible for us."

"I have been in the Pirate Worlds," Kan-Ten reminded him. "I know much of the man named Jordi Abdullah, and of the *La Sombra* cartel. Do you really think this man would be willing to help you take this world for the Tahni?"

"It suits his purpose. Of course, he has a selfish motive; I would not trust him if he didn't. But his plans run leg-by-leg with ours: he wants to be rid of the Commonwealth government on this planet. Once that is done, we may have our own land with our own laws, left to our own devices by Jordi Abdullah and his band of criminals. I think it is a fair trade."

Vala-Kel stopped in his tracks and Kan-Ten nearly passed by him, dragging his feet to halt in time to face him.

"What say you, my brother?" Vala-Kel demanded. "Will you pledge your arms to our cause? Will you fight with us to make our own place on this world, free of the humans? Is this a worthy use of your talents, or do you fight only for treasure?"

Kan-Ten looked deep into the eyes of his oldest friend, wondering how much of what he was about to say was part of his cover, and how much was the truth of his spirit.

"I will fight with you until the end."

CHAPTER FIVE

Reality warped and stretched and tore like an old bedsheet, then did the same thing less than a second later, and Sandi pressed her lips together and swallowed hard to keep the gorge in her throat from escaping.

"Shit, that's getting old," Ash murmured, yanking the interface jacks out of the sockets implanted at his temples.

Sandi focused on the main display projection, where the mineral barge seemed to have lurched tens of thousands of kilometers back towards them, growing from a barely discernable dot against the stars to a massive, looming mountain riding a flare of star-fire. Their own fusion drive remained silent; there was no point in burning reactor fuel on the physical drive when they could continue the micro-Transitions every few hours to catch up to the cargo hauler.

Except that it would be so much more comfortable, she complained silently.

She didn't bother to say it because they'd both said it too much over the last two days. They both had years of experience with star travel, and a single Transition didn't bother either of them much; jumping in and out in quick succession however, did nasty things to human perceptions. It wasn't as bad when you were jacked into the interface, which was why they were taking turns in the left seat, but it was still beginning to leave them both with perpetual nagging headaches that were probably more psychological than physical.

"How many more days of this?" Ash wondered, rubbing both hands over his face. "This damned thing practically *crawls*."

"Another ten days until she does her deceleration flip," Sandi reminded him. "After that, there won't be much anyone can do to her short of ramming an asteroid into her."

"Another ten days of this and I'm going to go stark raving mad," Ash said into his palms, his voice muffled. If there'd been any gravity, she knew, he would be sagging in the chair.

"Well, we got another three hours before the next one," she sighed. "Why don't we get some sleep?"

"I'm not tired," Ash told her, shaking his head, his hair flopping side to side.

"Your hair's getting shaggy again," she told him, leaning over to run a hand through it. He usually kept it tightly-cropped, but there hadn't been time before they'd left for Brigantia and he hadn't asked her to cut it on the trip out. "You gonna' let it grow out this time?"

He caught her hand, turned it over and kissed her fingers.

"You gonna' let yours go back to brown?" he countered, nodding toward the red tresses that were hanging below her shoulders now.

"What?" Sandi demanded with a grin. "You don't like me as a redhead?"

"I like you however you want to be," he assured her.

"Good answer. You're not as dumb as you look, Carpenter..."

She yanked at the quick-release for her seat harness and pushed over to him, leaning in to kiss him softly.

"You know, there *are* advantages to having the ship to ourselves," Sandi pointed out, snuggling into his shoulder.

They were both in normal shipwear, T-shirts and shorts and soft boots, and it was easily shed. It orbited above them, floating on the air currents in the cockpit. Skin against warm skin, slick with a thin sheen of sweat and growing hotter with the friction, and then the alarms went off and the lights flashed red and they were tumbling apart in a whirlwind of arms grabbing at clothes and a torrent of fervent curses.

"Oh for fuck's sake!" Sandi bit off, yanking her shorts back on and grabbing at her shirt as she pulled herself into the pilot's seat ahead of Ash.

"Hey!" he protested, grabbing at the back of the acceleration couch. "It's my turn!"

"I agree, babe," she shot him a bawdy grin just as the interface began to close around her consciousness, "but you're going to have to wait until after the battle."

"Shit," he mumbled, and she had a vague sense of him strapping into the copilot's seat before she became one with the *Acheron*.

Diving the interface was the greatest drug humans had ever devised, and as addictive as any of them. Sandi was a silver eagle soaring through a sky full of stars, and some of those stars were man-made candle flames of burning hydrogen. The barge was close, so close it felt as if she could reach out and touch it, but the bogies were closer still, just a few thousand kilometers away. She sprinted to meet them, nine gravities of acceleration squeezing at her chest and reminding her for just a moment that she had a physical body somewhere inside that silver delta. The interface drew her back into its embrace once again, and the punishing boost took a step further away from her consciousness, like a marathon runner pushing the pain and exertion into a compartment so she could keep her pace and finish the course.

There was just one bogie, familiar to her from the mission brief, a converted missile cutter like so many that had been parted out and sold as surplus after the war, like the *Acheron*. She had an eye for such things by now, and she judged that the ship wasn't a junker assembled from spare parts, but a complete body. Was it bought stripped, refitted by its new owners with civilian parts? Or had it been sold on the black market by some corrupt Fleet supply officer on the take?

It might matter, if it still had the military-grade deflectors and Electronic Counter-Measure packets intact. Without shields, one shot from the *Acheron's* proton cannon would blast the cutter to vapors; with the electromagnetic deflectors, they could shrug off a hit, maybe two, especially at extreme range. Best to try to get close. Sandi cut the acceleration and an elephant shifted its weight off of her chest; she thought she heard Ash gasp in relief beside her, but she wasn't sure.

She was concentrating on the jump computations. Sandi had taken class after class on navigating Transition Lines, learned the formulae for calculating the power output for each T-space entry and the time needed for each distance interval. It had been a waste; the ship's computer did all that work for her, requiring only a destination and a pair of fully-charged capacitor banks. The *Acheron* slipped through the space between spaces, ripping shortcuts through reality with bursts of gravimetic energy and coming out only a few hundred kilometers from the barge, between it and the enemy cutter, just beneath the plane of the raider ship's approach. The railgun could only be fired in a straight line from the ship's vector, so he'd have to maneuver to get a shot at them and they'd get the first swing. Unfortunately, the *Acheron's* capacitor banks had both been drained by the double-jump, which meant no proton cannon until they recharged, so...

"Gatling laser, Ash," she murmured.

The remote laser turret was controlled manually by the right-seat copilot or crew chief; even with the interface, there was only so much the pilot could handle.

And it makes them think they're good for something besides spare parts.

The laser pulses were invisible in the vacuum, but the computer simulated them for her, painting a checkered line of red between the wing of the *Acheron* and the nose of the enemy cutter for over a second. A flare of vaporized metal bloomed from the pirate cutter and Sandi had barely registered it before she was kicking herself in the pants with a six-gravity boost. Simultaneously, she began pulling the nose up with the maneuvering jets at the *Acheron's* bow, staying in the enemy's blind spot but still keeping the proton cannon muzzle aimed their way until the capacitors recharged.

Just another few seconds...

Then the cutter disappeared in an explosion of polychromatic light, and Sandi whispered a curse. He'd jumped, and she doubted he'd be going far.

With a thought, she killed the boost and opened herself up to the sensor input, searching for a warp corona that wouldn't be more than a few light-seconds away. There, back toward the asteroid belt, still on the ecliptic for this system, and only a hundred thousand kilometers from her position.

"Hold on," she growled to Ash, then slipped them back into Transition space for a heartbeat.

"Shit!" he grunted as reality folded and spindled and spat them out again.

But he was ready with the Gatling turret and hosed down the other ship with a long burst, chewing a set of charred pockmarks down the underside of its port wing before her pilot turned her stern toward them and ignited her plasma drives. The view in the main screens and the view inside Sandi's head both whited out as a star erupted only ten kilometers away, but she ignored the loss of optical feed and followed their thermal signature, still visible like a torch in the darkness.

Three gravities, then six and she was wishing they were back in the Fleet wearing military flight suits to lessen the impact of the constant acceleration but she kept on the enemy ship's tail, knowing if she gave her the chance to turn on them for even a moment they could use that rail gun and core the *Acheron* like an apple at this range. She just needed one clear shot with the proton cannon, and while they stuck to the enemy's six, the capacitors were recharging.

Unless he Transitions again, she reflected absently. *How long does he want to play that game? What's the fucking point?*

She felt the tickle of the sensor data on the corner of her limits of perception, a warp corona opening up hundreds of thousands of kilometers away, back on the course of the ore barge, and it could only be one thing.

"Fucker!" she blurted, yanking at Transition Space with a force of will. "Goddamn motherfucker!"

She'd been suckered; she felt it like a kick in the gut that was a worse jolt than the quick double-Transition and she flogged the ship at the highest boost she could take short of blacking out. Ash would be unconscious, she was sure of it, but she had to get into position. The cutter was the fraternal twin of the rabbit she'd been chasing, battered and scraped in different spots but definitely from the same gene pool, unmarked and unregistered and modified for its task with weapons illegal in any commercial system.

The *Acheron's* capacitor banks were charging again even as the acceleration mashed her deeper and deeper into her liquid-cushioned couch, making it harder to concentrate on the interface, harder to think or plan or do anything but act on instinct. Fortunately, she had some good instincts. The two ships were less than a hundred kilometers apart when they fired simultaneously.

Time slowed and her brain manipulated the ship and the sensor input faster than any human body ever could, and with more precise judgement than the best artificial intelligences that computer science had been able to produce in two centuries of trying. The proton blast was moving closer to the speed of light than the coffin-sized tungsten dart from the rail gun, and when it struck the enemy cutter, the ship was engulfed in a crackling, coruscating ball of light that could only be the result of the particle beam interacting with an electromagnetic deflector shield.

Damn, they do *have military-grade defenses.*

She had one more charged capacitor and she was getting ready to unload on the cutter when it disappeared in a Teller-Fox warp corona and into Transition Space, unwilling to chance being taken out now that it had fired. Its rail gun projectile remained, though, a silent dagger in the dark, about to turn hundreds of thousands of dollars' worth of hardware and probably millions of dollars' worth of ore into a worthless and short-lived comet heading into the system's primary.

There was no way to stop it; it was too heavy and going far too fast for the *Acheron's* deflectors to affect its course, and a proton burst wouldn't do anything even if she could get into a position to hit it. Sublimated tungsten still travelling at a substantial percentage of lightspeed would do as much damage as the solid kind. Well, no, that wasn't quite true...there was *one* thing she could do.

The ship's belly jets fired, using a good percentage of their limited stores of maneuvering fuel, and the bottom of her seat pressed into her, squeezing her vertebrae together like a child's building blocks, and she felt herself getting centimeters shorter. Vectors and trajectories played out before her like a ballet, streaming green and red lines that curved with gravity and spacetime and she could feel the massive tungsten slug like a whisper from death itself breathing on her neck.

There would be a fraction of a second when their trajectories intersected, and nothing not made of electricity and neurons could have calculated the boost just right...and no computer would ever think to do it. The two bodies in space were only three meters apart when she screamed into the interface and the *Acheron* Transitioned yet again, using the capacitor charge she'd been saving for a second shot at the cutter. Earth-normal gravity returned for the first time in days and she took advantage of the lull of a few seconds to turn and look through her physical eyes at Ash.

He was staring at her in disbelief, somehow still conscious after all the brutal acceleration, his mouth hanging open, his eyes wide.

"Sandi," he said slowly, his voice a dry rasp. "You know I love you. But you're completely fucking nuts."

She giggled at that, and thought that it was probably the wrong response. The part of her still paying attention to the interface noticed the second capacitor bank had recharged and she brought them back into realspace, the Earthlike pull of the gravity field fading as the star-filled black replaced nothingness.

They floated nearly motionless in space, a million kilometers out from the barge. Beside them, tumbling slowly, its velocity stolen by a dimension where such things had no meaning, was the railgun projectile. It was harmless now, unless someone or something was luckless enough to run into it out here in the vasty deep.

"You're also the best damned pilot I've ever met," Ash admitted.

"You keep up that kind of talk," she said with a broad grin, "and I'm going to rip your clothes off again."

"Later." He waved a hand behind them. "We'd better get back and let them know we're not dead."

"Not yet." She looked back with the ship's eyes at the image of the barge, just a bright star among many, moving so fast and yet so slow. "Day's not over."

Jovan Fisher shuffled morosely, hands jammed into his jacket pockets as he paced the same three-meter stretch of pavement over and over. The street light was old, and half-broken, and long past the date it should have been serviced, and three meters was as far as its faded and attenuated glow would reach.

If Portillo came out to check on him, he'd yell at him for staying in the light, and he'd yell at him for having his hands in his pockets, and he'd yell at him for not being more like his old man, most likely.

Fuck him, Jovan thought, staring into the shadowed uncertainty of the back street. *This place sucks.*

It was hot in the daytime and freezing at night, and the bars and clubs sucked, and the locals were ugly as sin, and there wasn't anything to do even when Portillo or Lombard weren't sticking him with one stupid, pointless job or another. Like keeping watch on the warehouse's back entrance.

Who the hell is going to be breaking into some random warehouse in a whole street full of empty warehouses? It's bullshit. Portillo put me out here because he's never liked me.

A shudder went up his back and he cursed softly, pulling a cannabis chew from the bag in his pocket and sticking it between his cheek and gum. Portillo would get on him for that, too, if he saw it. He didn't like people using when they were "on duty."

"On duty," like we're in the fucking Marines or something.

At least they'd let him carry a gun. Its weight was solid and comforting on his hip, even if he'd only fired it a couple times. Maybe he'd get to kill someone while he was here; he knew some of the older types looked down on anyone who wasn't blooded. Maybe if he popped his cherry on this job, Portillo would cut him some slack...

Something hit him in the sternum, something so fast he didn't see it, something so hard it drove the wind out of him and left him breathless and helpless and curled in a fetal position on the cold, damp pavement. His thoughts were a haze of fiery desperation and agony; he didn't even try for the gun, and some small part of his mind that was still coherent realized that something was tugging at his belt, yanking the pistol from its holster.

"P..Portillo?" He tried to yell for the older man into the pickup for his 'link, but the word came out as an inaudible croak.

A finger pried the ear bud out and he heard a distant crack as it was destroyed, then something that must have been a hand, but gripped as tight and unyielding as an industrial exoskeleton, grabbed his ankle and began dragging him away from the back door of the warehouse. His jacket rode up, and his shirt beneath it, and pavement burned at the skin of his back and he wanted to cry out but lacked the breath. Darkness swallowed him up and he tried to thrash and grab at anything, but then he was being jerked to his feet and slammed against the cement block wall of one of the many abandoned buildings in the industrial district.

Someone loomed over him, tall and clad in black, his face lost in the shadows, and a grip as hard as steel clenched at his throat, squeezing just hard enough to warn him not to call for help. He finally managed to suck in a breath but it did nothing to alleviate his rising panic. No one could move that fast.

What the hell is he?

"Do you want to live?"

The voice was smooth, and deep, and sonorous, like one of the computer constructs that the news networks used to narrate the stories. But behind it, there was something sharp and cold and jagged, like broken glass.

"Yes," he mumbled a reply, nodding vigorously. He could feel the scratches on his back itching and burning, but he ignored them, trying not to move, not wanting to give the man any excuse to kill him. He'd discovered very abruptly that, more than women, more than drink, more than drugs, he wanted to survive this night.

The hand at his throat flexed and tilted Jovan's head back until their eyes met. A single ray of illumination fell across the face; it was bland and nearly expressionless, almost more machine than human, with dark hair cut close to the scalp. There was something strange about the big man's eyes, something uneven about the way the stray gleams of light reflected off of them, and Jovan guessed that one was biological while the other was bionic.

"Tell me again," the big man demanded, those uneven eyes boring into his. "Make me believe it. Do you want to live?"

"Yes," he repeated emphatically, trying to nod against the restrictive grip. "Yes, I want to live."

"That's very good." A lopsided smile twisted the bland face into something much less pleasant. "Then let's have a talk."

CHAPTER SIX

GALLATIN'S QUALITY GLASSWORKS WAS THE SORT OF place that simply didn't exist anywhere in the Core worlds. Korri Fontenot had seen its like in the Pirate Worlds, of course, but even in the Periphery it was something of a throwback. On Earth and the Core colonies, everything was transplas, and the only glass you'd ever see was an antique in the private collection of some Corporate Council executive showing off for their friends. But out here, everything that came from Earth or the Core cost money, including the machinery to manufacture transplas, and the petroleum needed for that manufacture, and the machinery needed to drill for that petroleum...

Silicon, on the other hand, was all around them, and turning it to glass was cheap and simple. Windows were crafted from it, and kitchenware, and artwork and furniture, and this place had all of that, out on display in rack after rack as if they were in 19th-Century London. Of course, each item could be fabricated to order, which was not so Victorian, but Mr. Gallatin also offered hand-crafted glassware for a substantial premium.

Fontenot decided that she liked the place...though it probably looked homier and more welcoming with the lights on, and without the smashed-in door. Michael Gallatin would probably have agreed, if he could have talked with the sole of her boot pressing down against his throat.

He was a heavy-set, older man, weathered and lined with the years in this dry, harsh climate and with a bit of silver in his bushy, dark hair, but still healthy and strong and probably very unused to being tossed around the room like a rag doll. It was hard to see in the low light, but he had the makings of a nasty bruise along his right jaw, and his left shoulder might be dislocated---she wasn't a doctor or anything, but it had that look. He had an apartment over the shop and he'd been down the stairs with a gun in his hand perhaps ten seconds after she'd busted through the door.

"Why you sleeping over your shop, Michael?" she asked softly, and his eyes darted toward her, fear beginning to set in, now that anger was fading. "I know you have a house outside town, a family there."

He didn't seem like he was going to answer, so she twisted that left arm just a little bit and he squealed and started babbling.

"Not...safe here in town, with the damn Tahni," he grunted. "Have to keep an eye on things..."

"Why would you have to worry about the Tahni, Michael?" Just one tiny bit of pressure on that arm again and Gallatin let out a high-pitched screech. "After all, you're the one paying the vigilante hit squads to attack them, aren't you?"

Fontenot took her boot off his throat, kneeling down to put her knee into his chest instead. It was a big chest, muscular beneath a layer of fat, but his ribs creaked under the weight of her. He tried to grab for her with his free arm, but she brushed it aside easily.

"I *saw* them come here, you know, just this afternoon. I recognized the big, good-looking guy from yesterday in the street, so I set loose a few insect drones and saw you pay him. Paper tradenotes, Michael?" she scoffed. "That's so cliched. Surely, even in a place like this, you could have come up with a dummy account and done the transfer remotely."

It didn't seem as if he was going to reply to that, but just a slight squeeze on that left arm was enough to get him talking again.

"It's how Antonio wanted it!" he insisted. "He gives me the cash, I hire the men!"

"Now we're getting somewhere," she said, satisfied. She even let up a little on his chest. "Who's Antonio and why can't he hire the men himself?"

"He's an off-worlder." The words were grudging, but the man finally seemed as if he understood just how much trouble he was in. "He came here a few months ago for a visit and asked to meet with me. Said he'd heard about my shop down in the Tahni district being burned down, and thought that wasn't right, so he agreed to bankroll me to help me get through it."

His expression was almost apologetic and she tried not to snicker at how ridiculous his bushy hair looked pushed down under his head on the hardwood floor. "I was close to going under, without the trade from the other shop...there are people off-world who want Tahni crafts, and barter at that shop was the only way I could get my hands on them."

"And hiring the thugs was his idea?" she guessed. At his nod, she went on. "So, where's this Antonio now? How do you get in touch with him?"

"I don't know! I never contacted him...he seemed to know when I needed more money and he'd just show up."

Shit, she thought sourly. *This might be a whole lot of trouble for nothing, then.*

"What does 'Antonio' look like?" she asked. It was a long-shot, but she knew a lot of the *La Sombra* enforcers by sight. If she at least knew who she was dealing with, she might be able to get inside their decision loop.

"He's dead sexy."

Korri Fontenot was a soldier; she'd been one for over a century. She didn't freeze at the unexpected voice, even though it seemed impossible that anyone had been able to get by the insect drones she'd left on watch. There were ways to jam those. She just moved, throwing herself forward into a shoulder roll and trying to yank her pistol out of its holster as she flipped into a crouch facing back toward the door.

The sonic hit her before the gun was halfway clear of the hand-tooled leather, slamming into her like a physical thing, a screaming brick wall of sound that blew her backwards off balance into a display case. Glass shattered all around her, but she barely noticed it, convulsing helplessly as consciousness began to fade.

The last coherent thought she had before the darkness closed in was that she knew that voice. You'd never mistake it once you heard it. Her bionic eye recorded the face that went with it as he loomed over her, smiling cruelly. He was a sharp-edged man, with not a hair on his head, not even an eyebrow, and a dark light in his eyes that spoke of untapped depths of depravity. And his name wasn't Antonio.

It was Jordi Abdullah.

Kan-Ten felt the need clawing at his spirit, growling and spitting and thrashing inside his chest, barely contained. His fingers clenched against the rough, jagged edges of the rock wall that separated the males from the females and he tried to use the pain from the sharp lines of granite and basalt digging into his skin to force his brain to work.

It both helped and hurt that there were so many females—twenty-four of them, three times the sacred eight, clustered in a layered defense, youngest on the perimeter and the planetary Matriarch at the center, guarded and protected above all else. They swayed in the traditional dance of warding, its motions designed to distract the gathered males from the chemical fires blazing brightly inside their endocrine system. The blend of the colored strips of cloth in their robes waved with the motion like a calming tide crashing against him. With so many together, it was difficult to separate them into individuals, to find one on which to focus his uncontrollable desire. But the combined scent of so many females also sought to overwhelm his control, to drive him to madness.

He could see that same struggle in the eyes of his brothers on this side of the wall, see tensed shoulders and combative stances as they began looking at each other warily, cautious of challengers. No weapons were allowed in a Concord for just this reason, though his hand ached for one and paranoia gnawed at him.

Concords were rare and he was surprised that Vala-Kel had been able to convince the Matriarch to agree to one. She was under no obligation to listen to anything the males had to say, and his friend was a comparative newcomer to this settlement. He looked over at Vala-Kel, having to tear his attention away from the females to do it. The warrior stood tall, controlled and composed, and Kan-Ten wondered if he had taken drugs to calm his need. They were available, but they were known to dull the mind and were forbidden by the priests back when there had been priests, and most males avoided them...though there had been a growing percentage of males who'd taken to them as recreation since the war.

Vala-Kel's features flickered and writhed in the dancing shadows of the torchlight that was the only illumination inside the Sanctuary. The torch-pits were dug every one-eighth of the distance from the center pit, where the Flame of the Path burned always, kept up by the priests. Well, it *used* to be maintained by the priests, before the humans had outlawed their caste for inciting the Tahni to uprising. Now, lay volunteers kept the Flame, the same ones who maintained the Sanctuary building. Everyone in the colony, male and female, had worked in turn constructing the Sanctuary; it would be the first structure built on any new world, a place for the sacrament and the Concord.

Here, on a world shared with the humans, the Sanctuary was built as far away from the city of Gennich as possible, nearly thirty kilometers distant from the center of town. It had taken an hour to reach this place over the rough, dirt roads even with the all-terrain trucks the settlement council had provided, and Kan-Ten was fairly certain he couldn't have found his way back through the winding, canyon roads without the aid of the navigation program on his 'link. The females had arrived before the males, before dusk, as was the tradition, and their vehicles were parked on the opposite end of the Sanctuary's lopsided ovoid so that they could leave through a different exit, on the other side of the meter-high wall.

"Leader of the council," the Matriarch's protégé called, standing above the older female, arms outstretched. She was middle-aged herself, but strong and comely still, and she would make a good replacement for the Matriarch when the older female passed. "You have called for Concord! Why do you bring the male and female together, if not to mate?"

Her tone was harsh, and when the head of the Council of Males, Rya-Jan stepped forward to reply, the set of his shoulders and the tilt of his head was suitably apologetic.

"I humbly beg the pardon of the Matriarch," Rya-Jan spoke

the traditional phrase, "but the Path requires the Collective Will of all for such a decision."

The Matriarch was ancient, her skin lined and leathery, her eyes nearly invisible under brow ridges grown more pronounced with the years. She seemed skeletal inside her flowing robes, but when she rose from her stool, it was with a graceful, effortless motion that spoke of a strength of body and of will still not completely sapped by time. She stepped up behind her protégé and rested a hand on the younger female's shoulder for support, head tilted backwards as if to get a better look at Rya-Jan and the others.

"I am present," she said, her voice raspy and harsh, but still strong and carrying. "Speak your piece, warrior."

It was an honorific, Kan-Ten knew. Rya-Jan had never been other than a craftsman, either here or back on Tahn-Skyyiah.

"A warrior comes who would lead our people on this world," Rya-Jan said. He brought Vala-Kel forward with a motion. "Shin-Tan-Vala-Kel is a true follower of the Path, a servant of the Will of the Emperor. I would have you hear his words."

"Things cannot continue as they are," Vala-Kel began without preamble. His voice carried like a professional orator's, Kan-Ten thought with a bit of envy. "The human colonists grow bolder every day without their government's forces around to keep them in check. Eventually, there will come a point where they no longer fear their own law enforcers; and when that day comes, they will move on our district, and on the female compound."

He inclined his head. "I know we all will sell our lives dearly, but they outnumber us four or five to one in this place, and many of them have guns, while we are not allowed to possess them, and the ones we do have could be seized by their Constabulary at their pleasure."

"What you say is true, warrior," the Matriarch acknowledged, signaling impatience with a spreading of her fingers and a shifting of her stance. "But what would you have us do?"

"We need weapons," he declared. "We need enough weapons to tip the balance. And you, oh Matriarch, know where those weapons can be had."

The dance of the females ceased abruptly and they stared at him as if he had defecated in the Pit of the Sacrament. The protégé actually took a step toward him, as if she intended to vault the wall and attack him, and a few of the males made gestures of shock before she controlled herself. The Matriarch motioned the other females to remain calm, and regarded him with a cool fury.

"Male, you speak of things you should not know, particularly as a newcomer to this world. This is a secret that was shared with me in the strictest and most holy confidence. The only ones who know of this are in the group around me. Has one of them strayed from the Path and betrayed my trust?"

"You forget something, honored Matriarch," Vala-Kel said gently. "There was one other who knew: the male who entrusted you with the secret to begin with, Colonel Gar-Shan-Tan-Ro."

"He survived the final battle here?" The female seemed shocked. "He swore to me that he would die rather than surrender."

"And he nearly did. But the Will of the Emperor was that he survive his wounds, and he and I wound up in the same internment camp on Tahn-Skyyiah after the war's end."

"Why would he share this thing with you, Vala-Kel?" she demanded, her stance skeptical. "Even if you speak the truth, why would he tell you of this?"

"Because he, too, understood that we have been betrayed." Vala-Kel's tone was as harsh and unyielding as a blade to the throat. "We were led astray by a False Emperor, a liar who took us away from the true Path and brought a civilization that had lasted ten thousand years to ruin, brought our people to their bellies at the feet of a conqueror who knows not the Path or the Will of the Emperor."

Even the Matriarch seemed taken aback by the warrior's vehemence and fury. Kan-Ten looked at his old friend and tried to recall if he'd ever seen that anger before. He couldn't remember anything but comradeship and bravado when they'd been in battle together, but that was before they had lost the war.

"He gave me his secret," Vala-Kel continued, "and I probed for its like from others there in my prison, who'd been stationed on other worlds. I know, honored Matriarch, that the Colonel entrusted to you the location of the weapons he cached for the final push against the humans, the one that never came. I know it's hidden in these canyons, and I know you alone have the entrance codes."

"And you wish to use these weapons against the humans here." It wasn't a question, and Vala-Kel didn't bother to answer it. "Do you think their military will ignore this? That they won't come back here and kill each and every one of us in retaliation? Or kill all the warriors and send the rest of us somewhere worse, somewhere the sun never shines through the clouds and the water is frozen most of the year? Do you honestly believe they'll regard us here, ruling one of their worlds, and do nothing?"

"If my plans were so simple and child-like, you would be right to mock me, honored Matriarch," he said smoothly, as if his earlier anger had been affected, an act for the crowd. Was it? How well, Kan-ten wondered, did he actually know his old comrade? Vala-Kel shot him a reassuring glance before he continued.

"There is a human named Jordi Abdullah who leads one of the criminal cartels out in the Pirate Worlds. He wants to use this colony as a new base for his operations, but he lacks the people to conquer it himself. That is," he corrected his words, "he could possibly conquer it, but he couldn't control it for long. Not without help."

"You would ally us with a human?" the protégé blurted, talking out of turn but past caring. "And a criminal at that?"

The Matriarch slapped the younger female on the arm sharply, shooting her a reproving glance.

"It is a good question, Vala-Kel," the leader of the females admitted.

"As you say, honored Matriarch, we cannot simply take this place under our rule. We will act as the foot soldiers for Jordi Abdullah, and he will take control of this city. By the time the human authorities get wind of anything, his people will be in place as the new planetary Constable and colonial governor, and the records will show they were rightly elected...because he will write the records. And no one here will question it openly, because we will be here, and we will be armed, and autonomous, and ready to put down those who would threaten this arrangement."

It was, Kan-Ten reflected, a good plan. It was simple and relied on the self-interest of all involved, which was brilliant, because plans that counted on the benevolence of others were doomed to failure. He thought he saw those same thoughts pass across the face of the Matriarch.

"This course of action has its appeal," the old female admitted. "But what guarantee do we have that this cartel boss will not grow tired of sharing this world with us and simply take everything for his own?"

"We will be armed. We will not give up our weapons, and to fight us would cost him much. Better to have us as a partner on this world than as yet another enemy."

"My son," the Matriarch began slowly, and Kan-Ten felt a

tinge of disbelief---for the Matriarch herself to call a warrior that invoked high status and regard. "My son, I believe you when you say you have faith in this course of action, and there is much to be commended in its daring and its simplicity. But a voice speaks to my fears and says that it would mean the end of us all. It is in just such an underestimation of our enemy that we found ruin so recently."

"Give council to your fears and you allow them to rule," Vala-Kel quoted the Truth of the Path to the Matriarch and again, there were expressions of shock. That was impertinent.

"Yet to whom I give council," the old female returned with a fire that belied her advanced years, "is my decision, as is to whom I allow access to these weapons, young male."

"Warriors!" That was Rya-Jan, his voice raised in alarm, the expression on his face nearly frantic. "I have received warning from the watch! Vehicles are approaching up the road!"

"Humans," Vala-Kel spat, and a panicked rumble ran through the thirty-two males present.

Kan-Ten jumped to the top of the wall, the biochemical storm of lust suddenly gone, replaced by something even more atavistic and primitive.

"Get to your vehicles," he called to the Matriarch, motioning urgently. "We will hold them off until you're safely away from here."

He'd barely spoken the words when the rear doors on the female side of the Sanctuary burst open and dark, shadow-clad figures poured through them. They were dressed in black to blend with the night, and Kan-Ten had time to think that the vehicles were a distraction, that these men had crept up on them and drawn the sentries away with the trucks coming up the road to give them an opening to reach the entrance. Then thought deserted him and he threw himself down off the wall and through the crowd of Tahni females and slammed into the lead human with the full weight of his shoulder.

He could hear ribs crack at the impact, and felt the force of it rock him backwards even as it sent the human tumbling head-over-heels to trip up two of his fellows as they crowded through the choke-point of the narrow entrance hallway. Three more of them were on him immediately, and he swung wildly, trying to keep them away as the closest raised a blade, ready for a downward strike that would slice right through him.

Then Vala-Kel was there as if he'd materialized out of the smoke from the Flame of the Path, catching the knife-hand at the wrist and wrenching sideways, yanking the human away and into the shadows. Kan-Ten longed for a weapon, but there were none inside the Sanctuary, so he used what Fontenot had taught him over the years and kicked at knees, chopped at necks, gouged at eyes and threw himself into the humans as they tried to crowd through the door. They might have guns, but if he could stay close enough, they wouldn't dare use them.

Blows rained down at him as he tried to engage three of them at a time, but most were ineffectual, and he ignored them either way; as Fontenot liked to say, there were no "time-outs" in combat. One of them went down after a kick to the knee and he pistoned a heel down into the human's face as he moved past him, grappling with the next. There was the hiss-crack of a gunshot, a mini-rocket pistol he judged, and another, a deep-throated boom from a flechette gun, but it didn't hit him and it didn't hit the man trying to kill him, and he couldn't be concerned with anything else.

Others were crowded around and he felt a morose certainty that he was about to die, about to go down beneath their numbers and be stomped to death or stabbed or shot on the ground. When that didn't happen, when fewer blows rained down rather than more, he began to realize that the others around him were Tahni males, that they'd followed him and Vala-Kel over the wall to defend the Matriarch. A surge of energy seemed to flow through him at the knowledge that he wasn't alone and he yanked the human off his feet and slammed him to the ground, pounding the man's face and neck with hammer-blows from his fists until bone cracked and blood spattered him.

Human blood, he thought not for the first time, smelled and tasted much like Tahni blood. It couldn't be a coincidence; the gods were at work here, or the Predecessors the humans always harped on, the ancient aliens who had engineered living worlds like this one ,and then vanished eons ago. What would they think if they saw their legacy, writ in blood across the worlds they'd made?

He shook the esoteric thoughts away with the realization that he'd taken a blow to the head, perhaps more than one, and his mind was beginning to drift. He tried to find someone else to fight, another target, but there was more shooting...and he could see the flashes of tiny rocket motors heading towards the entrance hall, see the miniature starbursts of the warheads igniting against the dark camouflage clothing the humans wore. Two of them went down, thrashing and spasming in their death throes, and then the ones that remained were fleeing back through the rear door, tearing at each other in their haste to retreat.

Kan-Ten sagged, supporting himself against the rough-hewn stone of the nearest wall, sucking in an unsteady breath. Five humans were sprawled on the dirt-covered floor, arrayed around the rear exit like a sacrifice, some shot, some beaten to death. Beside them, two Tahni males were down as well, their lives claimed by the flechette guns the humans had brought. He looked over to Vala-Kel, who was standing firm and resolute, a large and menacing handgun clutched in his left fist, curls of smoke still rising around him from the rounds he'd fired.

"You have brought a weapon into the place of Concord." That was the protégé; she stood in front of the Matriarch in a stance of protection, her tone full of outrage. "It is a violation of sacred tradition!"

"It *is* a violation of tradition," the Matriarch affirmed, stepping past the younger female, her voice less accusatory than deeply sad. "And yet, this is a time when tradition may not save us."

She stepped carefully around the bodies, her sandals sticking briefly and then pulling free of the growing pools of blood with an obscene, viscous sound, and stopped only centimeters from Vala-Kel, eyes boring up into his.

"Perhaps," she said, "we must face the truth that our traditions need to change."

"But Matriarch," the protégé said, sounding scandalized, "if we abandon our rituals, if we break our own laws, what are we?"

"What we are, child," the old female answered her, never looking away from the warrior, "is a people with very little left to lose."

CHAPTER SEVEN

Korri Fontenot woke from a nightmare of being crushed again, of being buried under the walls of the base on Andalusia after the missiles had penetrated the defenses and brought down the barracks. She'd been trapped under tons of debris for days, and what they'd dragged out barely resembled a human. They told her she'd begged them to let her die, but she didn't remember that, didn't remember anything but the pressure, the crushing pressure of the metal cross-beams bearing down on her arms and legs and chest...

She forced herself through the residual pain and confusion of the sonic stunner and realized that the nightmare was real. Her left shoulder, the bionic half of her, was pinned, trapped beneath something large and flat and metal, and she felt a surge of nearly uncontrollable panic, barely suppressing the whimper that seemed to want to claw its way out of her chest.

"Wakey-wakey, Fontenot. Time we had a talk."

It was Jordi. She'd recognize that voice anywhere, and then he was in front of her, leaning over sideways, a look of mockery on his dark, hairless face as he met her eyes. They were in a shop of some kind, the walls bare corrugated aluminum set in a concrete slab floor, machine tools and metal cutters and fabricators cluttered together, all with the air of disuse. Jordi's people were cluttered together as well, huddled in folding chairs or cots or just on blankets stretched out on the floor, some watching her, some absorbed with card games or videos or ViR goggles.

She was, she gradually realized, pinned beneath an industrial stamping press of some kind; and as strong as she was, not even her cybernetics could overcome that sort of pressure. She'd been played.

"Have you been following me since I landed?" she asked, trying to keep her voice even, trying to keep the fear and rage and the burgeoning panic out of it.

"Only since you visited the Constable," he corrected her, not caring that he was giving her information, not caring that she was stalling. That wasn't a good sign. "We've been keeping an eye on Mr. Freeman; he's far too capable a man to take lightly. Imagine my surprise when I saw *you* walk through those doors..." He laughed and reached out a hand to run a finger over the synthskin on the left side of her face. "Although I must admit it took me a moment to recognize you after your makeover. Was that Hollande's idea? To make you blend in more, attract less attention?"

He shook his head, leaning against the side of the machine. "She's a clever bitch. She even managed to turn that mad dog Singh against me, though God knows how." His smooth, cocky smile faded for a moment, replaced by something dark and bitter. "Everyone seems to have gotten the idea that I'm weak, that they can hurt me now, that this is their opportunity."

There was something different about the man, she thought. He seemed less smooth and sharp and polished now, rougher around the edges. She thought she saw new lines of stress on a face that had once been perpetually young, and there was a harried look to him, to the set of his eyes and the lay of his clothes.

"I'm not running with Hollande anymore," Fontenot insisted, knowing he probably wouldn't believe her, but deciding it was worth the effort anyway. "We parted ways; I'm on my own now."

"Really?" His voice was heavy with skepticism and she saw his fingers tapping on the side of the press, just above the control panel. "Then what the hell are you doing here? That's an awful coincidence, isn't it, the two of us being here at the same time? You think it's fate, or bad karma? Maybe it's the universe's way of getting back at you for betraying me?"

"I'm just working a job. The planetary government put out a call for gunfighters, anyone who'd be willing to help them with their Tahni problem. I was between gigs and I needed the money."

"Oh give me a fucking break," Jordi said, laughing sharply. "You, the only one of us that Tahni freak Kan-Ten would even talk to, suddenly deciding you're going to go find some Tahni colonists to shoot? Do you think I'm a fucking idiot, Fontenot?"

He touched a control and the press hummed to life, its gears churning as it began pushing against her shoulder even harder, the metal of her prosthetic creaking with the added pressure, coming closer to buckling, coming closer to pinching into her flesh. She closed her eyes, her teeth clenched as she readied herself for the pain.

The hum died away and she slowly and reluctantly opened her eyes and craned her head back to look over to where Jordi had hit the control again, halting the press. He leered at her, his finger poised over the touch pad, twitching as if he might hit it by accident.

"Would you like to try again?" He slid his handgun from its belt holster and touched the cold metal of its muzzle against the side of her face. "You're going to die, Fontenot. You and I both know that. The question is whether it's clean, fast, easy..." He motioned with the muzzle of the heavy pistol. "...or slow, and messy, and oh, so painful."

Someone laughed nearby. She couldn't see them, couldn't see much except a cockeyed version of Jordi Abdullah and a small section of the shop floor, but the laugh was harsh and bawdy and male, and she wanted to rip the man's throat out.

"I know you don't have much actual human left in you, bitch," Jordi hissed so close to her face that she could feel drops of his spittle on her cheek, "but I'm perfectly willing to keep cutting and burning and crushing until I get to the soft, creamy center."

His finger touched the button again, just a teasing glance for a half-second and Fontenot grunted, halfway to a scream as the press pushed downward another fraction of a centimeter.

"Last chance. Where are Hollande and Carpenter?"

There was a booming crash, the unmistakable sound of a door being kicked in, and then a crackling hiss; before Jordi could even look up from her face, she could already see the black smoke, smell the bitter, burning fumes. He moved quickly, dancing away from her narrow field of view, and she saw a confused collage of panicked motion before the smoke began to close in, and all that could penetrate it was sound. There were shouts and yells and scurrying, and the clatter of overturning chairs, and the scrape of feet on the rough concrete of the floor, and when the shooting finally started all she could wonder was why it had taken so long.

Mini-rockets hissed in all directions, and at least one pulse laser weapon was firing, but through the yells and the racket and the shooting, she could make out a peculiar, high-pitched hum overlain with the snap-snap-snap of multiple projectiles breaking the sound barrier so close together they could have been one, continuous stream. It was a Gauss machine pistol, a needler some called them, adapted as a civilian weapon from the KE-guns the Tahni used during the war. They were expensive and rare and she'd only known one man who'd actually owned one...

A black-gloved hand reached through the smoke and slapped against the red emergency release button on the machine's control panel, and the heavy slab released with a pneumatic hiss, the pressure lifting from her shoulder so abruptly she almost passed out. She slid from beneath the massive, two-meter-long press and coughed fitfully at the thick, black smoke. It shut out the light, visible and infrared, and somehow even made the thermal imaging and auditory analysis from her bionics harder to interpret, and she felt an unfamiliar disorientation that somehow angered her more than Jordi's threats.

Something was pressed into her hand, something heavy and metal and coldly comforting in its familiar, lethal lines: her own Gauss slug-shooter.

"Follow me, and stick close."

The voice was as familiar as the gun, though not nearly as comforting. But it was all she had at the moment, and she went with it, grabbing with her free hand to grasp his and letting him lead her through the smoke and clamor. She couldn't see the door other than as a slight thinning of the smoke, but he led her to it as if he had the layout of the place projected inside his head...and, for all she knew, he did.

Then they were outside, and the streets were just as dark, the streetlights sabotaged and inoperable, but she could see on infrared now, see that they were somewhere in the industrial district, somewhere the buildings were closed and boarded up. Outside the walls of the shop, she saw the bodies of the sentries Jordi had left, their heads looking back over their shoulders, necks snapped.

They ran. They ran as fast as she'd ever run, and he led her at that speed, which was something he never could have done before but she didn't want to distract either of them with questions now. The streets seemed empty, but Jordi Abdullah was nothing if not forethoughtful, and she didn't dare bet that he hadn't left a trail of drones or remote cameras or paid informants in his wake. But blocks became kilometers, and closed-down shops and warehouses and factories became shut-down bars and restaurants, and some that weren't shut down, and their pace slowed to a simple run, then a jog, and then a casual walk.

She holstered her pistol and dragged her heels to halt them both, gripping his hand tight enough that he couldn't let go and keep walking. He turned, his face blocky and expressionless, and somehow, miraculously, whole again. The last time she'd seen Jagmeet Singh, the bounty hunter had been carrying half a face full of metal, to go along with the left half of his skull, his left shoulder and left arm. It wasn't a simple synthskin camouflage job like hers, either; she could see on thermal that it was flesh, and so were the arm and shoulder.

"You've had quite the makeover, Singh," she told him, cocking her head appreciatively.

He still had his sidearm in his hand, but after taking a quick glance around, he shoved it into a holster beneath his black, armored duster. It wasn't just the skin that was new; he had a short, close-cropped beard as well, and a fashionable, swept-back haircut that nearly made him look a new man.

"I owe it all to you," he told her, his voice smooth once more, lacking the lazy slur that had marked it when half his jaw had been metal. "Consider this repayment."

He started to turn, but she caught his arm with a hand, shaking her head.

"If you think I'm letting you walk away from me without you telling me what you're doing here, perhaps you haven't learned as much from me as you might believe."

His eyes narrowed and he seemed to consider it for a moment before he jerked his head down the street.

"Not here. Come back to where I'm staying and I'll explain." He smirked, something of the old bastard she knew him to be shining through his new look. "Unless you're afraid this was all an elaborate trick to lure you somewhere private and kill you myself."

"Shit," she drawled, turning the word into something with three syllables as she glanced at him sidelong. "I'd love to see you try, boy."

"Ah, Fontenot," he sighed, turning back down the sidewalk and waving for her to follow. "I've missed you." He chuckled. "I'll aim more carefully next time."

———

"They're back," Ash muttered, half to himself, knowing Sandi wouldn't hear him over the alarms. He hit a control to silence them as he plugged the interface jacks into his sockets. His touch lingered on the cold metal still, after all these years. He wondered if there would ever come a time when it didn't.

"Son of a bitch," Sandi swore, louder than he would have, maybe louder than she would have when this trip started.

She had a worn, haggard look that came from too much time in zero-g and not enough rest; she'd been trying to sleep in the cockpit when the alarms had sounded. And he knew she wasn't just mad because the raiders were back, she was mad that they'd come back when it was his turn in the left seat.

"That's less than forty hours turnaround time! Are these different ships?"

"Not according to the sensor readings," he told her, then he dove beneath the interface and was beyond conversation.

Space shrank, or perhaps his perceptions grew, to the point where he was a giant kilometers tall, floating in the dark firmament. Even the ore barge seemed tiny beside him, the length of his stride measured in light seconds. And there they were, the intruders again, slipping into their midst like coyotes squeezing through the fence into a sheep fold for the third night in a row, driven by the persistence of hunger. It was the same two boats, there was no doubt; their drive signatures were identical to the ones the sensors had recorded during the last attack.

He could see the Savage/Slaughter lighter's fusion drive flaring to life, trying to move into a position to intercept them, but she was on the far side of the barge; she would never make it in time, and she couldn't micro-Transition the way the *Acheron* could, lacking her multiple jump capacitors. They didn't even have a clean firing solution for their beam weapons, and none of their missiles could intercept before the enemy ships got into position for a railgun shot.

He had very little time to think, but he forced himself to take it. If he jumped in, he'd have empty capacitor banks, and all they'd have to engage the predators would be the Gatling turret and their limited ammo supply for it. By the time the capacitors were charged enough for a volley of proton cannon fire, the two cutters could jump back out. He had to try something different, something risky, something potentially stupid. Something Sandi would do if she were flying this boat...

"Aw hell," he muttered. He wasn't sure if he'd said it aloud.

The *Acheron* Transitioned, just a step around the corner as his old instructor used to say, a micro-jump that was hard to control as exactly as he was attempting. That was why this was risky, maybe stupid. If the ship's navigation systems were a hair off, just centimeters off, they could slam right into the barge or one of the cutters, and they'd never even know they were dead. Just an eyeblink and then...whatever. Darkness, void, nonexistence, Heaven, Hell, reincarnation?

None of the above, he had time to think, ignoring the blaring of the proximity alarms, ignoring Sandi's surprised squawk from the right-hand seat.

They were three hundred meters from the closest of the cutters, in line between her and the barge...and the enemy vessel was burning right into the mouth of the *Acheron*'s fusion drive coils. With a thought, Ash ignited the drive and a star-hot plume of fusion plasma washed over the enemy cutter nose-on.

They weren't destroyed; Ash knew that wouldn't happen, not at this range, and he couldn't have cut it any closer. But when he tapped into the barge's exterior camera feed, he could see the cutter's electromagnetic deflector screens were awash in flames, a glowing Christmas-tree ornament, for a good two or three seconds before her belly jets lifted her above the bore axis of the *Acheron* and out of her exhaust. The raider vessel's bow was black, her nose armor ablated and her maneuvering thrusters damaged...and most importantly, her railgun emitter melted to slag.

She'd cut her boost and so had he; the burn had taken the *Acheron* too far for the drive to be an effective weapon. The enemy ship hung there, looking still and helpless in relation to them, despite the fact that they were both traveling at hundreds of meters per second. Ash saw the capacitor indicator lights going green and had barely had time to think about flipping the ship around for a shot at the other cutter when they Transitioned.

She blinked out of realspace in the rainbow ring of a warp corona; it was what Ash had expected and he was already swinging the nose around, killing his drive and aiming the proton emitter at the second ship. They were turning as well, trying to line their railgun up with the barge. He'd figured the other crew would at least try to fire off a shot at their target, that they'd give him the chance to take them out rather than give up on the attack altogether. They didn't disappoint, but he shot first.

The proton beam took them in the nose, and at this range, even their deflectors couldn't shed the full strength of the blast. BiPhase carbide armor sublimated in sheets centimeters thick, and he could see the bow of the cutter being blown to starboard by the sudden jet of vaporized metal. Then they were gone, ripping a hole in space and pulling it in after them, and there was nothing left of them except a glowing cloud of ionized particles.

Ash sighed and fired off a corrective burst from the fusion drive almost absent-mindedly to correct their attitude toward the barge. Sandi surprised him by grabbing hold of his chair and kissing him firmly and passionately.

"That was brilliant," she said, the exhaustion and exasperation temporarily banished from her eyes in a rush of adrenalin-fueled passion. "That was *exactly* what I would have done."

He caressed her cheek but couldn't keep the frown of dissatisfaction from tugging his face downward.

"What?" she demanded. "What's wrong, Ash? You just kicked their butts; it'll take them days to repair that ship."

"They *have* days," he pointed out, trying not to take his frustration and anger out on her. "And eventually, they're going to get through our escorts and take this barge out, just like all the others." He shook his head, eyes going hazy as he accessed the ship's sensor web over the interface. "We're going at this all wrong, Sandi. We're playing their game, letting them choose the time and place for the battle. You don't win that way."

He found the data he'd been searching for, and his vision snapped back to reality.

"We need to talk to those Savage/Slaughter mercs. It's time to take the fight to the enemy."

CHAPTER EIGHT

Korri Fontenot eyed the rickety chair uncertainly and in the end, decided she'd rather stand. The wooden floor creaked miserably under her feet as she shifted her weight, and she began to wonder if standing was a good idea either. There was a scraping sound as Jagmeet Singh pushed the door shut, then a solid thump as the locking bolt shot home.

"I love what you've done with the place," she said, gesturing around at the one-room apartment.

It was barely four meters on a side and most of that was taken up by the bed, which sagged in morose resignation on a frame of faded and splintering wood. Above it, the gossamer blades of a ceiling fan turned slowly clockwise, the only light in the room coming from the bulb that hung beneath it. The spiteful tap-tap of a bad gasket in the sink faucet echoed off the thin, panel walls, and she guessed that the toilet and shower were behind the plastic curtain that hung across a narrow doorway in the corner. There was nothing else to the room; no window, no closet, no entertainment console. Just a tiny, round table with two chairs she didn't trust.

"It's cheap," Singh commented, stripping off his duster and throwing it on the bed. Beneath it, his clothes were all black, a mixture of spacer's leathers and utilitarian work gear, and the nylon straps of a shoulder holster ran across his chest, supporting the weight of his Gauss machine pistol. "And the bar downstairs is about two weeks' receipts from shutting its doors permanently, so they were happy to have the money."

The big man shrugged. "I don't spend much time here."

"Do you have a ship?" she wondered. "How did you get here?"

"No ship. Too expensive and I've never been much of a pilot." She thought she saw a dark shadow pass over his face, and she remembered that it had been his late wife who'd flown their ship...the wife Ash Carpenter had killed in aerial combat. "Anyway," he seemed to visibly shake off the memory, "I invested most of my accumulated liquid assets in some physical improvements."

"I noticed," she admitted, nodding. "And not just that you had your bionics replaced with cloned tissue; you were running as fast as me out there. You're jacked."

"I was having the work done anyway," he motioned toward his repaired face. "The docs who were fixing me up told me they could boost me, for a price. Bionic servos in the joints, bone laminants, boosted reflexes, an implant 'link and a headcomp to run it all. They offered some more exotic stuff, like implant blades but..." He shrugged, making a face. "I didn't want things to get too complicated. And I was already pushing the limits of my various bank accounts. I barely had enough to buy a ride off the books with some old acquaintances heading this way."

"But why'd you come out here?" she insisted. "I know you said you weren't going to work for Jordi anymore, but I didn't think you were going to war with him."

"I didn't declare war on him," Singh corrected her, easing down cautiously to take a seat on the bed. It squeaked plaintively at his weight, but held. "He declared war on me. When I showed up back in the Core worlds without his ship or his people, he put a price on my head. I've been dodging bounty hunters and hit squads for months now, and yes," he eyed her with a sour expression, "I *am* aware of how ironic that is, before you say anything."

"You decided to take him out." A grin spread across Fontenot's face almost of its own accord. "I'd bet you're the one who organized the other cartels against him."

"I contacted the right people," he allowed, tossing his head as if it were no great thing. "The sentiment was already there, they just needed some encouragement. Then I heard about this place." He snorted a humorless laugh. "I have to admit, for a desperation move, it's genius. If he could pull it off, he'd be in position to control the black market for the whole Periphery. No one else would have the connections, the proximity, the political pull that he would. We can't let it happen; he'd be nearly unstoppable. I gather your friends in Fleet Intelligence have come to the same conclusion."

"Yeah, if only they'd bother to help," she muttered with just a trace of bitterness.

"Things are complicated right now," Singh allowed. "I've heard rumblings of it; everyone with connections has. The Corporate Council is making some sort of power play; their Corporate Security Force is swarming all over the place in the Core worlds."

"Sorry," Fontenot said with an indifferent shrug. "I only have a vague idea of what exactly the Corporate Council does."

"Yes, you *have* been out in the sticks for quite a while, haven't you?" There was something in the look that he gave her just then, something like curiosity. "They were a product of the First War with the Tahni, an emergency stop-gap to get around monopoly regulations and let the economy run more efficiently to help with war production." The corner of his mouth quirked upward. "And of course, since it made everyone involved very, very rich, that 'emergency measure' became permanent. The Corporate Council Executive Board controls all major industry in the Core worlds; and over the years, they've developed an unhealthy amount of influence with the Patrol Service and the DSI as well...not to mention the office of the President. Apparently, it's all coming to a head, and it makes some cartel power-play in the middle of nowhere too small-time to worry about."

Fontenot grunted in distaste. "Makes me glad I live out here. We have enough to worry about without all that back-room political shit."

"Yes, this is *so* much better." Fontenot recognized the sarcasm but let it go. Singh leaned back, seemingly determined to get through with his story. "I've been watching the port, and in the last three or four days, I've seen shuttles coming in, bringing down one load after another of what looks to me like hired muscle from the Pirate Worlds. I don't know how long Jordi's been here, but he's getting ready to make his move."

"People like that," Fontenot said, shaking her head in confusion, "they gotta' have records. The Constable didn't strike me as a careless man; you'd think he'd have noticed."

"That was the whole point of stirring up the Tahni," Singh pointed out. "So he wouldn't have time to notice. But I think you're missing the bigger question here, Ms. Fontenot."

She sniffed, spreading her arms in a welcoming gesture.

"Enlighten me, Mr. Singh."

"Where," he asked, "are they going to get weapons for all those people?"

———

The road played a rhythm under the tires of the old cargo truck, the ruts and ridges notes written by time and erosion. Kan-Ten wanted to let the song of the road and the grumble of the engine and the darkness of the cab lull him to sleep; it seemed like forever since he'd slept. He'd had to keep his guard up since he'd arrived here, unsure of who to trust. If he listened to Fontenot's advice, it would be fairly simple; she'd tell him to trust no one.

He looked sidelong at the driver, who was chanting a mnemonic to keep himself awake. He was a young male, too young to have fought in the war, but he wore his cue wrapped around his neck as if he were a warrior. He probably thought himself one now, because he'd engaged in a few street brawls with human vigilantes.

Fool.

He was surprised at the harshness of the thought. He hadn't believed that the war still haunted him; yet here, with Vala-Kel, he knew it did. His old comrade sat on the other side of the cab, staring out the window into the absolute darkness of the high desert, silent for long kilometers now. Up ahead of them perhaps a hundred meters on the hard-packed dirt road, Kan-Ten could see the lights of the rover, the Matriarch's private vehicle, leading them into the unknown.

"Will there be time to train?"

It felt blasphemous to break this almost worshipful silence, but the question had to be asked, both for appearance's sake and because it mattered to him. Vala-Kel turned away from the window and peered at him in confusion.

"With the weapons," Kan-Ten elaborated. He indicated the driver. "Many of our males have never fired military weapons before, or had limited experience in the war. Will there be time for them to train before we move?"

"Not much," Vala-Kel admitted, indicating apology and regret with a gesture. "Our enemies will have no military weapons, and little training as well. We will overwhelm them with firepower and they will break before us." He took hold of Kan-Ten's shoulder and touched foreheads with him briefly in a gesture of comradeship and comfort. "Do not worry, brother. The Spirit of the True Emperor has ordained this to be."

"You are so sure of this," Kan-Ten mused. "Are *you* the True Emperor, brother? Are you his physical form with us? Do you believe this to be so?"

Vala-Kel didn't respond immediately, and Kan-Ten wondered if he was pretending to be considering the question, but he knew his old friend's face better than that. He *did* believe it, and he had for some time.

"Who can say?" the warrior finally answered the question with a question. "Would I know if I were? This is a mystery that can only be solved by action. We must hold onto faith, do as the Spirit Emperor would wish, and wait for him to manifest himself."

"You sound as if you harangue the crowds at a war rally." There was more scorn in the set of Kan-Ten's shoulders and feet than he intended, and he hoped that the darkness concealed it.

Vala-Kel looked as if he were about to give in to anger, but controlled himself with a visible effort.

"Brother, I understand why you worry. Believe me, I do not intend to throw our males into a fire and hope that fate smiles upon us, the way our commanders did in the war. We are going to hit the Constabulary building, take them by surprise and take control of the fortifications there. Once we have an unassailable position inside their fortress, we can send probes out to seize control of the fusion reactor, the water treatment plant and the data and communications center." He interlaced his fingers, clenching his hands together in a motion of strength and unity.

"Once we have control of this city, the work is done; the other towns lack the troops and the firepower to oppose us. When Jordi Abdullah puts his people into position in the planetary government, the other humans won't have any choice but to fall in line."

"I will trust you, brother," Kan-Ten told him, making signs of apology. "I pray you do not give me cause to regret it."

"She is stopping." That was the youth, their driver, and at his words, Kan-Ten's eyes went to the distant running lights of the rover, saw them drawing closer as the vehicle slowed.

They'd followed the road into a box canyon, its red-tinted sandstone walls bleached white by the headlights of the vehicles, and now they were nearly at the end of it, and the end of the dirt track. Only a few car-lengths ahead, the headlights splashed into a steep rock face that climbed upward for twenty or thirty meters before merging into the edge of a plateau. Shadowed crevices in the rutted wall promised hidden mysteries, and it was to one of the recessed pools of darkness that the Matriarch went.

The middle-aged protégé exited the rover first, lithe and graceful, her twin braids swinging back and forth like pendulums across her back. Kan-Ten found it hard to keep his eyes off of her as she leaned back inside to offer a hand to her mistress. He shook himself, trying not to let the need control his thoughts. It had been years since he had mated and the idea of it was becoming hard to suppress, even when his mind should have been occupied with so much else more important.

The Matriarch seemed unsteady on her feet after so long in the car, and she leaned heavily on the shoulder of the younger female while another of her followers shut the door behind them. The car stayed in place, its headlights still illuminating the rock wall ahead for them as they walked.

Kan-Ten thought for a moment that Vala-Kel was going to

remain in the cab of the truck and watch them, but he merely waited until the two females were a respectful distance ahead before he threw open the door and dropped to the rust-colored dirt below. He still had the pistol, tucked into a sash at his waist, and his hand strayed toward it, head darting around as if he expected an ambush. Kan-Ten climbed down behind him, still watching the females.

The Matriarch was feeling her way along the stones of the rock face, fingers dancing across them as if she were searching for a certain shape, remembered only by touch. Kan-Ten found himself feeling impatient with her, growing increasingly uncomfortable in the dead-end canyon. The walls seemed too close, the darkness too oppressive. Even the sky was overcast this night, as if it wished to slam shut the door of a trap and pen them inside, and his hands longed for a weapon.

"I have found it."

The Matriarch's voice drew his eyes back to the rock face, except it was different now, the shadows deepening in a section four meters tall and nearly as wide. He could hear the scraping of metal over rock and suddenly his perspective shifted and he perceived that part of the wall was fake, a camouflaged door that was swinging back into its dark recesses. The opening was like a black outline drawn on the rock, the headlights unable to penetrate more than a meter or so into its depths, and the utter darkness of it drew his gaze against his will.

Vala-Kel switched on the flashlight he'd taken with him from the cab of the truck, shining it into the blackness and revealing a matte grey door that stretched the whole length of the opening. Kan-Ten took a step closer, running a palm over the surface of the barrier; it was cool and smooth, with the feel of massive solidity to it, and he was sure it would stand up to anything short of a proton cannon.

The Matriarch slid her shoulder along the cold metal of the

door until she reached the far-right side of it, then felt again with her fingertips, tracing a line downward until sections of the wall lit up in multicolored patterns. He thought he saw her face brighten at the display, but it might have just been a trick of the light. She weaved a complex pattern with her fingers along the lights, one he couldn't follow or ever hope to duplicate, and he marveled that she'd been able to recall it after all these years. There was a tone that issued from the door or from the rock around it, rising and falling like the call of a night-flyer, and the lights flashed eight times before the heavy door began to rumble aside.

The driver was standing beside him, Kan-Ten realized, and more young males were moving up behind them from the second truck, an almost worshipful awe on their faces, but they stayed back and let him and Vala-Kel cross over the threshold first. Lights flickered on automatically with their passage, and walls too far away to see in the dark solidified into mosaics of green and white tile, inscribed with warnings about unauthorized access and stored explosives.

The sight brought back memories, most of them unwelcome, of endless days huddled in underground shelters on one planet or another, waiting out orbital bombardments for the landings that would, inevitably, come. He could imagine dust showering from the ceiling as Gauss cannon rounds and proton beams smashed down at them, imagined the fearful eyes of young recruits watching the support columns shake, and praying for them to hold up, and then fighting and running and endless retreating to the next world, to do the same thing over again.

Here, the only dust was collected on the surface of the packing crates stacked in cylindrical shapes in ordered, even lines across a section of flat, unfinished concrete. There were sixteen crates in a cylinder, sixteen cylinders in all. He walked over to one and flipped the top; it was stacked with KE rifles, "needlers" the humans called them. They were fed from a drum filled with tantalum slivers, powered by a bank of capacitors in the stock, fired fully automatic from superconductive coils of electromagnets. Liquid hydrogen stored in a fat cooling jacket around the barrel kept the superconductors at a workable temperature.

He reached in and pulled out one of them; it had the familiar feel of an old and well-used tool and a quick check revealed that the capacitors were still charged after all this time. Vala-Kel checked another stack and held up a spare ammo drum, excitement and satisfaction writ large in his stance and his expression. Vala-Kel tossed the drum underhand to Kan-Ten and he caught it easily despite the weight, slipping it into a pocket of his shoulder bag.

"With these, brother," Vala-Kel motioned, "we are unstoppable."

Kan-Ten's gaze went slowly past the rows of stacked crates, past a cluster of eight support columns, and into the dimmer lighting of the next chamber over and a feeling of elation welled within him, mixed only a heartbeat later with a cold, shuddering dread.

"No, my brother," he corrected his old friend, pointing behind him, into the shadows. "With *those*, we are unstoppable."

Vala-Kel turned and saw what Kan-Ten had seen, but his reaction was unreserved, almost maniacal glee.

Hunched over like ancient stone guardians, they loomed in the shadows, their dull grey camouflage blending with the slate-grey walls. Four meters tall and three wide, their humanoid shapes distorted by centimeters of layered honeycomb boron armor, the two High Guard battlesuits watched them with dead eyes, arms hanging at their sides. Yet it seemed to Kan-Ten that they beckoned to him, that they'd been waiting for him for all these years.

He'd come so close to dying inside that metal box so many times, had felt as if he'd cheated the Will of the Emperor when he'd emerged that last time alive.

I should have known...no one cheats death forever.

CHAPTER NINE

"You want to do *what?*"

The holographic image of Trisha Nassir's face was screwed up in disbelief, her long, drawn, low-gravity features looking like a funhouse mirror version of a real person. The lightspeed delay only added to the absurdity of the image, since her reaction was seconds later than the words that had precipitated it.

"It's a sound plan," Captain Alcala insisted, arms crossed over his chest, feet anchored to the deck of the Savage/Slaughter lighter's bridge by the magnetic soles of his ship boots. "And Captain Carpenter's reasoning is air-tight."

Michael Alcala was the mission commander as well as the captain of the *Warlock*, and Sandi had to admit she was impressed by the ship. Most lighters were slapped-together pieces of shit, with bypassed power routing cables hanging everywhere, and maintenance panels left off or thrown away because the weapons systems they'd jury-rigged onto what had been a light freighter were always shorting out. The *Warlock* was neat and tightly-run, and the crew were professionals, even if Jacobson was a bit of a douchebag. The bridge was quieter and more squared away than many of the Fleet cruisers she'd had the chance to visit during the war.

Alcala himself was a spare, short, unassuming man with wavy, dark hair that was barely regulation for a paramilitary organization like Savage/Slaughter, and a dark, unlined face that probably would have been ageless even without the nanite treatments. She thought he'd been Fleet during the war, but he was wearing a sidearm in a hip holster even here in deep space, which was the sort of deep-seated paranoia you usually found in Marines.

"Okay," Nassir admitted after the obligatory signal delay, "I'll admit that it's likely that the raiders have a base in the system. There's nothing else close enough for the turnaround times they've been pulling. But we *need* the *Warlock* and the *Acheron* on convoy duty! What happens if you go off on this wild goose chase and they come back and finish off the barge before you return?"

"We did some serious damage on this last attack, Ms. Nassir," Ash told her. He looked uncomfortable there on the bridge of the lighter, and Sandi knew it was impatience; he thought it was a waste of time docking with the *Warlock* and speaking in person. He was itching to go hunt down the raiders and finish them off. "They'll need forty or fifty hours for repairs, minimum, not counting downtime. We have a chance to root them out and put an end to this now."

"Listen, lady," Sandi interrupted, getting tired of the back and forth, "Ash and I have about exhausted every fucking trick we ever heard of keeping this barge in one piece, and it's only been two engagements! The bottom line is, either we go find their base and kill the shit out of them, or your barge is toast." She shrugged. "I get paid either way, I'm just letting you know."

Ash shot her a reproving look, but she could tell he was smothering a grin. Alcala seemed amused as well, and wasn't trying to hide it, but the rest of the bridge crew was studiously paying attention to their stations, and Sandi had the sense that it was because they didn't want to piss off their captain.

Nassir sighed in resignation, scratching the back of her head in what seemed like a nervous tic.

"All right, where do you think they're hiding?"

"We've been going over the data from your intelligence files," Alcala told her, touching a control on his 'link and calling up a map of the system that was projected beside Nassir's image. "Anywhere in the asteroid belt is out of the question, of course; with all the mining activity there, someone would have noticed. Same goes for the primary gas giant and its moons; even though you don't have any major mining operations there, you have the test facilities, and again, that sort of activity would be noticed."

"It's out at the ice giant," Sandi cut in, earning a dirty look from Alcala. She didn't care; he'd been milking the whole thing for dramatic effect. "The larger of its two moons has solid land mass, and water ice, and a thick enough atmosphere to hide their thermal signature from long-range telescopic scans."

Alcala adjusted the projection and it zoomed outward, past the belt, past the system's lone gas giant to the ice giant out near the cometary halo. It wasn't much, as planets went, not as large as either Uranus or Neptune back in the Solar System, and it had only two moons worthy of the designation unless you counted a few small captured asteroids.

"We're betting it's in this area," Alcala brought up a land mass near the moon's north pole. "There's water ice there, and some thermal activity that would keep the heat up enough that you could be outside in a regular vacc suit for a few hours without worrying about frostbite."

"I'll take the *Acheron* in on the opposite side of the ice giant," Ash said. "Keep the drives cold until I can orbit around and get a good scan of the place, then transmit back to the *Warlock*. Then I'll run air cover while the *Warlock* Transitions in and Sandi...Commander Hollande...flies a Savage/Slaughter trooper lander down with an assault team."

"Don't you have your own lander pilots?" Nassir wondered, frowning.

"I do," Alcala acknowledged, "and they're both very talented, but neither has the sort of real-world combat experience that Commander Hollande does. Since we have her, we may as well put her to work."

"Ash volunteered me," Sandi accused, making a face at him, "just so he could get more stick time on the *Acheron*."

She was lying, of course; Ash would be worried sick about her taking the troops in. But she'd known if she hadn't volunteered, that he would have, especially since it was her turn to fly the cutter.

He's too damned noble for his own good.

Ash didn't respond, and she was fairly sure he knew exactly what she was doing and wasn't happy about it. But he wouldn't say anything, because he also didn't want her to think he was being overprotective.

We have such a good relationship.

"I guess we're doing this." Nassir didn't sound excited about it. "I'd better start coming up with a good justification for the Board of Directors." She shook her head. "And a resignation letter, just in case."

Sandi wanted to feel sympathy for the harried woman, but couldn't muster any. If Nassir wound up resigning, that would very likely mean they were all dead.

———

The door exploded inward from the impact of the sole of her boot and Korri Fontenot launched through the opening, throwing herself down into a shoulder roll and coming up to a knee, Gauss pistol outstretched.

Nothing. The room was dark and unoccupied, and no alarm sounded. It held no furniture, only stacks of plastic storage bins up against a wall, covered in layers of dust and discolored with age. Just what you'd expect for a utility room connected to a roof access door.

She stood, ducking back through the door and waving for Singh to enter. He was crouched on the ledge, looking down off the third floor of what had been a fabrication center before the economic collapse. The alleyway below was clear; no one had seen them climb the wall, and she hadn't seen any sentries posted. She wouldn't have expected Jordi to be so sloppy.

Singh was inside the room in a single, bounding step, pushing the door shut behind him, not looking the least bit inconvenienced by the pitch blackness inside despite the fact he wasn't wearing any night vision gear.

More implants, she thought. *Unless the eyes are still bionic.* She perversely hoped they were. It didn't seem fair that he could do most everything she could do without the prosthetics. She idly wondered how much it had cost him.

"Down," he said softly, motioning with the barrel of his Gauss machine pistol toward the next door over.

Fontenot kept her handgun trained on the room's other exit as she reached out with her other hand and cautiously yanked on the handle. The battered, cheap plastic door creaked open on old hinges, revealing a narrow, twisting flight of stairs heading to the next floor down. She winced as the wooden steps groaned beneath her weight, but there was nothing to be done about it; if no one had reacted to the door being kicked in, they probably wouldn't hear this, either.

By the time she reached the next landing, she knew something wasn't right. When Singh had busted her out, this place had been packed with troops, Jordi's hired guns from the Pirate Worlds. If what Singh had told her about the shuttles coming in was accurate, there should have been dozens of them, maybe over a hundred. But the next floor down was dark and deserted; no sound filtered up the stairwell, no buzz of voices, no scrape of shoes on the floorboards, just a gently flickering light.

They'd suspected it from their recon of the outside of the building, and now it was certain. Jordi was on the move. She just hoped something he'd left behind would tell them where. Her steps were a drumbeat on the stairs now and if anyone couldn't hear them, they must be in a coma...

Or a netdiver deep in the interface.

She saw them the second she hit the bottom stair, three of them arrayed in a semicircle around a quantum stack, settled into form-fitting "easy chairs" with the interface cables jacked into their implant sockets. Two of them were men, the third a woman, but in looks they were nearly identical: heads depilated, skin pale to the point of translucence, blue veins visible through it, loose clothes hanging like rags off their skeleton frames. Not just your average professional netdivers then; they were obviously ViR addicts as well, working for the cartels to feed their need for illegal ViRware that would directly stimulate the pleasure centers of their brains.

What they were, though, wasn't nearly as interesting to her as what they were doing. There were cheap, obsolete, flat-panel displays mounted on the wall above the quantum computer stack, each about a meter across, showing the video feed from what could only have been a swarm of insect drones. It was early morning, well before dawn outside, but the view on the displays was as bright as noon, thanks to night vision filters and computer interpolation. The view on one screen was somewhere on the road out of the city, at least that was her guess from what little she'd seen of it. The plains outside Gennich were red and rocky, and barren but for a few hardy, bioengineered plants brought from Earth decades ago and the even hardier lichen left behind as a terraforming tool by the Predecessors hundreds of thousands of years before that.

The road that cut through those wind-swept plains turned quickly from pavement to gravel to graded dirt, and the convoy of vehicles rumbling down that road were throwing up a cloud of dust that challenged even the infrared filters and the computer enhancement. There were ten of them, she thought, most of them passenger vans, though she saw two cargo trucks and a smaller rover as well, and she would have been willing to bet that Jordi was in that car. That was enough vehicles to be carrying the whole lot of them, and where they were going...

The middle screen was showing a seasonal river bed, a *wadi* she thought they were called, crossed by a crude, stone bridge barely wide enough for one of those cargo trucks to pass over it. The bed was dry at this time of year, though she thought she might have seen a hint of mud from a light rain somewhere in the hills above. The road and the bridge were deserted, the lonely stand of genetically engineered Earth cottonwoods a dozen meters off the edge of the dirt track the only sign of life. Yet they'd taken the time to put it under surveillance, and she had no doubt that was where they were heading.

The third screen showed their quarry, their target, rolling the opposite direction much further down a turn-off of the same road, coming out of a deep canyon system over the pass through the hills and up near the distant plateau halfway to the next settlement. Dust roiled into the air behind them, though not as much nor as dry as the cloud around Jordi's convoy. There were only three vehicles: two large, twelve-wheeled cargo trucks, lurching as aged and under-maintained transmissions changed gears to compensate for the downhill grade. Out in front a beat-up rover led them, and through the front windscreen of the smaller vehicle, Fontenot could make out enough of the driver's face to see that they weren't human.

"Oh, son of a bitch," she muttered.

As if the words broke a magic spell keeping the two of them invisible, one of the men blinked, his eyes focusing suddenly on her and Singh, and growing wide with fear and shock.

"Stay where you are," she was saying, but the words hadn't quite made it out of her mouth before another man, one they'd missed, burst out of a narrow doorway in the corner of the same shop floor where she'd been held prisoner only hours before.

She had less than a second to evaluate the threat. He wasn't a netdiver, she could tell by his healthy complexion and shaggy hair, and his clothes were cheap flash from a cheap fabricator. The belt around his multicolor pants was unfastened and she had the absurd thought that they'd caught him on the shitter. There was nothing absurd about the heavy machine pistol in his hand, though, and he'd started firing before he came out of the bathroom.

Fontenot fell to a knee, knowing instinctively that the netdivers were between her and the cartel gunman and feeling confident he wouldn't shoot them. And then he did. The gun was ancient, a primitive slug-shooter older than her, and from the chatter of its discharge it still used conventional gunpowder propellant. The bullets it fired did a fine job on the female netdiver just the same, punching through her torso cleanly before they flattened themselves into Fontenot's chest armor with bruising impact.

She fired by instinct, a two-round burst that took him in the chest. The pistol was loaded with anti-personnel rounds rather than solid tungsten slugs, and the wire-wrapped, frangible ceramic loads spent themselves inside his body. He jerked and spasmed, the gun dropping from strengthless fingers before he collapsed forward to the concrete slab floor.

Singh was moving, running past the dead gunman and into the back room, leaving her to deal with the remaining netdivers. They were both retreating from the interface now, yanking in panic at the cables that attached them to the quantum stack, and starting to climb out of their backwards-tilted chairs. The third one, the woman, was clearly as good as dead; her body thrashed and shook, blood gushing from her multiple gunshot wounds, from her mouth, from her nose.

Fontenot grabbed the nearer of the two survivors by the throat, slamming him back into his seat hard enough to send chair and man crashing to the floor. The last, distinguishable from his fellow netdiver only by a small tattoo of a unicorn on his left cheek, ran to the corpse of the cartel thug, trying to grab for the machine pistol laying on the floor next to the body. Fontenot bit back a curse and lunged across the room, knowing instinctively that she wouldn't be able to reach him before he picked up the gun, counting on the probability that it would take the jackhead a second to figure out the weapon.

She was still a good meter from him when his head disappeared in a spray of red, and she dug in her heels, scrambling to keep from winding up wading through what was left of his brain. Singh was standing in the doorway of the back room, his Gauss machine pistol extended. He brought it back to low ready, his face as neutral as if he'd tossed a can into a recycler.

"I had it handled," she snapped at him, stepping back from the wreckage of the netdiver.

The one she'd slammed to the ground was gasping for breath, attempting to roll off the chair and crawl away. She pinned him down with a boot between his shoulder blades, still glaring at Singh.

"We didn't need him." The bounty hunter tossed his head

dismissively. "We have that one, and from the looks of things," he motioned at the view on the monitors, "we don't have much time."

She grunted by way of reply, stepping off the netdiver's back, then grabbing him by the collar of his loose, baggy shirt and hauling him to his feet. This close, she could smell him; he stank of sweat and fear and stale piss, and his clothes were coated with overlapping stains of various ages and provenances. He was panting, his mouth hanging open, and it was a close thing whether his breath odor outpaced his body odor; his teeth were dark yellow, lacking the basic hygiene that even most Pirate Worlders could afford.

"You're coordinating drone surveillance for Jordi," she snapped, jabbing a finger into his chest hard enough to make the netdiver gasp in pain. "Where's he going? What's he after?"

He started to shake his head and she slapped him lightly across the face. Lightly for her meant that she merely split his lip and knocked out a tooth instead of breaking his jaw. He groaned and spat blood, and she scowled as drops of it splattered on the sleeve of her jacket.

"Let me ask the question again, in case you didn't hear me right the first time," she said, grabbing him by the back of the neck and squeezing just slightly. "Where is Jordi going? What is he after?"

"He'll kill me..." The words were slurred through split and swelling lips, blood dribbling out of his mouth as he spoke.

"What the hell do you think *we'll* do to you, boy?" Singh demanded, leaning in over her shoulder. "At least this way, you'll have a chance to run."

"Do I tell you how to do *your* job, Singh?" Fontenot growled at him and he stepped back, raising a palm apologetically.

"It's guns," the netdiver blurted.

Fontenot turned back to him, pulling his face closer to hers. He whimpered at the proximity, eyes going wider.

"Say again?"

"It's guns," he repeated meekly. "Jordi is going after the guns." He pointed at the screen with the smaller convoy still navigating the canyon road. "The Tahni are getting guns and stuff from a stash their military hid during the war, and Jordi's gonna' steal them."

"That's what this was all about in the first place," Singh declared, his face slack with the abrupt realization. "That's what he's been after...it's why he stirred up trouble between the humans and the Tahni."

Fontenot shook her head in reluctant admiration.

"He's one clever son of a bitch," she said. She focused her gaze on the netdiver again, giving him a gentle shake as a reminder she was still there. "You tell us one more thing and you can walk out of here alive. You get me?"

The hairless, skeletal man nodded as best he could with her metal hand wrapped around his neck.

"Anything," he insisted, wiping blood away from his mouth with the back of his hand.

"That," Fontenot said, turning his head toward the middle display, the bridge over the wadi, the cottonwoods, the deserted stretch of road. "I need you to tell me exactly where that is. And how much time we have left before both sides reach it."

CHAPTER TEN

The bed of the cargo truck sagged under the massive step of the battlesuit, and Kan-Ten thought for a senseless, panicked moment that the vehicle wouldn't take the weight, that he'd tumble off the back and wind up unable to recover. He'd seen images on the entertainment streams aboard the *Acheron* of a hard-shelled Earth creature called the tortoise; sometimes, they'd be shown having somehow fallen onto their back, help-less, their legs kicking slowly in the air. That's what he would look like, he thought ruefully, some stupid, slow-moving animal.

The on-board gyros did their job, though, and the truck's suspension held under the weight of his powered armor just as the other cargo bed had held up for the suit Vala-Kel had loaded onto it. He moved into position behind the stacked weapons crates, leaned the upper body forward, then squeezed the correct combination of the finger controls, and the servos powered down and left the suit frozen in place. Another control and the chest plastron slid downward and he scrambled out of the suits metal and plastic embrace eagerly, trying not to hyper-ventilate as his feet slammed down on the steel plate of the cargo bed.

"Get it strapped down securely," he ordered the two males who'd come along as cargo handlers, riding in the back of the truck on the way here.

Kan-Ten looked down at himself, at the black control garment he was wearing, and felt a wave of disbelief that he'd put one on again after all this time. It had been stored inside the battlesuit, and while any of them could have worn it, only he and Vala-Kel had experience operating the machines. There'd been no choice, but that didn't make him feel better about it. No choice. Destiny, the humans called it, those who believed in it. Fate. The Will of the Emperor, the Path, his people termed it, but it was the same idea. An inescapable outcome. Death inside one of those damned suits.

"It's just like old times, brother!" Vala-Kel exulted, stepping down from the bed of the other truck. He looked at home in the black garment, as if he'd worn it yesterday rather than ten years ago. "Have you missed it as much as I have?"

"We should leave now," Kan-Ten said, rather than answering the question. He lowered himself to the ground, leaving the cargo handlers to their task. "I'm uncomfortable being out here in the open." He looked over to where the Matriarch and her protégé waited at their vehicle, a proper distance away, deep in a conversation that he couldn't overhear.

"Who would know where we were going? We need not fear any more...it's the humans who should fear us!"

"Yes." Kan-Ten showed nothing in his stance or the set of his shoulders. He started to yank at the fasteners of the control singlet, but Vala-Kel put a hand on his wrist.

"Leave it on, brother," he insisted. "Get used to its feel again." He motioned at the computer modules on the waist. "You know the longer you wear it, the more accurately it will read your motions."

"I am aware." He chanted a calming mantra inside his head

to keep from venting his anger. "I will leave it on if we can depart now."

"As you will." Vala-Kel seemed disappointed in him. "I will ride in this truck." He motioned at the one he'd helped to load. "You should stay with yours, with your suit."

"It is not my suit, brother." He turned away and headed for the cab of the truck, not trusting himself to say any more. The KE-gun he'd taken earlier was wedged in the floor of the passenger's side, and he shoved it aside, falling into the ripped, worn seat and slamming the door.

He waited in the cab until he heard the other truck's alcohol-fueled engine rumble to life. Even then he didn't look aside at it, worried that Vala-Kel might meet his eyes and see the fear in them. The Matriarch and her protégé noticed the truck starting as well, and slid into the front of their own rover, the doors lowering shut with a grinding squeak. The rover scratched across the sand and dirt on knobby tires, this time taking the trailing position behind Kan-Ten's truck, following closely as it lurched into motion with a grinding of the old transmission.

The road back seemed rougher than the road out, and Kan-Ten guessed it was from the massive load of weapons weighing down the truck's suspension, but eventually he began to grow used to it. It was a deeper, stronger rhythm than before, but all rhythms were part of the Path, and he tried to submerge himself into it, but something nagged at the corner of his vision. He turned and saw the driver staring at him sidelong every few seconds.

"What?" he wondered.

"I feel as if I am in the time of legends," the young male admitted, "in the company of the giants of old." His tone was full of an almost religious awe. He motioned to the truck ahead of them. "Do you really think Vala-Kel is the rightful Emperor?"

"I suppose if he is," Kan-Ten reasoned, "then our cause can't possibly fail, can it?" He made a gesture of equivocation. "Of course, if he's not, then we will be too dead to realize our mistake."

The driver seemed scandalized by the idea and he fell silent, but at least he stopped constantly staring at Kan-Ten. It was very late and he was beginning to adjust to the day-night cycle of this part of the planet, which was inconvenient since it meant he was growing weary, and the cab of the truck wasn't the most comfortable place to sleep. But if years in the High Guard had taught him anything, it was how to sleep wherever and whenever he could. He rested his head against the window and began to drift off.

"What is that up ahead?" The driver's voice woke him, like a buzzing insect droning in his ear.

He pushed away from the door, straightening in his seat and staring out the windshield. The earlier overcast had cleared as they left the canyons, and between the light from Brigantia's moon and the headlights from the vehicles, he could see the road up ahead several hundred meters. They were approaching the bridge they'd crossed earlier in the night, and just past it, behind the stand of cottonwoods, he could see vague, dark shapes blending with the shadows of the trees.

"You have a keen eye, warrior," he complimented the driver, then picked at the pile of clothes he'd left in the cab when he'd changed into the control garment, finding his 'link still attached to the shoulder of his tunic.

"Vala-Kel," he called. "Do you see that up ahead, just over the bridge?"

"I see nothing." The reply was terse, which seemed very unlike his usually effusive comrade, and Kan-Ten felt a curious sensation of foreboding, a grim certainty that something was wrong.

He saw Vala-Kel's truck slow as it approached the bridge,

saw its suspension shift as the front wheels hit the near side of the span and suddenly the shapes through the trees jumped into focus. They were vehicles, a large group of them, parked in the shadows, their lights off.

"Stop!" he yelled at his own driver and into the 'link, but he was seconds too late.

It wasn't much of a blast, certainly not the HyperExplosives the military used; more like something homemade, an "Improvised Explosive Device," as he'd heard Fontenot refer to it. It was mostly flash, probably gelled petroleum or potassium nitrate or something, but it was more than enough to lift the cab of the lead truck off the ground nearly half a meter and dislocate the front axle, sending both the wheels spinning off the side of the bridge and down into the wadi.

Kan-Ten felt the concussion inside his chest, then felt the seat restraints yank at him as the driver slammed on the brakes. Stars filled his vision from the flash of the explosion and the violence of their abrupt halt, but he could see well enough to spot the humans running out of the thicket of cottonwood, pistols and carbines in their hands, the vehicles pulling out from behind the trees and advancing across the open plain.

This was a trap. They were after the weapons.

"No!" he yelled at the driver, grabbing his shoulder and pointing down at the wadi. "Head down there! Get us out of here now!"

"But the others...," the male protested.

"If we stay here, they," Kan-Ten pointed at the oncoming humans, "will concentrate their fire here! We need to spread them out! We need to get the Matriarch to safety! Get us out of here!"

The driver shifted the truck into a lower gear, jammed on the accelerator and twisted the wheel to the right. The truck shuddered and there were banging sounds from the cargo compartment as the boxes shifted in the back. Kan-Ten was tossed against his restraints again by the wheels leaving the road, but he pushed himself up and grabbed the KE-gun from the floorboards. He hit the seat belt release and threw open the door, stepping out onto the running board, holding the KE-gun against his left hip as he held onto the safety handle with his right hand. The surface of the wadi was hard and smooth except for a few stretches of mud, and once they were down in it, the jolts and shudders settled enough for him to keep his balance.

The Matriarch's rover was following them, but she wasn't going to make it off the road before the humans reached her. Already they were firing at his truck and at her vehicle, the meteor trails of mini-rockets streaking through the night, their warheads splashing against the stone of the bridge as they went wide of their targets. Kan-Ten aimed the KE-gun in the general direction of the approaching vehicles and held down the trigger. The weapon bucked in his hands despite the weight of it, spitting out hundreds of tantalum needles at thousands of meters per second.

He couldn't tell if he'd hit anything, but he did see some of the vehicles swerve and the others slow, a few of the runners throw themselves down. The Matriarch's rover nearly flipped on its side when it went over the bank of the wadi at top speed, but the wheels slammed back to the ground in a spray of sand and mud, and it was quickly accelerating after the truck, sheltered from enemy fire by the banks. Back on the bridge, there were the flares of exploding warheads from the mini-rockets, and Kan-Ten thought he saw one of the cargo handlers go down under the enemy fire before they were too far away to make out details.

Kan-Ten swung back into the cab and yanked the door shut, closing out the rush of the wind and the rumble of the engine. The driver's face was tense, with the look of one trying to keep his concentration on what he was doing, despite the fear and panic doing its best to distract him. The wheels were sliding back and forth on the slick surface of the wadi, one or another spinning wildly when it hit a muddy spot.

"The Matriarch is following us," he assured the young male, trying to remember how he'd spoken to young warriors during the war. "You've done well."

"Kan-Ten!"

It was one of the cargo handlers in the back of the truck calling him over his 'link. He touched a control to answer.

"Are you all right up there?" Kan-Ten asked.

"The vehicles are moving to cut us off," the male told him, his tone urgent and desperate. They had a higher viewpoint up on the cargo bed than he did in the cab, he realized. "The banks of this river bed get lower up ahead; they're going to reach it before us!"

"Get weapons from the crates if you can. Get ready to fight."

Kan-Ten clutched at the driver's shoulder, getting his attention.

"You have to go faster."

"We'll go out of control," he protested. Then his face seemed to firm up, along with his resolve. "I'll try."

He pushed the accelerator down and the engine grumbled with the effort, surging as he shifted gears. Kan-Ten checked the digital readout of the KE-gun and realized that he'd emptied most of the drum. He bent down to retrieve the spare he'd taken from Vala-Kel inside the underground cache, had to steady himself against the dash when the truck began to slide again. He needed to put his seat harness back on, he thought, grabbing the reload and ejecting the nearly spent magazine. The fresh one seated home with practiced ease, rote memories learned from long hours of repetition as a young recruit.

He'd just begun to reach for the seatbelt when the driver blurted a half-formed warning and the truck went from thirty-five kilometers per hour to zero in less than a second, slamming Kan-Ten against the dash hard enough to stun him. The engine roared and the wheels whined as they spun up, throwing thick gouts of mud into the air, some splattering against the side windows.

"Get us out of this!" He tried to shout the words, but the breath had been knocked out of him, and he barely gasped them.

"I'm trying, sir!" the young male said, shifting the truck manually into a lower gear and hitting the accelerator again. More roaring, more spinning, more mud, but no motion.

By the time the driver had shifted them into reverse, Kan-Ten was back in his seat. The entire length of the cargo hauler jerked backwards as the wheels spun the other direction, but it was stuck fast.

"Stop," Kan-Ten instructed, throwing open his door and dropping to the ground.

His legs sank half a meter into the mud and he nearly went face-first into the muck before he caught the edge of the door and steadied himself. The truck, he could see immediately, wasn't going anywhere. All of the wheels, from stem to stern, were buried half their height into the thick, soupy mud and it would be an hour's work to free them...and they had seconds.

"Are we stuck?" That was Tran-Coh, one of the cargo handlers, leaning over the railing of the truck bed, staring down at him.

"Do you have a weapon?" he asked the male by way of response.

Tran-Coh blanched at that, but held up the KE-gun he'd salvaged from their cargo. The other male in the back---Kan-Ten couldn't recall his name---held his own rifle up as well, looking more confident than his fellow.

"Go protect the Matriarch," Kan-Ten directed them, waving back at the rover, still twenty meters behind them.

She was out of her vehicle now, and the younger female was beside her, a compact slug-shooter in her hand and a resolute fearlessness in the set of her shoulders. That one would have made the mother of great warriors, he decided, had she not dedicated her life to the path of a Matriarch. Even this far away, he could feel urges pulling at him, his animal brain screaming at him to drop his weapon and run to mate with her...he could see it on the faces of the males in the back of the truck as well.

"They're coming for the weapons," he told the females. "You two should move along the river bed and find a place to wait them out while we hold them off."

"I brought this on us," the Matriarch declared. "I will see it through."

"Honored Female," Kan-Ten said respectfully, "your presence will distract us from the fight. Go now, while there is time."

"Listen to him, Mother," the protégé urged. "Your life is more important than these weapons...or proving a point."

She didn't seem happy with the idea, but the Matriarch was, by definition, the wisest of them, and she saw the wisdom in this argument. Kan-Ten turned and made his way through the mud back to the truck, climbing into the back with the cargo handlers.

The driver was leaning out the door, looking over the edge of the banks of the wadi, watching the vehicles approach. They'd figured out that the cargo truck wasn't moving and they'd abandoned their attempt to cut them off, turning back to head directly for their position.

"What about the battlesuit?" the driver asked him, gesturing to the bulky machine, still bowed forward as if it was genuflecting to them, bright red loading straps crisscrossing the length of it, securing it to tie-downs set in the cargo bed.

"It would take too long to unstrap it and restart the reactor," he said with a motion of negation. "Longer than we have."

Was that true? Could he have done it if he'd thought of it immediately when they'd stopped? Or had he not because he still resisted the idea of walking the thing into battle?

Humans had a curious notion of how to dispose of the dead. Well, some of them did; their beliefs and customs differed alarmingly from one group to another. But he'd met those who insisted on burying the dead in the ground in a box called a coffin, which had always struck him as a morbid and wasteful practice. The battlesuit, though, reminded him of one of those coffins, reminded him of death and waste.

He shook the thought off; the vehicles were less than a hundred meters away now, the cloud of dust from their wheels rising over the plain, shining in the bright moonlight. The dismounted troops were another hundred yards or so behind them, too far to aim without computer assistance, which none of them had.

"Target the vehicles," he told the others, leaning the cooling jacket of the KE-gun against the railing and lining up the electronic sight with the grill of a passenger van.

It had been slapped together from parts fabricated on patterns decades old; newer patterns would cost more if you acquired them legally, and out here, it was easier to run your own alcohol still for fuel than to pay for high-end capacitor banks, and then to pay again to replace them if they failed. Power was cheap, of course, with the colony's ubiquitous public fusion reactors, but ways to store it were not. Not out here.

That made the targeting easier; he aligned the sighting reticle with the grill, knowing that if he could take out the cooling or fuel lines, he could take out the vehicle.

"Shoot them," he ordered, touching the trigger button.

The stock pushed against his shoulder insistently, and a hundred tantalum slivers blasted out across the flat plain beyond the river bank, the crack of their passage trailing the sight of their impact on the front of the van. He sent most of the burst into the grill before rising his point of aim to the windshield; steam and smoke poured out of the engine and the vehicle ground to a halt, skidding sideways, its plastic windshield in tatters. The rear double-doors flew open and panic-stricken humans began piling out; he hosed them down without a thought, except, perhaps, the reflection that it *did* seem just like old times. One after another jerked and fell, the light armor they wore no match for a military-grade weapon such as his.

The warning light flashed in his optical sight, helpfully letting him know that the drum was empty. It was only then he noticed the incoming gunfire, though he was sure it had been ongoing for several seconds. Swarms of mini-rockets trailed fiery red exhaust plumes over their heads and Kan-Ten ducked down instinctively. Tran-Coh's body was sprawled out beside the stacked crates, blood from the gaping wound in his throat pooling beneath him, his KE-gun nowhere to be seen; Kan-Ten guessed it had fallen over the side panel of the cargo bed. The other male, the one whose name he still couldn't recall, was huddled beside his friend, the KE-gun cradled against him, the halo of the reload warning light blinking against his chest.

As far as he could tell, neither one of them had hit a thing, but a quick glance over the bank showed him that the enemy advance had slowed with his destruction of the van full of troops. The vehicles had pulled up short and the remainder were concentrating on pouring fire at him. He ducked back down. This was less than half of the force he'd seen back at the bridge, which meant the rest had stayed with Vala-Kel's truck, and his friend was most likely dead.

I suppose he wasn't the True Emperor after all.

Kan-Ten crouched low and moved over to the tied-down crates, checking to see if he could find a reload for his rifle, knowing even as he did that the enemy would likely be on him in seconds.

When he heard the whining hum overhead, he thought at first his ears were playing tricks on him, battered by the near-constant eruption of mini-rocket warheads all around. But it only got louder, closer, and then he could see it coming in low against the stars, glinting in the moonlight: a hopper. The ducted-fan helicopter was old, battered, a patchwork quilt of spare parts; he could hear the pitch of the fans vary every few seconds. If it was Jordi's men in it, though, his life expectancy had grown even shorter than he thought.

"Kan-Ten." The call on his 'link was barely audible from the shoulder pocket where he'd stowed it. He pulled it out, trying to hold it closer to his ear to offset the gunshots, and the whine of the hopper, and the grumbling alcohol engines all around him.

"Kan-Ten," the voice went on insistently. It was Korri Fontenot. "If you can hear me, stay in the river bed and keep your head down."

Fontenot... He glanced up again at the hopper and realized that it must be her. But how had she known? And why hadn't he told her? He pushed that thought off for later.

The hopper banked low over the vehicles, then shuddered in mid-air as one of the doors popped open and a stocky, black-clad figure leaned out, one hand filled with a weapon of some kind. Ionized air flashed white, turned to plasma by the energy of the laser pulses from the carbine, and the bursts began to chop across the front of one of the remaining passenger vans. Sparks and flames shot from the hood of the vehicle as the laser pulses pierced its engine compartment, and it caught fire.

Kan-Ten turned away from the battle, ripping through the

storage boxes tied down in the bed, throwing one after another open until he finally found one packed with loaded ammo drums for the KE-guns. He grabbed one and tossed it at the male who still sat crouched on the floor by the body of his friend. The drum hit him hard in the chest, and he glanced up in confusion and anger.

"Reload that weapon," Kan-Ten growled at him in a voice that had made new recruits wish for their mothers not so long ago. "Get back into the fight."

He ejected the spent drum from his own rifle and replaced it with a fresh one, then threw himself up on the left-side panel of the open cargo bed. The hopper was circling now, bobbing up and down and trying to make itself a harder target as the troops on the ground had begun to fire up at it. Kan-Ten aimed at the biggest clump of them; they were poorly disciplined, and tended to group together instead of spreading out properly. That was the trouble with most hired guns; if they were competent, they wouldn't have to hire out to someone like the cartel.

The KE-gun spat a stream of hypersonic needles at the mercenaries, slicing through them as if they weren't there, and passing on through. One after another of them toppled, some dead and silent, some wounded and screaming. Humans had such odd screams, he thought. Nothing like a Tahni sounded, not even a female...maybe a child. He'd heard females and children die before; the humans hadn't been targeting them, but things happened in war, and missiles intended for point-defense turrets sometimes hit the people those turrets were defending.

The cargo handler was beside him now, he could see it out of the corner of his vision. He propped his weapon across the next panel over and opened fire; Kan-Ten wouldn't have been willing to bet his life on the male's accuracy, but he didn't need to hit anyone, just let those hired guns know someone was shooting at them. He could see them falling back now, some trying to shoot as they retreated, the others simply running. Fontenot was shooting again from the hopper, and the combination was too much for the mercenaries; the vehicles began to reverse, to turn around and head back to the bridge, to the other cargo truck.

The hopper was descending now, coming down right next to the bank. Kan-Ten lowered his weapon, reaching down to where he'd left another loaded drum at his feet, swapping them out and leaning the rifle against the side panel of the truck. The cargo handler was staring at him, his weapon empty and held limply at his side.

"These are allies," he told the male, motioning toward the hopper. "Don't make them shoot you."

Fontenot jumped out of the hopper before it had even touched ground, landing heavily in a crouch and running towards them. She vaulted the bank of the wadi and landed in the truck bed with the tone of a massive gong being struck with a clapper. The cargo handler jerked backwards, fumbling for his gun before Kan-Ten slapped it out of his hands and sent it tumbling across the bed.

The driver finally reappeared from where he'd been hiding inside the cab, glancing around in awe. Kan-Ten wanted to be angry with him, but he knew the young male hadn't had a weapon and had never been in combat before.

"I appreciate your superb timing, as always," Kan-Ten told Fontenot. "How did you find us?"

"I had some help," she pointed back at the hopper. "The real question is, why didn't you call me?"

He knew her as well as he knew any human, and he thought he could read her facial expressions after all this time. She wasn't happy, and he couldn't blame her.

"I was under observation," he said, and wasn't sure if it was true.

She eyed him sidelong, but finally nodded.

"I saw a couple of Tahni on foot heading down the wadi," she told him, gesturing in the direction they'd been traveling. "I assume those are friends of yours."

"If you could go retrieve them, I will get to work on freeing this vehicle from the mud. Jordi Abdullah already has half our weapons. We can't wait around for him to return for the other half." He stared back in the direction of the bridge. "I believe we're going to need them."

CHAPTER ELEVEN

"Lander two-zero-four, you are cleared for launch."

The last word was still ringing in Sandi's ears when the *Warlock*'s mooring clamps released and the shuttle's belly jets kicked her free of the docking bay. The bare metal womb of the bay dropped away and she was swallowed up in darkness, the dull greys and whites of the ice giant below them only visible due to the computer interpolation of the views from the external cameras. The moon was a smaller circle passing across the larger arc of its parent world, shadowy and indistinct, hiding its mysteries under layers of nitrogen clouds. Yet it had already given up one of those secrets to Ash Carpenter and the *Acheron*...

"Prep for boost," she warned the Savage/Slaughter mercenary platoon arrayed behind her in the rows of acceleration couches. She thought she saw Lt. Benitez scowling at her through the faceplate of his pressure suit's helmet from the right-hand chair. Oh well, she would have been mad, too, if she'd been kicked out of the pilot's seat for a stranger.

The main engine flared behind her and four gravities pushed her back into her seat with sudden brutality; she retreated into the interface, trying to shut out the discomfort and distraction, concentrating on the bird, on the flow of power through her body and the flow of data into her mind. She could see the traces of the raider base now, just hints on thermal through the clouds of the moon as it rotated beneath her...and she could see the fusion burns coming up through that atmosphere, two of them rising quickly to meet her.

It was the pirate cutters. It couldn't be helped, they'd had to Transition at the minimum safe distance, then burn in on the *Warlock*'s fusion drive until they'd been close enough to launch the lander. It was too long, too far; they'd all known the enemy would see their warp corona, see the thermal signature of their drive and have time to scramble the cutters. They could shoot her down before she brought her human cargo to the ground, which was worrisome of course, but they could also just run the hell away. *That* they couldn't allow, because then they'd just come back at their leisure, in two weeks or a month, or three months.

This had to end today. And Ash was going to end it.

"They're on their way up," she told him, forcing herself back into her body long enough to speak. "Take them out."

She could see his drive flare burning around the terminator from the other side of the moon, and she had to smile. He always said she was the better pilot, but when he was jacked into the *Acheron*, he was truly alive, and she couldn't imagine him ever doing anything else.

His reply came in a moment later after a second's delay at the mercy of the speed of light.

"I got 'em."

———

Ash felt his lips skinning back from his teeth against the boost of nine gravities, the pain and pressure forcing their way past even the separation of the interface. It was almost a relief, after nearly fifty hours spent in zero gravity, alone, waiting in a depowered ship for the orbit around the gas giant that would give him a view of the moon. He was beginning to think that Sandi had volunteered to pilot the shuttle just so she wouldn't have to do the scout mission. At least the waiting was over...now he got to go let some nutcases try to kill him.

Unless I can kill them first. The thought still bothered him sometimes, despite everything he'd been through, despite the war. On the other hand... *If they didn't want to get killed, they should have picked another line of work.*

The atmosphere of the moon was thicker than usual for a body this small and this cold; the external cameras of the *Acheron* showed nothing but an endless field of grey clouds, and the sensors didn't show much more. The thermal flares of the two cutters ascending through the upper atmosphere were beacons, torches in the mist, but they seemed to hang just out of reach, and he was beginning to imagine the crushing boost would never end. Then, as if by magic, they were leaping ahead at him and he cut his acceleration to a more manageable two g's, bringing the proton cannon online and slaving the Gatling laser turret to the ship's computer for point-defense use.

They were going to spot him any second now...

And there it was; the ships split off from each other, breaking their ascent trajectory and beginning opposing arcs back toward him. They weren't total amateurs; he knew that already, from their last encounter. They had balls and skill and he'd had to think way outside the box to beat them.

Don't think too much, he warned himself, remembering the words of his flight instructors. *Just do.*

He lowered his consciousness beneath the interface, the feel of the acceleration couch and the view from inside the cockpit fading away, replaced by a different sort of awareness that he could never adequately describe to someone who'd never experienced it. The *Acheron* was his body, an extension of his thoughts; its fusion reactor was his heart, its engine his lungs. Banking away into a new trajectory wasn't a matter of math and applied physics and firing maneuvering rockets; it was as simple as shifting his weight and turning a corner. Jacked into the interface, he wasn't a pilot, he *was* the ship.

They were trying to trap him in a pincer, limit his avenue of retreat and catch him in their firing arc. He didn't believe they carried missiles; they'd yet to use them against the barges, and he had to figure it was because railguns were cheaper. They might have lasers as well, but probably not military-class Gatling lasers; more likely a jury-rigged mining laser, something they could steal and plug into their reactor. Either way, it wouldn't cut through the *Acheron*'s hide quickly enough to be a threat, so his main worry would be the railguns; and to use those, they'd have to angle the nose of their ships for a head-on shot.

It's practically a propeller-age dogfight, he thought ruefully. *What I wouldn't give for some heat-seekers...*

He couldn't go down because then he'd be giving them the chance to get away, get to Minimum Transition Distance before he could catch up; instead, he lifted the nose and headed out of the atmosphere, trying to put a hard ceiling on their ascent vector. The push of the extra g's added to the sensation of sprinting uphill, squeezing his chest with the effort, the view from the ship's cameras tilting and shifting as grey gave way to star-crusted blackness. Through the pressure and the disorientation and the thinning atmosphere, he still retained a knowledge of where the enemy was, the data from the sensors simply there in his perception the same way you knew where your arms and legs were without looking.

They were matching his move, angling up for suborbital space again, trying to line up for a shot. The warning wasn't a computerized voice, wasn't a flashing light in his vision, he just knew the shot was coming the way you knew when you saw an arm cocking back to throw a punch. He dodged, as natural as sliding a foot to the side and shifting his weight, even though it involved cutting thrust to the main engine and hitting the belly jets and the fore and aft port maneuvering thrusters for a long second before reignition of the drive.

Acceleration hammered at him along with a wash of micro-gravity, the battering his inner ear took nearly dragging him out of the interface, but when the railgun fired, the round passed ten meters from his port wingtip. He cut the main drive again, firing both aft belly jets and spinning the *Acheron* end for end, far enough up now and in a thin enough layer of the atmosphere that the move didn't send the ship out of control. The opposing thrust from the bow belly jets cut the spin short and left his nose lined up with the cutter that had fired on him.

Pale white lightning, barely visible in the thin layer of atmospheric nitrogen, crackled across kilometers and struck the pirate boat amidships. Their deflectors lit up in a coruscating globe of fire, yellow and purple and white like an aurora, and he could see a flare where the shields yielded to a point-overload, star-hot plasma arcing through the portside delta wing. Vapor-ized metal and flaming atmosphere shot out in an impromptu maneuvering jet and the ship went into a spin, the combination of uncoordinated thrust sending her banking back away from him, trailing glowing clouds of thruster fuel and escaping air.

Ash didn't try to follow the wounded ship's track with his full attention; he knew the other boat would be maneuvering, cold-bloodedly taking advantage of his distraction with the shot to line up his own main weapon, because that was exactly what he'd do. He flipped the *Acheron* end for end, punching the main drive and the starboard belly jets at the same time, banking away from the undamaged cutter's trajectory but staying above him. Wind caught at his virtual wings though there wasn't enough atmosphere to produce it, a simulation of the ship's motion in a way his instincts could grasp without thought.

The world was a network of patterns, of angles and trajectories and velocities in tangled lines, and the data washed over his brain through the interface, transforming into movement and hunch and guesswork. He remembered watching old movies, reading old novels about how a brain-computer interface might work, stories written before it had become reality, and they'd never approached the actual experience. The computer wasn't a personality, because time and experimentation had shown that computers with personalities were unreliable, unstable; they were artificial intelligence, but they weren't artificial *human* intelligence, and treating them as if they were had driven them insane. They didn't speak in words because words took too long to communicate data, slowing down the decision-making process.

No, when the interface had finally worked, it worked because thinking wasn't necessary, because talking was ineffcient, because communication was redundant. The patterns of the sensors and the mathematics of the vectors and angles and probabilities all became motion, filtered through the greatest computer in the history of biological evolution: the human brain. Only conscious thought could slow it down, so the split-second decisions were often made unconsciously, which was why experience and repetition and training were so crucial.

These guys had the experience, he could tell that, and undoubtedly some training, but they hadn't been where he'd been, hadn't been squadron leaders who ran simulations twelve hours a day until they were ready to send down to the rest of the flight crews. So, when the opportunity came, his subconscious mind saw it and took it long before his opponents even recognized that it was happening.

It was just a slight change of angles, a small mistake that would take seconds to recognize and correct; he couldn't have pinpointed it to someone watching, couldn't have explained it later. But in the space of two heartbeats, the *Acheron* was rocketing straight to starboard and for just an instant, the undamaged enemy cutter was passing through the targeting reticle of his boat's proton cannon at a distance of barely three kilometers. The weapon fired with a caress of his thoughts and speared the pirate cutter through the portside of the control deck, burning through the deflector shields like they weren't there at this range.

Atmosphere flared and burning metal flashed and people died, vaporized without a trace they'd ever been. Most of the nose of the ship was gone, yet it kept accelerating, the drives frozen in ignition. They'd run until the reactor fuel went dry, and by then the ship would be heading for interstellar space, a cold and dark memorial.

He felt the *Acheron*'s plasma drive punch him back into his acceleration couch and didn't know why for just an instant until the data reached his thinking mind. The damaged ship had returned, and a railgun projectile, twenty kilograms of solid tungsten, had screamed less than a meter from the stern of the *Acheron*, a nanosecond from turning the ship into an incoherent cloud of plasma.

He banked starboard again, diving back into the atmosphere, but the ship was still on him, not badly damaged enough to keep it from matching his nine-gravity descent. The maneuvering thrusters were sledgehammers beating against the wings of the ship, flinging the massive delta shape port and starboard in an erratic course. Another railgun shot, this one nearly as close, and the atmosphere was thick enough now that the friction ionized it into a fiery meteor.

Shit, he had the time to think. *At least Sandi has a ride home.*

That was when he saw the shuttle. It was burning in on his starboard side, rising on a fiery torch of exhaust, and its Gatling laser was firing even as he watched. A perforated line of flaring white pulses shot from the weapons multiple emitters, focused by the central crystal, and the rear cameras showed them striking home on the nose of the enemy ship, ignoring the electromagnetic deflectors.

The bow maneuvering thruster fuel tank burst in a glowing white globe of fire, and the raider ship nosed downward, spinning seemingly out of control. Ash didn't take a chance this time; the pilot had already burned him once. He pulled the nose of the *Acheron* up, the maneuvering thrusters pushing against the bottom of his acceleration couch, and the rapidly descending cutter filled his gunsights. The proton accelerator struck like Zeus' thunderbolt through the thickening atmosphere, and the pirate boat vanished in a plasma plume hundreds of meters across.

Ash felt the *Acheron* shudder as shockwaves traveled upward, and he banked away urgently, feeling the static electricity crackling around the ship.

"Thanks," he called to Sandi, rasping, his mouth full of cotton.

"I can't take you anywhere," she chided playfully, her laugh hoarse and somehow incredibly provocative. "Cover my descent; they might have anti-aircraft defenses down there."

"Aye, ma'am," he said, feeling a grin spreading across his face just at the sound of her voice. "I got you covered."

"I take it all back," Benitez said quietly over their command net.

Sandi glanced sideways at him, keeping just a small section of her consciousness submerged in the interface to watch for rising missiles. The younger man was staring at her through the visor of her helmet again, but not with a scowl this time; it was more like a sour smile.

"What?" she wondered.

"Everything I've been thinking since they put you in the left seat," the copilot clarified. "You deserve to be there. Hell, both of you are better pilots than I ever will be. I don't care what either of you say, you both got that Medal for a reason."

Sandi grunted, but she smiled inside her helmet.

"Let's see if you feel that way after my landing."

The lander was a goony-bird compared to a Fleet assault shuttle, but it seemed about as agile as the *Acheron* here in the soup, and Sandi felt herself slipping into the length and breadth of it, her consciousness spreading out through its wings and control surfaces. There was a weight to the bird, a solidity that she could appreciate, and it had as much boost as any other shuttle. The boost pushed against her with a welcome pressure, the body of a lover descending upon her, and the mists parted as the wings split them.

Razor-edged mountains of ice reached up at her, menacing in their beauty, lifeless and brutal. She followed the edge of them, staying as low as she dared, hunting for the thermal signature Ash had detected, the launching point for the now-destroyed cutters. The track led her to a pass through the mountains, and she could almost feel the cold off the surrounding peaks as the lander roared through it.

She could see it then, the sensor readouts of it, the thermal signature, the lidar return. It wasn't huge and it wasn't fancy, but it was sizable for a place like this, for an operation like this. It could be that the base was automated, that the cutter crews had been the only personnel on the world, but she doubted it. Automation cost money, both to buy and to transport and to maintain. It wasn't something you saw much in the Periphery, rarely in the Pirate Worlds, and never among two-bit raiders like these.

There was at least a maintenance crew down there and likely hired guns as well, she could feel it as much as she felt the lift of the atmosphere on the shuttle's wings. When the Gauss cannon opened up on her, she wasn't surprised, not by the ground fire or the choice of weapons; electromagnetic slug-shooters were cheap to make and cheap to feed. She shoved the nose down, burning in nearly vertical, feeling the turbulence in the wind around her from the passage of the slugs, seeing the streaks of fire where their sheer speed ionized the atmosphere around them.

"Ash," she bit off through teeth clenched against the acceleration.

"Got it," he replied tightly.

It was too many seconds later for her peace of mind, but a raging streak of furious energy fell out of the sky and lanced into the canyon of ice where she knew the flat section of ground held a landing field and three dome-shaped buildings. A half-globe of white fire arced static electricity, and a dark and roiling cloud followed it upward into the death-grey sky.

"You're clear," he said, sounding satisfied at having returned her favor.

She was three hundred meters up when she began firing the belly jets, throttling down the main drives and levelling out the shuttle's descent. She kept a close eye on the sensors, but there was no more incoming fire; the Gauss cannon had been their only point defense. There were tiny figures pouring out of one of the dome buildings, growing larger as the shuttle powered in nearly on top of them. They were in armored vacuum suits, camouflaged grey and white against the snow and ice, firing up at the lander with hand-held weapons. It was desperation, but they had reason to be desperate; they had nowhere to run that wouldn't kill them in hours, and the only transportation out of here had just been turned to atoms. They might have a cargo ship scheduled to come pick them up at some point, but it wouldn't be anytime soon.

"Take them out, Benitez," she said, her voice even and businesslike.

The Savage/Slaughter pilot had the controls for the Gatling laser turret slaved to his station, and he played the weapon across the gaggle of armed pirates, razors of coherent light slicing through them. Gouts of steam rose from flash-heated ice instantly sublimated to a gas, and three of the armored figures were chopped to pieces before the others retreated back into the white, buildfoam dome beside the landing pad

"Poor fuckers," Benitez murmured, as if he was unaware his mic was still live.

"They'd do the same to us, and laugh about it," Sandi reminded him. She switched her mic to the general platoon frequency and addressed the men and women strapped into the back of the lander. "Prepare to un-ass the vehicle. We're down in ten seconds."

It felt like less; she brought the shuttle in fast, trying to avoid any further last-ditch attacks, the belly jets screaming in protest. The landing gear barely had time to lock before they were slammed into their seats and she came up short as her straps locked into place.

"Get out of my bird, you damned ground-pounders," she drawled.

She heard a gentle whoosh of air as the belly ramp lowered, letting the thicker on-board atmosphere escape into the low-density nitrogen mix outside. Everyone was suited up, ready for it, but it made her feel strangely vulnerable.

"We're out, ma'am." That was Jacobson, the platoon leader, sounding in a much better mood than the first time they'd met; he was actually going to get the opportunity to shoot someone. "Don't leave without us."

She made no promises, but she powered back her acceleration couch, then loosed its catches and spun it around before yanking the quick-release for her seat restraints. There was a small locker affixed to the bulkhead just between the cockpit and the rows of troop seats; she pulled it open and grabbed two pulse carbines, handing one back to Benitez.

"You think we'll need these?" the man asked, hefting the weapon dubiously.

"If I knew when I'd need a gun," she replied, leaning against one of the passenger seats, the carbine cradled across her chest, "I'd never need one."

———

Lt. Emil Jacobson licked dry lips as he waited beside the inner airlock door of the buildfoam engineering shack. The platoon had broken into squads to search the buildings, and he'd stayed with First, since their squad leader was the youngest and least experienced of the three. Sgt. Arkala was overseeing the planting of the door-buster charge that would get them inside, and Jacobson didn't know if he trusted the woman to do that any more than he did to lead the squad into combat. But everyone had to start somewhere.

"Ready," she told him. He couldn't see her face through the helmet of her vacc suit, but he could imagine her nodding to him, her elfin nose scrunched up with the tension.

"Kick it, Sergeant," he told her, trying to sound confident.

She ducked to the side of the sturdy, metal airlock frame set in the buildfoam. The raiders had left the outer door open, putting the whole atmospheric pressure of the interior air against the inner door, which would make it impossible to open manually, so blowing it was the only thing they could do. He just hoped it didn't blow them up with it.

"Fire in the hole!" Arkala called in timeless warning. "Fire in the hole! Fire in the hole!"

There was a dull crump, not nearly as loud as it would have been in an Earth-normal atmosphere, tinnier and higher-pitched than Jacobson was used to, but the results were just as spectacular. What was left of the inner door blasted outward on a column of flame that roared ferociously out of the airlock tunnel for long seconds, flickering out as pressures equalized and the oxygen burned off. Before the final orange and yellow fires had died out, Jacobson was slapping the squad's A-team leader on the shoulder.

"Go!" he barked at her, and she lunged through the ragged, charred ruins of the airlock, her pulse carbine at her shoulder.

The rest of her team peeled off the wall and followed her inside, and crackling flashes of actinic white marked the firing of pulse guns. Jacobson trailed after the fire team just a heartbeat later, feeling the same druglike jolt of adrenalin that he remembered from the war. If this were a conventional military operation, there would have been a Captain sitting back on the shuttle, watching the view from the helmet cams and coordinating the attack. In Savage/Slaughter, things were a bit more old-fashioned and a platoon leader still controlled his platoon, and he preferred it that way.

The engineering and maintenance building was a dome twenty meters tall at its highest point, and thirty meters across, and it was basically a large workshop for rebuilding parts of the pirate cutters or presumably anything else that broke down out here. It was a crowded, messy place filled with several industrial fabricators and all the equipment necessary to lift and manipulate anything they could build, which gave anyone inside lots and lots of cover. The enemy troops were taking full advantage of that, spread out among the heavy industrial gear and popping enough shots off to keep the fire team he'd sent in first pinned down near the entrance.

Corporal Shiffrin, the team leader, was edging along the shadows of the right-hand wall while the rest of her team laid down covering fire, the bursts from their laser weapons sending brief, colorful flares of sublimated metal spalling off the casings of the fabricators and the support girders of an industrial crane. It wasn't going to be enough, he could already see that; a hail of return fire was smashing into the wall just in front of Shiffrin, forcing her back. Even as he watched, one of the spin-stabilized mini-rocket warheads slammed into the armored pauldron over her left shoulder, and her cry of pain echoed over the team net, and she spun to the floor.

"B-team!" he yelled over the platoon net. "Get in here and lay down some fire!"

Then he was rushing in after his fallen team leader before he had time to think better of it.

Jacobson *should* have ordered someone else to do it; that was what they told you in Marine Officers' Basic Course, that leadership meant keeping a cool enough head to stand back and control and direct, not run in guns blazing. He'd never been that good at the whole cool head thing, which was exactly why he was a platoon leader in Savage/Slaughter instead of a staff officer in the postwar Marine Corps. He switched his laser carbine to his left hand, cradling it against his hip and emptying the magazine as he ran in and grabbed Shiffrin by the carry handle built into the back of her vacc suit's neck yoke.

She was alive; he could see the health readings from her suit on his helmet's HUD, one among a long list, expanding from the rest as he glanced at it, pulsing a deep yellow as it indicated she needed immediate medical attention.

Working on it, he thought.

His carbine vibrated against his palm, letting him know the magazine was drained, but he didn't have the time or the free hand to reload. He gritted his teeth at the whip-crack of incoming rounds splashing spears of plasma off the buildfoam walls around him, concentrating on dragging the woman back behind cover and wondering if he'd make it.

Then Arkala was beside him, carbine at her shoulder, leaning forward as if she had to compensate for recoil; that was a relic from her Marine days, he knew, when they'd been issued Gauss rifles. The pulse carbines Savage/Slaughter used had no recoil, which made them handy for work in microgravity, but he missed the penetrating the Gauss rifles had afforded. Still, the added pressure of Arkala and the squad's B-team was enough to drive the enemy back.

The incoming salvo of rockets died to nothing, and as he got Shiffrin around the safe side of a stack of storage crates loaded down with metal shavings, he noticed two of the pirate ground troops lying sprawled in the aisles between rows of fabricators, nasty holes burned through their pressure suits.

And then he noticed the rear cargo doors rumbling open...

Shit. He hadn't thought about them. They were ten meters square, massive, metal barriers meant for occasional use bringing in or taking out equipment too large to fit through the main airlock. He hadn't considered them because they could only be used if the dome's atmosphere had been evacuated...just like it was now.

He realized he'd reloaded his pulse carbine without thinking, was startled when he heard the faint clatter of the empty magazine off the poured cement floor.

"Trang," Jacobson snapped at the B-team leader, "take care of Shiffrin. Arkala, you're with me!"

He wasn't sure why he'd chosen the squad leader, other than she was the nearest to him and she'd been there when he needed her. She ran beside him through the maze of machinery, her carbine pointed the opposite direction of his, no hesitation in her step. He half-expected the pirates to have left someone behind to ambush them, crouched in the shadows and half-light of the dome, but they were running scared and not thinking about fighting.

"Where are they going, sir?" Arkala asked him, the sharp rasps of her breath coming through the transmission.

"The shuttle," he told her, and his gut twisted with the realization, the answer coming to him in that instant. "It's the only way out of here."

"Ma'am," Lt. Benitez was asking, his voice soft and pensive, "have you ever..."

"Benitez! Commander Hollande! Look out!"

The call was frantic, high-pitched, and it brought Sandi's head around. She'd been sitting, waiting in the back of the lander for long minutes, trying to keep track of the action using the command display on her helmet's HUD, watching IFF transponders scuttle from one place to another like swarming ants. It was frustrating, as waiting always was for her, made doubly so by the fact she was enclosed by the cloying grasp of the vacuum armor. She'd had to borrow it from Savage/Slaughter; all the pressure suits on the *Acheron* were utilitarian rather than tactical. And like any pressure suit that hadn't been fitted, it bound and chafed and made her itch in all sorts of maddening places.

She'd let her thoughts drift off to Ash, wondering if she should check in with him and make sure there wasn't a lighter or armed shuttle out there that they'd missed, and of course that was when the attack came. At the warning cry over the command net, she allowed a pilot's instincts to betray her, glancing back at the cockpit rather than the boarding ramp. It wasn't a huge mistake, only the hesitation of a moment, but it was enough.

There were four of them sprinting up the lander's ramp, their pressure suits mismatched, their armor jury-rigged, the only commonality between them their weapons, the ubiquitous carbines so easily fabricated everywhere in the Pirate Worlds and the Periphery. Unguided, dumb and obsolete, the spin-stabilized 12mm rockets could still do nasty things when they hit you. Sandi fell backwards, the utilitarian grey bulkhead of the lander blurring around her, the falling-star streaks of the mini-rockets passing by only centimeters over her head, and flaring violently as they struck home in the fuselage and the overhead behind her. Finally, the training Fontenot had drilled into her over the last few years took hold and she made herself hold onto her weapon and not attempt to break her fall.

Her shoulder caught the edge of the step to the cockpit and she felt herself bounce off of it, the armor of her suit absorbing the blow and then absorbing the second impact as she hit the deck. Her finger was tightening on the trigger pad already, the scintillating flashes of the laser pulses darkening the automatic filters inside her faceplate. The long burst chopped sideways as she rolled instinctively onto her side to try to make a smaller target, jets of vaporized plastic and metal flaring off the bulkhead on either side of the boarding ramp and sprays of superheated blood erupting like volcanoes from the burn-throughs on the pressure suits.

She hadn't killed all four; even at this range, that would have been too much to ask, particularly for a semi-trained shooter like her. But two were falling backwards, tumbling down the ramp in slow motion in the one-third-normal gravity; the other two seemed to falter, the violence of the counter-attack and the air leaking from the laser-burns in their suits making them forget all about shooting for just a heartbeat.

They were backing the way they'd come, but they were also bringing their guns back up, and she was desperately trying to shift her weight and shift her aim to target them, and every nerve in her body was on fire with the certainty that she was going to die. When the flash of white lit up the boarding ramp, she was sure it was them firing at her and she braced for the pain and the darkness...instead, the two pirates jerked and spasmed as bursts of laser pulses cut them down from behind.

She was beginning to hyperventilate from the dose of adrenalin and she forced herself to hold in a deep breath until she got her heart rate down and her breathing under control.

"Are you two all right?" It was Jacobson again, coming up the ramp with another of his troops in tow, carbine at the ready.

"I'm okay," Sandi assured him. She pushed herself up on one hand, cradling her weapon with the other. "Benitez, are you..."

The words froze in her throat when she turned her upper body so she could look through the visor at the mercenary pilot. He was lying on his right side, his carbine forgotten on the deck beside limp and nerveless fingers. A warhead had punched through his throat with a pencil-thin spear of plasma, and his blood had pooled around him like a dark ocean, quickly freezing and crystalizing.

"Shit!"

She lurched over to the man, fumbling at his left wrist for his suit's control pad; the first-aid features should have been trying to stop the bleeding, trying to stabilize him until they could get him to an auto-doc. She punched at the diagnostic tab frantically but it blinked red at her, beeping an unhelpful error message.

"Aw, Benny..." Jacobson knelt by the body of his friend, shoulders sagging, leaning into his pulse carbine, its butt resting on the deck.

"Help him!" Sandi blurted, grabbing his shoulder in a surge of desperate anger. "Get this damned suit working!"

"Ma'am..." He trailed off. His visor was reflecting the lights of the cockpit and she couldn't see his face, but his voice was heavily laden with deep sadness. "It's too late."

She sat back heavily, the air going out of her. She stared at Benitez, unable to see him.

It's these damned suits, she thought inanely.

You couldn't see anyone's face. It didn't seem real if she couldn't see him, didn't seem as if he'd ever been there. The pirates she'd shot, the ones Jacobson had killed...they were faceless and lifeless and they could have been machines for all she could tell.

"He was trying to tell me something," she murmured. She didn't know if she was transmitting the words, didn't bother to check. It didn't matter.

"Ma'am?" Jacobson asked her, close enough now that she could just barely see his eyes through the visor. They were confused, maybe by what she'd said, or maybe by the death of his friend.

"Benitez was trying to tell me something when they started shooting. I wasn't listening. It feels like I should have been listening." She felt the shrill edges of the words tearing away at her control and she grabbed at it, unwilling to let loose. She pushed it back behind something hard and cold and far too calloused.

"I have to go check on the ship's systems," she told Jacobson, and the voice seemed harsh and alien, the words belonging to someone else, a stranger to her. "The gunfire might have damaged them."

She stepped carefully around the frozen blood, climbing into the lander's cockpit, leaving him there, standing over the body of his friend.

CHAPTER TWELVE

"I don't like having humans here." The Tahni stared at Fontenot and Singh with an expression that could have been anything but was probably contempt.

Fontenot noted that the male had spoken the words in English, which meant that he'd taken the time and effort to learn the language, and that he'd wanted them to understand it. She didn't remember his name, didn't even remember if he'd offered it in the frantic work to get the cargo truck under the cover of the old industrial garage before dawn revealed it to the rest of the city. The building probably dated to the first War with the Tahni, constructed to maintain vehicles just as obsolete and dated as the one used for the pattern of the locally fabricated cargo truck, but now the ancient, sheet-metal building was abuzz with activity.

At least ten or twelve Tahni males were busying themselves unloading the truck, stacking crates of weapons and ammo in a cylindrical pattern beside the battered suit of Tahni powered armor. Kan-Ten had walked that down out of the bed of the truck himself, and she didn't need to be an expert translator to discern how much that had bothered him.

"Without these humans," Kan-Ten told the older male, "we wouldn't be here, and these weapons would be in the hands of our enemies."

It seemed strange to see him in the black control singlet, she thought. She'd met him when he'd been a drifter in the Pirate Worlds, a gun for hire, and seeing him as he must have been when he'd fought her people in the war was disturbing somehow, a reminder of something she would rather have forgotten.

"Jordi already has half the shit you took out of that old stash," Fontenot reminded the both of them. "That's bad enough."

"Bad enough that he may be able to take this world," Singh said glumly. He stood with his arms crossed, eyes glancing around at the Tahni as if he thought one would attack him without warning. They'd left their pulse carbines in the hopper, tucked into the back lot outside the building, and Fontenot knew his hands were itching for the weapon. "I don't know that we have the forces to stop him."

"Where did you get the hopper?" Kan-Ten asked her. "From the bounty hunter?"

"The bounty hunter," Singh commented with acid scorn, "doesn't have the money to buy hoppers anymore."

"We stole it," she admitted easily, "from the Constabulary motor pool." She shrugged. "He wasn't using it, and he seemed like the type who'd be eager to help."

"Kan-Ten!" The call came from one of the sentries they'd left outside. He was running towards them, clutching the old flechette gun across his chest like it was some family heirloom. "It's Vala-Kel!"

"What about him?" he asked. They were speaking Tahni, but Fontenot could follow the conversation.

"He is here."

That wasn't the male with the flechette gun, it was another, younger and taller and wearing a battlesuit control singlet identical to the one Kan-Ten had. He walked through the vehicle entrance with a commanding stride, the sunlight filtering in from outside stretching his shadow ahead of him. He watched her and Singh carefully as he approached, a KE-gun held in his right hand by the carry handle.

"I feared you were killed in the attack, brother," Kan-Ten said. Again, Fontenot was no expert translator, but she thought from years spent with the Tahni that his body language wasn't all warm and fuzzy.

"I managed to escape on foot," he explained, "unlike the others in my vehicle. I found a barely-operational vehicle left behind by the humans who attacked us, and managed to get it into town before it broke down from the damage." His gaze bored into Fontenot and Singh. "And I find more humans here at this secret place, among us."

"Without the help of my friends," Kan-Ten spoke in English, making a point, she guessed, "the Matriarch would be dead or captured instead of alive and with us." He gestured toward the private office up a short set of metal, grillwork stairs at the far end of the building. "Without the help of these two humans, I would be dead and the half of the weapons I guarded would be in the hands of Jordi Abdullah, the human *you* trusted, who betrayed you and killed our brothers."

"The humans who attacked us were not my allies," Vala-Kel declared, switching back to Tahni, making a point of his own. "They must have been the vigilante force organized and armed by the Constable."

"Constable Freeman is not responsible for the attacks on your people," Fontenot interrupted, making her best attempt at speaking Tahni despite vocal cords not evolved for it. "He only wants an end to the violence."

"Of course, *you* would say this," Vala-Kel addressed her for the first time, in English again. "You were seen in his office; you likely work in his service, betraying us to him."

"And I killed his men and rescued your friends why then, exactly?" she demanded, trying to keep anger out of her voice, knowing it would be lost on him. "Your words make no sense in either language." She switched back to Tahni for a proverb she'd heard from Kan-Ten several times through the years. "You flee the truth for the light it would shed on your misdeeds."

Several of the workers who had kept at their tasks despite the distractions stopped now, staring at the two of them. Vala-Kel began to bring up the weapon he held, but Fontenot's Gauss pistol jumped into her hand as if it had always been there.

"Just give me an excuse, motherfucker," she said, not caring if he missed the subtleties of the human expression.

"Vala-Kel," Kan-Ten said, stepping between the two of them, "I would like to know how you think our enemies knew of our mission to retrieve these weapons."

"What do you accuse me of, brother?" He still had his weapon held at the ready, the muzzle halfway between them. "Do you side with the humans now?"

"I side with my friends, whether they be human or Tahni. I wish I could believe you were among them."

"If you are accusing me of betraying our people," Vala-Kel said, tossing his KE-gun to the floor, the hard plastic and metal clattering loudly at his feet, "then there is only one remedy." He made an elaborate gesture that Fontenot didn't recognize, beginning with his hands palm-out over his head and ending with them clenched at his sides. "I challenge you, Kan-Ten, in the name of the True Emperor, for the sake of the Path, and may the truth favor its own."

"What the fuck does *that* mean?" Fontenot demanded, her pistol still in her hand, but held down at her side.

"It is a fight, as you would say," Kan-Ten told her, eyes locked with Vala-Kel's. "With bare hands and to the death."

She felt her guts tie themselves into knots at the thought. Fair fights were for suckers.

"I didn't know you guys did that kind of shit." It sounded a bit primitive even for the Tahni.

"It is not something that has been done in a long time," he admitted. "And when it was, it was between claimants to the title of the True Emperor...in stories of old times."

"Then don't *do* it," she suggested, throwing her hand up in disgust. "It's like some asshole challenging me to a joust or some shit."

"We don't have time for this nonsense." Singh's voice was flat and full of disdain, his Gauss machine pistol somehow already in his hand, and Fontenot thought for a moment that he was going to shoot Vala-Kel right then and there.

She noticed the other Tahni closing in around them, a few of them already armed with the KE-guns taken from the crates, and she put a restraining hand on his arm. He paused, glancing around with a scowl and an obvious estimation of whether he could kill them all before they got a shot off at him.

"What transpires?"

The turn of phrase was odd, and in English accented all to hell, Fontenot thought. She looked over to the staircase leading up to the garage office and saw the Matriarch coming down, her younger assistant at her side. It had been the assistant who'd spoken; she doubted the Matriarch would bother learning English.

"There has been a challenge issued, Matriarch," Vala-Kel called to her. "I await a response from my opponent."

"Do you believe this is the time of legends?" That was the Matriarch and in her own language. Trying to follow the conversation was giving Fontenot a headache. "Do we not have enough enemies without creating them in our own ranks?"

"I accept," Kan-Ten said abruptly, throwing down his own weapon and stepping up to Vala-Kel, stopping only centimeters from the other male.

"Are you fucking nuts?" Fontenot asked him, grabbing him by the shoulder and spinning him around to face her. "What the hell are you trying to prove?"

"Do you want to stop the violence in this city?" he asked her. "You seek to solve one half of it. This," he gestured at Vala-Kel and the other males who surrounded him, "is the other half. If I allow his version of the truth to go unchallenged, there will always be those who believe it."

"And some half-assed gladiator match is going to change that?" she asked, shaking her head.

"To them, it will." His beady black gaze locked with hers. "This must happen, and you must not interfere. Promise me that you won't, Korri."

She let her hand fall off of him, rolling her eyes.

"You're a fucking idiot."

"If this foolishness is to be done," the Matriarch said, coming no closer to the party of males, "it will be done as I dictate. You will fight until one either yields voluntarily or is no longer able to go on, but not to the death. This is my command."

"Very well," Vala-Kel acknowledged, and Kan-Ten gave what she recognized as a gesture of assent.

"You males," the old Tahni female ordered, "form a ring, weapons out. Let no one interfere."

"No one" meaning "us," Fontenot thought, giving the old biddy the stink-eye.

The collected group of workers and guards who'd gathered in the garage to unload the shipment clustered around Kan-Ten and Vala-Kel, leaving them a circle about ten meters across of bare concrete floor. Two of the males retrieved their fallen KE-guns and pulled them away, while another checked to make sure neither carried any other weapons, then retreated into the curving line of onlookers. The males held their newly-acquired guns awkwardly, pointing them at the floor or the ceiling or, in a couple cases, each other, and Fontenot thought sure they'd wind up shooting someone by accident.

There was enough of a gap between the males that she could see Kan-Ten squaring off with his old friend within the ring they'd formed. She paced back and forth, nervous energy propelling her as much as the isotope power packs that ran her cybernetics. She should, she knew, just kill this asshole and back everyone off; they didn't know how to use those guns and wouldn't be that hard to intimidate. Then she could drag Kan-Ten out of there and go find Jordi. That's what Sandi and Ash would want her to do.

"You want to make a play," Singh hissed in her ear, as if he were reading her mind, "I'll back you."

She considered it, wondering if she could trust the man to pull it off without just slaughtering the Tahni. She looked at Kan-Ten, saw him looking back at her and knew he'd never forgive her.

"No," she ground out by way of answer to the bounty hunter. "We have to let him do it."

"You're as big of a fool as he is," Singh muttered, but he stepped back, seemingly surrendering to the inevitable.

One of the older males, the one who'd complained about her and Singh's presence earlier, stepped into the ring of guards and put a hand on the necks of each of the fighters. He said something in Tahni, something she didn't recognize from her limited experience with the language. When he stepped back among the other males, Vala-Kel lunged at Kan-Ten, hands held in a high-and-low stance that seemed awkward and unnatural to Fontenot.

She felt herself tense up, but Kan-Ten stepped easily aside from the rush, and she recognized the martial arts stances and motions she'd taught him over the years in his technique. He slapped aside Vala-Kel's clawing fingers, then swung his right forearm in a clubbing strike across the other male's neck. Vala-Kel grunted as he stumbled aside, and Kan-Ten surged forward to follow up, but his old comrade was fast and experienced at his own form of fighting. He caught Kan-Ten by the wrist and twisted him into a hip-toss, throwing the other male across the floor, rolling into the legs of two of the guards.

Fontenot's stomach muscles knotted with the effort of not running in to help her friend as Vala-Kel stomped down towards his face. He managed to catch the descending boot in the crook of his arm and twist Vala-Kel's leg, bringing him to the ground and lunging on top of him. Kan-Ten's right hand came down in a hammer-blow that caught Vala-Kel square in the chest, and Fontenot could hear the breath leave his lungs in a pained whoosh of air.

Just as she'd taught him, Kan-Ten followed through with his advantage, ramming his knee into his opponent's side again and again. Vala-Kel caught some of the blows on his arms, and he managed to throw Kan-Ten off of him in a desperate thrashing of arms and legs in ways that human joints couldn't have bent, then scrambled to his feet.

"Damn it," she murmured. Fights that lasted longer than a few moves usually wound up indecisive, and they *needed* this fight to be decisive.

Kan-Ten jumped up in time to avoid another rush, circling around the perimeter of the surrounding Tahni males, watching Vala-Kel carefully, his eyes on his opponent's center of gravity. She'd taught him that, too. People---humans and Tahni---could couch their eyes, could fake you out with their hands or their feet, but they couldn't fool gravity. If they were going to make a move, it would show in their hips first. When Vala-Kel went for a low leg sweep, Kan-Ten dived over it, his arm sweeping across the other fighter's chest and slamming him back to the floor.

"Now," she whispered as if he could hear her. "Finish him."

She'd coached Kan-Ten in the Brazilian Jiu-Jitsu she'd learned in her youth, but she'd never been sure how much use it would be grappling with one of his own people. Tahni joints bent different ways, had different tolerances than human ones, and the leverage had to change along with those differences. One thing was the same for humans and Tahni, however: they still pumped blood from a heart in their torsos up through their necks to their brain. So sinking an arm into the arteries of a Tahni's neck still cut that blood supply off, with predictable results.

Kan-Ten moved with speed gained in long, arduous practice sessions, sliding around to Vala-Kel's back and catching his neck in a vice-like grip between his upper and lower arms. Vala-Kel jerked and thrashed and struck backwards with futile and strengthless blows, but Kan-Ten's head was tucked into his shoulder, and the strikes spent themselves without doing any damage. Slowly, excruciatingly slowly, Vala-Kel's struggles grew feebler until he went limp, and still Kan-Ten held him in the choke until the Matriarch spoke.

"Let him go." Her voice was clear and piercing even from forty meters away across the building.

Kan-Ten disengaged, letting Vala-Kel's unconscious deadweight fall away from him as if he was discarding something distasteful. He stood, looking over at the old female expectantly.

"The Truth has emerged victorious," she declared formally. Her stance shifted into something that seemed less hieratic and more exasperated. "And now, if you males have finished with your boyish contests of strength, we have more important things to do..."

Fontenot felt a relieved breath hiss out of her, as if she'd been under acceleration in the ship and they'd just throttled back to one gravity.

"That was pointless," Singh was saying quietly beside her. Then he paused, brow furling thoughtfully. "Unless this was..."

...a delaying tactic.

The building exploded. That was how it seemed to Fontenot. There was an overpressure that slammed into her with a hammer-blow of hot wind, and she stumbled backwards, metal shrapnel slicing into her arms as she threw them over her face, ripping through clothes and synthskin but ricocheting off her metal limbs. The pressure was followed by a wave of heat and a billow of black smoke, and only her bionics kept her on her feet, only her thermal and infrared filters letting her see anything at all.

She was the only one left standing, though Singh had fallen catlike into a crouch beside her; everyone else, all the other Tahni, were laid out on the cement floor, a few of them bleeding from minor wounds, and some obviously unconscious, while others were rolling and coughing fitfully. Her bionics had kept her upright, but the blast had stunned her and she felt as if the fog and smoke and clouds of particulates drifting through the garage had penetrated through into her thoughts as well. The only thing that pierced the veil of the concussion was the sight of Kan-Ten, writhing in pain and confusion on the floor beside the Tahni warrior he'd just defeated, barely in better condition.

She forced herself into motion, cybernetics acting when biological limbs would have failed her, and lunged forward to grab her friend by the arm, yanking him to his feet with her left hand as her weapon jumped into her right. Her natural ear was ringing, nearly whistling, but the pickups in her bionic audio disc heard the heavy footsteps of the troops on the concrete of the garage's entrance ramp, and she knew she had seconds before they were inside...and she also knew there'd be too many to take with just the two of them.

Kan-Ten was tall, and broad, and very heavy, nearly two hundred kilograms, but she threw him over her left shoulder as if he weighed nothing, and ran. Her first instinct was to head for the rear exit, but she knew they'd have that covered, so she sprinted for the stairs. The Matriarch was still at the head of the staircase, collapsed atop her protégé, both of them barely conscious. She wanted to help them, wanted to make sure they got out; but she knew that she couldn't, that there wasn't time, and she passed them by.

Singh was behind her, she realized, following her either in affirmation of her sound tactical judgment or simply because he couldn't think of a better idea. Her steps were ringing gongs off the metal grillwork of the stairs, where his were the soft kiss of a pouncing cat, and she was sure he could have gone faster if he wanted to; but he kept with her, and in a second, they were up on the landing of the catwalk where the sheet metal construction of the office was bolted into the exterior walls of the garage.

Below her, she felt more than saw the attackers pouring through the garage's main entrance, heard their shouts and one or two shots echoing upward and wasn't certain if they were aimed at her or at the Tahni. They'd come for the rest of the weapons, she was sure, and they'd been led here by Vala-Kel. She knew it in her gut, and she figured Kan-Ten had as well. Vala-Kel might want to keep the Matriarch and the others alive for his own purposes, but if the three of them were captured, they'd likely be killed out of hand, or turned over to Jordi for a less pleasant death.

She knew there was a fire exit from the second-floor catwalk; she remembered seeing it from the outside of the building, also recalled that it was on the opposite side from the office, and she turned that way off the landing, hoping against hope that Jordi's thugs would be so busy with the others that they wouldn't notice her. He'd be somewhere down there too, she knew. He'd never trust an operation this important to a subordinate, not as paranoid as he was.

There it was, the fire door, a metal hatch with a paddle lock across it; if it was still connected to the automatic alarm that the ancient warning sticker promised, everyone was about to know exactly where they were.

"Hey!" a voice called from the first floor, rough and petulantly insistent. "Up there!"

Fuck it, she thought, slamming the sole of her boot into the door with an impact that shivered her through her spine. *That's torn it.*

The door swung open with a wrenching, squealing scream of rusted metal and the golden light of dawn shone through, nearly blinding her. She knew the hopper was right below the fire exit, and she knew just as well that they wouldn't have time to take the drop-down ladder. There was a metal gate across the railing where the ladder went down, and she stepped atop it with a single bound, then dropped straight down.

She fell six meters, but it felt as if her stomach stayed at the second-floor platform, only catching up when her boots slammed into the hard pavement below with enough force to crack it. The servos in her bionic legs whined plaintively with the effort, Kan-Ten's weight compressing her chest with a rush of outgoing breath. Her surroundings rushed up to meet her senses with as much force as her feet had impacted the concrete. She was standing next to their stolen hopper, marked with the faded crest of the Gennich Constabulary, and surrounding it were the same vehicles she'd seen back on the road to the Tahni weapons stash.

Most of Jordi's people were inside, but he'd left a small guard with the vehicles, just four of them that she could see, three men and a woman. They'd heard her fall and turned toward her, their appropriated KE-guns swinging around at the new threat. The kick of her Gauss pistol was a packet of data sent through the neural feedback of her artificial hand, barely registering, her attention fixed on the one she'd instantly deemed the biggest threat. He was lean and ragged, but he had a look to him, the look of a stone killer, a look she knew well from her time in the Pirate Worlds...and from her mirror.

He wasn't wearing a helmet, and the tungsten-wrapped ceramic slug erased that look, along with most of his head. She was shifting to the next in her snap-judgment priority list, but a blast of tantalum needles sliced through the woman's chest armor as if it weren't there, and she stumbled forward, dead before she hit the ground. That was Singh, still trailing her and still as deadly as ever. They split the last two, killing both of them before either got off a shot, and she was about to head for the hopper's cockpit when Singh rushed by her towards a parked rover.

She was gathering a breath to yell at him when a badly-aimed burst of KE-gun fire stitched across the cockpit of the ducted-fan helicopter, punching through the polymer with little effort, and she realized that he was right. There was no way they could have gotten the hopper's fans spun up in time to take off before the troops inside reached them. She followed the bounty hunter to the small groundcar, throwing open one of the rear passenger doors and laying Kan-Ten's prone form out across the seat, shoving his feet inside and pushing it shut.

Another burst of tantalum shards from the fire escape platform chewed away a rear corner of the rover's roof with a sharp, ripping crack, and she felt the vehicle beginning to surge forward before she even had the front passenger's side door open. She put a foot on the running board and yanked herself inside, feeling the seat moorings creaking at the impact of her weight as the door slammed shut from the sudden acceleration.

Singh ducked instinctively as another burst of gunfire bit into the front corner of the hood, but then they were on the road, bouncing along the ruts and cracks with the wild abandon of a stolen car. She settled back into the seat, trying to catch her breath while she cursed in four languages, including one that technically had no swear words.

"Is he all right?" Singh wondered, his eyes fixed on the road as he guided the battered old vehicle with its manual steering wheel.

She suppressed an amused snort, wondering why the hell Singh would care. She checked on her friend, anyway, and saw him moaning softly, his head lolling, still semi-conscious.

"I think so," she estimated. "Tahni have thick skulls."

She looked down at the pistol still in her hand, considered holstering it, but decided against it; given the events of the day so far, it seemed smarter to hold on to it for now. She looked over at the bounty hunter, deciding that he looked pretty good with his bionics replaced. Maybe she should consider doing it...she certainly had enough money now, stashed in accounts all over the Commonwealth. She hadn't bothered to check the balance on most of them in twenty years.

I'll think about that if I live through this.

"Where are we going?" she asked him.

"My place," he told her. "We can hold up there and wait this out."

"Wait what out?" She shook her head.

He looked at her with an eyebrow cocked in obvious disdain.

"Jordi has all the weapons he wanted now," he reminded her. "What the hell do you *think* he's going to do with them?"

CHAPTER THIRTEEN

REALITY SWAM INTO FOCUS BEHIND A HAZE OF INTENSE pain, and Kan-Ten thought for a moment that the dim light from the apartment's rickety lamp was a laser beam boring into his optic nerve and turning his brain into an expanding ionized gas. His hands went to the sides of his head and he moaned with the misery of a dull ache that seemed to come from everywhere.

"Where am I?" he asked, unthinking. If he were in the hands of his enemies, it might have made more sense to remain silent.

Korri Fontenot loomed over him, hands on her hips, and what he'd come to know as a relieved expression on her face.

"About time you woke up," she said. "I was beginning to think you had a brain bleed, and we're fresh out of auto-docs."

"I used my portable medical sensors on you, but they're not calibrated for Tahni." That was Singh, standing just behind the woman, gesturing with the small device. It wasn't something most people would carry around, but it made sense that he would.

"Where am I?" he repeated, slowly pushing himself up. He

was on a rickety, narrow bed in a small, one-room apartment, dingy and poorly appointed even for the Periphery. "What happened?"

"Jordi Abdullah has made his play," Fontenot told him, grim-faced. "Watch."

She pulled out her 'link and propped it up on the small table, setting its internal projector to display on the wall, a white rectangle of light that highlighted the web of cracks in the old plaster. Jordi Abdullah's face replaced the bare white, his coldly savage visage broken by those same cracks and split by a fierce scowl.

"Citizens of Gennich, I am Jordi Abdullah and I am in control. For those who doubt that statement, allow me to demonstrate."

The view shifted from the closeup of his face to the exterior of the planetary Constabulary headquarters, its fortress-like lines presumably intimately familiar to anyone who lived in the city. The front doors were open and two dozen men and women in the characteristic dark blue uniforms of the Brigantian Constabulary were lined up single-file a few meters from the entrance, on their knees, hands clasped behind their heads. A couple looked as if they'd been beaten, while another had a makeshift bandage tied around a wound in her upper arm, the white rag soaked with red. Jordi's hired muscle guarded them, most holding Tahni KE-guns, but a couple armed with weapons seized from the police armory.

Another line of deputies was arrayed a few meters ahead of the captives, this one unguarded and unmoving. There were ten of them, some torn to pieces by explosions but most shot down, their uniforms and armor stained with drying blood. Kan-Ten didn't see Constable Freeman among them and he wondered if that was because he had yet to be captured or he'd left no intact body behind to display.

"My forces occupy the planetary Constabulary," Jordi's voice spoke over the images, "as well as the fusion reactor complex."

The image shifted again, this time to the bulging white curve of a dome somewhere outside the city. The cooling towers and steam pipes that ringed the building were typical of the sort of cookie-cutter fusion reactor that powered cities on dozens of colony worlds just like this one, slapped together a century ago from fabricated parts by the old Colonial Authority. They were easy to build, easy to maintain, and reliable as the tides. There would be some isolated homes and businesses and planetary services that generated their own power through solar panels or handy hydroelectric or geothermal units, but nearly everyone in this city and the next two settlements over would rely on the fusion reactor.

Jordi's men patrolled the outside, making a show of manning the guard station, and when the broadcast traveled inside to one of the control rooms, the technicians there were also under the watchful eyes of the cartel troopers.

"We also hold the water treatment plant and the data center," Jordi continued, the image shifting back to his face. Kan-Ten thought he was trying to appear confident and satisfied, but the effect was lost on him. "Things do not have to be unpleasant. All business can carry on just as before." He smiled. "In fact, I expect the economy to experience a sharp upturn in the near future. Just go to your jobs, stop at the local bar, relax in your homes, everything as usual...but do *not* attempt to interfere with my people." The smile disappeared. "Individuals who try to disrupt the smooth and orderly transition of power will be dealt with harshly. Anyone who gives aid and comfort to my enemies will be put in a cell, their goods and their businesses forfeit. Any attempts to organize a resistance against me or my people will be put down; you've seen our weapons, but that isn't the half of it."

This time the image in the projection was a view of the sky over the plains outside the city. A pair of shuttles screamed overhead, low enough that Kan-Ten could make out the hardpoints where weapons had been affixed.

"We have armed air support, and if there is any show of armed resistance, we *will* use it. I'm sure you all believe that the government will come along and set everything right soon. Good. Go on believing that, let them take care of it. That way, whatever happens, you'll be alive to see it."

The man was oily and persuasive when he wanted to be; Kan-Ten had seen it before, back when he and Fontenot had been in his service.

"As for the non-human residents of this city," Jordi went on, "I have a special message for you from my newest lieutenant, whom I've appointed as your representative."

Kan-Ten leaned forward, his fingers clenching in the surface of the bed, pulling himself to his feet. The view on the screen had shifted to the right side, away from Jordi's face to Vala-Kel. He stood beside the cartel kingpin, in Constable Freeman's office, his stance a Tahni reflection of the smug confidence on the human's face.

"My people," Vala-Kel began, speaking Tahni, and Kan-Ten wished a thousand times that he'd killed the male when he had the chance, "Jordi Abdullah is our ally and friend. He seeks to free us from the oppression of the Commonwealth military, and has begun this by deposing the planetary government. Now that the shackles we wore have been removed, we can begin to build a home here, a place for others to come and join our struggle."

He shifted his shoulders, moved his hands in a way that would be meaningless to most humans but spoke volumes to

Kan-Ten and other Tahni watching. It was a subtle hint of threat, a promise of punishment.

"I know there are those who would seek to use this situation to further their own agendas, to spread lies about me or our new allies, but I trust that you all will do the right thing and reject these selfish and unworthy blasphemers who deny the True Emperor and oppose his will. Know that, in this matter, I have the complete support of the esteemed Matriarch." He reached out a hand and pulled the old female into the frame of the shot, and Kan-Ten felt a jolt of shock go through him at the casual indecency of it, of a male touching a female in public, of *any* male touching the Matriarch.

"The Matriarch is well, as you can see," Vala-Kel announced, "and she will remain well as long as no one chooses to interfere and bring her to harm."

Kan-Ten could see the abject hatred in the old female's body language, but she spoke not a word, and he wondered what threat they held over her to prevent her from condemning their actions. He felt himself begin shivering with impotent rage, and very nearly didn't register Jordi Abdullah's final word of warning for the citizens of the city to avoid congregating in the streets in groups of more than four until further notice. He barely noticed when the recording ended and the projector went dark.

"We've failed," he said, bitterness heavy in the words and in the center of his being. "With the life of the Matriarch at risk, the Tahni here will never risk opposing Jordi Abdullah, and he's already neutralized the only other armed and organized resistance on this world by taking out the Constabulary."

"Yeah," Fontenot admitted, putting her 'link back on her belt. Her tone was quiet, her manner subdued. Kan-Ten couldn't remember seeing her this way before. "Even if Ash and

Sandi accomplish their mission and take out the Pirates in the belt, it's a *fait accompli* now. Jordi owns the town and the *Acheron* couldn't do anything even if they took down those shuttles. We don't have a way to unseat *La Sombra* from the Constabulary building."

"Well, aren't you two the cheery bunch?" Singh commented, leaning back against the wall by the bathroom door, arms folded across his chest. "So, we're just giving up, are we?"

"No one said anything about giving up, Singh," Fontenot snapped, impatience writ on half of her face. "It's just more complicated now."

"Killing Jordi Abdullah would uncomplicate it," the bounty hunter said, stroking his beard with the fingers of his left hand, as if both were still novel to him.

"You try to waltz in there and take him out, you'd better make peace with whatever gods you pray to. He's a paranoid at the best of times, and you can bet your ass he won't set foot outside the fortress until he has things well in hand out here."

"Then we'll get into the fortress," he suggested. "There's got to be a way." He grinned lopsidedly. "Perhaps I could turn you into him for the reward and regain his trust."

"I think I liked you better when you were trying to kill me."

The knock on the door was hard and abrupt, and so was the reaction to it. Fontenot and Singh drew their guns with a speed Kan-Ten wouldn't have believed except that he'd seen it before, both of them moving out of the line of the entrance. Kan-Ten glanced around for a weapon and found a pulse carbine propped up in a chair; he grabbed it and went down to a knee, training it on the door.

There was silence for a long moment, as the three of them waited for a boot through the thin door, or a shot, or a breaching charge.

"Open the fucking door."

The voice was authoritative but also hushed and brittle, pained. Kan-Ten didn't recognize it, but he saw in Fontenot's eye that she did. She held up a hand to him and Singh, then moved slowly and carefully over to the door, her pistol held up at high ready as she reached for the latch. Kan-Ten saw her suck in a breath and grit her teeth before she yanked it open.

A human nearly collapsed through the opening, stumbling into her supporting grasp. He was a big man, solid and brawny from the look of him, though Fontenot held him up as easily as if he were a child. His skin was coal-dark, his hair long and grey and tied into a ponytail down his back, and his tan jacket was stained with blood, at least some of it his own. A battered and well-used rocket revolver hung from the wounded man's left hand, as if he'd forgotten it was there and only held onto it from habit. Kan-Ten rushed forward to close the door behind him, glancing carefully down the narrow stairwell to make sure the man hadn't been followed.

Fontenot sat him down in one of the rickety chairs and it creaked dire warnings under his mass but somehow held. She pulled open his jacket, slapping aside his feeble attempts to stop her, and found what looked to Kan-Ten's eyes like a through-and-through wound from a Tahni KE-gun just below his floating ribs on the left side. The shirt beneath it was soaked red and she ripped it free with a casual, impatient tug and tossed it away.

"Get me something to stop the bleeding," she told Singh, pulling the revolver out of the big man's hand and setting it on the table. The bounty hunter nodded and began foraging through his medical kit. "I figured you were dead by now, Constable."

Constable, Kan-Ten thought, his suspicions confirmed. This was Freeman, the man Fontenot had visited upon their arrival. He hadn't seen him, but he matched her description.

"I figured I was, too," Freeman rasped, eyes half-closed, panting softly, pain written on his face. "Turned out I was exaggerating."

"How did you know to find us here?" Singh wondered, leaning over the wound in the Constable's side with a small medical device Kan-Ten didn't recognize. Something flared at the contacts on the business end of the thing and the Constable gasped, then fixed his teeth in a snarl against the pain until he finally relaxed. When Singh withdrew the device, the slow flow of blood had ceased, and a line of charred skin and blood showed the wound had been closed. Then, before the Constable could pull away, he slapped a drug patch on the man's neck, a painkiller, Kan-Ten guessed.

"Shit," Freeman moaned, slumping back heavily in the chair. Then he seemed to remember the bounty hunter's question. "I'm the damned sheriff of this town."

Fontenot barked a laugh. "You're a planetary constable and you're loopy. I think you've lost too much blood."

"Whatever you want to call it." Freeman shrugged, eyes blinking fitfully as the drugs began to take effect. "Someone like you comes around, Ms. Fontenot, practically announcing that you're here to stick your nose into my business, I keep an eye on your comings and goings." He looked at her sidelong, one eye closed as if it was an effort to keep her in focus. "Why do you think it was so easy to steal that hopper?"

"You got away from Jordi Abdullah," Singh said. "So why come here? You thought we'd be willing to hide you?"

"No, Mr. Bounty Hunter," the big man said, grinning broadly. "I came here so you could help me take back the Constabulary building and kill that cartel motherfucker."

———

"That son of a bitch," Sandi slapped at the control to end the playback, freezing it on the smug, smirking face of Jordi Abdullah. "He played us, led us around out here until it was too late."

She wished she could hit something, but all it would accomplish in zero-g was to send her floating across the cockpit, and the *Acheron*'s cockpit wasn't that large; she'd wind up banging off the overhead and it would be embarrassing. She wiped Abdullah's face off the viewscreen and the external camera view of the asteroid base replaced it, the glittering, silvery metal of the docking facilities reflecting the far-off rays of Belenus.

"We should be heading back there already," she told Ash, and she realized the words sounded like an accusation even though that wasn't how she'd intended them.

It wasn't his fault that the Savage/Slaughter Captain had insisted on a detailed, recorded report of Benitez's death. She fought back a muttered curse at the memory of exactly how painful and awkward *that* had been. And it had taken *hours*, excruciating and mind-numbingly tedious.

"He can't have more than a couple shuttles...we can take them out and blow that fucking 'fortress' of his to shit in a half an hour."

Ash was belted loosely into the pilot's seat, and he looked handsome and intelligent and disgustingly reasonable, hands clasped in front of him, brows knitted in thought.

"That would probably feel good," he admitted, "but it wouldn't solve the problem. He's holding the whole city hostage, including the Tahni Matriarch, and we'd probably wind up killing them." He sighed. "Not to mention the fact that he might have control of the defense lasers."

"I don't think so," she argued. "If he did, he'd have bragged about it in his little propaganda video." She waved a hand demonstratively at the screen where they'd played the recording. "He can keep anyone else from using them, but the planetary government probably has some pretty strong biometric locks on the firing codes." She pulled her hair out of her face with a sweep of her hands, wishing she had something to tie it back with.

It's getting too long, she mused idly. Then, *It's been red a long time. Wonder if Ash is right, and I should let it go back to brown.*

"I wonder if he's got enough of a handle on the communications network that we couldn't get a message through to Korri's 'link."

"He doesn't have to block messages to track them," Ash reminded her, infuriatingly correct. "She's probably laying low..." He winced. "Assuming she and Kan-Ten aren't sitting in a cell in the Constabulary or..."

"They're fine," she insisted flatly, not willing to hear it. "Korri knows how to take care of herself."

"We could get help from the mercs again," Ash suggested, his expression brightening with the idea. "The mining co-op won't pay them, but the planetary government sure as hell will, if they help take out Jordi."

"Hell, Captain Fox will pay them, if I have to get Korri to squeeze his head like a grape until he does."

Ash was nodding and she could see his mind working behind his eyes, feeling it meshing with hers, the way it had since they were in the Academy together.

"They may not have the laser defense systems online," he pointed out working the problem, "but they have those armed shuttles. That means they might have a ship in orbit that launched them, too. We can't take on their starship and guard the Savage/Slaughter landers at the same time."

"We need to get the shuttles coming after us," she agreed. She frowned. "It'd be just like Jordi to hold one of them back in reserve, though."

"None of this is going to work unless we get some intelligence about what's happening on the ground. We need to find a way to contact Fontenot and Kan-Ten."

A notion suddenly blossomed into a thought in Sandi's imagination, and a grin spread across her face. She reached out a hand and grasped Ash's shoulder then pulled herself over to him and kissed him solidly.

"What?" he wondered. He was smiling, too, maybe because he'd liked the kiss, or maybe because he knew her well enough to figure out that there was something fiendish and devious going on behind her dark eyes.

"Jordi's paranoid," she explained, her lips beside his ear, "but more than anything else, he's a vindictive prick. And there's one thing that's guaranteed to make him throw everything he has in one attack, and that's me. I'm going to send him a little message."

She chuckled, her breath whispering against his face and she felt his hand slipped down the small of her back, pulling her closer.

"Easy, tiger," she said, but didn't pull away. "First, I think I've figured out a way to reach Korri, too." She nodded at the main control panel. "You still have all those multimedia documentaries about the First War with the Tahni in the ship's memory?"

"I think so," he answered, blinking in surprise at the question. "Unless Kan-Ten erased them again to make room for more nature shows."

She leaned over him to access the controls at the pilot's station, typing the search in manually. Ash was convinced that voice control was easier, but talking computer systems freaked her out and she'd vetoed the idea every time he'd brought it up.

"What are you looking for?" Ash asked, trying to sneak a look over her shoulder.

"Who do we know," she reminded him, "who might be familiar with a military encryption from the First War?"

CHAPTER FOURTEEN

"T‍ELL ME SOMETHING, CONSTABLE FREEMAN," JAGMEET Singh asked sourly, "if you're such a know-it-all frontier badass, how the hell did Jordi kick your ass and take over your station so easy? And why didn't you go down fighting in true cowboy style?"

The Constable downed the last of the water, then handed the glass back to Fontenot for a refill before he turned and regarded the bounty hunter with a dubious glare. His face looked less ashen than it had when he'd arrived at the door, but he still hadn't recovered from the blood loss.

"You waited until I came down off the painkillers just to ask that?" He made a show of checking the time on his 'link. "It's been, what? Two hours?"

"Four," Fontenot muttered, taking the glass from him. "But who's counting?"

"It's not as if we've had any place to go, or anything else to think about," Singh pointed out. He was sitting on the bed, arms over his knees, watching the Constable with suspicion in his eyes.

Fontenot sighed, holding the glass under the sink spigot for a moment and handing it back to Freeman. Singh had been brooding the whole time, mostly silent but with the occasional complaint, and only the fact that they were crashing in his rented room had kept her from smashing him through a wall.

"Give it a rest, Singh," she snapped.

"If I lay off him, I might just start remembering how you and the Tahni," he jerked a thumb at Kan-Ten, who leaned against a wall, in a stance that she'd come to know spoke of impatience at their inaction, "basically handed Jordi Abdullah everything he wanted on this planet in the space of a few days."

She controlled herself with difficulty.

Use your words, Korri, she reminded herself, *not your Gauss pistol. It's too messy.*

"He was a lot further along in his operation here than I thought," she admitted. "If you were so interested in killing him, though, it seems to me that you had the perfect chance back when you busted in on the shop where he had me prisoner."

"I was a bit preoccupied saving your ass." He sniffed, his look showing how much he thought of her for getting captured in the first place.

"Yeah, why'd you do that, anyway?"

"It seemed like the right thing," he snapped, looking off to the side, not meeting her eyes. "I've been experimenting with doing the right thing lately."

"And how's that been going for you?" She couldn't help the grin, even though she knew it would piss him off. Or maybe because.

"I wanted to stay and fight," Freeman interrupted, answering Singh's question, his voice strained, a haunted look in his eye. "My people were getting killed all around me, and I wanted so bad to stay... But there was a chance I wouldn't get killed, and I couldn't let them take me alive."

"Why not?" Singh demanded. "What's so special about you?"

"I'm one of three biometric signatures required to unlock the controls for the planetary defense laser." Freeman drained the glass in one long pull, and Singh fell silent, understanding passing over his face. "So yeah, I ran. My chief deputy told me if I didn't, he'd kill me himself. I saw him die before I got out." He paused, working that memory through his mind, visibly wringing the pain out of it.

"Anyway," he went on, "Abdullah can kill our power and take away our water, but he can't shoot down any ships, and we need to keep it that way." He looked at each of them, as if evaluating their worth. "Now, what I have in mind is I got out of the Constabulary through an escape tunnel we dug after the war, and that's just how we can get back in."

"Get back in and do what?" Singh asked.

"That's what's gonna' take some planning." The Constable spread his hands. "I figure we got maybe two days at most before he finds us. We need to come up with something before then."

Fontenot felt a vibration from her 'link and checked it reflexively, then realized that the others were doing the same thing. She saw the readout and frowned. A wide-band broadcast was coming in, something keyed to activate the emergency announcement settings on every 'link and console on this side of the planet. That had to be a beam from a satellite or...

She grinned and keyed the 'link to receive, then set it to project and laid it on the table in front of Freeman, letting the image display on the wall again.

It was Sandi, the smirk on her face smug and taunting and just perfect.

"Jordi, you low-life piece of shit," she said, shaking her head. "You thought you had this all figured out, that your hired guns could stop the ore shipments and starve the Brigantians long enough to destabilize the government and take over. It must have seemed like easy pickings after you got your ass kicked by every other Pirate World cartel, and had to run your sorry little group of losers to the Periphery to find a place you could hold up. But you didn't count on one thing, asshole." She touched her chest with two fingers.

"Me. Me and Ash took out your pirate friends, and now we're coming to take you out, too. You can skulk and hide in your little castle, but it won't save you from us. You should have stayed home and died like a man fighting your enemies, Jordi. You've come a long way just to get put down like a rabid dog." The smirk turned to a sneer. "We're coming for you so you'd better get your ass ready."

There was a burst of static at the end of the recording, just a half-second long, but incongruous enough to catch Fontenot's attention for reasons she couldn't consciously identify. She was still staring at the projection when she noticed Singh rising off the bed, shaking his head in disapproval.

"What was the purpose of *that*?" He threw a hand up demonstratively. "She obviously wanted to piss him off, but why? What does she think she's going to accomplish?"

"I take it you know this woman?" Freeman asked, cocking an eyebrow in an obvious invitation for an explanation.

Fontenot ignored the question, fingers tapping out a control sequence on the keyboard of her 'link, her mind working feverishly. If that static wasn't static...

"She could," Kan-Ten speculated, "have been attempting to draw him out, keep him from just sitting under the protection of the fortress and counting on our fear of civilian casualties to prevent us from attacking from the air."

"The shuttles," Singh decided, pointing a finger overhead. "He has those armed shuttles. Hollande and Carpenter are trying to get him to commit them to combat so they can take them out."

Still looking at the screen of her 'link, Fontenot began to laugh softly, drawing curious looks from the others.

"That's not all they're doing," she said, touching the screen and projecting the data there on the wall. The code sequence she'd initialized was represented in the display as a series of horizontal grey bars, shrinking as each was decoded, revealing a sequence of numbers which transformed slowly into words.

"What *is* that?" Singh asked, peering over her shoulder. "Was that attached to the recording?"

"Not attached to it, embedded in it," she corrected him, feeling his warmth against her shoulder. It bothered her for some reason, like an ache from an old injury. "It's a worm program, dates back to the First War with the Tahni, decades ago. That burst of static at the end, that was a signal to look for it."

"Don't tell me you fought in that war," Freeman said, eyes narrowing. "How the hell can you be that old? Shit, even nowadays, people out here don't get the same medical treatments that they do in the Core worlds. Back then, it was even worse."

"I'm from Earth," she said, blowing past the questions that was going to bring up. "And yes, I was in the Marines during the First War, and this code was used to get through to colonists and intelligence assets on occupied worlds."

The grey lines were disappearing more quickly now, running across the display from side to side, and the numbers were following them, switching to letters and revealing just a few sentences.

"We're attacking in thirty-six hours," she read them aloud. "We'll draw their air assets away to clear the landing for two shuttles full of mercenaries. One platoon will land at the fusion reactor, the other at the Constabulary. If you can penetrate the fortress and get the ground forces a point of ingress, it would aid in avoiding civilian casualties. The garage entrance would be best, since it's got less of a choke-point. Also, if the defense lasers are working, we're fucked, so give us a heads-up. Take care of yourselves. S&A."

"Well, there you go," Freeman said, leaning back in the chair, his hands clasped over his belly, the grin on his face satisfied and slightly taunting. "A plan."

———

Jordi Abdullah stood from the bed, grabbing the woman's clothes and throwing them at her with casual disdain.

"Get out," he told her, not bothering to turn on the lights.

It was daytime here, mid-afternoon he thought, but his internal clock was still set for another set of Circadian rhythms and he kept the windowless room dark. It had belonged to the Constable, Freeman, and he'd likely kept his spare room deep inside the fortress for security reasons, but it worked fine for Jordi. The only illumination was a small chemical strip-light across the top of the heavy, metal door, but it was enough for him to see the prostitute's bare shoulders disappear under the darkness of her shirt, to see a glint from her eye as she watched him.

The scornful sneer on her face was probably just his imagination, but his fingers brushed against the butt of his sidearm where it lay on the bedside table, longing to grasp it, to put a round through her face. Instead, he picked up the small wad of Tradenotes and tossed them underhand to her. Even in the dim light, her hand snatched the bundle of cash out of the air as fast as a snake striking. She was smart enough not to say anything as she pulled open the door, letting in the glaring white light of the outer hallway.

She'd barely had the chance to close it behind her when he heard the knock. He ground his teeth against the curse that tried to force its way out; he needed to seem in control.

"Just a minute," he said, loud enough for it to carry through the door.

His clothes were on a chair beside the door. He pulled them on slowly, taking his time, slipping into his shoes and buckling on his gunbelt, and then taking a deep, shuddering breath and slitting his eyes before he touched the main light switch. He blinked anyway as the glare stung his eyes, then turned and pulled open the door.

Medina was on the other side of it, nervously shifting from one foot to another the way he did when he had to relate bad news. Since he was a large man, a good six centimeters taller than Jordi and at least fifteen kilograms heavier, with bushy blond hair and a forked beard that gave him a fairly sinister appearance, the childish fidgeting seemed even more ridiculous.

"What is it, Francis?" He didn't bark the question; Medina was a bit fragile around the feelings, and he didn't need the man retreating into a shell before he told him the news.

"You gotta' come to the comm room, boss," he said, motioning back across the hall. "There's a message."

Jordi sighed heavily, making a herding gesture to get the big man moving. He wasn't in the mood for this.

"Uh, boss," Medina hesitated, still filling the doorway. "You got a…" He trailed off, pointing to the side of his neck.

Jordi cursed under his breath, feeling around on his own neck until his fingers found the drug patch he'd stuck there before he'd called for the working girl, and then forgotten after. He peeled it off and stuck it in his pocket. Medina gave him a disappointed look that made rage blossom in his chest.

"What?" This time he *did* bark.

"You never used to sample the product, boss," he responded,

the concern in his voice more infuriating than any insubordination or disrespect.

He wanted to slap the man, wanted to yank him to the ground and kick the shit out of him. But he didn't have enough loyal soldiers left to ruin one of them now. Maybe after this job panned out, after this city was his, this world.

"A lot of things are different now," he growled, pushing past Medina and heading for the Constabulary's operations center.

It was down the hallway from the office, a large room, the largest on the floor. It was a combination conference, briefing and communications room as well as a tactical command post for teams in the field, and it was packed with display screens that could be slaved to drone feeds or helmet cameras. The rest of the space was taken up by a holographic mapping table surrounded by chairs, and a holotank hooked up to the communications array on the roof of the fortress.

There was only one other person in the room, one of his netdivers plugged into the tactical control stations, her baggy clothes hanging off her skeletal frame. Her eyes were open, but unseeing, lost somewhere inside cyberspace.

"So, show me," Jordi demanded, waving at the holotank.

Medina nodded, moving quickly over to the controls and scrolling back through the menu until he found what he was looking for, then poking at one with a fat, meaty finger.

Sandrine Hollande's face filled the holotank, lifelike enough that he could have reached in and strangled her, and he so badly wanted to. She was the cause of all this, she and her insufferable, straight-laced boyfriend...the cause of the loss of face, the loss of confidence, the loss of the fear the other cartels had for him and for *La Sombra*. They'd robbed him of his pipeline of stolen military weapons, killing his major source of income, robbed him of Singh and turned the bounty hunter against him.

It had all been downhill since then, his enemies emboldened against him.

He was weak, he was vulnerable, and now he was an addict, and it was all that fucking bitch's fault.

He very nearly didn't hear her words, didn't register the meaning until finally they penetrated.

"Me and Ash took out your pirate friends and now we're coming to take you out, too. You can skulk and hide in your little castle, but it won't save you from us. You should have stayed home and died like a man fighting your enemies, Jordi. You've come a long way just to get put down like a rabid dog." The smirk turned to a sneer. "We're coming for you so you'd better get your ass ready."

He didn't remember drawing his pistol, didn't remember making a decision to shoot; the hiss-crack of the spin-stabilized mini-rocket startled him, and in the next instant the holoprojector was flaring and sparking and exploding, and the image in the holotank flickered and faded away in a sea of static.

Medina was staring at him, wide-eyed, but he ignored it the same way the netdiver was ignoring the gunshot and the smoke and the insistent hooting of the smoke alarm in the background. She was totally absorbed with whatever obscure corner of the data-stream had caught her attention, and he was absorbed with rage, with hatred. He pushed it down with all the willpower he had...all he had left. He shoved the gun back into its holster and turned to Medina.

"Get the shuttles up," he ordered curtly. "I want a constant patrol over the city, day and night. Arrange for refueling and keep them both in the air."

"But that's a lot of hours," Medina protested. "Those birds aren't exactly military assault shuttles off the line, sir..."

"Constant patrols, day and night," Jordi reiterated in a tone that would brook no arguments. "Tell the lighter crew to break orbit and stay at the minimum Transition distance, be ready to engage the *Acheron* when it arrives."

"Yes, sir," Medina acknowledged, his expression glum but his tone obedient.

"What's the situation with the Tahni weapons?" he asked, trying to flog his brain into analytical reasoning. It seemed to take more effort to do that every day...maybe he needed another hit.

"Everything that can be operated by humans has been handed out to the troops, and we have crew-served weapons surrounding the perimeter of the fortress." The big man shrugged. "Of course, we can't figure out how to get those battle-suits to work for us; you gotta' have one of the control singlets, and they only work for Tahni." He brightened with a sudden idea. "Hey, we could let that Tahni guy Vala-Kel operate it if you want. He has the control jammies."

Jordi considered it for a moment, but then shook his head.

"No," he decided. "He's of use, but he has his own agenda. I don't trust him enough to give him a weapon more powerful than anything we have." He sucked in a breath, trying to let the air calm his thoughts, but there was too much smoke drifting through it and he coughed convulsively.

"Get the ships up, and double the guard. When they come, we're going to end this shit." He coughed again and spat on the floor carelessly. "We're going to shoot that piece of shit out of the air and kill that bitch."

CHAPTER FIFTEEN

To be outside the universe was a meaningless phrase; the universe was, by definition, all there was, the whole of spacetime. Ash Carpenter's Academy physics instructors had chided him whenever he'd used the term to describe the Transition Drive. They'd made serious, academic noises about how Transition Space wasn't another universe, it was merely a "rolled-up dimension not normally accessible to four-dimensional constructs," as if *that* made any more sense.

Nevertheless, any place you literally couldn't see because your mind hadn't evolved to make sense of it, any place where the laws of physics were so different you could make your own gravity and travel faster than light, was close enough to outside the universe for him. It scared some pilots. They didn't want to admit it, but being in T-space scared them. You could see it in their eyes, the subtle claustrophobia of being stuck inside a small bubble of realspace, at the mercy of a technology most of them didn't understand and couldn't hope to repair beyond swapping one part out for another. One malfunction, one energy surge at the wrong time, and you'd just cease to exist.

That wasn't what scared him, and he'd never really understood why being in T-space with a bubble of spacetime between you and death was so much different than being in regular space with a thin layer of metal between you and death. Vacuum could kill you just as dead as losing atomic coherence because you lost the spacetime bubble.

Dying wasn't that scary, except in an abstract, philosophical way, at least not dying on a ship where it was likely to be quick and clean. What was scary, what knotted his guts and kept him awake at nights, was the idea of being helpless, of having to sit there and watch as his friends, the people he loved, died.

This sucks, he thought.

Oh, he realized it made perfect sense. Savage/Slaughter was down a shuttle pilot, and it was the two of them who'd asked the mercenaries to get involved in this. When the Captain of the *Warlock* had requested that Sandi pilot one of the landers, she could hardly have said no. But somehow, she was going to be the one flying down into the teeth of the enemy again while he was stuck as air cover.

He bit off a curse and shunted himself and the *Acheron* back out of Transition Space.

Gravity faded and light exploded across the breadth of his expanded senses, data rushing in through the ship's cameras, lidar, radar, thermal scanners and spectral analyzers and coalescing into a coherent picture his brain could interpret. Brigantia was a dark circle against the glare of fiery Belenus, and the planet's moon lit up a bright white off to the side in the view from the optical cameras.

He concentrated, looking deeper into the picture, and the smaller details began to manifest. There was the orbital industrial processing facility, abandoned and unpowered, and a glittering web of communications satellites floating over the surface, most of them on the night side of the planet, facing him.

And even closer, so close he felt he could almost touch it, so close it was nearly in optical range, was the *La Sombra* lighter.

It was probably the last starship they had, he mused. If Jordi had more, he would have brought them along. He took the measure of the craft in an instant; it was typical of the converted freighters that passed for gunships out in the Pirate Worlds or the Periphery, though not as professionally assembled as the Savage/Slaughter ship had been. Thermal readings showed the leakage where power feeds were inexpertly routed into makeshift weapons mounts, and the armor layered over the ship's hull was bulging and ugly.

That didn't make it any less dangerous, though, and that was the reason he was sitting alone in the *Acheron* while Sandi was still on board the Savage/Slaughter ship, waiting a micro-Transition away for him to clear this heap of junk from the board. He watched the cartel ship with half his attention, the other half plotting a course to an insertion orbit, then hitting the drives. Fusion plasma roared out of the *Acheron's* drive coils and flattened him into his seat, sending the cutter leaping ahead, lunging for the planet.

The lighter had been waiting for him, sitting out on sentry duty probably for days now, but it still took nearly a minute for the crew to see him and react.

Amateurs. He heard the word inside his head in Fontenot's voice.

The exhausts of the missiles launching from their bolted-on weapons pods were signal flares in the night, half a dozen of them screaming towards him at twenty g's. He cut the ship's boost, breath rushing back into his lungs, then hit the bow thrusters, spinning the ship around to face the flight of laser-guided weapons coming in from the portside at about forty degrees off his line of travel. He had neither the time, nor the fuel, nor the inclination to attempt to out-maneuver the missiles, so he'd go with the trickier, riskier, and much quicker option.

The Gatling turret opened up at the very edge of its engagement range, controlled by the ship's computer systems; the long burst of laser fire was a broken line of red in the enhanced view over the interface, and there was just the slightest flare of vaporizing metal where it touched the closest of the missiles. There was no explosion, but the targeting system assured him that the missile's maneuvering thrusters were badly damaged, and it moved on to the next in line. He couldn't wait that long. The lighter was swinging around, trying to line up his cutter with the railgun on a fixed dorsal mount down the length of the cartel ship. At this range, he had a chance of dodging the unguided slug, but they'd be trying to drive him into the missiles, to keep him from maneuvering.

The Gatling laser was already firing again, but he ignored it and kicked the nose of the ship a degree starboard, and fired the proton cannon with a touch of his thoughts on the trigger. He was well out of range for a shot at a fighting ship with deflector shields, but he didn't have to penetrate shielding or thick BiPhase Carbide armor. Those missiles probably weren't even stolen military inventory, not with Jordi's black market sources drying up; they were home-made with fabricated designs and local materials, and BiPhase Carbide was too expensive to use for armor on anti-ship missiles.

The range was great enough that the proton blast didn't have the energy or cohesion left to violently convert the warheads to vapor, but the particles still penetrated far enough to ignite the propellant remaining in the fuel tanks. Two of the missiles expanded into white balls of flame as propellant and oxidizer mixed in one last, violent chemical reaction, and the blasts were close enough to knock out two of the other weapons, the fragments impacting them and throwing them far enough off course that they lacked the fuel to correct in time.

That left one missile intact, and his Gatling laser was still slaved to point defense and still firing without his interference. In seconds, the board was clean of threats and he was accelerating again, this time directly at the lighter. She could have launched another spread of missiles; he was sure the weapons pods grafted to her flanks had a battery full of them. But he was getting close and boosting at three g's. If they didn't intercept him on the first run, they wouldn't be able to correct and lock on again until he was in slugging range of the lighter. Trusting home-brew guided missiles not to lock onto your own ship when fired at close range was a gamble, and apparently not one this captain wanted to take.

He knew what was coming next; the range was still too far for beam weapons and too close for missiles. He couldn't see it on optical, but his lidar picked up the incoming slugs from the lighter's railgun when he was only a hundred kilometers out, too close to maneuver away from the shots. He tensed up, teeth grinding, the sudden concentration pulling him out of the interface just slightly, allowing the pressure of the acceleration to slide past his guard and squeeze the breath out of him.

Three slugs, each solid tungsten, a meter long and half a meter wide, burned in across the distance in less than thirty seconds. Any one of them could have sliced through the *Acheron's* armor as if it weren't there, but they were metallic and exactly the sort of thing military-grade electromagnetic deflectors were designed for. Fusion-fed EM fields diverted the course of the rounds, sending them careening off to be someone else's problem. The cartel ship's captain would see that, too, and since he was fighting this battle like an amateur who'd only ever faced other amateurs, Ash knew what his next move would be.

He started the cutter into an axial spin even before the laser fired. It was a re-tasked mining laser, not a heavy Gatling, and he'd expected that, too. Gatlings needed constant resupply of ammo, and it wasn't easy to produce out in the Pirate Worlds; mining lasers just needed an occasional recharge of the reactive gas, and a reactor to power them, and they were plenty to take out some half-assed, slapped-together cartel-rigged assault shuttle.

Ash could feel the laser playing over the ship's armor like a sunburn on his naked skin, but the spin kept it from burning through the BiPhase Carbide, and just about the time he figured he couldn't take the spin and stay conscious anymore, the ship was in range. The proton cannon fired almost of its own accord, his instincts riding the interface even as his conscious mind was starting to black out. He barely retained enough coherent thought to ignite the maneuvering thrusters and stop the spin.

He killed the drive, the sudden microgravity threatening to bring his stomach out through his throat, but the cutter and the lighter were still heading straight for each other at pretty healthy velocities. He sensed rather than saw the damage he'd done, the sparking, hemispheric glow of expanding gasses from the spot where the lighter's port weapons pod had been, and knew it wouldn't be enough to take the cartel ship out of the equation. He had one more crack at them before they passed by each other and headed out of range again; the capacitors wouldn't recharge in time to get off more than one shot.

He could easily have put that shot right through the lighter's bridge; at this range, even if they had deflectors, nothing would stop the proton cannon from burning right through it and killing everyone on board. He shouldn't have had any problem with that; these were criminals, murderers. He'd killed men like them before, so many times.

He didn't make the decision consciously; he was still reeling from the spin maneuver and operating on gut-feeling and instinct. He felt as if he were along for the ride when the cutter spun laterally on a reverberating bang of maneuvering thrusters, turning her nose to keep it facing the lighter as they passed only a few hundred meters from each other.

The proton cannon fired one, final time and a flash of vaporized metal and a firefly swarm of fragments flew away into a ring-like orbit, and the lighter's main drive was nothing but slag. She kept moving the direction of her travel, heading into interplanetary space trailing a small cloud of plasma.

He watched them drifting helplessly away, drawing back from the interface and seeing the image with his physical eyes on the screen. They couldn't turn and follow, and he didn't know if they could even use their Transition Drive with that sort of damage...but they could use maneuvering thrusters to set themselves on a course into the asteroid belt. It would take weeks, maybe even months, but a ship that size should have the supplies to last that long.

The miners out there would spot them and send a ship to intercept. If they wanted to kill them, they could do it themselves. Like the loose railgun slugs, they were someone else's problem. He submerged under the interface again and knew that his trajectory was carrying him towards planetary orbit, but so fast he was going to skip off the atmosphere and never be able to land. He spun the ship around with the resonant banging vibration of firing maneuvering rockets, and started a two-g deceleration burn.

With the fusion flame between him and the planet, he couldn't see sensor data camera feeds, but he knew the shuttles were coming. Like the lighter, they'd been waiting for him, and their pilots would be panicking at how quickly he'd disabled the bigger ship. They'd hang in the upper atmosphere and try to take him there, looking to take advantage of their greater maneuverability in the soup.

He activated the ship's main antennae, pointed at a specific coordinate a light-minute away, and pulled out the interface long enough to speak into the audio pickup.

"I'm going in," he told the Captain of the *Warlock*. "It's time."

"Roger that, *Acheron*," Alcala responded two minutes later, his voice phlegmatic and even. "Transitioning in five minutes."

Ash switched to Sandi's private channel, running the message through the *Warlock's* receivers but coding it for her 'link.

"Be careful," he said, knowing she wouldn't have time to respond before they Transitioned and he was in the soup. He resisted the urge to call her "honey," or "baby" or anything else cute and romantic. *She hates that shit.* "I love you, so it's not okay if you get killed."

He knew, as he knew his own name, that the ship's velocity had slowed enough. He turned into the darkness of the Brigantian night, and rushed headlong into the fight that awaited him.

———

Sandi grinned, the countdown to Transition fading into the background as she listened to Ash's words a third time over her 'link's ear bud. The man knew how to get to her; he always had, even back when they'd only been friends.

"It's not okay if you get killed either," she murmured back to him, not transmitting it. She didn't want to distract him.

"What?" Jacobson asked from the seat next to her, glancing over. He wasn't really a qualified co-pilot for the shuttle, but they'd decided to squeeze as many ground troops into each lander as they could, so every acceleration couch was filled with an armored trooper.

He didn't have his helmet on yet, probably feeling a little lax about it since they were headed for a habitable planet, and she could see the confused frown on his squared-off block of a face. Sandi wondered how he felt flying with her; she'd gotten his friend killed not that long ago. At least that was how it felt to her, despite everyone assuring her there was nothing she could have done.

I could have insisted on taking the shuttle back up after the drop-off, she argued again in her head, where there was no one around to debate with her about it. Sure, Captain Alcala had said to stay on the ground in case they needed a quick exfil, but he wasn't her boss and she should have followed her own instincts.

"Just talking to myself," she told him, only half a lie. She gestured at the digital countdown on the main display screen. It was already below ten seconds. "Get ready."

He nodded, pulling his helmet on quickly, slapping down the lever-lock on the seal just as the counter reached zero. Reality lurched, and then almost instantaneously did the same thing again, and suddenly, they were close enough to Brigantia for the dark circle of the planet's night side to fill the main viewscreen, shadowed and backlit by the primary star.

"Prepare for high-g boost," Alcala's voice came over the PA speakers and her 'link's ear bud simultaneously.

He didn't wait long; the echo of his announcement was still ringing off the bulkhead when the acceleration pushed her back into the pilot's seat with six times her normal weight. The ship rumbled and shook as the fusion drive roared silently into the vacuum, and she could see the planet growing in the viewscreen's as the minutes crept by. She fought for breath, wondering how long they were going to boost, knowing that eventually, they'd have to decelerate in order for the landers to be traveling at a safe velocity for atmospheric entry.

I guess he doesn't want to give the ground forces much time to react to us, she reasoned.

"Deceleration in ten seconds." Alcala could have been sipping a glass of whiskey in his stateroom for all the strain he let into his voice.

The fusion drives cut off and there was a violent, cacophonous series of bangs as the ship's steering thrusters skew-flipped the *Warlock*, spinning it 180 degrees. She sucked in a deep breath and held it, and then the drive cut in again and the pressure was back, worse than before, turning her thoughts into a hazy, formless cloud. Her vision began to narrow to a dark tunnel and she thought she passed out for just a moment, because the next second the weight was off her chest and the view in the lander's main screen was swinging around to face the planet again, and she didn't remember hearing the maneuvering thrusters fire.

"Lander crews," Alcala said in her ear. "Separation in ten seconds."

"Lander Two-Zero-Four, acknowledged," Sandi replied, her voice dry and raspy from the brutal acceleration.

She grabbed the leads of the interface cables off the spools set in the control console and jacked them into her sockets, one on each side of her temple. The interface traveled up the leads and into her head, sucking her back down the wires and into the computer like Alice through the rabbit hole. The narrow confines of the cockpit expanded into a starscape of high orbit around Brigantia, the colors of the planet muted and dark with the night, the moon a massive white orb reflecting the unseen primary star Belenus...and the metal embrace of *Warlock* still cradling the lander.

"Landers cleared for launch."

A flex of her muscles and the lander separated from the lighter, the steering jets adding to the scorch marks on the docking cradle that were mementos of previous launches. The main engines kicked in once they were a few hundred meters away and the other lander fell into formation beside her.

Somewhere below, Ash was already in the upper atmosphere, probably engaging the *La Sombra* shuttles, clearing a path for her. A part of her noticed the thermal signature of the *Acheron's* jets down there, and wanted to search for the exhausts of the shuttles; but he had his job to do and she had hers, and this time she couldn't afford to screw around trying to watch his back. Fontenot and Kan-Ten were down there and they were counting on her.

She thought of Benitez and tried to come up with a suitable military quote for the occasion, but the best she could think of was "Victory is a thing of the will," and she didn't know if the man would have appreciated a quote by a French general.

Then it came to her. Patton had said it, and she'd loved to scandalize the military history teacher in her sophomore year at the Academy by quoting it.

"No dumb bastard ever won a war by dying for his country," she mumbled aloud to herself, and to whatever part of Benitez might still be hanging around to listen. "He won it by making some other dumb bastard die for *his* country."

"What?" Jacobson asked in inane counterpoint to his earlier question. He had his helmet on now, but she could tell he was staring at her like she was nuts.

"I said," she lied to him, "let's get to work, Lieutenant. We got a war to win."

CHAPTER SIXTEEN

Kan-Ten banged his head against the roof of the tunnel for the fourth time in half an hour and fervently wished for night-vision goggles. Neither Singh nor Fontenot needed them, his old friend because of the infrared filters in her bionic eye and Singh most likely from lens implants, though he hadn't bothered to ask the man. He found his very presence discomfiting and would have argued against it if circumstances hadn't necessitated calling on his aid for this operation.

Freeman had his own night vision gear, but it wouldn't have done Kan-Ten any good even if he'd been willing to loan it to him. Tahni eyes saw things in just a slightly-shifted spectrum from humans, enough that the output from human optical gear never worked quite right when he used it. He had his own, of course, but it was on the *Acheron* and he hadn't been able to come up with a good justification for bringing it with him.

There was Tahni night vision equipment among the weapons stash they'd salvaged as well. Perhaps, if this tunnel came out as close to the Constabulary garage as Freeman had promised, they might be able to grab some from the cargo trucks parked there. The Constable's sources had told him that was where the gear they hadn't already issued out was being stored.

If he has so many sources he can trust, Kan-Ten wondered, *why are none of them willing to pick up a gun and help us?*

Not that they had that many guns to go around, he reflected. The human pulse carbine he was carrying felt unnatural and awkward, his fingers going to the wrong places over and over. The grip angle and the placement of the firing controls made his hands cramp, but it was a better weapon than the others had; they all carried nothing but sidearms, and Singh had said more than once that he thought the idea of taking on a small army of cartel soldiers with four people, three pistols and a pulse carbine was absurdly suicidal. Fontenot had told him to shut up and grow a pair of balls, though Kan-Ten still wasn't clear exactly what the expression meant.

The tunnel entrance had been concealed under a maintenance storage shed well outside the security perimeter around the fortress, in the corner between a memorial to the colony's founder and what had once been a decorative garden that had fallen into disrepair and was mostly sand and rock now. The path to the shed had given them a clear view of the defenses, bared and blatant under the glare of security floodlights mounted on the walls. Crew-served heavy KE-guns were mounted on mobile turrets at each corner of the Constabulary building, and he imagined there'd be at least one more at the main entrance. Foot patrols shuffled through the night in plain view, their heads down, their weapons held loosely. They didn't want to be out at this time of the morning, and lacked the discipline to hide it.

It hadn't taken much effort to avoid being seen by them; it had been much harder to actually access the tunnel, since the hatchway had been buried under a pallet of organic fertilizer, and the wheel that unlocked it had been frozen with rust. Singh and Fontenot had managed to get it open, but the squeal of release had been loud enough that Kan-Ten was sure they'd be discovered. The biggest danger so far, though, had been to his head and his pride.

Singh was shining a compact visible-light flashlight ahead of them, but the beam was mostly to give their light-intensifying lenses something to work with, and he kept it pointed down at the floor to minimize its reach. Kan-Ten gave up trying to keep both hands on his weapon and let the fingers of his left hand trail against the ceiling, warning him when it dipped downward below two meters.

How long is *this tunnel?*

The thought barely had time to bounce from one side of his head to the other when they came to an abrupt halt and he nearly collided with Korri Fontenot's back. In the gloom of the single, narrow-beam flashlight, he could just make out the shape of the door, heavy and solid and sealed with a formidable locking lever.

"The other side of this is in a cleaning equipment storage closet in the back of the basement garage," Freeman reminded them, his deep voice kept low without whispering. "I don't *think* anyone will hear it opening, but that's just a guess."

"Kan-Ten," Fontenot said to him. "Get up here with me while I open it. You've got the weapon with the highest rate of fire."

He ducked to one knee behind her, giving a signal when he was in place. She braced herself in a deep stance, then grabbed the locking lever in one massive, metal hand and pushed upward. There was a scratching, squeaking clang as it popped free, and the door edged outward a few centimeters. He moved in front of her, pushing at it with his left shoulder, the pulse carbine cradled across his body. It swung slowly open and he rolled through with it, hitting on his shoulder and tumbling into a crouching stance in the darkened closet.

A sliver of light came from underneath the door to the storage room, revealing the innocuous shapes of cleaning robots and pallets of the chemicals used to fill their tanks. They were jammed into cheap, stamped-metal shelves bolted into the block walls and then squeezed into every available nook and cranny in the room, and the path to the door was a shadowy maze. He let Fontenot move ahead of him and negotiate it with her cybernetically enhanced vision, while he followed, a hand on the back of her shoulder to guide him. She stopped beside the exit, resting the cosmetic façade of her left ear against the thin, plastic door and letting the bionic amplification disc inside it absorb the external sounds and paint a picture for her of what was on the other side.

The technology was so handy; he'd often wondered if he'd strayed far enough from the beliefs of his fathers that he would consider having himself augmented with cybernetics. It was a taboo worthy of death for the Tahni, but those beliefs had given them the war with the humans and then lost it, two unforgivable sins, and the last more than the first. He'd discussed it with Fontenot and tried to come up with a comparison to a human taboo, and the closest they'd been able to come was incest. And somehow even that, which she obviously considered obscene and disgusting, wasn't a powerful enough stricture to match the Tahni aversion to altering the form that the True Emperor had given them.

Or perhaps he was being overly optimistic about the chances of living through the next few minutes.

"There's someone out there, moving around," Fontenot reported quietly. "At least two people, but they're pretty far from this door...maybe on the other side of the garage."

"Let me slip out and take them down," Singh offered. "I can

pass for one of them for a few seconds before they look too close." He motioned toward Fontenot. "Or you could. It's too obvious what these two are," he added, gesturing at Freeman and Kan-Ten.

"All right," she said with a nod, surprising Kan-Ten with her willingness to trust someone else. "We'll watch from here. Try to keep it as quiet as you can, but those troops are going to be on the ground in less than five minutes if they're on schedule, and we have to get the garage entrance open. So, if it goes to shit, we're making a push for that door no matter how much noise we make."

He nodded silently, then holstered his Gauss machine pistol, shoved the door open, and brazenly stepped through it. The light out in the garage seemed obscenely, painfully bright after the long trek through the dark streets and then the longer crawl through the tunnel, and Kan-Ten found human lighting garish in the best of situations. He squinted as he watched Singh sauntering across the garage, brushing past battered, well-used rovers with the Constabulary seal painted on their doors, past a pair of hoppers that looked as if they'd been thrown together from about a dozen nonfunctional models, and past the massive, aging hulk of an old cargo truck still partially loaded down with Tahni storage crates.

In the center of the broad parking area, a wide space around them as if anything else was afraid to get close, were the two Tahni battlesuits. They hunched over on the concrete floor, naked to the harsh, overhead light, the worn and cracked spots in their metal clearly visible, like the wrinkles and lines in the face of an elder. Even Singh seemed to hesitate at the sight of the monstrous golems, edging around them.

Kan-Ten could see the cartel soldiers now, the ones Fontenot had heard. There were three of them, huddled together near the garage entrance, the tallest of the three leaning against the flexible metal shutters of the closed vehicle door. All humans pretty much looked alike to Kan-Ten, but the tallest one was a male, and at least one of the other two was female, if he read the visual cues correctly. All three were armed with Tahni KE-guns, and he thought that the weapons' hand-holds had been modified somewhat to make it easier for humans to fire them.

They paid no attention to Singh's approach, and Kan-Ten marveled that they could be so unobservant; but as Fontenot had assured him, looking as if you belonged was half of not being challenged. He was only six or seven meters away when the tall one finally looked up; perhaps he thought Singh was one of his superiors and didn't want to be punished for shirking, Kan-Ten mused. Either way, the expression on his face changed as he got a clearer look at Singh, possibly in realization that he didn't know the man.

Singh shifted into an entirely different speed, as if he were on a recording being played at three times the normal rate. Whatever he'd had done to himself to replace his bionics was faster and smoother and far less clunky and awkward, and it had to have involved wired reflexes. He hit the one leaning against the wall first, the one who'd noticed him; his right hand shot out faster than either human or Tahni eye could follow and struck the man in the throat. Kan-Ten couldn't hear him choking from across the garage, but he saw him double over, rifle clattering to the floor as his hands went to his neck, and Singh turned to his next target.

The other two were trying to react now, moving far too slow to match Singh's inhuman speed; he'd produced a knife from somewhere and suddenly, it was buried in the female's left eye and deep into her brain. She collapsed, blood and other, less colorful liquids spraying from her socket as the knife withdrew. The last man didn't have time to get his KE-gun twisted around to aim at Singh, but he was squeezing the trigger convulsively, a scream forming on his lips. The scream died in a wet gurgle as the knife flashed across his voice box and the gurgle faded into a grunt as the blade sank home in his heart with surgical precision.

It was too late; the cartel soldier was dead on his feet, his life spilling from his throat and chest, but the KE-gun was firing with a hum-snap of its electromagnetic coil, its tantalum needles spewing wildly across the garage, smacking into the cement block walls with sprays of white and grey powder, and punching through the cab of the cargo truck before the man's hand went slack.

"Shit," Fontenot muttered beside him as they watched through the half-open door. "We need to…"

"Shoot him! Shoot that motherfucker!"

The voice echoed through the garage, ricocheting like the needles off the steel and concrete, but Kan-Ten thought it had to be coming from the corridor opening off to their left, running back inside the fortress. Singh was drawing his pistol, spinning towards the voice when the first burst of KE-gun needles began chewing at the garage door just above him, hosing downward. Warning klaxons began to scream, their warbling sirens accompanied by the flashing red of light panels set in the walls.

Kan-Ten was moving, feeling Fontenot beside him, running out from the storage room and heading toward where he thought the firing was coming from. He could see them coming out of the hallway, at least half a dozen of them, with probably more to come now that the alarm was sounding. Some wore makeshift armor, adapted from the suits of it that were in the wartime weapons cache or pieced together from Constabulary gear, while others seem to have jumped right out of bed, their shirts off, their hair untied and flowing wildly in multicolored flares across the grey walls.

Undisciplined and untrained, they sprayed gunfire across the garage, hitting the vehicles and the battlesuits and the walls, and most of them not seeming to know who they were actually supposed to be shooting at. Singh fell into a crouch that put him below the level of the vehicles and began firing from beneath their undercarriage, but the tantalum needles were eating right through the thin, sheet-metal bodies of the rovers, and getting closer to him.

Kan-Ten raised the pulse carbine to his chest and tried to aim through the human optics as best he could, touching the trigger pad with his middle finger and pressing it down. There was no kick, just a vibration against his hands as hyperexplosive cartridges pulsed heat energy through semiconductive lasing rods, and flashes of ionized atmosphere trailed the actual laser pulses as he squeezed off a long burst, walking it onto his targets.

Flares of vaporized concrete shot fire and steam from the wall, and then one of the cartel mercenaries was jerking backwards as the laser pulses pierced through his Constabulary armor vest and then blew through his throat in a steaming, boiling spray of superheated blood. Another went down from Fontenot's Gauss pistol, the first tungsten-wrapped ceramic slug shattering against the Tahni chest plate but the second taking him square between the eyes. His head disappeared in a red mist, and then the rest were scattering and the rocket rounds from the Constable's big revolver passed through the crowd of them as they parted, not hitting anything but the walls.

"Where are the controls for the doors?" Fontenot barked at Freeman, pausing to fire a round at a foot sticking out from behind the concealment of a cargo truck wheel. The slug took it off at the ankle and someone screamed, the high-pitched shrieking devolving into loud sobs.

"The office is over there," Freeman gestured with the barrel of his revolver at a doorway just to the right of the corridor.

Glass windows had lined the small office, but they were cracked and splintered and shattered now from the gunfire, and the lights inside were flickering where the panels had been hit by tantalum needles or mini-rockets. Fontenot veered off toward the office, Freeman at her heels, while Kan-Ten walked backwards behind them, keeping an eye on the remaining three cartel soldiers still hiding behind the vehicles. There were sounds leaking through from outside, vague rumblings through the massive, sheet steel doors, and he wondered if that was the landers coming in. The humans had an expression about the clock ticking; it had never made much sense to him since clocks didn't make any particular noise that he could hear, but this would be a time to use that expression. If that door wasn't open in the next few minutes, whoever was trying to attack the fortress would be slaughtered.

Kan-Ten was still facing backwards when he heard the shout, the warning coming from Singh as the man sprinted past him towards Fontenot and the Constable. He spun on his heel, seeing just a glimpse of the man, the familiar, depilated head and the cruelly angular face. Jordi Abdullah stood at the end of the hallway into the fortress, dressed casually as if he'd been in bed, his hands filled with a weapon that had been taken from the Tahni cache, but not a KE-gun. This one was something more specialized, something Kan-Ten had seen but never fired. It looked awkward on the shoulder of a human, as if it was teetering on the edge of toppling over with all its weight thrown to the rear behind the ray shield; it was meant to be fired from the prone, but Jordi stood, legs spread for balance, the muscles in his shoulders taut with the effort. Kan-Ten tried to swing around his carbine, knowing he wouldn't be in time...and he wasn't.

The electron beamer was a slow-firing, clumsy weapon that took nearly a minute to recharge, but it could penetrate heavy armor and it was absolutely devastating in the enclosed space of the garage. The light and heat hit first, washing over him like he'd stepped into a furnace, an instant sunburn over any part of his body not covered by the control singlet he still wore. At this range, the delay between the heat and the concussion was mostly imagined, yet he still felt there was a heartbeat-length of time from the roasting heat and the actinic light to the blast of hot air that drove him off his feet and sent him tumbling across the floor, the carbine slipping out of his hands.

There was a ringing in his ears that was more a whistling, and when he tried to suck in a desperate breath, there didn't seem to be anything but smoke and fire in his lungs, but he knew he had to move. He had a dim realization, not so much from what he could see, since he couldn't see anything but smoke and flame and blinking purple after-images, but from a general sense of where he'd been and where the shot had gone, that the office didn't exist anymore. He didn't know if Jordi had targeted it, or it had just been collateral damage from trying to hit Fontenot and the Constable, but where the office had been was nothing but a flaming pile of wreckage.

He couldn't see any of the others, and couldn't afford the time to find out if they'd survived. He had to move, and there was only one direction worth moving. He scrambled to his feet, ignoring the dull ache that seemed to come from everywhere, ignoring the burning in his lungs, and sprinting across the debris-littered floor to the second battlesuit.

He'd chosen it rather than the first because it had more concealment and potential cover with the other suit and the cargo truck between it and Jordi's position, assuming the man was still there. Kan-Ten was sure he saw KE-gun needles punch into the side of one of the hoppers as he ran past it, but he still couldn't hear anything, even his own labored breathing. Just one of the needles in the right place, just one and his long journey would be over right here, and would that be so bad? How had he wanted it to end? This would be as good a way to finish it as any.

But it didn't end before he reached the suit. The smooth, polished surface of it was cold even in the heat the electron blast had left behind, yet it held a life, a warmth to it that wasn't obvious to anyone who'd never been inside. He touched a control and the chest plastron began its slide downward, agonizingly slow; he crouched down behind the massive legs and chanted a calming mantra as he watched something traveling thousands of meters per second smack into the back shoulder armor of the suit and career away faster than he could follow.

His hearing was starting to return, and there was the distant clamor of shouts, and the distinctive hum-snap of electromagnetic slug shooters, and the whoosh-crack that could only be the Constable's revolver firing. At least one of them was still alive, then. The plastron stopped in its descent and Kan-Ten wriggled into it with a twisting motion that seemed childishly easy now; it had taken him months to perfect it in training, and he'd been the fastest for three cycles running by the time he'd earned his own platoon.

He thrust his hands into the arms of the suit and grasped the finger controls; at his touch, the plastron pulled inward toward him automatically, folding him into its embrace like the arms of death herself. Interior lights flickered to life, the Heads-Up Display cutting through the smoke and haze and showing him the roller door just ten meters ahead. Warnings flashed, not in the humans' choice of colors but in something more sensible, more meaningful, letting him know he was being targeted by incoming fire.

"I am aware of that," he said softly, powering up the isotope reactor.

Talking to himself was another bad habit he'd learned from

humans. His own people would think him possessed by evil spirits if they'd heard it, but they were the least of his problems. If Jordi's weapon recharged before he got this battlesuit working, that beamer would tear right through its armor at this range.

He checked the display, saw the heat sources scattered around the room, barely distinguishable from the fires still burning in the office, but the computer put the slight heat differences together with sonic input to paint him a picture. At least a couple of the others were still alive, and firing at Jordi and his troops. More and more of those troops were flooding into the corridor entrance, though, and they, perhaps, had even less time than he did.

The thermal signature of the assault beamer was distinctive, and the computer knew it; he could see from the threat readout in the HUD that the weapon was fully recharged. If Jordi Abdullah had any sort of tactical sense, he would ignore the distraction of Fontenot and the others, would take whatever chance he had to in order to take out the battlesuit before it powered up. It would be a spear of white heat and then he'd be flash-roasted in half a second.

The isotope reactor came online without warning, nearly surprising him, and the servos whined to life as he lunged forward instinctively. The High Guard battlesuit was a big target, a power hog which demanded a logistics train that, perhaps, far outweighed its worth; but in combat it was a marvelous machine in ways that made him forgive its shortcomings. Both the suits they'd found lacked any major weaponry; they had been stored without missiles or KE-gun ammo and the electron beamers built into the left arm, of each were deadlined, long ago stripped for parts to make another suit work. But it still had the vibro-cutters extending from each wrist and they hummed to life with a clench of his fingers on the right controls.

And it still massed 500 kilograms, and worked very well as a battering ram.

Kan-Ten thought about running, let those muscles flex---and the battlesuit ran. Long, loping strides, deceptively fast and then he leaned forward and jumped and thought about jumping *hard*. Intakes at the top of the suit's "backpack," the armored housing for the reactor, sucked in air through miniature turbines and fed it through the vents surrounding the isotope power pack, heating it and expelling it through jets at the bottom.

He wasn't sure how fast he was going when he hit the door, but he felt it buckle, felt it bow outward, heard the wrenching squeal of metal even through the armor. He brought both arms up, vibro-cutters extended, and sliced downward. Stressed metal parted like wet parchment, shrieking in agony, and the blades came free, leaving gaping rents in the battered and bent surface. He took two steps back then slammed into the three-meter-wide stretch between the two slices.

Behind him, the electron beamer fired again and there was a white flare of raw energy, and a clap of thunder, and a flash of breathtaking heat, but the steel of the door gave way with one last scrape of metal talons on armored shoulders, and he was through...

CHAPTER SEVENTEEN

Boost. His whole world was boost, acceleration, high gravity pushing him, battering him, punishing him. It felt as if it had been the entirety of his experience for as long as he could remember. Ash took comfort from it at times, at the pure, unbridled power it represented, power under his control, a part of his body. But after too long, after too much acceleration at too many gravities for minutes that dragged like hours, he just wanted to breathe again, and he wasn't sure when that would happen.

The *Acheron* rumbled and roared and shrieked and groaned and vibrated around him and he felt every strain, every gram of stress, every bank and loop and dive as if her skin was his, her effort his own. The night sky over Gennich was a cloudless mass of stars, the kind of sky that could disorient you, get you turned around, but the interface kept him focused. He knew where he was instinctively, knew where the shuttles were, knew where the surface was.

The *La Sombra* birds were trying to get away from him, trying to get to the Savage/Slaughter landers, now that they'd noticed them. The cartel aerospacecraft were fast and slippery, sliding through his targeting lock, silver, metal fish wriggling out of his fingers. They were too low, too close to the city, too close to Sandi's LZ, and he had to draw them away, force them to target him.

His problem was his training, he decided. A shot from a proton cannon took the full charge of one of the ship's two capacitor banks; doctrine, pounded into pilots and crews from day one, was never to waste a shot, because once those banks were drained, it took a long time---up to thirty seconds, forever in combat---to recharge them. But he was in atmosphere, and a proton blast didn't have to hit to get their attention.

He angled the *Acheron* into a dive, following them down, trying to get his targeting reticle centered on the portside of the pair, watching the bird dance back and forth. The pilot might not have had military training, but he had plenty of experience shaking bogies off his tail in gunfights in the soup. Ash only needed him to be within a few dozen meters, though...

He'd fired before he realized it, lashing out with the cutter's main weapon, the shot ripping apart the atmosphere, seeming to tear at the fabric of reality with a lance of pure white energy as powerful as any lightning bolt. The air around the blast super-heated, and the expanding cylinder of plasma sent shockwaves of turbulence outward from it, slamming into the shuttle and sending it tumbling into a wild spin, angling down over the high desert outside town. Ash banked after the out-of-control craft, intent not so much on finishing it, although he would if he could, but on making the other shuttle pilot *believe* he was about to finish it.

It worked. The rounded wings of the tumbling shuttle were beginning to slow in their rotation as the pilot began to power out of the spin, but he was still seconds away from getting a target lock on the bird when he sensed the second shuttle burning hard upward, coming in at his nine o'clock. Ash tried to hold his course just a few seconds longer, thinking maybe he could scratch one of them now and be able to concentrate on the other, but the incoming bogie wasn't taking "no" for an answer. Narrow flares of heat bloomed on thermal as the flight of four missiles streaked from the shuttle's weapons bay, tendrils of white smoke glowing incandescent in the moonlight, seeking him out.

Had Ash been forced to think through his actions and implement them manually, he might have died in the next instant; but the interface coupled with years of training and experience allowed him to act without conscious thought, without intention. He fired the proton cannon again, even though it was degrees away from being aligned correctly, just another shove to keep that shuttle off balance. The blast of charged particles had barely left the ship's accelerator before Ash spun the cutter end for end with a kick of maneuvering thrusters and boosted out of the path of the missiles. The *Acheron* seemed to moan with the strain, the jet engines roaring in protest.

It was risky using the maneuvering jets in the atmosphere; the *Acheron* wasn't fresh off the production lines, and there was always the danger that the stress would rip the wings right off of her.

Not this time, Ash thought ruefully, clenching his stomach muscles against the sudden rush of g-forces. The interface kept him conscious and focused, but it was a close thing.

The missiles were struggling to make the turn, lighter and able to take greater g-forces than a manned ship, but not nearly as powerful or maneuverable. They weren't military-grade; again, like the weapons the lighter had launched, they were fabricated in the Pirate Worlds for use by amateurs against amateurs. Ash climbed away from them, his fuel only limited by the reactor, his reaction mass superheated air sucked through the intakes and out through the engine exhaust. The missiles had onboard chemical propellant tanks and it would only last them just so long, particularly trying to maneuver in the atmosphere.

The shuttle followed him from a careful distance, not wanting to get caught in the explosion of its own warheads, but he felt its presence through the interface as if by some sixth sense. The other one was kilometers farther back, finally out of its wild spin and climbing again, and he cursed as he saw it going back after the landers, as persistent as a dog with a bone. He sank further into the interface, opening himself up to all the data it was feeding him, felt the distance from the missiles, felt their speed and velocity and how long it would take them to catch up to him. He didn't have to think about it or calculate it, he knew it like the way he understood when he threw a baseball how far it would go and where it would hit.

He pulled an Immelman turn, a maneuver not designed for a starship one hundred meters long, but still effective, cutting his thrust and letting the boat drop back downward, steering into the dive and then shifting power back to the jets again. The missiles lunged at him with renewed vigor, as if they somehow realized they had a chance to reach him now, and the Gatling laser turret in the cutter's wing hummed to life on its own accord, guided by the ship's computer. He knew there couldn't be much ammunition left in the Gatling's hopper, not after the fight with the lighter, but he didn't interfere; it wasn't as if he could turn what was left in for a refund.

There was an explosion off to his two o'clock, then another further back as the laser pulses sought out and dispatched two of the heat-seekers, red and white eruptions in the darkness. Two left...and then a red warning flashed in the perimeter of his vision, letting him know that the Gatling laser had, as they used to say back in the military, gone Winchester; it was totally dry on ammunition.

"Fuck," he muttered, more inside his head than out loud.

Only one thing to do; he throttled up the jets, feeling nine g's-plus stomping him into the seat. The lower of the two *La Sombra* shuttles was just a few kilometers ahead of him now, and less than three hundred meters below his altitude. Blackness tunneled in on his awareness, threatening to send him over the edge into unconsciousness, but he fought it, knowing it meant death. The ship's flight systems would pull him out of the dive automatically, but that left the pesky missiles, and they wouldn't play fair and let him take a time-out.

The missiles were less than a kilometer away and closing; they'd detonate automatically at a hundred meters, firing off a shotgun-blast of penetrators aimed at his engines. The *Acheron* was armored, but each sub-munition would have its own quick-burnout rocket motor and a plasma warhead designed to burn right through BiPhase Carbide. If they'd been black market military hardware, they wouldn't just be heat-seeking, they'd be capable of tracking his lidar and thermal signature and he never would have been able to pull this off. He didn't have time to line up the proton accelerator with the shuttle trying to target Sandi's lander, but he didn't *have* to use the proton cannon; the cartel pilot had given him another weapon.

Two kilometers from the shuttle now, nearly even with its altitude, and only a thousand meters from the deck. The missiles were about 300 meters out and descending at a shallower angle, cutting off his avenue of escape upward. This was one of those moves that would have horrified his trainers, but then, he'd never met a military trainer that really appreciated what was possible with the interface. Just a combination of the angle of the flaps, the vector of the exhaust, a slight nudge from the belly jets, not planned or thought through but felt in his gut and expressed as a motion of the ship-as-his-body...and suddenly the *Acheron* was standing on its nose, sliding forward, nearly scraping wings with the shuttle.

And the missiles were a hundred meters away. They both detonated as one, and suddenly the shuttle was bombarded by a hail of molten metal, spears of plasma that sliced through its skin and into the fuel tanks. The explosion was a hammer-blow that nearly knocked the *Acheron* out of the sky, and Ash was struggling with her now, pushed out of the interface by the blast wave and the shock that tossed the ship, and him, into a spin. He dove again, submerging his mind and subsuming it back into his meld with the ship, powering out of the spin with the belly jets and climbing again.

The other shuttle was waiting for him up there, and he knew now that he had the pilot's undivided attention. Below him, Sandi was taking the lander into the teeth of the enemy, but he'd done what he could for her.

"You don't get to die," he reminded her softly, then he climbed to meet his enemy in the black sky.

———

Sandi caught the explosion out of the edge of her perception and knew immediately that it was one of the enemy shuttles, not Ash. If the *Acheron* blew up, it would have been a fusion blast that blotted out the sky and possibly killed them all; this was the explosion from solid rocket fuel going up. She hissed out the breath she'd been holding and concentrated on the landing zone.

There was already anti-aircraft fire rising from the corners of the fortress, streams of electromagnetically launched tantalum slivers crossing back and forth, hosing down the sky around her. She jinked the shuttle in an irregular, choppy pattern, but she knew the only reason she and the other lander hadn't been shot down was the lack of computer control for the weapons. They were Tahni weapons and the targeting was manual, the readouts in a non-human language and she knew the operators were firing by guess and by God...and it was still coming too damned close.

"Get ready," she murmured to Jacobson. "Gonna' get rough." Then she switched to the frequency for the other lander's pilot, a short, disagreeable man with regulation-length hair that was nonetheless purple and in corn rows. "Filipe," she said. "I'm going in and drawing their attention. Slip on by to the fusion reactor while I have them distracted."

"Roger." His reply was curt and laconic, just like everything else he'd said to her over the last two days.

You're fucking welcome, she thought at him sourly.

Then she threw the lander into a barrel roll, and past the layer of unreality that the interface provided, she thought she heard Jacobson puking into his helmet. Her own dinner stayed firmly in place, but the g-forces jerked her forcefully against her seat restraints as she took the aerospacecraft down over the fortress in a steep, tight spiral. The lander had a Gatling laser turret in the wing and she cut loose with it as she descended, trying to put fire on the air defense turrets as best she could. She wasn't sure if she'd hit anything; the aerospacecraft was going too fast and her attention was too focused on bringing it down as close as she could to the garage entrance.

Sandi hit the belly jets nearly simultaneous with the low altitude warning sounding, and the bone-jarring deceleration felt as if it were going to drive her through the deck of the lander. The airframe shook violently and she thought for a second she'd badly miscalculated and the bird was about to break in two...and then they were hovering two meters off the ground, drifting slowly sideways on a column of fire, sand and dust and debris billowing around them in an obscuring cloud, and the belly ramp was already on its way down.

"Go! Go! Go!"

She wasn't sure if she was yelling, or if Jacobson was, or both, but the words echoed back through the rear compartment of the lander and through her 'link's ear bud, and the ground force platoon leader was already unstrapped and heading out to lead his troops off the belly ramp. The Constabulary fortress loomed ahead, harshly illuminated in the glare of the floodlights, its high walls ugly and threatening. She could see the closest of the crew-served KE-gun turrets and she played the Gatling laser over them, flares of ionized air passing across the front of the building, leaving a row of strobe-light flashes in their wake from vaporizing metal and concrete.

"We're clear!" Jacobson's voice was as loud as if he'd yelled the words from a few centimeters away, but she could see in a corner of the viewscreen that he and his platoon were rushing at the garage entrance...and she couldn't tell if it was open.

She bit off a curse and flipped the control to raise the ramp, then slid the lander sideways on the belly jets, still firing the Gatling. She could see the round counter in her mind's eye, projected through the interface, and she knew that she had maybe two to three more seconds before the hopper ran dry, but she needed to keep those KE-gun turrets suppressed to give the infantry a chance.

She didn't know where the shot came from, but she knew when it hit. The tantalum slivers punched through the portside air intakes, raking the wing and shredding the turbine inside it. Jacked into the system, watching with the slow-motion perceptions of the interface, she could observe every minute detail of it, could see each microsecond unfold as if it were a picture in a frame, but couldn't change the inevitable outcome.

The lander's port belly jets billowed black smoke as the

turbines tore themselves apart, their fragments taking the wing right off the fuselage, the thrust cutting off abruptly. She tried to feather the starboard belly jets manually, but the controls were damaged and it was far too late. The lander flipped over, belly up, and Sandi's world flipped with it, the interface spitting her out into harsh reality as the craft smashed to the ground with a shriek of rending metal and an impact of dull agony. Sound and feeling and sight all snapped off and everything was infinitely black.

———

She couldn't remember her old name. She'd simply been "the Matriarch" for long years now, and before that she'd been "the Protégé," and before that...before that, she'd been a young female, picked out of a house of other young females for her quick wit and quick tongue, and she couldn't remember what that young female had been called. What would that girl have said if she could have seen the end of her life? Would she have run away from the calling, had she seen a vision of herself confined to this tiny chamber in the human place, the place they called the Constabulary? Would she have believed that a warrior, a male who had served the Emperor against the enemy, would stand over her so brazenly, alone in that same, small room?

It was something so outrageous, so blasphemous, that any onlooker would have tried to kill him for it, even though it meant their own death. Yet he regarded her coolly, calmly, as if this were the most normal thing in the world. She'd tried to ignore him for the long minutes he'd stood there, backlit by the glowing panel in the ceiling, looming over her as she sat on the edge of the cot that was the holding cell's only furniture, but it didn't seem to deter his interest.

"What do you want of me, Vala-Kel?" she asked, risking blasphemy herself to end this ridiculous standoff.

"You are far too old to make a male lose control in your presence," he mused, still looking at her quite inappropriately, as a craftsman might regard a new tool. "I wonder why it is forbidden for an adult male to be alone with you?"

"Things are, as they have been," she quoted from the text they both knew from rote memory, the one impressed upon all of them as children. "Why do you question the Path? What has led you to betray your own people? You were a warrior, a respected male who could have led us."

"I *will* lead you," he corrected her. "That is inevitable."

"Must I repeat myself?" She hid fear behind vexation. "What do you want of me?"

"Now your protégé, Gen-Lya-Tal," he went on, as if from his original thought, ignoring both her questions and his answers, "she is not yet to that age."

The Matriarch felt alarm and fierce anger, and she rose from her seat on the cot to her still-unimposing height and stood nose-to-chin with Vala-Kel.

"How do you know her name?" she demanded.

"She has need of it again," he explained, putting a hand on her chest and pushing her backward. She squawked as she stumbled on the edge of the cot and fell heavily back on it, outrage battling with the still-growing fear. "Now that she is no longer eligible to be a Matriarch's protégé."

The Matriarch felt as if she were shrinking in on herself. That could only mean that Vala-Kel had mated with her.

"You drag everything we are, everything we represent through mud and shit," she hissed at him, the outrage finally winning out over the fear, "and you think we would follow such a one as you."

"When the choice is that or death, of course I do." He was

imperturbable, somehow. It was infuriating; everything about him was infuriating, but she knew that to attack him would mean her death, and the people needed her now more than ever.

She simply stared at the male, waiting for him to get to the point.

"Very well, I will tell you what I wish of you, you old, useless, feeble bitch." He stalked across the room restlessly, hands clenching and unclenching as if he wished to kill her and was having to restrain himself. "If you were to simply disappear in this place, to never be heard from again, your bones rotting in some forgotten hole, then there would be nagging questions. Those who might otherwise be useful cogs in our society would need to be killed, and I find this idea wasteful."

"You think I'd agree to support you? After what you've done?" She wasn't sure if it was the absurdity of the idea or his temerity in suggesting it that she found more objectionable.

"Not support," he said, making a gesture of placation. "Simply keeping your mouth shut."

"I assume there's a threat or a promise involved in this some-where." He would have to be stupid as well as mad to assume she'd cooperate with him otherwise, and she didn't believe him to be stupid.

"I'd think it's fairly obvious," he said, gesturing surprise. "They're your people, your followers. Every one of them I'm forced to kill would be on your head."

Her instinctive response was to tell him that his words were dishonorable, and she was about to invoke a traditional curse on him when the klaxons sounded and she looked around at the loud, annoying warbling, a human sound that was piercing and painful to her ears. He went to the door of the cell, yanking it open and sticking his head outside, yelling something in the human tongue, English, that she couldn't make out over the sound of the siren. When he stepped back into the cell, his expression wasn't alarmed or angry...it was satisfied, as if this were something he'd anticipated.

"Come with me," he said, seizing her wrist with the ruthless speed of a striking predator. She tried to pull away, but his grip was iron.

"Where are you taking me?" she asked, trying to dig in her heels and resist. It was useless; he dragged her out into the hallway outside the cell, heedless of her efforts. The walls were slate-grey down in the confinement level, grim and featureless. "I should have let Kan-Ten kill you."

Then he did pause, looking back at her, manic and feverish and insane.

"Yes, Matriarch, you should have." He yanked her after him with cruel insistence, pulling her along when she stumbled. "You won't get that chance again...and neither will he."

CHAPTER EIGHTEEN

Abel Freeman watched the world burn around him and waited for his turn.

The night sky was alight with the flames, choked and dark and cloudy with the thick, black smoke. The only home he'd ever known roared and cackled insanely, as if the fire were a demon, delighting in the chaos, destroying all it touched. It had consumed his mother and his younger sisters the moment the first missiles had struck, and the blast had washed away half their house like a wave, and left him trapped in a pocket of wreckage that had spared his room the immediate destruction. The fate had been cruel rather than kind, since it meant he would be denied the quick death of the explosion to savor the agony of burning alive.

His father had arrived like an avenging angel, the big man's massive boot crashing through what remained of his bedroom door with a billowing inrush of smoke and heat. George Freeman was on fire, the flames eating away at his clothes and his skin, and already burning the hair off his head in wisps of curling smoke. But he grabbed his son by the arm and sheltered him with his body as he bulldozed a path back out through the conflagration, through a heat so intense that little Abel thought it would burn him down to the bone. Then one final impact as the front door gave way, and they were outside, and he could breathe again.

His father had collapsed beside him out on the front walk, his eyes staring into infinity as the great, strong man had finally let his life slip away, his last task accomplished. Abel couldn't even cry; this wasn't real, this was some nightmare from which he couldn't wake. He stared dully at the barn collapsing just a few dozen meters away, across what had been lush grass, but was now charred and smoking earth. In the distance, a red glow lit up the dark horizon, and he wondered that it could be dawn already; it was too early.

When he heard the engine grumbling, heard the tires grinding on the dirt and ash, he couldn't even rouse himself enough to look up. There was the squeak of an ancient suspension, and a door opening, and heavy footsteps that came to a halt right in front of him, the battered work boots filling his vision. He finally looked up, into the craggy, lined face, the ragged, blond hair and the unkempt, blue uniform shirt.

"I'm sorry about your family, son," Constable Llewellyn Johansen said, hand resting on the butt of the big revolver holstered at his side. "But y'see that glow over there?" He pointed at the horizon. Abel nodded slowly. "Well, that's Kennedy City, and most of it's already gone. It's the Tahni, y'see." He waved upward at the sky and Abel heard the roar of jet engines overhead in the distance. "They swarmed through the Jumpgate and overwhelmed the orbital defenses and we just don't have enough ships insystem to stop them. I've been picking up survivors."

Abel stared at the battered, ancient, alcohol-fueled utility truck, and vacant eyes stared back at him. Many were little older than him, most of them still only teenagers. He wondered for a moment where their parents were, until he felt reality slap him in the back of the head like his father would do when he asked a stupid question.

"If you wanna' come with me, son," Johansen continued, softly but urgently, "then we need to leave right now. The Tahni are landing in the city, and they'll have patrols out here soon."

He reached out a hand, and Abel took it, the dry strength of it so much like his father's as it pulled him up to his feet...

Abel Freeman felt the world swim around him in a haze of pain and confusion, and a heat that seared his lungs when he tried to take a breath. He hadn't been unconscious...he didn't think he'd been unconscious...

Shit, he thought with rueful admission. *Unless all that stuff back on Aphrodite was a daydream, then I was fucking unconscious.*

He'd certainly at least had the wind knocked out of him by the force of the blast from whatever it was that Jordi Abdullah had fired. He'd never seen one before, and hoped like hell he never saw one again.

He forced his eyes open, forced his body to move despite the dull ache that seemed to engulf it, punctuated in places by sharper, knifing agony. The ruins of the garage office were scattered about, and under and on top of him, and pieces of them were still on fire. He jerked instinctively, despite the pain it caused in his back and shoulders, throwing the burning bits of wood and plastic off of him, leaving behind smoldering, charred patches on his jacket and jeans, and burns beneath that he'd have to ignore for now.

It was hard to make out anything through the smoke, particularly with half the light panels in the garage burned out, but he could tell that he was alone; there were no bodies around him, no dead or wounded, and no one shooting at him. That part was good, the rest not so much. Freeman pushed himself to a sitting position, searching around on the debris-littered floor for his handgun, but not finding it.

"Damn it," he mumbled. That had been Johansen's gun.

The sound of his own voice seemed off, and he realized then that his ears had been ringing, his hearing muted by the blast, but it was beginning to come back...and the cacophony of battle came with it. He looked up sharply, hearing gunfire, explosions, feeling the ground shaking. It all seemed to be coming from off in the direction of the garage door, and there was one spot where the sound was louder, clearer than anywhere else, a gap in the metal of the roll-up barrier. He could tell there was a source of fresh air that way, as well; the smoke was roiling out in that direction, starting to clear, though he still couldn't make anything out by the dim and flickering light of the fires.

He was willing to bet that Jordi Abdullah and his people had gone out there to deal with the attack; and, if Fontenot, Singh or Kan-Ten were still alive, they'd be out there too.

Should I go out and try to raise some hell on my own, he wondered, *or should I go cut my deputies loose from the holding cells first, and increase the level of potential hell-raising exponentially?*

He put that debate on hold when he heard voices coming down the hallway from further into the building. He thought for a moment his hearing was still messed up when he couldn't understand what they were saying, but he quickly realized that was because they were speaking Tahni. He'd heard it often enough back on Aphrodite during the occupation to get a feel for it, though he still couldn't understand a word of it, even after all these years on Brigantia.

He thought about Jordi's Tahni allies and rolled into a crouch, looking around again for a gun, or something he could use as a weapon. It was too late; their shadows emerged before they did, backlit by the undamaged lights in the hallway, projected across the layer of particulate dust and smoke floating across the garage. It was a male and female---together, which was odd---and it looked as if the male was dragging the female physically out into the garage. She was old, and oddly dressed even for a Tahni, and suddenly he realized that he recognized her from Jordi's broadcast video: she was the Matriarch, that Tahni priestess they were holding hostage.

The male, he couldn't place; they all tended to look alike to him. But if he was here, and allied with Jordi, and dragging the old lady around, Freeman figured he must be that Vala-Kel he'd heard about. And he didn't seem to be carrying a gun, which made Abel Freeman feel so much better about things.

They didn't seem to notice him there, crouched in the shadows, and he waited until they were almost even with him before he leapt to his feet. He charged the male, throwing his not-inconsiderable weight into a body block that took both of them down. The female's arm came loose of Vala-Kel's grip, and she rolled away from him and out of Freeman's peripheral vision as he focused on grappling with the big warrior. The Constable had fought Tahni hand-to-hand before, and he knew not to aim any blows at the head; the bone there was thick, and he was more likely to wind up with a set of broken knuckles than to do any damage. He also knew not to attempt any of the joint locks or arm bars he'd trained in for so long, since they didn't work well on joints that bent in slightly different directions than a human's.

Freeman went for what had worked for him before: strikes at the throat, and knees aimed for the upper thigh, but this guy wasn't sitting still for it. This Vala-Kel was strong, even for a Tahni, and when he blocked Freeman's attempted chops at his neck, it felt as if the Constable was ramming his arm into an iron bar set in cement. Freeman didn't even see the blow coming; one second, he was on top of the Tahni, pounding away at him, the next he was rolling off across the floor, his right shoulder pulsing with a flare of pain, like it had been dislocated.

The Tahni was up before Freeman tumbled to a stop; he could see the alien springing to his feet with an inhuman litheness to his motions, and he knew he'd bitten off far more than he could chew. He was clawing for purchase in the wood and bits of concrete on the floor when the fingers of his left hand brushed against a polished, wooden grip; his hand closed around the revolver and he rolled onto his back and fired by instinct. There was a flash from the rocket's exhaust, a red glare that left an afterimage across his vision, and the Tahni was spinning away, clutching at his right shoulder.

The Constable tried to follow through with another shot, but Vala-Kel was already running behind cover, and the warhead plowed into the side of a rover, already peppered with KE-gun needles, as the Tahni dropped from sight. Freeman cursed, trying to push himself to his feet and hold onto the gun simultaneously with one hand, the other useless from his injured shoulder. He saw the wounded Tahni dash between vehicles and fired off another snap-shot at him, but he was unsteady and rushed, and the warhead flared impotently against the roll-up door at the far end of the garage.

Freeman coughed, unable to hold it in, the smoke scratching at his throat, the barrel of his revolver wavering at the motion as he held it out in the direction he'd last seen Vala-Kel. Shadows flickered between the vehicles, but he couldn't be sure if it was actual movement or just a trick of the flames. He nearly stumbled as he tried to shuffle across the wreckage-strewn floor, sliding over to where the old Tahni female crouched behind a vehicle charging station.

"Do you speak English?" he asked her, his voice dry and raspy. He needed a drink, and at this point, he'd even take water as a second choice.

"Some." The word seem to wrestle its way out of her, like it hurt to say it.

She was, he decided from close range, one ugly mother, even for a Tahni.

"We gotta' get out of here." He motioned towards the distant hole in the garage door. "That's the most direct way out, but the shit's going down out there. And there's your boy somewhere over there, too. But I'm going that way, so I'll cover you. If you head back," he explained, motioning up the hallway, "you might run into more of Jordi's people, and I don't know that you'll find an open exit...and you'll be on your own."

She was silent for a second, and it seemed to be entirely too long of a second for Abel Freeman. His eyes darted back and forth, sure that Vala-Kel would spring out of the shadows any moment and lunge at him.

"I'll go with you," she decided finally.

"All right," he sighed. He turned back towards the front, left side-on, revolver extended like an old-time duelist. "Follow close."

The noises from outside were getting louder, closer, and he knew that meant the fighting was going to be in their laps soon. He sacrificed caution for speed and led the Matriarch up the left side of the garage, trying to use the two rovers parked end to end there for cover. He glanced beneath and inside each of them carefully as they passed, wary of an ambush, but there was none. Nothing moved, nothing but the eddies of smoke curling through the gap in the roll-up doors, and the shadows flickering in the light of the slowly-dying fire.

Then there *was* a sound, somewhere off to his right, the grinding hum of servomotors, and for a second, he thought that someone had remotely triggered the garage door, that it was about to open and expose them to the violence outside.

But no, the door remained motionless; the sound was coming from somewhere closer than that, somewhere by the cargo truck...

A cold emptiness filled his gut as he saw the trollish bulk of the remaining suit of Tahni battle armor begin to shift on its massive, pillar legs.

"Run!" he yelled at the Matriarch, pushing her ahead of him roughly, ignoring her protests.

Her feet were invisible under the hem of her striped robes, but the material flapped in counterpoint with their movement; she could run much faster than he'd thought from looking at her. But not quite fast enough. The battlesuit ducked its shoulder and slammed the rear end of the cargo truck aside, metal crunching and tires squealing in anguished protest on the bare cement of the floor. It had the angle now; it would be on them long before they reached the giant, three-meter high rent in the door.

He stumbled and banged his left shoulder on the side of a rover as he stopped, and he saw the Matriarch look back at him with what might have been uncertainty.

"Go!" he urged her, waving at the exit. "Go, now!"

He steadied himself, then stepped out from behind the rover, levelled the revolver and fired off a round directly at the faceplate of the Tahni High Guard battlesuit. The round hit true, the blowtorch-hot plasma spear igniting right in the center of the opaque visor, leaving behind a dimpled pockmark, but failing to penetrate the thick transparent aluminum of the face-plate. The suit turned his way, the treads of its broad, circular foot pads scraping on the floor.

"Well, this sucks," he muttered, trying to aim for the same spot again, hoping maybe he could weaken it enough that...

Whatever he was hoping, the powered armor moved faster than his trigger finger. The last thing Abel Freeman saw was a massive, metal fist swinging downward at his head, blotting out the light forever.

———

Kan-Ten nearly plowed his battlesuit into the pavement of the loading ramp as he stumbled through the jagged rent he'd made in the garage door, and it took him two or three stomping, jolting steps before he regained his balance. The picture the helmet was painting for him was abstract and difficult to read, and it was a long moment before his mind began to filter it through his senses in the old way, to make sense of the data input and translate it into an image he could interpret. It was well before dawn, but the glare of the security floodlights around him were brighter than mid-day, and they illuminated the finest detail of the line of *La Sombra* fighting positions on the defensive wall that guarded the Constabulary's perimeter.

He was looking up at them from the bottom of the ramp; the garage entrance was sunken nearly a full story below ground level and steps led up another two meters to the fighting positions set in the ten-centimeter-thick duralloy reinforced concrete of the wall. There were two soldiers in each of them, armed with weapons stolen from his people, firing out at the forces Sandi and Ash had brought with them from the asteroid belt. He remembered that Jordi used to stress uniformity, professionalism, each soldier in the same khaki fatigues, carrying the same weapon. These troops were dressed in piecemeal bits of civilian clothes and old military uniforms and whatever else they'd come across that struck their fancy, like the criminal gang they were, rather than the army Jordi Abdullah had wanted them to be. If Kan-Ten had as much as a light KE-gun, he could have killed every one of them in minutes.

As Fontenot says, I guess we'll have to do this the hard way.

The turbines screamed, loud and close enough that their vibration blurred his vision, and the armor bounced upward shoulder first, straight into the nearest fighting position. The suit slammed into the unyielding concrete of the wall hard enough to crack it, hard enough to bounce Kan-Ten's head off of the padded lining inside the helmet, but between armored shoulder and reinforced wall was the fragile form of a human. Bones splintered and organs ruptured and what slid down off the edge of the platform was bent and folded in ways no human body ever should have. Kan-Ten couldn't tell if the thing had been a male or female, could barely tell it had ever been alive.

The other cartel soldier in the fighting position was screaming, face covered in blood and contorted in horror, his KE-gun hanging forgotten in one hand. He tried to jump off the platform, desperate to get away from the leering metal golem, but Kan-Ten lashed out with instincts he'd forgotten he had, grabbing the human by the skull and catching him in mid-air, his legs dangling down, kicking helplessly. Kan-Ten squeezed his hand into a fist and the skull burst between his fingers. He let what was left of the human drop the two meters down to the pavement, not looking at it, grateful the suit didn't pass actual sensations through the skin of the giant, metal fist, not because he feared it would fill him with revulsion...but because he feared it wouldn't.

The suit teetered on the ledge of the fighting platform and Kan-Ten grabbed at the top of the wall, steadying himself as he looked out across the open fields between the Constabulary and the spaceport. He knew the mercenaries Ash and Sandi had brought in were out there, but he couldn't pick them out on thermal or infrared, not even with the security floodlights blazing; whatever stealth armor they were using, it worked superbly. Their weapons were low signature as well, probably the Gauss rifles the Commonwealth Marines had used during the war; he heard the loud cracks of electromagnetically launched slugs smacking into the wall all around, but there was no trace of their source.

What he *could* see, jagged and angular and half-buried in a mound of plowed-up dirt, was the lander that had brought the mercenaries down from orbit. It lay twisted, and shattered, and inverted a hundred meters or so away from the wall, smoke roiling up from the tattered and shredded portside wing.

He was frozen with indecision for a moment. He knew that either Sandi or Ash would have insisted on flying the lander, which meant one of them could be out there, trapped inside the wrecked aerospacecraft. But he also knew that the mercenaries they'd brought in to take the fortress wouldn't have a chance of making it past the wall without his help. He decided that Ash or Sandi, or whoever was flying the lander would have wanted him to put the success of the mission first. Though, he realized, if it was Ash in the lander, Sandi would want Kan-Ten to rescue him, and vice versa.

Tahni didn't have the same concept of profanity that humans did, but he'd picked it up from Fontenot over the last few years, and it felt very satisfying at times such as these.

"Shit."

He knew what he was going to do: he'd take out the next two fighting positions, make a gap in the defenses the attackers could exploit, then he'd go check on the pilot while the defenders were occupied. That felt correct, ethically and tactically, like something Fontenot would do; he was flexing the knees of the suit, getting ready for a jump to the next platform over, when he glanced back down at the cargo ramp and froze in place.

The Matriarch was climbing through the hole he'd made in the garage door, clumsy and awkward, her robes catching on the jagged edges, everything about her face and her carriage speaking clearly of desperation and panic. Someone was chasing her.

"Shit," he said again, this time trying to put the exasperated tone into it that he'd heard from Sandi. She was almost as good at profanity as Fontenot.

The old female pulled free of the door, leaving scraps of cloth from her robes hanging on the jagged edges, and ran up the ramp to the walkway that circled behind the wall, heading off to his left. Maybe, he thought, she would be okay. The cartel soldiers from that side would be coming towards the garage to meet the attack...

There was a sound like a lost soul crying out in despair as the metal of the garage door was torn and ripped like paper along the length of the hole, and the other battlesuit exploded through the gap, arms spread, blades extended. He didn't have to guess who was inside it; no one else could use it, no one else would still have the control suit and be in a position to have access to the thing. It was Vala-Kel, and he was turning on his heel, poised to lurch off in pursuit of the Matriarch, and suddenly there was no doubt at all what Kan-Ten's priorities should be.

He activated the helmet's external speakers and bellowed loud enough to echo off the fortress walls and across the plains.

"Vala-Kel!"

The oversized caricature of a humanoid paused in mid-step, staring up at him in a stance that bespoke disbelief.

"Kan-Ten," Vala-Kel's amplified voice boomed upward, its tone almost jovial. "How appropriate."

Kan-Ten extended the vibro-cutters from his armor's wrists, then leapt off the ledge of the fighting platform to meet his old comrade one last time.

CHAPTER NINETEEN

Korri Fontenot tasted metal and blood, and smelled burnt hair and flesh. Someone was carrying her, she realized, and she didn't *want* to be carried; she thrashed and struck out, but something just as strong as her grabbed her arms and held fast, and lowered her gradually to her feet. She opened her eyes...well, her eye. The other one was "open" semi-permanently, but she'd been ignoring what it was telling her.

She was in a dimly-lit corridor somewhere inside the Constabulary, and Jagmeet Singh held her forearms tightly, concern in his dark eyes. His sideburns had been mostly singed away along with his eyebrows, and she could see a raw, open burn on his neck. His armored jacket had held up, but leather had been charred away from the duralloy lining beneath it all across his right shoulder.

"Jesus," she mumbled, her mouth dry. "How bad do *I* look?"

"Well," he allowed with a philosophical shrug, "you're gonna' need some new synthskin, but the parts of you that were flesh and blood are still pretty much flesh and blood, so I think you'll be all right. As long as you don't get a brain bleed from the concussion before we get you to an auto-doc."

She pulled away from him and looked down at herself; the sleeves had been burned off both her arms, along with most of the synthskin that had covered her bionics. The bare, silvery metal seemed odd to her, somehow, despite the decades she'd had to grow used to it. Wearing the biomechanical cover over the cybernetics these last couple of years hadn't just changed how she looked, it had changed how she thought about herself. The idea made her uncomfortable, and she shoved it aside, looking around for her Gauss pistol and not finding it.

"Where's my gun?" she wondered aloud, then glanced around again at the featureless hallway. She felt momentarily dizzy, and only her bionics' internal gyros kept her from stumbling. "And where the hell are we?" Another look behind them, and again in front; no one was in sight. "And where's Kan-Ten and Freeman?"

"I don't know," Singh admitted. "After Jordi fired that fucking Tahni whatever-the-hell-it-was, the two of us were on one side of a bunch of burning shit, and they were on the other and I couldn't find my gun, or your gun, or anything but you, and you were basically on fire." He shook his head, seeming a bit embarrassed if she was any judge of men. "I got you the hell out of there, figured we could regroup when you were conscious again."

She wanted to berate him for a coward, wanted to yell at him for abandoning her friends, but she couldn't bring herself to do it. She didn't know Singh all that well, but in all her experience, she'd never known him to show fear for his own safety. Which meant he'd been afraid for *her*, and that thought was so odd that she simply put it aside. She patted at her belt, was surprised to find her 'link still there and still intact.

"I'm not synched with Freeman," she explained, scrolling through screens until she found the right one, "but I should be able to tell where Kan-Ten is, assuming he didn't damage or lose his 'link."

A map of the building and the area around it projected out of her 'link and onto the wall, and she could see the green dot that represented the Tahni's datalink; it was outside the building and moving...fast.

"The action's out there," she said, shutting off the projection. "And we should be, too."

Singh grinned crookedly.

"Honest to God, Fontenot," he said, "if it weren't for all the shit where we were trying to kill each other for a couple years, I might kiss you."

She grabbed him by the back of the neck and pulled him into a quick kiss, and he was too surprised to resist.

"I've lived a long time, Singh," she told him, letting him go and heading down the hall. "If I ruled out everyone who'd tried to kill me, I'd never get a date."

———

"God damn it, we can't just sit here!" Sgt. Arkala muttered, ducking instinctively as another burst of tantalum needles tore up the sand and rock only a meter ahead of her.

She'd left her helmet comms on the command frequency and hadn't realized it, Jacobson thought. Well, he was giving her the benefit of the doubt there; otherwise, she was showing poor discipline and judgement by whining in front of her platoon leader.

Slightly in front, he thought with a touch of irreverence, *and a bit to the right.*

Her squad, First, was arrayed in a broad arrowhead, with her at the center and him just behind, while Second was out to their right in another wedge-shaped formation. His Platoon

Sergeant had gone with the other squads in the lander that was hitting the reactor, and he hoped the man was having an easier time of it than they were. He glanced back at the wreckage of the lander and winced. It was possible Commander Hollande was alive back there, but if he sent his people to get her out, they'd be cut to pieces.

"Sgt. Arkala," Jacobson chided gently, aiming his Gauss rifle as he spoke, and carefully firing off a round that actually grazed the emitter of one of the cartel KE-guns, sending up a shower of sparks and making the man withdraw back beneath the rim of his firing position. "If we charge that wall willy-nilly, this stealth armor won't do a damn bit of good; they'll see us in two seconds and we'll all be dead."

It was a good thing Captain Alcala had the foresight and initiative to bring the Gauss rifles along in the *Warlock's* armory; this mission was supposed to be all low-gravity or micro-gravity, which was why they'd gone with pulse carbines. Firing a high-signature weapon like that down here would have been like tacking a "Please shoot me" sign on their backs. When the Captain had told him about the electromagnetic slug-shooters, Jacobson had felt like his birthday had come early.

"Second Squad," he transmitted to Sgt. Petrucci, off to his right, "move up ten meters, maximum stealth speed."

That wasn't just a buzzword, it was a calculated speed of how fast these suits could move in certain light conditions without being seen. They were expensive, and uncomfortable, and not as effective as regular armor at actually protecting them from projectiles, but the light-bending, sensor-absorbent tech made it a trade-off he was happy to accept at the moment.

"Moving," Petrucci confirmed.

"First, lay down covering fire," he added.

Privately, he agreed with Arkala; this was taking way too long, and the longer it took, the more could go wrong. They didn't have air cover anymore, and *damn it*, someone was supposed to break through that garage door and give them an opening...

Something moved on the wall, something *big*. Jacobson zoomed in with his helmet optics, focusing on the fighting position at their 12 o'clock, the one that had been pinning them down for minutes now. A gargoyle figure loomed over it, towering a meter above the edge of the parapet, grey and massive and splashed with patches of dark red fluid that might have been blood. It was, he realized with a sudden clenching of his gut, a Tahni High Guard battlesuit. He hadn't seen one since the war, but it wasn't something you'd forget.

Shit.

He kept the curse silent and private with a great deal of effort. If the cartel had scrounged up battlesuits, they were all as good as dead; the Gauss rifles wouldn't even scratch their paint. He was about to order a general withdrawal, but paused as the powered armor suit shifted, raising its oversized left arm. Something dangled from the fist, jerking and thrashing wildly, something that looked very much like a person. Jacobson's eyes went wide when he saw the blood squirt through the claw-like fingers, saw the dangling figure go still. The mechanical hand opened and Jacobson felt his mouth curl in a scowl of revulsion at what was left of the man's head.

The body dropped below the parapet, and a few moments later, the battlesuit followed it...and that entire section of the wall was left undefended. His lips skinned away from his teeth, and he felt the wolf rise in his heart.

"Everybody up!" he yelled, levering himself to his feet with the butt of his rifle, running forward. "Follow me!"

When he'd come of age and gone to the house of his father for his naming ceremony, Kan-Ten had been surrounded by a group of newly-named boys in a corner of the courtyard and pummeled by each of them in turn. This, too, was a ceremony of sorts, though not one he'd been expecting. He'd tried to fight back, but there had been too many of them. They hadn't seriously injured him, but it had been painful, and terrifying, and he'd thought it would never end.

This had the same nightmarish feel to it, the bare walls and barren ground that surrounded them, blocking off the rest of the world, the sense that it would never end, that his blows were ineffectual. He knew it wasn't true, that his strikes were just as strong as Vala-Kel's, that his old comrade felt the same dull ache from each impact of armored fist on armored helmet or chest; but it seemed that the featureless face was unchanging, unaffected. It glowered at him like one of the Angry Spirits in his father's stories, the reflected floodlights from the walls painting phantom images across the tinted, transparent metal.

Kan-Ten's head jerked to the side as a forearm slammed into his helmet, but he clutched at it, trapping the arm against his right shoulder and yanking backwards. He felt Vala-Kel go off-balance and he tried to slice upward with the vibro-cutter on his left wrist, but talons of steel clamped down on his left forearm, unyielding. They were locked together, neither willing to turn loose, each pulling the other a fraction of a step in one direction or the other. Metal pads scraped pavement with a nerve-grinding screech that seemed to echo inside his head, and Kan-Ten reared back and slammed his helmet into Vala-Kel's with as much power as the servos would give him.

The crown of his helmet struck in the center of the other male's visor and this time, he could feel it sink in, could feel the crack splinter outward from the impact. Vala-Kel stumbled backwards, his hold slipping, and Kan-Ten tried to surge forward, yanking his wrist free and plunging his vibro-cutter downward. Vala-Kel interposed his suit's right leg, bracing on the left and leaning into Kan-Ten's chest with the footpad, then pushing off, with a blast of superheated air from his jump-jets adding to the shove.

Kan-Ten felt himself flying backwards, and he had a brief thought to use his jets to right himself, but it was too late; he had already lost his center of balance, and when the weight of the massive suit hit the pavement, he could feel the surface crack beneath him. His head and shoulders slammed into the padding that lined the suit and the breath went out of him in a whoosh, as stars filled his vision.

Movement. He had to move; to indulge in his pain would ensure its quick end. Vala-Kel would be righting himself, leaping for the kill stroke; he could feel it even if he couldn't see it, playing out in his mind's eye like the animation from an instructional text at the Warriors' School. The suit jets would be firing; he'd be using them to boost himself off the ground, building the momentum he'd need to crack the armor with his vibro-cutter. He couldn't use his own jets, not with his back flat on the ground, didn't have time to roll off to the side, wouldn't have the leverage to block the blow.

There was one thing left to do, as obvious as it was insane; he brought his knees up to his chest, his feet outstretched. His control singlet read the motions and made the suit move in conjunction with his body, the tree-trunk legs swinging upward, the footpads meeting Vala-Kel's heavily armored chest as it descended, sending a ringing gong echoing off the fortress walls. The reverberating tone was loud enough that it nearly drowned out the gunshot snap as his right leg broke at the calf. Kan-Ten screamed, unable to hold it in as he followed through despite the agony, and tossed Vala-Kel backwards off of him, somersaulting his own armor to land heavily on its stomach on the pavement.

He was vaguely aware of the other battlesuit pinwheeling through the air, out of control, in an arc abruptly interrupted by the bare, grey wall of the fortress nearly five meters up. Kan-Ten was gasping, his own grunts of helpless pain drowning out the flat crump of metal on concrete, though the small part of his brain still able to concentrate noticed the impact crater in the wall, the splintered concrete sending clouds of white powder billowing outward. The suit slid down, scoring the grey with streaks of white until it landed heavily on its feet, swaying as the automatic gyros kept it upright.

Warning lights flashed at the edges of his vision, cautions that the suit's leg servos were badly damaged, barely operational. Kan-Ten forced himself to stand despite the agonizing pressure it put on his leg; at least the suit did the work, he just had to bear the pain.

"Pain is the enemy of weakness," he quoted to himself, bringing his breathing under control. "Pain is the ally of the Warrior."

These were the words of the Songs of the Path, the Will of the True Emperor...the words felt right, felt natural. Yet the True Emperor had deserted them; his promises were lies, his priests cowards, and his generals traitors. But perhaps truth remained truth even if couched in lies. The Imperium was dead, and it would never return; he'd known that since before the end of the war. But perhaps the Path had its own benefit even after the death of the society it had built, benefits that didn't require another Emperor to realize.

The steps of Kan-Ten's suit were jerky and hesitant, mirrors of his own motions, as if the armor felt his pain as well as its own damage. He shuffled resolutely, knowing his physical body and its mechanical counterpart wouldn't survive another clash like the last. The warnings in his helmet had gone from cautions of potential failure to portents of imminent doom in just a few steps on the strained joints.

Vala-Kel stood stock-still, his visor flat and unreflective from the star fractures in its surface, his chest plastrons dented inward from the unbelievable force that had broken Kan-Ten's leg even through the duralloy armor.

I hope he hurts as much as I do.

He hesitated in front of the motionless battlesuit, wondering if it was a trick, if Vala-Kel were waiting until he was close enough to deliver one last, debilitating blow. One step closer, yet still nothing. He reached up with the vibro-cutter on his right wrist, feeling the hum in the air as it activated, holding it just in front of Vala-Kel's helmet.

There was a barely-audible pop from explosive bolts, and the damaged visor abruptly fell away, along with the rest of the front half of Vala-Kel's helmet. It was, Kan-Ten knew, part of the suit's emergency medical systems, designed to make the wearer accessible for instant treatment if the primary chest access was damaged...which it was. Vala-Kel's head looked absurdly tiny inside the monstrous confines of the suit, resting against the padding at the side of what was left of the helmet, gasping fitfully for breath.

Blood caked his face from a jagged fracture in his brow ridge, but that was superficial. The foam-flecked blood that spewed from his mouth when he coughed out a breath wasn't.

Broken sternum, he thought clinically. *Pierced lung. Maybe internal bleeding.* You didn't dent the chest armor on a battlesuit without doing nasty things to the warrior inside. He felt something close to amusement. What was it that Sandi said when she fired on a ship? Something like "this is going to hurt you worse than it hurts me."

Vala-Kel tried to lift his head, tried to face him.

"You always were the best of us," he gurgled around the blood. "Why did you leave?"

The tone was the hurt of an abandoned child, and Kan-Ten had the sense that perhaps that was exactly what his old friend was. Kan-Ten had taken the pain of the betrayal, of the death of all they'd ever known, and run as far away as he could. Vala-Kel had tried to fight it head-on, but the Tahni no longer wanted to fight that war. It had been lost, and Vala-Kel had been lost with it.

He had no answer for the warrior who had once been his comrade, his brother. All he had for him was an end to the pain.

The cutter didn't slow as it passed through Vala-Kel's head.

Kan-Ten let his arm drop away, feeling the air go out of him. He tried to turn back the way he'd come, to go help his friends, but the suit locked itself into place as the servos in the hip and knee and ankle failed. If it moved another step, it would fall, and the safety systems wouldn't let that happen.

My part in this fight is done, he realized.

He hit the release for the chest access hatch and waited patiently for it to descend. His leg throbbed as he slowly and carefully drew it out of the armor, keeping it straight and loose as he lowered himself to the ground. He'd have to get it treated and set once this was all over...assuming he lived, and they'd won.

Right now, though, he needed to find the Matriarch and ensure that she was safe. He hobbled unsteadily, one hand against the wall of the Constabulary.

"Perhaps," he mused aloud, "I have run far enough."

CHAPTER TWENTY

JORDI ABDULLAH STARED AT THE SPENT MAGAZINE FOR A moment before he tossed it to the floor. The plastic clattered spitefully, mocking him with its hollow emptiness. Jordi glanced around instinctively, but the narrow hallway was empty, deserted. He checked his chest pouches one last time and found no more spares.

"Damn," he said mildly, as if it were a minor inconvenience.

He weighed the carbine in his hands, judging it for its utility as a club, then tossed it away as well. The sound it made was solid, substantial, metallic...disappointed, disdainful, telling him he'd regret leaving it behind. He should have taken the time to grab some spare magazines off of Medina's body, he knew. Or maybe he should have tried carrying more ammo instead of that Tahni blaster that weighed thirty kilograms and only lasted two shots before it shit the bed...and wound up killing one of his own guys in the explosion from that last round that had hit the rover and basically set the whole garage on fire.

It had *looked* so damn impressive though...

He sighed and pulled his handgun from its holster. It wasn't much against the Gauss rifles the mercenary troops were carrying, but maybe he could scavenge a Tahni KE-gun off of one of his own soldiers. There were plenty of them lying around. The mercenaries Hollande had brought in had bulldozed through them, illustrating, he thought bitterly, the difference between trained soldiers and hired thugs.

"It's your own fault, you stupid motherfucker."

His head snapped around to where the voice had seemed to originate, the gun moving with it, but there was no one in the darkened hallway. He turned back the way he'd been walking and saw his father standing there, arms crossed over his chest. He was a gaunt, sharp-edged man with a face like a hatchet blade, crisscrossed by a network of scars partially hidden by his thickly-curled dark beard. His eyes were dead black, as dead as they'd been the night Jordi had put a bullet through his head and taken over *La Sombra*.

Jordi felt at the drug patch he'd left on his neck.

Too much, he thought, picking at it, trying to pull it free. *I did too much.*

"You think it's the drugs, you little shit?" He laughed, circling around Jordi, shadowed eyes never seeming to move. "You think I need the drugs to get to you?"

Jordi's fingers tightened on the grip of his pistol, but he didn't bother to point it at the image of Malcolm Abdullah. He was an apparition, a ghost, already dead once.

"You think you could have done better, you worthless old fuck?" he demanded, knowing the futility of the question but asking it anyway. "You think you could have taken on all the other cartels at once and come out on top?"

"It wasn't the cartels that brought you down, little man." Jordi felt himself bristle at that, just like old times. He'd always hated when his father had called him "little man." "It was that bitch Hollande. You fucked up when you didn't kill her."

"I know I did." The admission hurt less since he knew he

was really making it to himself. "But what the hell can I do about it now?" He shook his head. "It's all over."

"She's out there somewhere, boy." The old man leered, baring yellowed, chipped teeth. "Go make sure she doesn't live to brag about how she got the best of you. Carve your fucking initials into her corpse."

Jordi grinned at the thought, vaguely realizing that if anyone was watching him, they'd think his expression was insane.

"Boss?"

Now he did raise his pistol, finger tightening towards the trigger pad, but hesitated when he saw that the half-dozen armed and armored figures approaching down the hallway were his people. The one in the lead was a woman, her hair twisted into twin braids, a holographic tattoo of storm clouds running across her left cheek. Her name was...

"Kessel." He frowned, lowering his weapon. "Where did you come from?"

"I think everyone else is dead, boss," she said hesitantly, trying not to point the muzzle of her carbine at him. The others seemed afraid to speak. "We were trying to stay clear of those mercs, hoping they'd give us a way out." She looked around uncertainly. "Is this a way out?"

Jordi looked behind him. The apparition of his father was gone, though it seemed less that he'd vanished and more that he'd simply stepped away.

"Yeah," he told her, nodding slowly. "This is the way out." He motioned down the hallway. "Come with me."

———

Ash hurt everywhere. The g-forces battered him from all sides, overwhelming the comforting cushion of the acceleration couch, overwhelming the sensory separation of the interface, too insistent to be ignored. There was the laser again, playing across his starboard wing, and he had to roll into a spin to keep it from focusing long enough to do serious damage.

Wincing in anticipation, he yanked back the nose, climbing into a barrel roll that took him to the edge of the atmosphere, hoping he could, at last, get the shuttle off his tail. It clung, it *latched*, a remora on a shark, just too damned maneuverable here in the soup for him to shake it. The planet passed by beneath them, a curved stretch of ruddy brown, deep blue and pale green, nearly forgotten in its irrelevance, a backdrop to the chase, and nothing else. The star Belenus was up where they were, and he vaguely realized that sunrise had been hours away when the fight had started.

He had to get back; he'd let the shuttle drag him away from the battlefield, drag him away from any possible air support. God only knew what was happening back in Gennich, and no one was answering their comms.

Well, there's one thing I haven't tried yet, he mused, a rueful grin twisting across his face in what felt more like a grimace.

He threw the *Acheron* into a dive, throttling back slightly, letting the shuttle close the distance between them to less than a kilometer. The shuttle opened fire with its jury-rigged mining laser, and yellow warning lights flashed in the perimeter of his perceptions as the rear armor began to heat up. He checked his altitude: five kilometers and descending fast. He sucked in a breath, then cut the engines and felt his stomach flip-flop at the sudden sensation of free-falling.

He didn't hesitate; the other pilot was good, better than most of Jordi's amateur pilot; and if he waited, this guy would twig to it quick. A combination of control surfaces and the judicious use of maneuvering thrusters spun the ship around lengthwise, then a burst of attitude jets to keep it stable, falling backwards, for just long enough to line up the targeting reticle over the nose of the shuttle. The bird was already moving, already trying to pull out of the dive, the pilot figuring out the maneuver faster than he'd thought.

The proton cannon fired. The shuttle was less than three hundred meters away, nearly point-blank for the ship-to-ship weapon, and when the blast hit, the bird simply ceased to be. The explosion was so close it whited out the cameras, filling his view with the light of a second sun; the shock wave hit a moment after, and suddenly, the *Acheron* wasn't stable anymore, wasn't just falling. It was spinning, a flat spin that threw Ash forward against his restraints with g-forces that would have made him pass out immediately without the buffer of the interface; even with it, he had to scratch and claw at consciousness.

Belly jets...he had the thought and they fired, together with the bow and stern maneuvering thrusters, and the ship groaned and grumbled and roared as the spin turned into an unsteady hover, only 800 meters above a rugged mountain range basking in the golden light of dawn. Caution lights were flashing again, warning him of structural strain that would need to be repaired before any more high-g maneuvers, warning him of possible stress to the vectored thrust nozzles.

The *Acheron* wasn't indestructible, even though they treated her like she was.

"Yeah, yeah, girl, I know," he mumbled, spinning the cutter end for end. "Later."

Acceleration, one last time. He ran away from the dawn, chasing the night.

———

"Poor son of a bitch," Singh muttered. Fontenot nodded silent agreement.

It had taken them a while to make their way back to the garage, and the fires had mostly burned out, the smoke clearing through the gaping rent in the garage door. Abel Freeman's corpse was sprawled not too far from that door, though the only way they could identify him was from his clothes. His head was gone, smashed to jelly, and Fontenot wondered what could have done it...until she noticed what was missing from the garage floor.

"Shit, the battlesuits," she said, gesturing. She saw comprehension in Singh's eyes as he stared at the place the powered armor had been standing.

Fontenot broke into a run, leaping through the gap in the metal roll-up door, large enough that one of the suits had to have made it. She sprinted up the loading dock ramp...and then stopped abruptly, hearing Singh skidding to a halt behind her. Two more bodies, these obviously Jordi's people, one with...his? her?...head crushed to a pulp, the other flattened as if he'd been hit by a cargo truck.

She frowned in confusion for just a moment, wondering why Vala-Kel, who was ostensibly Jordi's ally, would kill his men. A light went on behind her eyes and suddenly she understood that Kan-Ten had one of the suits. Nothing else made any sense.

"Kan-Ten?" she called over her 'link. There was no answer.

She gritted her teeth and picked up the KE-guns the dead soldiers had dropped, ignoring the blood and bone fragments splattered on them, and handed one to Singh. His lip curled in distaste, but he took the proffered weapon and tucked it under his arm, wrapping his fingers around the unfamiliar and alien firing grip. Fontenot looked up and down the perimeter wall, but saw no sign of friend or foe, though the pockmarks on the side of the fortress behind the wall told a story of Gauss rifle rounds burying themselves in ten centimeters of reinforced concrete.

"Where the hell is everybody?" Singh wondered.

"They retreated from the wall," Fontenot guessed. "The fighting probably went inside, or else the mercs followed them around the other side of the building." She cocked her head, listening for the sounds of battle with her cybernetically-enhanced left ear, but heard nothing. "I think it's over."

She jumped the two meters up to the fighting platform in one bound, grabbing at the edge of the wall for purchase, and Singh followed just as easily.

"What the fuck?" Fontenot blurted, seeing the crashed troop lander immediately, clearly visible in the security lights still burning along the roofline of the Constabulary. She felt a cold pit in her stomach as she realized that Sandi or Ash would be inside that thing...likely Sandi, if she knew the woman at all. "We've got to get down there..."

She moved without thinking, lunging forward, ready to throw herself down off the wall; Singh grabbed her by the collar and jerked her back a half-second ahead of a burst of tantalum needles that would have decapitated her. They spent themselves against the inner edge of the parapet instead, and she threw an arm up to protect her face from the spray of concrete fragments that exploded outward from it. She spat out concrete dust, yanking away from Singh's hand with an angry glare, but quickly reining herself in as she realized he'd saved her life.

"There are seven of them down there." He gestured at the wall, keeping his back against it as streams of metal slivers chewed away at the parapet, their impacts a staccato jackhammer that vibrated through the thick, metal-reinforced wall. "Moving west." He indicated the direction straight away from the garage door, toward the landing field. "One of them is Jordi Abdullah."

"You got that all in two seconds?" she asked, cocking an eyebrow at him as she checked the unfamiliar controls on the KE-gun to make sure her fingers were still positioned correctly.

"I'm very observant."

The firing died off, the rainstorm of projectiles slowing to a patter, then going silent.

Fontenot exchanged a look with Singh, then surged upward over the parapet and swung the muzzle of her borrowed weapon downward. She could see them jogging quickly across the open plain in a ragged line, heading straight for the wrecked lander, Jordi Abdullah at the front. He was nearly a hundred meters away, but she couldn't mistake him for anyone else; his face was burned into her brain. She tried for just a fraction of a second to put the rifle's targeting optics over his retreating figure, but gave up on it almost immediately; they were too different, built for eyes that didn't focus quite the same as a human's.

Have to use Kentucky Windage.

She leveled the weapon toward Jordi as best she could with no sights and had the sudden, prescient thought, *There's only five of them down there. Singh said seven.*

She ducked her head instinctively, jamming the KE-gun muzzle off to her right one-handed in her left arm and holding down the firing stud. The gun shook and bucked wildly in her grasp as it fired off a brief burst, then she felt a powerful, wrenching jolt in her left shoulder, saw a shower of yellow sparks. Suddenly, she was off-balance, falling backwards helpless to stop herself. Singh lurched forward, trying to catch her, and she wanted to extend her left hand to grab his...but her left hand wasn't there.

Two meters' worth of gravity drove her into the ground below, hitting on the metal of her right shoulder, but with enough force to crack her head against the pavement. Stars sparked in her vision and she cursed reflexively, knowing that

Jordi had dropped two of his troops back to guard the rear, and she'd fallen for it, quite literally. She tried to bring her left arm up to assess the damage, but it had been severed below the bicep, taking the isotope power pack on that side with it. Jagged metal and ceramic trailed threads of superconductive wiring at the very end of the bicep, but she couldn't see anything past that, couldn't see her shoulder, and it seemed like she had to twist her head around way too far just to get that much of a view...there was a blind spot that took up her whole left side.

She abruptly realized that her left eye had gone dark, the power to it cut when she'd lost the battery in her arm. She rolled to her right, pushing herself to her feet. At least her leg was on a separate power source, or else she wouldn't have been able to move at all.

Singh had dropped down beside her, looking as if he wanted to offer her help but had thought better of it.

Smart man.

"We have to get out there," she said, her words coming out slurred; she couldn't open her mouth all the way with the left side of her jaw unpowered. Her voice sounded muffled, like her ears were stuffed up and needed to be popped, and she knew that was from her cybernetic audio pickup not working.

"Get up." She glanced up with her right eye since she couldn't nod. "Give me cover, I'll jump the wall."

"Forget it," Singh declared flatly. "You're half the woman you used to be...about ten seconds ago."

She felt her temper flaring up, but he forestalled it by shoving his KE-gun at her. Her own had toppled over the wall along with half her arm. She took it by reflex, turning it awkwardly, one-handed, bracing it against her hip until she found the grip.

"You get up there," he suggested, "stick this over the side and open up." He waved demonstratively. "I'll go after Jordi."

"You don't have a gun," she reminded him, the Tahni weapon wobbling in place as she tried to steady it with her right hand, her center of balance off from what she'd grown used to over decades.

"I'll figure something out," Sing assured her, grinning crookedly. "I'll call you when I'm ready."

Before she could argue any more, he took off running down to the next fighting position, fifty meters farther down the wall. She cursed silently, since it was too much effort to talk, and looked up at the fighting platform. There was no way in hell she was going to be able to climb up to it without using her hand. She crouched, then leapt, trying to lean forward since she couldn't count on her arms for balance. Her right shoulder crunched against the interior of the recessed platform, smearing the wet, red stain where one of its former inhabitants had been messily killed, and she scrambled to find purchase with her feet before she fell back down again.

She found her balance and gasped in a breath, feeling the muscles on the biological half of her face tick spasmodically from the strain of moving the metal hinges of the left side of her jaw manually.

I'm half-blind, half-deaf, and mostly useless, she grumbled, crouching just below the edge of the parapet, waiting for the signal from the bounty hunter.

"Now." The word sounded tinny and artificial over the external speaker of her 'link, but the receiver in her cybernetic ear was useless, and the communications device knew it.

More cautious this time, she peeked the muzzle of the KE-gun over the edge of the wall, exposing as little of her arm as possible, and began spraying random gunfire in the general direction of the two sentinels Jordi had left behind. The answer was immediate, and two KE-guns could put out an impressive volume of fire; she jerked her weapon back over the ledge after feeling at least two tantalum needles strike its cooling jacket. Another three quick bursts dug into the wall in sprays of dust and fragments, then both fell silent.

"Let's go."

Singh's voice over the 'link startled her, but she didn't hesitate; she jumped up and stepped off the top of the wall, the night streaking past her as she fell the four meters, holding the Tahni weapon out to the side for a counterweight. The impact was jarring, even with the shock-absorption built into her bionic legs, and she had to roll forward into a crouch to keep from simply falling on her face. She scanned the horizon carefully, expecting Jordi and his group to stop and take a shot at her, but there was a slight rise in the ground just outside the wall, and she was sheltered from their line of sight.

Singh was twenty yards away, even with her on this side of the rise, kneeling over the corpse of one of Jordi's soldiers, stripping it of its weapons. It took her a moment to realize that the dead man's head was turned around 180 degrees from his chest. The second sentry was less grotesque, if no less dead. She had a combat knife buried in the base of her skull all the way to the hilt, and her eyes were still open, a dull expression of surprise on her tattooed face. Her KE-gun lay just past her outstretched and strengthless fingers, but the drum had been ejected and Fontenot could see it was empty.

Singh stood, a newly-procured Tahni KE-gun in his right hand, braced on his hip, a Pirate World-fabricated rocket pistol extended toward her. She tried to shake her head, then stopped.

"Got a gun," she mumbled, gesturing with the KE-gun.

"It's fried," he told her, nodding at the muzzle end.

She turned it toward her good eye and saw that one of the rounds that had struck it had peeled away part of the cooling jacket. She could see the electromagnetic coil beneath, and what was visible of it was blackened and charred.

Damn.

She tossed the heavy weapon down in disgust and took the pistol from Singh.

Easier to shoot one-handed anyway.

As Singh shifted his rifle, Fontenot noticed a slice through his armored jacket on the right side, over his ribs. She frowned and stuck her pistol in her belt to free up her hand. He tried to pull away when she reached for it, but she drew it back and saw blood welling from a tear in the shirt beneath. He'd been shot. She looked at him and he shrugged.

"It hurts," he admitted, "but it's not going to kill me unless something helps it."

She snorted and let the jacket go.

Singh took the lead, without her having to tell him why: she was half-blind and had no IR or thermal without her bionic eye, not to mention he had the more effective weapon. She hoped to hell someone in Gennich did repairs for prosthetics, or it was going to suck riding all the way back to Sylvanus like this.

Or just being dead. That would suck, too.

They topped the rise and she could see immediately that Jordi was almost to the wreckage. Singh didn't wait to be spotted; he took off at a dead sprint and she followed as best she could, her legs just as fast as they ever were, but the change in her weight distribution altering her stride. Ten meters, twenty, thirty, dirt and sand spraying up around the soles of Singh's boots as he drew away slightly.

She couldn't see in the gathering gloom further away from the lights on the wall, couldn't see it when Jordi's troops turned, but she could see Singh dive to the ground, and that was enough of a warning for her to throw herself down. Tantalum hail snapped over her head, a series of high-pitched cracks marking the supersonic passage. Fontenot pushed the pistol out in front of her and fired off three quick rounds, unsure in the dark whether she was actually aiming at anything but not wanting to die with rounds still in her magazine.

Singh must have been shooting too, and more effectively, because suddenly the cartel troops were firing less and running more. She came up on one knee, levelling the pistol and snapping off a shot at one of the fleeing backs, but they were already taking cover behind the broken-off wing of the lander. It had been tossed a good fifteen meters away from the lander when the craft had hit, and it was closer to the cartel soldiers than the rest of the wreckage.

One of them didn't make it; she saw a dark figure go down as the snap-crack of the KE-guns firing filled the air. That still left three of the hired guns…and Jordi. Her vision was adjusting to the lower light out here, and she could just make out the cartel boss's dark jacket flapping in the chill night breeze as he ran toward the cockpit.

Fontenot tried to get up, tried to go after him, but there was a staccato crackle and something slammed into her right leg low, near the calf. She went down, cursing, rolling onto her side and firing back.

"Singh!" she bellowed, the call a distorted wail of desperation. "Get him!"

The bounty hunter was already moving, despite the incoming fire. His KE-gun was out of ammo and he tossed it aside and ran, faster than any normal human could. She could already tell he wouldn't be in time.

CHAPTER TWENTY-ONE

Sandi heard the gunfire and tried again to move; she couldn't, and she screamed in frustration and agony. The sound came out as a rasp, dry and mewling and she hated the weakness of it nearly as much as she hated the fact that she couldn't move and couldn't see. The lack of movement was a physical problem; she was fairly certain that she'd fractured her spine. The lack of vision was more physics: it was dark inside the cockpit, the only illumination the intermittent flashing red of an emergency indicator somewhere back at the control panel.

She was still strapped into her acceleration couch, but it had broken free of its struts in the crash and left her propped up against the portside bulkhead...or maybe it was the starboard, since the lander was inverted. She didn't remember the crash, didn't remember anything until a few minutes ago. How long had it been? She didn't have any way of knowing; the interface cables had yanked out of her implant sockets under impact, and there wasn't much chance the computer was operable anyway. There was blood coating the side of her face; she could feel it there, still wet, but not dripping anymore.

At least she could *feel* her face. She couldn't feel much of anything else, couldn't feel her legs or her arms or anything below her chest, and certainly couldn't move it.

Spinal cord damage, she thought with a fatalistic certainty. Nothing irreparable, *if* someone got her to an auto-doc, got her stabilized before her systems started to shut down.

Should have let Ash fly this bird... But then, *No, I'd rather it was me.*

She felt a wave of agony wash over her, unfocused and generalized, followed by a rush of nausea. She clenched her teeth. If she vomited, it would wind up all over the front of her flight suit, and that wasn't the image she wanted to present to whoever found her, whether it was Jacobson, or Korri, or Ash, or...

She didn't want to think who else it might be.

There was a burst of gunfire, the unmistakable hum-snap-crack of electromagnetic slug-shooters of some kind, closer this time, and then impacts somewhere on the hull of the lander. Groans and creaks as someone's weight was put on some strained section of the lander's fuselage, a bang as some piece of wreckage was thrown out of the way.

Goddammit, if I could just get to my gun...

The dark and shadowy figure that lurched through a gap in the fuselage could have been anyone, but she knew by a gut she couldn't feel anymore that it was no one she wanted to see. A small flashlight snapped on, pointing downward, giving enough light that they could both see each other without blinding either of them.

"Oh, this is perfect."

The voice was as smooth and oily and artificial as the receiver of the pistol in his hand. His depilated head gleamed slightly in the reflected glare of his flashlight, and the shadows made his face seem even more sinister than usual.

"Hello, Sandrine," Jordi Abdullah said with a wolf's smile. "It's so good to see you again."

———

Yellow warning icons had turned to red, the turbines were screaming at him with anguished, overtaxed wails and the hull of the ship was groaning in protest, but Ash ignored them all, ignored the dull ache and the constant pressure that made even breathing difficult. It wouldn't make a damned bit of difference if he arrived two minutes late in a perfectly-functioning ship and fresh as a daisy.

He could see his destination just a few kilometers ahead, and a few more below, a glowing red halo on the satellite map that stretched out before him in his mind's eye. There was nothing in the air, no orbital activity and no communications in or out of the city, nothing he could detect on any of the sensors, as if the whole place was dead, a ghost town. No...there was one signal. It was an emergency beacon, flashing a distress call over and over, automated and low-power...like something you'd find on a troop lander. It pulsed an ugly yellow in the open field between the spaceport and the Constabulary, just where Sandi had been heading to drop off the Savage/Slaughter mercenaries.

He throttled back the jets, almost against his will, as if the speed had been a barrier to dealing with what he might have to see, then banked into a spiral that would take him down over Gennich. The turn was tight, pushing him sideways into the corner of his acceleration couch, but it was the quickest way to bleed velocity, and he needed to be down there.

And there it was. He could see the belly camera feed, the infrared and thermal and everything else blended into a single, seamless picture for him by computer systems working like a mute, inglorious Renoir in the background. The lander was belly-up, one wing ripped off and separate from the rest of the fuselage, but it hadn't exploded…it was basically intact. Someone *could* have lived through that; that was what he tried to tell himself, anyway.

Wait. There, in the cover of the broken-off wing, there were three thermal signatures, human, and another one twenty meters away, this one with the unmistakable glow of isotope power packs dotting bionic prosthetics. That was Korri, and she was shooting at the others. They had to be Jordi's men, and if they were fighting over the lander, then Sandi had to still be inside it.

It was a logical leap, he knew, but it was a straw and he'd be damned if he didn't grasp at it right now.

"Korri," he transmitted. "If you can hear this…"

Korri Fontenot hugged the ground, counting on an almost-imperceptible swell of sandy earth between her and the cartel soldiers sheltered behind the wing to protect her from the insistent bursts of metal shards tearing up the ground only a meter in front of her. Her pistol was empty, Singh was occupied with heading Jordi off before he reached Sandi, and she couldn't see a damned thing with her head buried in the sand. She could only hear half of it, a truncated, mono version of reality, with half the whining snaps of the KE-gun rounds, half the chopping impact into the sandstone just beneath the surface, half the…

She rolled onto her side, eye opening wide.

Half the distant roar of turbojets overhead.

"Korri." The voice was as distant as the jets, coming from her 'link at her belt. "If you can hear this, get away from that wing, 'cause it's not going to be there in ten seconds."

"Oh, shit," she hissed.

She couldn't just get up and run away, not without catching a round or ten in the back. She dropped the useless handgun and began high-crawling backwards, toward the lander, counting on its bulk to shelter her from what was coming.

Ten seconds. It wasn't long enough, it was no time at all... and yet it seemed to stretch forever, and it was only four seconds in when she finally thought, *Fuck it*, and started running.

Five.

The roaring wasn't so distant anymore, it was a rolling thunder just overhead, maybe a few hundred meters up,

Four.

She could see puffs of sand only centimeters from her feet, knew they had to be from enemy fire, but it was too late to stop now.

Three.

High-pitched pings sounded off the fuselage of the lander as she got closer to the tail section; they were shifting fire. Thank God the Tahni guns didn't have usable optics...

Two.

She threw herself forward, hitting on her right shoulder and rolling onto her belly just past the edge of the lander's tail, around the cover of the broken and folded-in vertical stabilizer and then...

One.

She had her eye closed, her arm thrown across her head, but she still saw the flash as clear as if it had gone off inside her head. The ground shook, and the wreckage of the lander rattled in the hurricane-force wind as the shock from the blast travelled outward, and a tornado of sand scoured across her, debris pattering against the fuselage. She shielded her eye and looked back at where the severed section of wing had been; it was gone, swallowed up in roiling steam and a bubbling pool of molten sand. She could feel the heat radiating off of it from behind the body of the lander; of the cartel soldiers, nothing was left but vapors.

"Shit, Ash," she said softly. "It was just three guys."

———

It was just her imagination---the light was too dim, and shining the wrong direction---but Sandi was sure she could see right down the barrel of Jordi's pistol to the miniature warhead affixed to the rocket in the chamber.

"My only regret," the cartel boss said, finger caressing the trigger pad, "is that I don't have time to do a proper job of this. A gun is so much quicker and less painful than you deserve."

"Just get it over with, you fucking drama queen," she sighed, letting her head slump back against the seat. "Or are you gonna' talk me to death?"

Whatever his response might have been to that, it was lost in a flash that flared through the gaps in the fuselage and an explosion that shook the cockpit like a bone in the teeth of a dog, sending Jordi stumbling against the bulkhead. Sandi's acceleration couch slid down to the side, leaving her hanging from the straps of the seat, and she gasped as agony shot through her, the only sensation left that she could feel. She gritted her teeth, trying to clear her vision of the stars that floated across it, and thought she was hallucinating from the pain when she saw the tall, dark figure coming through the crack where the fuselage had split on impact.

But it had to be real; Jordi saw it, too, and fired at it instinctively. The rocket round flared against the black, armored jacket but didn't penetrate, and in the light of its ignition, she saw the absolute last person she'd ever expected to: Jagmeet Singh. The bounty hunter moved fast, faster than he had any right to. Before Jordi could squeeze off another shot, Singh had snatched the gun away, yanking it hard enough that Sandi was sure she heard a couple of the cartel leader's fingers break as it came out of his hand.

Jordi cursed hotly, pulling back his twisted fingers, his eyes wide with shock, and he reached for the knife at his belt with his left hand. He gripped it with the practiced stance of someone who'd fought with it before, the black, leather-wrapped handle between thumb and forefinger. His flashlight had fallen from his grasp when the explosion had shaken the cockpit, and it finally completed its slow, clattering roll across the slanted surface of what had been the overhead and was now the deck, coming to rest in a corner and giving Jordi a clear view of the other man's face.

"Singh," he said in a gasp of disbelief, the knife wavering.

He took a hesitant step back, and Singh took the same step forward, the pistol extended in his right hand.

"The last regret you're ever going to have," the bounty hunter declared, his voice as flat and deadly as his expression, "is sending your hired guns to try to kill me."

Jordi blinked, cocking his head in confusion that made Singh pause in his advance.

"What the fuck are you talking about?" He raised his hands in a peacemaking gesture, though he didn't drop the knife. "I sent you after Hollande and Carpenter, and the next thing I knew, you disappeared for weeks...I thought you were dead! And when you got back, you were killing my people on every outpost you could get to!" Jordi shook his head. "You were my best, for God's sake, why the hell would I try to kill you?"

Singh blinked, thoughts bouncing off of each other behind his dark eyes, and Sandi saw him glance her way, a shadow of suspicion on his face.

"It's true."

Sandi barely recognized Fontenot's voice. It sounded

slurred and ancient, and when the woman emerged from the gap in the fuselage and stepped into the glow of the fallen flashlight, she looked even worse than she sounded. The synthskin was gone from her right arm and peeling off of the other side of her face like she'd been stricken with some sort of skin disease; the metal beneath it was gleaming obscenely in the reflection of the flashlight beam. Her left arm was gone below the shoulder, the ends of it jagged and twisted. She didn't look as if she could take on Jordi right now, much less Singh.

"It was us," the woman admitted, steadying herself against the side of the bulkhead as she stepped up into the cockpit. "Well, we didn't do it, personally. We work with Fleet Intelligence; we told you. Before that mission, the one to find the *Metaurus*, we had asked our handler for help with you; you'd ambushed us in the Pirate Worlds, almost killed us. We wanted you off our backs, and he said he'd take care of it."

Sandi stared at her, horrified. Why the *hell* was she telling Singh this? He was the only thing keeping Jordi from killing her, the only one of them with a gun.

"You knew?" His voice seemed hurt, vulnerable, and Sandi's stare flitted over to him, her mouth falling open.

What the hell?

"I suspected," Fontenot replied. "It wasn't as if I could call and warn you; it was a done deal by then. When I saw you here...well, I wasn't sure if I could trust you at first, and I sure as hell didn't know how you'd react if I told you the truth about the price on your head." There was a look that passed over Fontenot's face, one Sandi hadn't seen there before...regret.

"If I'd known then what I know now, I might have done things differently."

"Singh, come on, man," Jordi urged, interrupting the exchange. His knife seemed more like a pointer now than a weapon and he used it to single out Fontenot. "These fucks lied to you, betrayed you. You have just as much reason to hate them as I do!"

There was desperation in his tone, but cunning in his eyes.

"You kill them both now, and help me get out of here, and I'll transfer you everything I have left in my dummy accounts in the Periphery. That's gotta' be half a million in Corporate Scrip...it's all yours." He grinned with that old Jordi Abdullah cockiness. "Just do one last job for me, let me pay you to do what you want to do anyway. Kill these bitches, and you'll be a rich man."

There was a silence that lasted far too long for Sandi's taste, and shadows played over Singh's face as he looked aside at Fontenot. Finally, he met Jordi's eyes again, his mouth set in a hard line.

"Sorry, Jordi. The man you want to hire is dead."

The gunshot took Sandi by surprise, its target even more so. Jordi Abdullah stumbled backwards into the bulkhead, a third eye punched through his skull between the first two, something dark and wet splattering on the deck behind him. The man who'd once controlled more star systems than any other single individual in the history of the Commonwealth slid down the bulkhead on a trail of blood, and settled to the floor just across from Sandi. She saw a look of startled annoyance on his face, as if he'd suddenly remembered an important engagement and realized he was late for it.

Sandi hissed out a sigh, letting her head rest against the side of the acceleration couch.

"She looks pretty bad," Singh was telling Fontenot. "I think her back's broken." His voice was distant in Sandi's ears, like a conversation on the shore heard from a boat slowly drifting away. "Give me a hand, we need to carry her out of here."

When Fontenot answered, it was a whisper in a sea of

blackness that was closing around Sandi, threatening to pull her beneath it.

"I'll be happy to lend you a hand...since that's all I got left."

There was a jostling, and a shifting, and daggers of agony in her back, and she was sure she passed out more than once. But consciousness was persistent, and finally she saw a face...familiar, she thought. Jacobson. It was Jacobson. He frowned, and pressed something against her neck, something cold and sticky that she barely felt. Her head swam with sudden dizziness and dribs and drabs of sights and sounds blurred and swirled around her in a feverish kaleidoscope.

"...pressure on her spinal cord," she heard a voice that might have been Jacobson's. "Paralysis is temporary for now, but if we..."

"Get her on board." That was Ash, firm and trying to be commanding, but too shaken and concerned to pull it off. "Get her into the auto-doc."

The flurry of light and sound seemed to fade into a featureless background, and warm blankets of sleep buried her in endless comfort, with one, last hazy thought penetrating before all thought was gone: *Ash is going to give me shit for crashing the plane...*

CHAPTER TWENTY-TWO

ASH HELD ONTO HER LIKE HE WAS NEVER GOING TO LET GO. Sandi had the thought that she should push him away, scold him for being so clingy in a public place. After all, it had been over a week since she came out of the auto-doc *en route* to Sylvanus, and he was still constantly holding her hand, touching her like he believed she'd fade away if he let go for too long.

But she didn't scold him, and she didn't push him away, because she understood how he felt, understood the fear she'd put him through, and she wanted him to hold her, even here on a park bench in the Dolabella Memorial Gardens. It was a clear night, warm for this time of year, and hundreds of couples and families and solitary dreamers wandered gravel footpaths lined with flowering trees and looked up at the wonderland of stars. Tonight, she just wanted them to be two of those people, enjoying the night and each other.

Then Captain Fox came along and ruined it all.

"Good evening," he said with a nod and a genial smile, strolling casually down the sidewalk from the park's street entrance. He was dressed in one of his loud, colorful shirts, his hands tucked in the pockets of his baggy, grey shorts like he'd come to Sylvanus for a beach vacation five years ago and never left.

"Why the park?" Sandi asked him, feeling curious.

"The café has a new owner," he confessed, his expression turning morose, as if it were a tragedy. "She changed the menu. Plus," he added, face brightening again, "things are changing for us, as well, and I thought a new venue would be symbolic, somehow."

He glanced around them, his hooded eyes flickering to each shadowy bower of the park. "Where are Fontenot and the Tahni?"

Sandi shared a glance with Ash, letting out a slow breath that was close to a sigh. He shrugged, shorthand for him volunteering to be the one to tell the story.

"Kan-Ten decided to stay on Brigantia," he explained. "He missed being with his own people, I guess. He felt like they needed him there."

"Commendable," Fox allowed, dropping down into a sprawling seat next to them on the bench, taking up about half of it, his arm stretched along the backrest.

Sandi scowled and scooted closer to Ash, the rough wood of the seat scraping against the back of her bare thighs. Fox didn't seem to notice her discomfort, or perhaps that had been his goal.

"But what about our friendly neighborhood cyborg?" he went on. "Don't tell me, let me guess: she stayed too, decided to run for Planetary Constable?"

Sandi started to say something smart-assed, but then reined herself in. Fox did nothing without a reason, at least not when it came to his job. He also didn't ask questions he didn't already know the answer to. He wasn't *really* asking where Fontenot was, he was gauging their attitude about it.

"Korri needed some custom repairs done to her prosthetics," Sandi answered him calmly and factually, not giving him the emotional response he wanted because *fuck him, he should have just come out and asked what he wanted to know.* "She couldn't get it here."

He seemed to be waiting for more, and she noted dissatisfaction in the set of his jaw when he didn't get it.

"That's a shame," he said, spreading his hands. "I wanted to congratulate all of you for taking out Jordi...and to share some news." He smiled broadly but somehow without showing his teeth. "You've all kind of worked your way out of a job."

"What do you mean?" Ash asked, and Sandi saw his eyes narrowing cautiously, looking around with obvious suspicion at the people passing by on the walking path.

She understood his paranoia; she was half-expecting a squad of Patrol officers to rush out and arrest them both at any second. It was just the sort of thing she'd expect Fleet Intelligence to do to someone who wasn't of use anymore.

"Calm down, children." Fox chuckled, clearly amused by their reaction. "What I'm saying is, there's been some changes, a reorganization, you might say. That power struggle I mentioned before you left? Well, we came out on the right side of it, and suddenly I've got a lot more pull than I did a few weeks ago. And since we don't currently have a need for undercover operatives in the Pirate Worlds..."

"Oh come on, Fox," Sandi exploded, getting tired of the theatrics. "Just tell us, for God's sake!"

A couple of passers-by glanced over at her eruption, but she ignored them, and for a change, so did Captain Fox.

"All right, I won't draw it out any longer," Fox said, raising his palms in surrender. "All charges against both of you by the Patrol *and* Space Fleet have been dropped. Carpenter, your official Fleet personnel jacket will reflect that you've been on detached duty with Fleet Intelligence this whole time. You can report to Inferno for a new duty station if you like." He shrugged. "Or you can be honorably discharged as of now."

Sandi felt Ash sag against her, his jaw dropping in disbelief.

"My God." His voice was subdued, almost awe-struck.

She knew how he felt. It had been so long, so long looking over their shoulder, unable to plan for anything but the next assignment, because staying in one place too long would get them arrested by the Patrol or targeted by Jordi's bounty hunters. They could visit the Core worlds, even go back to Earth if they felt like it...

She looked sharply at Ash. Unless he wanted to go back into the military. It wasn't as if leaving it had been his idea, after all. She'd crashed in on his world like the meteor that killed the dinosaurs, and thrown his life into utter chaos.

"I'll take the discharge." He was speaking to Fox, but his eyes were on her. As always, he knew what she was thinking. "After all," he expounded, "I built the *Acheron* because I wanted to see the galaxy." He grabbed her hand and squeezed it. "Let's go see it together."

———

Korri Fontenot couldn't think of too many places she hated more than Belial. The hollowed out asteroid was home to just about every inane and pointless weakness of the human species, put on showcase and sold for a premium. Immersive ViR, drugs, alcohol, pleasure dolls, prostitution and dozens of other pursuits, all designed to help people avoid having to actually live their lives.

And obscenely overpriced food, she added to the list.

She was here for none of those, but that didn't make her feel any better about the visit. She stared at the holographic banner that advertised the wares of the clinic and wondered if she could go through with this.

Cloned organ and limb replacement, it read. *Augmentation available. Price on request.*

"It's time to stop running from your past," Jagmeet Singh said, putting a hand on her left shoulder, "and be whole again."

She looked at his hand, flesh and blood, against the bare metal of her bionics, visible below her black vest. She'd had the damaged arm replaced back on Brigantia, but the new one was slightly bulkier, and nothing she owned that had sleeves would fit it.

Yet another reason to do this, she mused with a mild snort under her breath. *I can finally wear clothes that actually fit me.*

"The past isn't too hard to run from," she countered, "since it doesn't want anything to do with me." She shrugged. "But maybe it's time for an upgrade." She smiled up at him. "You just want me to have more warm flesh, you lecher." He laughed. He wasn't a bad sort for a former contract killer.

"What can I say?" He shrugged. "I have a thing for older women."

About a century older. You're a cradle robber, girl.

"All right, Jag," she patted his hand with a metal one, then headed into the clinic. "Time to move on."

Time to see if all my scars were on the outside.

————

David Blackard scraped his trowel over the patch in the wall, smoothing the material down with the edge. Sweat poured into his eyes from under his brimmed hat, and he paused to lift it off his shaved head with his free hand and wipe his forearm across his face. The primary star was beating down on Gennich like the city owed it money, and the cloudless glare was a spotlight on every scar left from the battle.

He sniffed at the thought. "Battle" seemed a pretentious name for what had happened, but no one seemed to be able to settle on a name for it. It would probably go into the history files as some nonsense like "the Battle for Brigantia." In reality, it had been half a gangland brawl, half a revolution and half a race riot.

He frowned. That was three halves, which didn't sound right. He shook it off and got back to work. Whatever you wanted to call it, the whole nasty business had left twelve deputies and Constable Freeman dead, along with about thirty civilians, a couple of the mercenaries and every single damned one of Jordi Abdullah's hired thugs. He didn't know if any had tried to surrender, but they hadn't accepted any surrenders that night.

Things were taking steps towards normal now, after a couple weeks, but there was still a lot of work to be done. Raw materials were coming in again from the asteroid belt; but most of the construction robots needed to be repaired, and the fabricators to make those parts needed to be repaired, and the damned fusion reactor had been down for a week before the Belters had loaned them parts to repair *that* so they could get started with all the rest of it.

The upshot was, any of the big honking holes that had got shot into everything had to be patched by hand while they waited for the machines to fix the machines to fix the machines. He could see the civilians out in the streets, working on their own store fronts and hotels and bars with old-fashioned cement and concrete and stucco and boards and adhesive and elbow grease, most stripped down to tank tops in the mid-day heat. They waved every now and then, and a couple had brought him and his people drinks once or twice, but no one had offered to help; they had their own work to do.

The Constabulary had other problems that couldn't be solved by complimentary lemonade; there weren't enough deputies left alive and unhurt to police the town *and* patch the holes and fix the doors and board the windows, and the building had taken the most damage of any structure in the city. So it was him, and maybe one other deputy when they could spare it, but mostly just him.

"Shit," he murmured in disgust. *How would Abel have handled this?*

He didn't notice the Tahni until he heard the murmuring from down the street. He looked up and saw them coming, two groups of them with about thirty or forty meters between and he could tell immediately that the ones in the front were the males, the ones behind the females. Their dress was different than he'd usually seen them; their stripped, multi-colored clothing that seemed to be held on by positive thinking was gone, in favor of what looked like more functional, work-oriented clothing. They carried tools as well, shovels and trowels and wheelbarrows, most of which they must have bought locally since their own implements were much different than the human versions.

At the head of the first column were two Tahni, a male and a female walking together, which he thought was odd. But then he recognized one of them; it was the Matriarch, the head of all their females, the one Jordi had taken hostage in the Constabulary. Not that he could tell one Tahni female from another, but she was unmistakably, unabashedly *old*, maybe the oldest Tahni he'd ever seen.

The male...he was thinking that the male looked like about every other adult male Tahni, but then he noticed the brace on his lower leg and remembered the Tahni who'd come here with the hired guns and taken down Jordi Abdullah. What was his name? Kan-Ten? He'd broken his leg killing that other Tahni who'd worked with the cartel, and they didn't have the same medical technology available in Gennich for Tahni that they did for humans, which was why it still wasn't completely healed.

He tossed his trowel down on the piece of wood scrap board where he'd set the bucket of patching cement, then pulled the rag out of his back pocket and wiped his face and hands. He was wearing his sidearm, but he didn't make a move for it. If these people meant him harm, one pistol wasn't going to stop them all.

"Greetings, Deputy Blackard," the one in the leg brace said as he approached. When he and the Matriarch stopped, the other groups did as well, as neatly as any military unit he'd ever seen. "I am…"

"Kan-Ten, yeah, I remember," Blackard interrupted. "And it's 'acting Constable Blackard' nowadays," he added ruefully, though the intonation was probably lost on the aliens.

"Indeed," Kan-Ten acknowledged. "We all mourn the loss of Constable Freeman."

"He died preserving my life," the Matriarch spoke, her English accented nearly to the point of incomprehensibility. "We seek to do him honor."

"We are here," Kan-Ten told him, "to help you repair the damage to the Constabulary. Our females will work inside, while the males are outside." He made a gesture that looked human, or at least looked like he was imitating a human, an open palm toward the building. "We wish to help. It is the least we can do."

Blackard thought about it for a moment, wondering if it was a good idea. But hell, the weapons were all locked up, and most of the rest of the deputies were out handling one call or another. They *did* need the help.

"I would be much obliged," he said with a nod. Kan-Ten stared at him for a moment and Blackard added: "That means, yes."

He made the 'link calls to the few people he had working

inside the building, just so no one would freak out. While he did that, the Matriarch and Kan-Ten began issuing orders in their own language, sending their workers this way or that in a bustle of purposeful activity.

"With this many hands," he commented to Kan-Ten once everyone was on their way to one job or another, "we might be done with most of the work in a day."

The Tahni inclined his head, the closest thing they could come to a nod, another sign that he'd been hanging around with humans for a long time.

"So, if you don't mind me asking," Blackard went on, "why didn't you wind up leaving with your friends? You were with that group, right, the ones on that ship, the *Acheron*?"

"I was. I am, for they were my friends when I had no others. But these are my people, and they need me, for now." He regarded Blackard with beady, dark eyes that somehow seemed more readable and human to the Deputy than they would have a few days ago. "You are a man who serves the needs of his people, are you not?"

"Yeah, I guess I am."

"Then you know the duty I feel." He fell silent, watching the labors beginning to unfold around them. His ridged brows inclined toward the trowel Blackard had left behind. "May I?"

"Sir, you are welcome to it," Blackard assured him, laughing.

Kan-Ten didn't laugh; but then, he didn't suppose Tahni laughed at all. He picked up the trowel and began working on the next shattered pockmark left in the wall by a tantalum needle. The Deputy watched him for a second, then his eyes traveled to the other Tahni, working hard despite the heat, moving like bees around a hive, and then to the humans watching them from down the street. There was something new on those human faces, he thought. Maybe respect? Maybe. At least it wasn't the hate and resentment it had been a few weeks ago.

"So, how'd you wind up as crew on a boat like the *Acheron?*" Blackard asked, feeling awkward just standing around and watching the Tahni work. Kan-Ten didn't look up from the wall as he smoothed out a dollop of patching cement, but there was a look on his face, something that could have been a smile if he were human.

"Now there, as you humans say, lies a tale."

ALSO IN THE SERIES

THE ACHERON
THE PRODIGAL
HYBRID
EXILE

ALSO BY RICK PARTLOW

If you enjoyed The Acheron, you will love Wholesale Slaughter!

Start a new adventure today!

FROM THE PUBLISHER

Thank you for reading *The Acheron*.

WE HOPE YOU ENJOYED IT AS MUCH AS WE ENJOYED bringing it to you. We just wanted to take a moment to encourage you to review the book on Amazon and Goodreads. Every review helps further the author's reach and, ultimately, helps them continue writing fantastic books for us all to enjoy.

If you liked this book, check out the rest of our catalogue at www.aethonbooks.com. To sign up to receive a FREE collection from some of our best authors as well as updates regarding all new releases, visit www.aethonbooks.com/sign-up.

JOIN THE STREET TEAM! Get advanced copies of all our books, plus other free stuff and help us put out hit after hit.

SEARCH ON FACEBOOK:
AETHON STREET TEAM

ABOUT RICK PARTLOW

RICK PARTLOW is that rarest of species, a native Floridian. Born in Tampa, he attended Florida Southern College and graduated with a degree in History and a commission in the US Army as an Infantry officer.

His lifelong love of science fiction began with Have Space Suit—Will Travel and the other Heinlein juveniles and traveled through Clifford Simak, Asimov, Clarke and on to William Gibson, Walter Jon Williams and Peter F Hamilton. And somewhere, submerged in the worlds of others, Rick began to create his own worlds.

He currently lives in central Florida with his wife, two children and a willful mutt of a dog. Besides writing and reading science fiction and fantasy, he enjoys outdoor photography, hiking and camping.

www.rickpartlow.com

www.ingramcontent.com/pod-product-compliance
Lightning Source LLC
Chambersburg PA
CBHW020312160726
47992CB00004B/1508

Introduction

I'm a little scared to share this book.

My habit is to post every poem on social media as soon as I write it. It's a compulsion, really. When I write, I must share it, or I feel physically uncomfortable. I just can't sit on stuff. When the spirit of creation jolts through me, it must be shared right away, or I end up seared.

So, all this poetry *has* seen the light of day. I have gone through each piece and edited, and, I think, improved on it, and I've had it looked over by more competent eyes than mine.

But I'm not really scared that my poetry is subpar. I'm afraid of the great whole of this book. Sharing each piece individually didn't scare me. But putting this collection together – that, it turns out, makes me nervous as hell.

I feel like I'm opening myself up to criticism, and maybe even rage. These pages reveal the breadth of my experience as a white woman bridging the 20th and 21st century in America. I know that experience touches only a fraction of the female experience, but it is deeply what I know, and what I must share.

I've been flaying myself on poetry for thirty years, which is long enough to know that the vulnerability I feel right now is a good sign. The fear that clutches my chest, the lean towards self-sabotage, the second guessing of my experience, and the urge to shrink to be more pleasing – these are all indications that this is my most authentic art.

I have a desire to ask you to be kind and understanding. I want to assure you that, if what I say here glosses over your own experience, if I've somehow left you out when you deserve a place at this table because I'm naïve and privileged, and don't even know it, I didn't mean it. What if this project slaps you in the face instead of validates your lived experience?

But I can't ask that of you. You're going to respond exactly how you need to respond. And we will learn from that together. I've poured my womanhood into this book. I hope, at the very least, it inspires you to open the dam of your own lived experience and share it out as far and wide as it will go.

Thank you for honoring me with your attention to this book - with your attention to my heart. I look forward to returning the favor.

I love you.

Ingrid

The Poetry…

I hear about balance
and inner peace.

I'm told that
self mastery is

real and attainable.

And every morning I
wake up committed

to being more human
and every night

I fall asleep in
the trenches, muddy

bitter
shameful.

I'm told that co-
de-pendency

and a cocaine-
de-pendency

can be things of the past,

but I've never been
wired for the

straight and narrow.

I am

the twists
the turns
the gnarls

2

I am

the ghosts
the reaper
the dead

and I am not
ready

I still need
space to

die, before

I let you in.

All I ever wanted to do
was write

p o e t r y.

"You can't make a living
like that.

And what are you?"
is the

u n s p o k e n

question - if
"you're not

p r o d u c i n g ?"

So I left it -

(well

m o s t l y)

a long time

in search of
dollars and cents

and dollars
and sense

and worth

- y - n e s s
desperate

worth -
- less -
- ness!

Until, exhausted
from digging
for
purpose

I collapsed
hard
bitter
ruined.

And poetry - she

s a v e d

me from that
fate of
lifeless
waste.

It feels like water rising inside me.

I'm kicking my feet hard, I
have to keep my head above it.

But I can see the swell

rising
rising
rising

almost to my chin now.

It's coming up slow

like molten magma

unstoppable.

I am going to drown.

And yet

I kick
I pump
I sputter

because instinct won't release its

grip on me.

I wish I could just relax, even if

it means I'll die.

Baby girl
chubby cheeks
playing in mud
delighted squeaks

      "stop!"

Mother yells
baby starts
fearful cries.

"No, no, no!"

Picks her up
drops in tub

"we don't play
    in the mud."
"Shhh,
    stop
    that
    wailing."

Baby girl
    swallows
      her tears.

Little girl
runs at school
falls on asphalt
blood on tights.

"Little girl. What is this?"
    "You've ruined your clothes."
"Stop that crying!"

And
    stop
      that
        bleeding.

Little girl
        swallows
                her tears.

Young lady
standing stiff
old man
smells of barley

"Stand still!"
        "Don't fidget!"
"Wrong tone!"

Be straight.
        Be perfect.

Young lady
        swallows
                her tears.

Young woman
on a stage
finds the voice
from years ago.

Tears are flowing
song is ringing

the halls coo
        "yes, child.
It's safe here."
        Let it go, let it go."

Thunderous applause
a few shaking heads.

Reviews said
"she shouldn't have cried."
      "There's potential, tone it down."
"She's out
              of
                    control."

      "No more songs!"

She vows today
gripping the paper
with awful words.

Young woman
        swallows
             her tears.

Her eyes are dry
and the grieving halls
        oh!
            They ache, and
                    they
                        ache.

You were sinewed with me
weren't you?

All tangled up in my mess

telling me how relieved I felt
by your vinegar kiss.

Mmmm, and I believed you for so long.

Until you made me crazy.

Or was I already crazy?

And you just rode along?

Egged me on?

You know, people don't like me
because of you.

I remember
that rush to get home.

To kick off my heels,
and meet you in the kitchen.

Wrap my hands around your neck.

You purred when I got home
and we sat for hours.

Barefoot. Hand in hand.

Until you made me sad.
Or mad.

Or was I already those things

masked by our heady conversation?

I snuck home sometimes at lunch,
just to see you.

To touch your lips and slip away.

But you really started in, didn't you?

All that touching

understanding

waiting for me, enticing me.

I believed in you!

But I think they call that gas lighting.

Controlling. Abusive, even.

Intoxicating? Without a doubt.

Addiction? I met the criteria.

Oh, you horrible trickster.
I would have sworn you cared.

And now I talk about you
like a disease.

I replaced you with a whole group of people
to fill that hole.

And we talk about you
all the time.

I still long for you, sometimes.
I see you out there, sometimes.

On a patio table
or peeking into a bar.

You're making everyone laugh
like you made me laugh, before.

Anyone can be your friend, I guess.

But never your lover.

B e well. Farewell. Have a good one. Aloha. Adios.

I never want to see your fucking face again.

I'm saying all of these things, and in parting, this:

be brave.

Be. Fucking. Brave.

Go after those demons with everything you've got.

Don't let anything else slip and slide between
your fingers because

you can't look that devil in the eye.

Be brave.

Storm the gate that seals your doom.

Combat mano-a-mano
that fiend that's got you by the tail.

Be stupid brave.

Hold on in the rain while
the lightning strikes you.

Dive head first into that lake of fire
damn the jagged rocks that'll

crack
your
head.

Be recklessly heroic.

Don't walk – run into the black.

Stand unsteady at the tip of the needle
see the world and risk the fall.

And when the demon drops you
and doom is released

and when the fiend devours you
and the lightning blasts you

and when the lake drowns you
and the black takes you

and when you fall, my love
drifting to your death

the skies will rumble
with your triumphant laugh!

So be brave, my
once
beloved, and

defeat
your
nature.

That one is best admired from a distance.

Yes, she's got those
rumbling curves and flashing eyes.

Her smile will make you wilt
and stand taller, still.

I suppose if you must approach
keep her well contained.

But you watch her close, now!

Go on – enjoy her, for a while.
She'll stay put for a time.

But eventually, you'll see
she's scraping chains against rock.

Gnashing and writhing: she's bleeding for freedom.

You can try and keep her longer,
but I'm telling you, boy

in the end

she'll rip you apart.

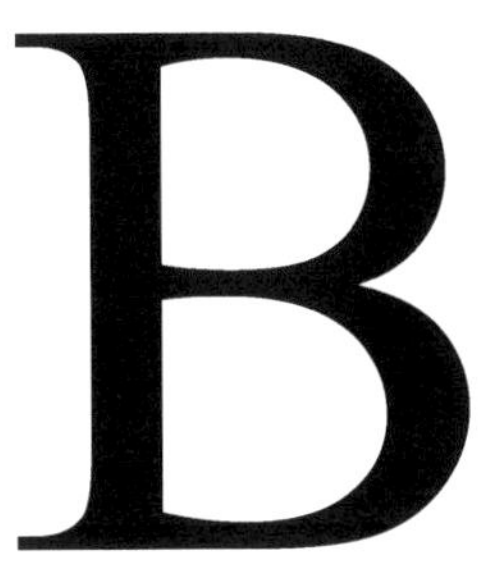

B

itch"

noun.

"a spiteful, unpleasant, or disliked woman."

and:

"a female dog, wolf, fox, or otter."

Yes, this bitch is spiteful
because she has had

countless
assassination attempts

on her love
on her power
on her prowess
on her care.

This bitch is unpleasant

having been

kicked like a dog
feared like a wolf
hunted like a fox
beaten like an otter.

This bitch is

disliked by the human who
would take her love for granted

sneered at by the human who
would belittle her as to control her

raged at by the human who
would throw rocks to stop her

begged for by the human who
cannot contain her.

This bitch is standing up for her capacity to

unconditionally love you, and
walk the hell away from you.

This bitch is standing up
raising her fist up

she is pumping her power
into the atmosphere

and for once you,
you cannot stop her.

This bitch is not
going to be still
for you to

belittle
rape
murder her

with your generations of entitlement.

This bitch will keep caring for
a world she was born to

mother
by first

caring for
herself.

She will

stomp and
scream

she will

march and
fight.

What this bitch will not do is

beg
bleed

open her legs

cry
or
die

at the behest of a millennia.

This bitch
has reached

the end
of the line.

I know that you didn't **slap my face**.

But you chewed on my heart.

I know you didn't shove me against the wall

but your face, it screwed so tightly, I knew...

you despised me for a moment.

I did my good girl part -

I didn't yell
I didn't curse

I didn't scrunch my face in retort.

I stood in the hurricane of your rage

and I thought at least

you'd say sorry
you'd reach out

you'd come back to me.

But you're still cold
across the bed.

You're blowing by me
in the hall.

Must I swallow this too?
Must I submit
yet again?

A **stray** black cat

slinks around my home.

It's not lost on me that

four hundred years ago
or so

this sort of consorting

would have resulted in me -
and probably the cat -

hitched to a stake and
burned. Alive.

Color inside *the lines."*

She made it seem like if
I broke protocol
with my crayon

something terrible would happen.
So, I did as I was told.

I colored inside the lines.
Very carefully.

I became excellent at
staying in the lines.

Precise.

I was praised my
whole life for

the way I stayed
inside the lines.

"You make it look easy!"
They said.

It is easy, I thought.
There's nothing easier than

following a line that
someone else drew.

One day I crossed a line.

I crossed it hard with my
red pen, and

I was so surprised that
nothing happened.

No bad thing came
smashing down on me.

No devil came to
take me to hell.

So, I grabbed my black pen,
and I did it again.

I pressed hard and drew
right through the line.

This time something did happen.

The lines, they
started acting stupid.

I couldn't take them seriously, these
lines upon lines, making

the same shapes over and
over and I just

laughed so hard, and they
got so mad, these lines, but I

couldn't listen anymore! I
traded my pens for

paint and I took whole
pails of the stuff and

threw all the colors at those
stodgy old lines and

danced in my world of chaos
and mess, and I could not

stop laughing, now that I
painted over all the lines, but

people were angry now!
I tried to explain, I said

hey! The lines are a lie! Come

dance with me and you'll
certainly see! But they wouldn't.

They stood at my borders and
criticized me for coloring

outside the lines. They said,
"you took the easy way out, you're

doing it wrong, and you
are dangerous now."

 nd suddenly
        come middle age
I am very
       angry at every
con-
descension

I swallowed whole
      from every man
I have passed

and
      known

in my

petite
    and
wholesome
     life.

I'm spending too much time
in the corners of my mind

where it's dark
dusty
filled with   dank.

I've been wallowing where
all my regrets are stored

meant to be
forgotten and   left alone.

But I so often find myself
pulled into that black past

riding a sick
merry-   go-round

hoping my attention will
bring scraps of repentance -

relief from
this mental   flogging.

I've never been a girl to give up.

I was raised by strong men,
and stronger women.

We don't give up.

We fight the live long night -
we march forward on orders.

We crawl if we have to.

I've never been a girl to give up.
Until today.

When you said to me -
Please. Let me go.

And I did.

Because I love you more
than I am strong.

I'd do anything for you."

Is it love
      when he comes home late
drunk

having spent the money
      for rent

on brews and babes?

Are you the better
      woman

when you just love him
      through it?

I'm so ready for real"
she sighs, selecting Crema overtones.

"I need it raw"
she weeps, rubbing lotion into her thighs.

Craving essence, she really is
while she clutches a blanket to her shoulders,

her nudity ruined
by stretches and dimples.

"Love me for me!"
She takes a verbal stand

and eats food she hates
and moves in ways that hurt.

Sobbing
standing over the scale.

Dear Son,

It's a good thing you don't know
how deep this well really goes.

It's a very good thing, I believe
you don't see my turbulence,
my searing disquietude.

Because if you could see - if you
really knew - the screeching

terror in a mother's heart
I believe you'd never move
from that spot, in case you

unwittingly killed me off.
I fear you would make a box

too small for your inde-
pendent charge. And that, my
sweet boy, would be deva-

stating - my son: cata-
strophic, my wild heart.

We're coy with each other
          in this great ballroom -
      music filling the space
          wafting to the ceiling.

              I'm doing my best to
      avoid you, pretend you
don't exist. Certainly
      not here! It's a masked

ball though, so you could be
          any of these guests, patrons,
barons - sneaking around, trying
          to pull at my skirt, embarrass

me. I know you, but I
          deny you. Hopelessness - that's
your name. You slink around these
          great celebrations - a

predator, spreading your
          sickly charm on women
and men in gowns and rags alike.
          You don't care who you devour.

I'm dancing hard to the
          cellos and violins, the great
piano, and tiptoeing
          along the strings of distraction
so, please - don't. I'm hoping

you'll lose interest, you
          bastard, you fiend, you amoral
trickster. Leave me alone!
          I want to love this life,

but you want to imprison
          me, in that invisible

cell, to cage my mind and heart,
      silence my screams so all the

ladies and gentlemen,
      they never hear my pleas
for release, and you can
      laugh at my demise because

there's no hope of rescue.
      You twisted devil, hopeless-
ness, by many names -
      despair, misery, rejection,

death. You have caught me, because
      I could not face you. I
ran from you, and then,
      because I would not look, you

snuck into my circle,
      after all this time of
cat and mouse, and you
      are victorious, indeed.

Enough.

Stilettos that make our
legs long but
deform our feet.

Contour and shading, rosy
cheeks and knockout lips, but
can't take a lover for a night.

Enough.

Soft, silky, scent-filled
creams for our
thighs because

sitting in an office with
staff and vodka, to entice
carving our face back to twenty-five.

Enough.

Straddling a boy on
one hip, and strapping
the girl to servitude

climbing over a glass
ceiling and dodging
pats on the ass

Enough.

Being told to "smile!" by
old men, and grinning
through the rage, because

can't say no to sex
because boys get
mad, and that's consent.

Enough.

Fear of the night, and
speaking up, and
saying no, fucking thank you

crippling compromise, and
terrorizing and
traumatizing, and sitting down.

Enough.

There will be no more
holding back the
tears and the screams, because

Enough.

The women
have had
enough.

I knew I'd
              done okay as

your mom when I
          saw how

beautifully
          delicately
lovingly

you treat your
          woman.

I am so sad for you
                because

no one taught you to
                be brave.

No one taught you that
                courage

is just fear that is
                dancing.

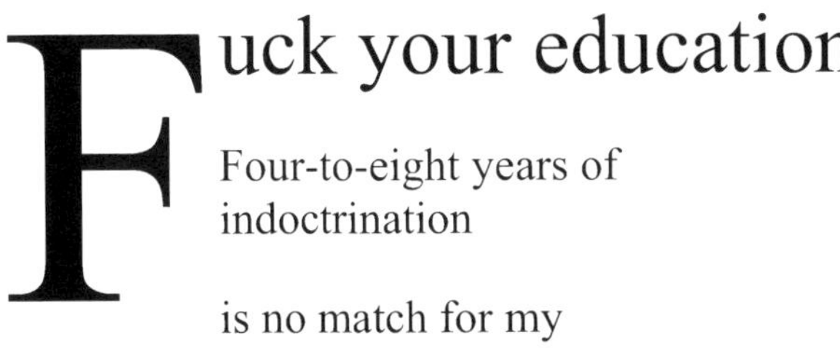

Fuck your education.

Four-to-eight years of
indoctrination

is no match for my

wheeling and
dealing

falling on my face, and
deciphering a world without

textbooks or
worksheets, or

a letter to define my

brain power, or my
legitimacy as a

thinking
bleeding

creature
feature.

To hell with your ivy league breeches

give me my
ride or die

bitches

because while you're
sipping wine, snug in your

gated community

I'll be riding, open top

across the country

flying, like you dare not
down the highway of

fast living.

You can pontificate on your
theories and judgments about

people like me, and

I'll be the wind rustling your
hair, and making you

real nervous while I
conquer fears you

did not know you had.

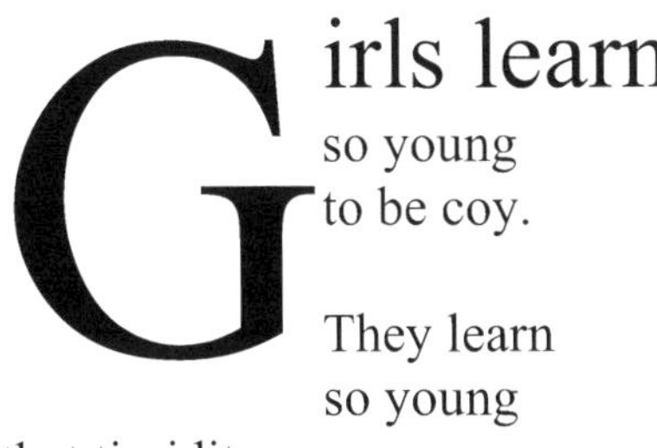

Girls learn
so young
to be coy.

They learn
so young

that timidity

wins. That
avoiding
the eyes

is correct.
They learn
so young

to mute,
and that
their roles

are just
smiles
and sex.

Hey man, I know you
don't hate me.

I know it's that you
hate the way you

lose control when you
catch the curves

of my ass at just
the right angle.

I know you hate that
my odor can

make you dizzy, and
you can't really

fathom why I should
have so much

command over you, when
you need to get

shit done. You're a
man! And then I

come along and disrupt
your focus, and

all you can think
about is how

my breast would
fill your hand, and

imagine the shape
and depth of my

vagina, and how
your cock would fit in it -

shit, you know there are
other holes too, and

fuck! You *bitch* -
tempting me from

my very important
work, you *whore*. They're

right, your existence
must be obscene.

Get to the bedroom
shut the fuck up.

I can't stand the way
you play me like

a puppet on
a string just by

looking at me with
those baby blues. I'll

use my weight to
hold you down while I

fuck your pussy, and
fuck your life, and

make sure you have
no rights. I'm not good

with you having
sovereignty over

your body, when you

rob of me of my mind.

I need your love and
your sex, I'm losing

my shit with my need
for you, and now I'll

lose my faculties
too, just to look at

you, smell you, even when
I think about you. You

will mind me woman,
and if you don't, I'll

make your life a
living hell, I'll chain

you up. If I can't
have you in my

basement, I'll have you
under my thumb,

you won't win this war
in my head, you

cock-sure bitch, I'm
ready to destroy

you and I will get
what I need from you.

"Move closer to the edge."
The voice says.

"I can't."
My feet tremble.

"Move closer to the edge."
The voice insists.

"I can't."
My stomach turns.

"Move closer to the edge."
The voice demands.

"I can't."
Now gravity pulls me.

I step.

I fall.

And that is how I grew my wings.

I always thought you
were the one I could
blame

for all my rage and
all my pain.
But today, you

reached out,
tenderly, and I
recoiled

even as I am
desperate for your
touch, your

affection, your
need.
And that's when I

realized I just
use you to
self destruct.

I am a **wild** thing
caught sometimes in the

net of your
           expectations.

I don't do well
clawing at lines of

reason. Hook me once
       with a word

but you can't trap me -
not while I glide in

oceans of
       weird
wonderful,
       and wise.

I'm hiding.

I'm intermittently suffering, but that is my choice.

I wend through the maze of my mind for a chunk of the day before I remember all I have to do is

stand up!

And step out of the puzzle that only exists in my head.

I'm hiding out while I work up the courage to kick over this corn maze

and leave behind the struggle for good.

Heavy though it is, there's a certain warmth to the enduring,

so I am detaching in pieces.

And that is okay.

My breath is the true me, my mind is the game, and we all like to escape ourselves and play games every so often.

And thusly, the human experience is born. The struggle is real.

I wonder what will happen to the game when I finally kick down the mental hay bales that make crude barriers for my anxiety to skitter through -

and end this toiling for good?

I am afraid and, at once,
I am free.

I have a mouthful of shame.

My cheeks are bulging with it as I
try and

stuff it
swallow it
chew it.

Anything, oh anything, but
never to

spit it
speak it
spew it.

Oh God, this shame has legs.

It skitters in my mouth
bounces on my cheeks
presses against my tongue.

It just keeps

popping
        popping
                popping

I'm so afraid one day it will
pop out and

the whole world will know.

It's waking up
cracking open guilty eyes
close them! Ouch…

For shame
crawling up my naked back

pelting head and beating mistakes
damn bottles, scattered about.

I know why Hemingway wrote in the morning.

Lilting words
rocking from my pen.

Get me high, imagination
heavy storytelling

this drug tingles
makes me stronger

(what an adrenaline junky)
that's a rush!

This day got better.
So, yeah.

I know why Hemingway wrote in the morning.

I remember the boyfriend who
gave me a book of poetry.

On the surface, this exchange,
it was thoughtful, kind -

because I love poetry, and I
write it all the time.

The book was a
compilation of verse

by a black queen, I can't
remember her name now.

I regret that, because the
poetry, it was beautiful!

But the comment my
boyfriend slid between

the pages when he
handed me that book -

he said, "this is for you.
Like *you* will relate to *her*."

Like that - sarcastic and mean,
underscoring my naivety and

privilege and making sure I
felt his disdain for me, mixed

up with his attraction for me,
and hating me for all of it.

He was right, of course -
I didn't relate to the

woman whose world leapt
off the pages at me,

but she took me for the
ride of my life, nonetheless,

driving me around on a
lyrical tour of a world I

had no access to, and I
was enthralled and

educated, and my boyfriend,
he was just mean, and

I'm glad he's well behind
me, but I sure wish I'd

kept track of that queen,
because her realm, it

expanded me
exponentially, and

I try to remember
that instead when I

think about that
man and that mean.

I'm being called out my window.

The wind is pulling at me,
whispering, "leap."

My feet are already
leaving the ground

as I throw open the window
and follow the

song of the cold. An unknown
ravine is utter-

ing a promise that my wings
will grow as fast as

I fall. I believe it must be so,
so I extend my

arms for flight and follow
the voice of the night.

I'm gaining weight again.
This time I don't care.

I'm busy nowadays,
surfing inconstancy

dancing my burgeoning
bottom through the city

delighting in anything
new and outside of me.

I'm so thrilled with my world
the way it shifts daily

like sand. I don't give a
damn that I'm rounding out

or that my age is
courting gravity -

or that my skin is dull,
because my eyes sparkle!

To hell with youth, and tone,
and sheen, I'm frolicking

in fuck-offs and go-to-hells,
and I'll tell you this, girls -

I'll take my ass over your
thigh gap any day, while

this husk, crackles and
breaks apart – most fully.

I'm not interested in you.
I have no ill will, no

animosity, I'm just
disinterested.

I'll be genuinely happy for
one minute when you

cross my path and
I see you're doing well. I

am all for all of us getting
what wins we can out

of this rickety life, but
I'm not interested enough

to keep tabs and study you
when you're winning and

try to be like you, and
I'm certainly not

interested enough to
glower and gloat if you

fall on your ass -
my god, who among us

stands tall all twenty four?
I am busy keeping my

balance, and taking my eyes off
the spot on the ground in

front if me will definitely
make me to lose my

equilibrium, then it's goodbye
doll, it's topple time, and that

would be because I gave
too much attention to your

spot on the street.
Look, don't take it badly, I

really hope you're as
uninterested in me, because

hey man, we are all in it
together, sure, but we're

walking ourselves home, not
each other, so, friend -

I'm super happy to see you
doing well, having a level

sort of experience, and
buddy: I know it can be

rough out there, but
hang in there, okay? It's

going to get better, the
thing about life is, it's

dynamic as fuck, and we
gotta learn to roll with the

waves, not try to brace
the tsunami of life with our

tired little bodies. So, you
focus on you, and I'll

focus on me, and when we

pass each other on the

interstate of humanity, I
hope we wave and

smile, and have fond thoughts
but we keep our eyes on the

road, so we don't crash into
each other and lose the

rush of the wind in
our hair, and the

rolling of the pavement
underneath our feet.

I'm so angry at you!

I'm so angry, I
beat up against you -

I yell, I beg, I
shake with rage, and

when it all drops
to my belly, I –

I see it now.

I'm stunned into
silence, because I'm

not angry at you.

I'm angry at me
for continuing

to ask permission

to live my life
to be who I am.

You don't make it
easy, but

why should you?

Hurling my pain at
you, and watching it

smack like Jello
on a dart board

it's the only way
I'd ever see that

I give all my power
to you, and to

anyone who

might shield me from
this terrifying

leap that will destroy
me and all at

once, set me free.

I'm so tired of helping
The Men.

All my life I've seen

my mother
my aunts
my idols
my rivals

pander, prostrate
        hand-wring, and

self-
    negate

for fathers
for uncles
for sons
and neighbors,
                too.

In
        fact!

Just this moment
                        ago

I gave up my chair

and sat
        on
                the
                        floor

because a Man
had nowhere
        to sit.

What possessed me!
To conclude that
          a Man

(any
    man!?)

is more deserving of a
          warmer
                    ass
                              than
                                        I?

I'm thoroughly enjoying
my last years of beauty.

I'm sitting squarely between
maiden and crone.

I look in the mirror and
I see half of me in

zest and
red lipstick and
cleavage, and

The other half is in
linens with
long hair that is

long gray.

I didn't enjoy my beauty
when I was young

because

I was taught to be ashamed
of my sex and
my hunger.

But I've got these
few years yet -

to be raunchy with my
head and heart and

all things below
the waist.

So yes, I am enjoying my
last bit of beauty, before

I re-emerge a
new thing: a

wise thing. And

this wise woman, she
is present enough

already, that I

am able to hear her,
and she tells me

enjoy! And I

listen to that
wise thing,

poking at me below
the surface of my

last years
as this
carnival, this
creature, this

beauteous thing!

I am **too damn tired**
to shrink myself for you.

It's exhausting, this
stuffing into a box.

I don't fit in pastels
or bridal gowns

and I am too fucking
lazy to work so

hard for your comfort
at your derision.

Leave me alone to
spread myself as wide

and loud, as thick and
      proud
           as I
                damn
                     well
                         please.

Indignation -
this a

pitiable cowl
worn by a

weakling, who
feigns haughty

virtue over
there, and

flies the coop
while you're

busy in
defense of

bluster and
half truths.

It heavy
                heavy
     it so   heavy.

          I carry it
from birth

I carry it
to mother

I carry it
to father.

It heavy
                    heavy
it so   heavy.

I carry it
to school

I carry it
for you

I carry it
to church

I carry it
so much.

It's heavy
                    heavy
it so   heavy.

I carry it
to wed

I carry it
to bed

I carry it
in love

I carry it
in grief.

It heavy
                    heavy
it so   heavy.

I carry it
inside

I carry it
outside

I carry it
to death

I carry it
                    heavy
it so   heavy.

I have a friend who has it all:

attentive husband
diamonds on her hands
and pearls around her neck.

I saw them out for dinner one night.

He pulled out her chair
and kissed her cheek

and I pretended not to look
pretended not to care.

I told her the next day
I saw you out with him

you look so happy.
I'd die to be you, lady.

She said

it's better from a distance.

That cheek kissing,
and chair pulling,

there's a price, dear.

I have to call ahead
and not be out too late.

I can't have too many friends
or he'll feel badly.

But I can't give it up
she said

what if no one else
can love me?

I'd rather be you
she said

free to roam
free to be.

I smiled at her and I said

It's better from a distance.

I have more room in my bed
but I get cold at night.

I don't have to answer to,
but I don't have love either

to share and swear
and sweat and bleed.

I'd give it up
I said, I guess

if it was right.

One day
on a job

I met a woman

with willowy legs
pouty lips,

a star-dazzled smile.

She whisks on through with

a body that curves
and shudders.

She walks on glitter
in stilettos, and

all the pretty boys
and the ugly ones, too

they look at her
and heave a sigh.

Guess I do, too.

In her presence
(when I found my voice)

I said

you're so lovely

I'd die to be
as lovely as you.

And she curled her glossy lips
and smiled at me.

She said

it's better from a distance.

I don't want this wretched body.
I'm losing my soul

but I can't give it up
she said
or they won't love me.

(even when she cried
she was lovely)

I'd rather be you,
she said

and live free
to be me.

And I almost,
I very nearly replied

it's better from a distance.

But, instead

I closed my mouth
put my hand on her back

and cried beside her.

Judgment is
sour cover

for a marked
lack of courage.

K. NERVA"

Your badge
glistened in the sun, while you
wrote my ticket, and
all I could think while you wrote
was: hard? Angry? Rage?

UN-NERVA-ING! My fear, it

breaks my heart we fear those
who swore to us
to protect and to serve,
but – I submit.
Insurgency is too
damn expensive.

You asked me yesterday
do I miss you being little?

"All cute and diapers and shit."

You said it like that
and it made me laugh.

I'm not sure how to say
both yes and no to you.

Sure, I miss little kid cuddles
but I love big kid conversation.

Yes, I miss those
unabashed belly laughs

but now I rather love
your awkward starts and

stops as you traverse
the end of childhood.

I miss you running
into my arms, but

I am so proud of your
level head and steady heart.

I miss our intimate
yesterdays but,

I root for all your
tomorrows and hereafters.

It's hard to explain, how
I love you even more

the day you move out, then

the day you were born.

So yes, I do miss my baby boy
but oh, I am gratified by

this man, in front of me,
standing tall, with that

wild heart of gold,
and unbridled spirit.

Loose lips
sink ships

so they say.

But darlin' -
these lips?

Well.

Maybe I just
don't care, but
maybe I do.

I'm a fish
flopping on a rock.

I can't decide
if I care if
I live or die, because

I'm totally
out of my element.

If I have to
stay here, I'm
ready to stop, but

if you can push
my slippery,

wriggly carcass back
into the river, I'll
relax, and come alive -

I'll shoot down
rapids and rocks, you'll

see me leap into the
air, showing off
for both worlds,

as long as I
can land in water, and

dive deep into
the silt at the
bottom, burrowing

back to safety. See,
I'm not so brave, its

just appearances, really,
but does anyone
have to know?

Maybe later.
            I'm a little
untethered, I'm
                  needing light feet,
not bound by

promises, or
      responsibility.

My heart needs to
      bounce, and my legs
need to leap, I'm
      sorry, it's a

maybe for me –
      today at least.

Misunderstand me. Please!

Your hatred will destroy me
and then fuel my fiery rebirth.

In the end your words will topple
silent, undisturbed in your grave

while my brazen will scorches on
becoming a new world's rising sun

long after my body
is rotted and undone.

I walked my mother to the beach today.

We went slowly
because she hobbles
with a cane.

It took us ages to get across the blacktop -
my patience wearing thin.

At last, her sandaled feet sunk into the sand

and she paused
        even at her pace
and she breathed
        even at her pace.

She breathed more deeply, perhaps
then she'd ever breathed before.

And she stepped again
        with a foot.
And she stepped again
        with her cane.

I barely touched her elbow

as she made her
dearest way
to the edge of the world.

Don't think about it too much, darling.

Don't think about this
about us
about me.

I don't want to get to the bad news, and darling -

it's always bad news.

Let's just play
and laugh
and get
giddy

in the
here
and now

because I'm loving your

softness and your
ferocious want
of me

and I think you
are feeling that way too.

So, let's not rush to the bad news
to the inevitable conclusion of this

delectable
morsel of a
moment.

Stop asking questions and building for
a fantastic future, it

will never get better than this.

Every time your face
flashes across my screen, I
pop a little inside. You're
so beautiful, but not in the

traditional sense, I mean
yes, you're handsome and

I like your face, but it's
your energy or maybe just

my fantasy. I have this moment
every time you post something

reflective, with depth, I just
have a moment where our

whole lives span before my eyes -
we're sitting together at night and

drinking red wine and
reading poetry and

laughing, because life is
sweet since we found this in

a huge world, thanks to...
I don't even remember how?

It's usually just that flash and I
flick my screen and our life is

gone, relegated to the
chambers of my imagination, but

I have to admit - sometimes the taste
of cheap wine and what I

imagine is the dark and rich

complexion of your voice, it

lingers - it wafts through my
duties, my kids, my husband, this

job, and sometimes it stays, it
stays for days and days.

Mom. Please!

Take up space.

Lay yourself out -
all of your

emotions
your heart
your grief, your

indomitable Spirit!

Mama, please!

Take up more space.

You need to be
big, and
bold, and
fearless, so

this daughter can
find you, and

follow a map to
her own

loudness
prowess
brashy sense.

Don't leave the
daughters of the
century

floundering, trying to
make their way through
a shrinking mother.

Speaking of -

Mother! Please!

Take up the
god damn space!

Be bigger
be more
be all of you

for all of me
for all of us

for all the
rest of all the
daughters of all
eternity.

I don't know, there's just
	something about curves on a body and
crevices on a face.

There is just
	something about the depth of time and
the dark of fate.

I just need
	something imperfect, gnarled, damaged
put through the wringer.

I want to
	sink my teeth into something tender and
marinated, well cooked.

I think you're
	beautiful, the way you're broken and
mended and broken and mended.

My mother has worn the same
lipstick for years.

I remember watching her in the bathroom

painting the circle around her mouth.

She'd catch a glimpse of me

peering around the door, and she'd wink.

I remember the pink stains on her favorite mug.

The band of color on her cigarette.

Her lips were full when I was a kid -

celebrated with that lipstick.

Now she's older, smaller, and

her lips are fine, like pencil.

But she still wears that pink. She still

leaves lipstick marks on coffee cups

although she gave up the cigarettes.

She doesn't wink at me, but she smiles

when I pull up - she smiles big and pink

and wide and says "welcome home, child of mine!"

I don't feel like it.

In fact, I don't feel like a
goddamn thing today.

I'm busy. My mind is
not here. So please: stop.

You're just annoying me with
your grabby hands

clawing at my waist, yanking
my hair, what is this?

I don't feel like it.
And I dearly wish you'd

leave me alone!
Get your hands off me, I'm

trying to go miles
from here, and you're

tethering me to chores that
I didn't ask for.

Go away. Let me be.
Why do you insist on

interrupting my reverie
when surely you can see

I don't want you.
I don't want you anywhere.

Not anywhere at all.

Most men want to break a
confident woman.

She struts in and turns them on with
sass
and class

and an open invitation to build a

pyre
beside her.

But the warmth of possibility, it soon becomes

rage
in a cage.

Her struts aren't provocative, now they're provocation for

blame
and shame.

"A man can't care for a woman like that!" she's a

conniving
a contriving

witch
bitch
whore.

Darling -

thank you,

for not being
most men.

This
       juxtaposition of
  sunshine
      and rain

    makes my whole
world all
make sense,
   and I just

dance and
    dance in circles
around you
    laughing at your

dizzy and
    confused
perception of
    my feral glee.

My head is full of spiders today.

I can feel them crawling in the shadows of
my

torn

up
psyche.

No. I haven't seen them!

But I know they're there.

That creeping, sideways hustle is

agitating my brain. My mind is bending
to avoid the sensation of

tickles from arachnid feet, I'm
violently retracting from the

potential bite that will
surely poison what little

grip

I have left

on this
mephitic
reality.

Heartbreak.

Heartbreak. What a relief
a broken heart would be.

Instead, my heart is bending,
kept pliable by hope.

You're sitting so close to me
on the narrow edge of

misunderstood, separated only by
one perspective shift.

But my body isn't long enough
to bridge a gap of things

misspoke, too often, rushed
left unsaid, hanging.

This bed is leagues of desert
dried up passion, rotten fruit.

"I would give anything" - so says
that saboteur, a hopeful heart.

I have learned nothing
but this: my beggar's heart is

grossly

   compulsively

      predictable.

I remember the refuge
of my mother's arms.

I remember the relief
when I sank into her

flesh and skin, so warm and safe.
I never gave it a thought.

I remember being carried
for ages, and then

being made to walk. I was
angry, stamping my foot

when she said "you're a big girl.
You have to walk now."

I remember marching, glow-
ering, then running

and running away from
my mother's embrace.

I remember her wanting
to hug me, and, embarrassed,

moving away from her.
The sting on her face, it

lasted just a moment, then
she covered it with a laugh.

I remember her respectful
distance when I made it

clear I didn't want her near.
I remember when we started

laughing together at
grown up jokes.

I remember the hugs outside
her house, visits that ended in

"see you soon, mom."
And I remember

glancing up at her in the
rearview mirror

waving goodbye, her grin
was proud, a mile wide.

I remember the autumn
she told us the news

I remember sitting by
her bed, holding her

frail, spotted hand, noticing
arms that had been my

childhood fortress, now
thin, wrinkled, and pale.

I remember lifting her up
and washing her body.

I remember hoisting her
off the bed and carrying

her to the car. She was so
fragile in my arms and

I was so scared I'd break her.

I remember the sharpest

intake of breath

I'd ever heard her take.
I remember the exhale,

the one I never
wanted to end.

She was gone, I remember,
and I cried harder that day

than the day she made me walk.

I scooped her body in my arms
retching grief all over

my empty mother. My safe
space gone forever,

and I regretted every
time I avoided her embrace.

My poetry doesn't rhyme
      because my
life is a rhythm
      of mismatches.
Not serene
      like silk
unless it's crushed -
      life's a bit like that.
Poetry feels like it
      ought to take you
for a bamboozled
      ride down a
bumpy lane and
      pour you into a
vat of ice and
      you don't know
if the cold it
      refreshes and excites
you or snatches
      your breath
because it
      shocks you and
hurts you.
      Life's a bit like that so
my poetry, it's
      a bit like that.

My shame is showing.

Rotting my teeth
carried on my breath

poking from inside
bulging my veins and

blemishing my skin
ruddy purples and browns.

My shame is showing

and I'm trying to cover it
with veneers and spit

caked powder not
quite the right shade.

I'm hiding in rags
hiding my fading light.

My shame is showing -

more than that, it's
eating me from the inside.

It's feasting on me, it's
smacking its lips

day by day, chomping
slurping, sucking, laughing.

My shame is showing

and I am done hiding.
Let it annihilate me

destroy my sense of
pretty, good, and right.

I'm ready to rip apart
and begin again.

It's a one-way ticket to paradise", he said.
"You won't want to come back," he assured.

He cocked his head, and toothed a grin
nudging me toward the train.

I got to paradise, alright.

And paradise is dry.
And thirsty. And a little bitter.

The train dropped me off in Mojave

someone's adobe idea
of bone peace, I guess.

I wish I could get back to greener pastures
with moisture for my cracked lips

and barrels of rain for my raspy throat.

Promised me someone else's dream
and they never wanted to leave.

"It'll be yours too," he said,
with a grandfather's wink.

So, he offered me a one-way ticket
(which I took)

because I believed. I believed.

I think it's
           only
    a mother who

     can sit
              drenched
in hurt

stare into the
         deluge
of rage,

hold on in the
           hurricane
of fury

and keep afloat with love
          love
                   love.

Only love.

I think
         only
a mother can

marry her
         pain
to another's anger

and build a
         partnership
that

somehow
         feeds
the world

a sustenance of love
        love
                love.

Only love.

I can see
        now
it's only a mother

who's
        compassion
sighs on the wind

who pours
        ardor
with the rains

who beams
        pride
along the sun:

a dwelling place of love
        love
                love.

Only love.

Peace. It falls out of
          my head, like
loose sand.

     It's so
          warm for a
moment, until it

evaporates! With the
          wind. So harsh, it
blows out my

inner sanctum.
          I am so far from
comfortable, from that

elusive peace. But -
          I can also see, it's
just out of reach,

because my mind
          twists these things
into gales of

expectation, and I
          nosedive into
misery, and I am

gone. I am always gone.

Pleasure. Is that a dirty word?

How did this, our

human
birth
right

become a
full shame
thing?

Don't move that way.
        Don't laugh so loud.
                Oh, grow up!

Shame!

This is your
        duty, it's
                your job, to

work hard you
                lazy git!

All of those
        dirty thoughts
                and sinful

drives, just

synonyms for
pleasure.

All of that
        pious
                censure, just

another expression
of shame.

So, you – don't
      put your
            shame
                  on me.

Pretty girls all look the same.

Petite.
Contained.

Neat inside the lines.

Turn me on with the wild ones!

With the crazy hair
and a grin a mile wide.

Light my fire with a cynic

some rage
and a ride or die.

Tickle my bare feet with

a beer
and a bonfire.

Teach me to howl at the moon -

I want to be just like you

grabbing big thighs
and laughing with loose lips

sinking ships, and
swimming in the undertow.

The pretty girls they can
watch from the bleachers

lined up one by one

we're gonna dance out of step
we're gonna sing out of tune

we're gonna fill a spittoon
from this vantage point of

not one fuck given.

I would love
to be
held and adored
squeezed and reassured
lilted to perfection
given a new perception
by you.
But,
failing all that
I'd really like
to smoke a cigarette.

Remember when good looks
were all you had?

Remember fretting
hovering at the mirror
picking at your face?

Ha!

Today you toss your hair
in a loose ponytail

and greet the day with
wisdom, kindness
and grace.

Your husky sex appeal
has been gently replaced

with the depths
of outer space.

Remember when all you had was beauty?

There's a **scream**
coiled in my belly.

It feels like miles
of flaming ribbon.

I think it'll twist
higher and higher

to the moon?
To the sun?

She may do a
three sixty

around Pluto, and
make her way back

to Mars. She's
rising and I

can't stop her.
Like a cobra

she is poised
ready for me to

slip up: to open
my damn mouth.

Then she will
catapult - I feel it!

I'm so scared to
let her out.

I don't know when
she'll stop, and

my voice is not
strong enough

to track a scream that
raps on the stars.

How can I be
moving so fast in a

box that doesn't
move at all?

Is it possible my
personal momentum won't

collide with a
world's inertia and

blow its lid, ejecting me
right along with it?

Hey! Space cadet!
Can I keep vibrating at

this electric rate without
destroying my people, my

planet, and it's quiet
servitude? Is anyone else

ready to self destruct?

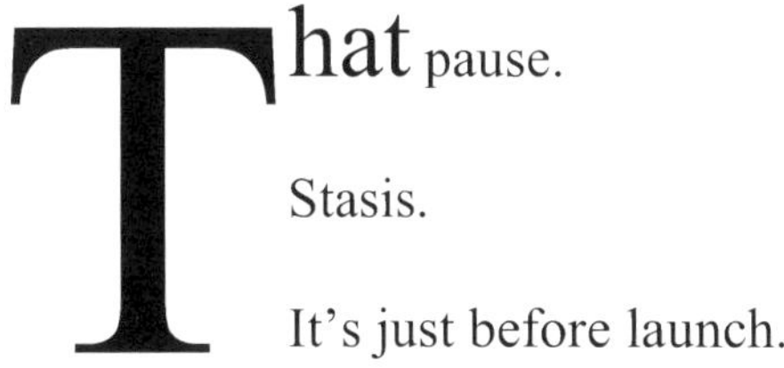

That pause.

Stasis.

It's just before launch.

I am
  ready.

Alert.
  Piqued.

This world has
no idea, and I'm

on tenter-
hooks, because

I know.

I finally
    fucking
know.

Stupid girl.

Gave all your power
and your faith to
anyone who had
a smile for you pass
across their face.

Stupid girl.

Nose to the grindstone
feet on the ground.
Toiling and yelling,
passing on the spin
like it's your own.

Stupid girl.

Mistaking coworkers for
friends, fancying loyalty
from foes. Letting your
hair down. Dancing.
Vomiting in your bed.

Oh, brave girl!

I see now, I see you're
getting ready to believe
something more about you,
a new life without strife
forget the lies, could it be?

Brave girl!

You left it in the dark -
don't know what it is
don't care to pack it up.
You're starting to edge
along the cliff - could you die?

Brave girl!

Sniffing now, at the
possibility of
leaving behind that
sensitivity, while your
toes are hanging off the rim.

Woman!

What if you took the
leap? Did you know that
you can fly? They told
you all the time, you're
stuck with them for life.

Woman!

You've sprung out your shoes
hurdling through the dark.
You don't give a damn
where you land because
you're equipped for every bit.

Woman!

You are an anthem!
Take flight and never let
the mice on the ground
deny your right to your
happy and your free.

Lady!

You drive a hard bargain against defeat.

Life twists us all up
in her gnarled branches

and you, dear;

you spin right out
with a triumphal curtsy.

Lady,

you are Cheshire Cat in the face of overwhelm.

Chaos catches us all
in her slippery whirlpool.

But you, dear:

use just a finger
to turn the tide.

Lady, lady:

you are draped in silver and jewels, I swear!

And I could always tell you
how much I admire

your grace
your talent
your fierce
your pride.

But I'd rather just sit with you, I think

And wrap myself with a corner of your silver.

Why do I smell you?

It's been months since I've seen you.
Longer since I touched you.

It's your cologne, clinging
to my clothes, wafting through the air.

Subtly rich, and sweet; lingering,
like pipe tobacco.

Why do I smell you?

How long has it been since I kissed you?
I don't even miss you, really.

Except, why do I smell you?

There's a hint of sweat, all mixed in.
Acrid. Nostalgic.

Reminds me of sex with you.

That scent! It's hugging my sleeves
sitting in the car next to me.

Brushing my hair.

Why do I smell you?
I don't even fucking like you.

I have torn through
the nucleus of shame.

You cannot bind me
with your tribal ties.

I have stumbled
and stood

and stumbled
and stood

in a jungle of fear
on no path but mine.

I have stood up
and limped on

more times than you
have sniffed at children

who do not bend, at
women who do not mind.

Snobbery is mediocrity
in fancy dress.

I do not need you
to save me a seat

at that table of
traditions and platitudes

for a meal of marked
and malicious cowardice.

I am still tumbling
through my mistakes

and I am still
falling on my face.

I have my scars
and my empty belly

but I will not partake
in this ornamented feast

to devour the visionary:
the architect of peace.

Oh, damn it.

The day slipped away again.

I got lost somewhere between

a novel and bed sheets.

It's too late in the afternoon for anything now.

I suppose I'll prop up my feet

drink my coffee.

Write some poetry.

Smoke a cigarette.

Except I quit the smokes...

...which, today

I kind of regret.

The flowers you bought me are pink.

Pastel.
Friendly.

Of course, I want to exclaim delight

but the fact of the matter is
the flowers you bought me are pink.

Pastel.
Friendly.

What drew you to these in the store?

Absent-minded thoughtfulness?

Pink says:

chatty.
Surface.

Let's keep it light.

Our whole life is pink.

Don't you see me craving red?

Deep.
Carnal.

Can't you see through my pretty smile
to my husky needs?

Do you not see my jaw clenching?

Do you not see my hands
scraping my needy thighs?

Why are you set on pink?

Pastel.
Friendly.

When I'm dripping with red over here.

I'm clawing my way up this
shaft, this well, and the sides are
rutted from the nails of

the warriors, the
explorers, the captives who
lurched this way before me.

If I look up, there's light, and
they say I'm getting closer, but
I just can't tell.

If I look down, it's black, and
they say it's a long fall, but
I just can't tell.

I'm shimmy-ing up this pit,
hanging on with my teeth
inching up, up, up!

Something, something in me

will not stop, it will not give,
so my life is lived with

my face looking at stone,
living in inches, until
I reach the top, until

I see the light, because

they say there is nothing
like it, nothing like
the light at the top.

I love watching the older women
the ones with no fucks given.

The ones who realize their bodies
are for moving, and their mouths

are for back talking. The ones
whose minds are crafty and moves

are extra nasty. I love
watching the older women

who remind me that life
is for fuckin' livin'!

You know there's a time that comes
in life

and I hope this is true for you -

When you stop living for
anything else.

When you stop living for
your family
your friends
your critics.

When you look balefully past
your beliefs

and see magic on the other side
of doubt.

There comes a time in life

and I hope this is true for you -

when you step out of fantasy, and
onto the shore

when you stop wishing and
start doing.

When you walk ahead
instead of enduring.

There comes a time in life when

movement supplants stagnation, and
life begins.

And I dearly hope,

I hope this is true for you.

I hope this is true for you.

detailed

dedicated to
the story
    of me.

And I'm not done with my deeds yet!

These lines will
deepen
and splay

and oh - my lord
if you learn the
        language

of these lines

you'll buckle to a story of

torture
devotion

rage, and
rapture.

Immersive
inescapable -

these lines
on my face

will wrap you up
like a spider

in her web

and eat out
your bleating
        heart.

It's dark here.
In between.

Between what was and
what will be.

I'm lost here
in the black.

I told everyone -
"this is it, it's

what I want."
But now I'm here and -

shit. I'm afraid.
I can't go back,

because amnesia.
I can't remember.

I'm driving forward
incessantly, towards

the void - helpless.
I can't stop, and

I'm flailing. Hard.
It's no use. I'm

committed to
whatever lies ahead.

I hope I can see
again. Very soon.

Because I do not like
this night without stars.

I'm tired in my bones today.

Heavy
like cement
mixed with brass.

I'm a dud
dredging under water.

I'm tired in my bones today.

Lost, tossed
like discarded
fish and tacks.

I'm ashes
snuffed myself out.

I'm tired in my bones today.

On dizzying heights
or in gasping lows

It is only ever the depth of experience.

Sink into madness
rise in exalted form.

Catch the sky with your breath.

What you seek lurks deep
quivering in anticipation of you.

Feeling the god damn walls closing in on
me.

The walls of a misfit.

Too old
too fat
too skinny
too young.

too much of anything and

I find myself

squeezed
by walls I can't

point to

or diagram
or explain
or mention.

It's the walls of
too much

and I'm

so sexy
so strong
so brash
so crass

but here, being anything
more than
just so
means a

squeeze so tight

I just know
I'm gonna blow

from all that
normalizing pressure
coming down the

pipes of the
good and right.

These unsighted walls

they tell me

"you're crazy for seeing
walls where they aren't."

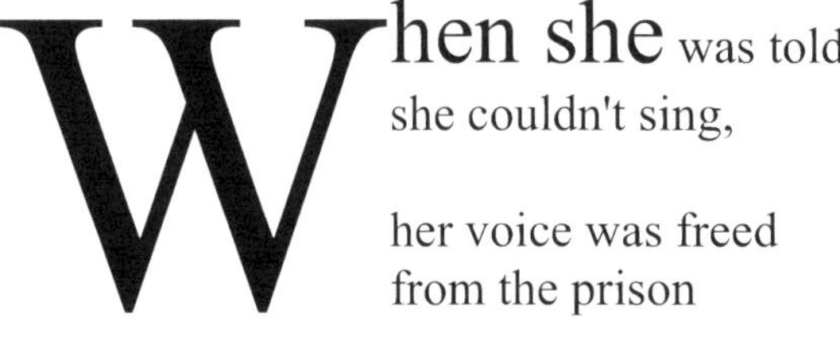

When she was told
she couldn't sing,

her voice was freed
from the prison

of timing
and technique.

Now the Gods -
they sing through her,

for a voice that
is free - at last -

from refinement,
is one to be

savored by the light
upon the lights.

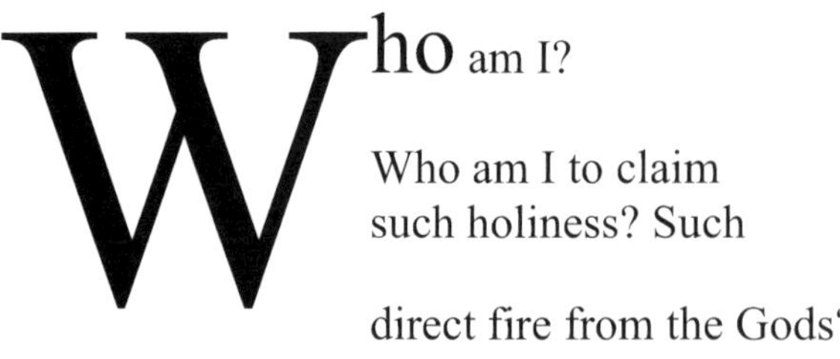

Who am I?

Who am I to claim
such holiness? Such

direct fire from the Gods?

I'll tell you.
I'll tell you right now.

I am the vessel.

I am woman, with my
yawning opening to

God's cock.

I am the one
holy capable

of the mystical orgasm.

I am the one
empowered enough to

catch the eye of Creation

to be seduced by
exploding stars and raise

light years of galaxies.

I am the one secure,
grounded, earthy enough

to hold space for
divine intervention.

You huddle in the corner
of a dank cave

shaking, hating me -

this woman!

The one who laughs in
the direction of a north star.

My cauldron is full
to the brim

with the heat and lust
of Creation.

Who am I?

This is who I am.

I am your mother
your wife
your daughter.

I am all the creatures

not like you

who wield Creation
and mirror back

your own
willful poverty.

My heart
can't be broken.
But it sure can
bleed.

Why does today feel like
a fun house?

Is it my perception that's
morphed, wobbled?

Am I seeing those waves, or
is this a trick?

"Go with the flow" you tell me,
but letting go of

my sanity feels like death
to me. How can I

trust you with that cheshire
cat grin, it's too

big for your face? Another
illusion? I just can't

reconcile this mazing
of events, I'm

confused. Can I even
trust myself? I'm not

seeing clear, I'm not perceiving
like I did. Can you

help me? I can't believe
those bobbly eyes

are a reliable source
of practicality

and I'm not comforted.
This place scares me, my

mind is not bending with
shattering glass, I'm

not laughing at the clowns,
frankly they freak me

out! I just want my dad, I
want to see him in his

weathered jeans, I want
my hand in his

weathered hand, I'm con-
vinced if I could

resurrect him from the dead,
the world would ease back

into straight lines and blacks
and whites, and

manageable splashes
of colors and light.

You told me I laugh in my
sleep. Like, a lot.

I'm glad you told me, darling.

I'm glad my dreams carry me to
frolicking fancies, while my

waking life is heavy right now.

I feel relief that I seem to
break away when I

sink below these weighty days.

I'm glad you told me how I
laugh when I sleep.

I'm relieved to be made aware that

my mind is still a happy place, even
when I'm exhausted, dredging

up this gravel and this granite, it's

so fucking heavy, my love.

I have years of tears to cry today.

I'm crying for the babies
        gunned down as freedom rings.

I'm crying for the soldiers
    helmets too big for their heads.

I'm crying for the lands
        frozen and boiled like ice and eggs.

I'm crying for our leaders
        lost within, caverns of hate.

I'm crying for the whole damn world
        and I'm crying hard for mine

crumbling as it is
        I'm so sorry, child of mine.

I left because I got tired.
I got tired of asking you

to ask me, "how
are you, dear?"

I wasn't tired of cooking or
cleaning. I got tired of

reminding you to say
"thank you, dear."

I could have made the bed
every damn day, and

danced barefoot and naked in
our kitchen forever, except

it's the hundredth
time I noticed that you

didn't ask about my day, and
now I'm exhausted.

So, I'm leaving.
Because your

forgetfulness with
words and questions and

sweet nothings has become like
an anchor around my feet. I

can hardly move
from the weight of all the

emotional connection that
ought to be divided between us.

I'm leaving because I

have to step out of these

shackles and give myself a
fighting chance to

be whole - not obese with
carrying the intimacy of two.

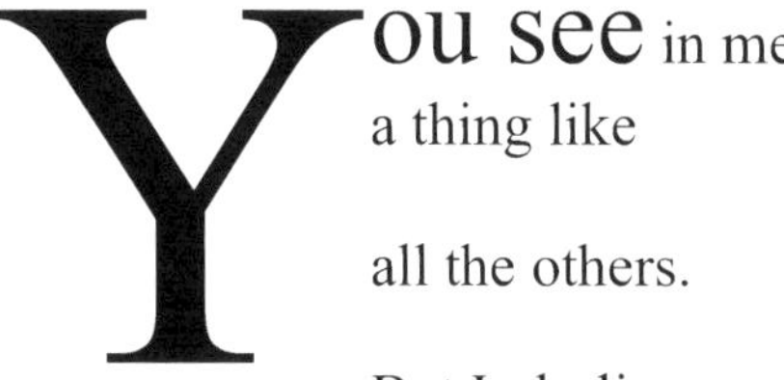

all the others.

But I, darling,

I am

a creature
just too

beautiful and

grotesque for
a mind

like yours.

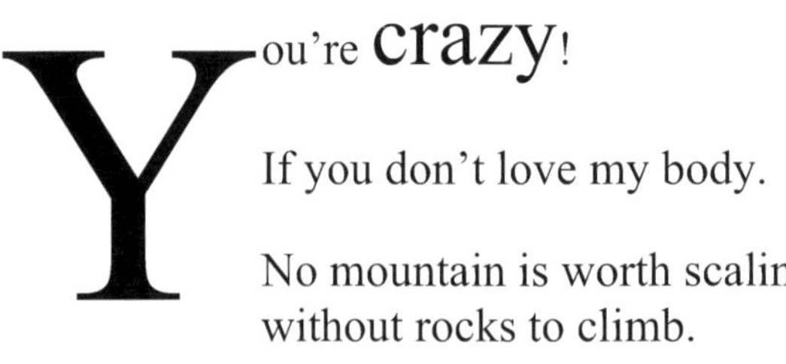

You're **crazy**!

If you don't love my body.

No mountain is worth scaling
without rocks to climb.

You're insane, I tell you!

If you don't see this wild beauty
ascending in stretches up my thighs.

You just don't understand grace

if you don't kneel at my fire, and
feel the warmth of my experience

while you're running your fingers
up and down my spine.

You're just out of your mind

if the weather on my face and
the clouds in my eyes

don't take your breath away.

More Books from Ingrid

Words.Love

Ingrid's debut book of poetry, published in 2017. This compilation is a smattering of Ingrid's heart, spanning subjects from love, to spirituality, to grief.

Buy on Amazon: bit.ly/words-love

Locked in Love

A book of inspiring messages and profound tidbits for the spiritually minded.

Buy on Amazon: bit.ly/lockedinlove

Posters and Prints

Don't forget, you can get a free poster when you join my inner circle!

Go to www.ingridhturner.com/poetry-circle

Scan the QR code below to see the posters and prints I have available.

You can also visit:
 www.ingridhturner.com/bitch-collection

Made in the USA
Middletown, DE
13 November 2022

14663574R00097